Hell has no fury

Dean Hamid

Published by Dean Hamid Presents, 2020.

While every precaution has been taken in the preparation of this book, the publisher assumes no responsibility for errors or omissions, or for damages resulting from the use of the information contained herein.

HELL HAS NO FURY

First edition. September 30, 2020.

Copyright © 2020 Dean Hamid.

ISBN: 979-8986593340

Written by Dean Hamid.

Hell Has No Fury
A Novel
By
DEAN HAMID

Editor - Writaz BLOC Inc.

Formatter – Brenda Wright, Formatting Done Wright

Library of Congress Control Number:2019911119

About the Author

The author Dean Hamid was born and raised in *Brooklyn, New York*. In his youth he would read the works of *Donald Goines, Iceberg Slim, as well as Richard Wright, throwing in the poetic banter of James Baldwin* over and over while hiding these books tucked away from his parents. Growing up in *New York City's hardcore Bushwick-Hylan Projects*, his writing is not necessarily intended to glamorize the quote-unquote gangsters, or even the street life; but to emphasize the presence of the drama that was involved and surrounded around it.

In the past ten years, he's been writing articles, commentaries, short stories, and has managed to write five novels; *Hell has no fury, Lovin Safari, Lovin Safari II, Lost Boy, and Cold hard wind*, and presently working on more. Given the opportunity to correspond with published authors, it's been said that his work swings towards what is described as Urban Fiction Drama genre, with a strong propensity towards a slick old school literary voice.

Dean Hamid started writing under his own title, Dean Hamid Presents, and hasn't looked back since. He works hard and tirelessly to keep his work as professional, and gritty as it can be, but yet stay literally solid. His work successfully proves and drives home this point. He looks forward to creating a legacy for himself in the Writing community as well as the Publishing business.

Hell has no fury...

Shakespeare once wrote, '*Hell hath no fury like a woman scorned...*,' well, Mya has finally had enough of the physical abuse, disrespect, shame and mental melt-downs. She's tired of hiding bruises with makeup. She's fed-up. Her old man, Aziz, and his cohort Miles, hustle heroin together. As top lieutenants, they're trying to prove their self-worth in a narcotics collective: running crews of young wayward thugs to moving product, and collecting money owed to Joker, the big boss. They're diligent, independent contractors competing for respect, power, and a chance to move up a vile and ever scathing dope chain.

Joker is a twisted mobster with the reputation for the brutal enforcement of rules that he makes up as he goes along. If you owe, not only are you in jeopardy, but so are the members of your family. Peanut crossed the line, and unfortunately, regrettably, found out all too late.

Mya's girlfriend Skyler has eyes for Steve, an old school flame who works with her at a midtown Manhattan graphics company. Skyler's high maintenance and gold-digging ways, have Steve lacking. He desperately needs a come up, and Joker's stash may just be it.

Somebody wants revenge! Joker, Miles, and even the dope fiends they use are potential targets from an indiscriminate, deranged killer;

as Aziz's own fate hangs precariously, unbalanced in the winds that blow high across the East River. Will Mya finally get even? Will Peanut get some get-back at Joker? Will Skyler save Steve from his own self-impending doom?

You'll be turning the pages in this suspenseful saga of urban drama set in the gritty, hardcore section of New York City's Lower East Side.....Alphabet City.

chapter 1

THE MORNING AFTER LOVEMAKING, unlike any other, starts out like flowers that bloom on a warm spring morning, quiet, cozy; taking on the moment of the period regardless of the glorious bright climate. The yawning, turning, starting over and mentally embracing each other usually tends to excite one to a point where what seemed like a dream, becomes the meaningful plot to a magnificent night. The song of birds in the trees, the sun striking the ground, and the reality of it all from the sweetness of the dawn; is it morning already? Yeah, that's usually how it starts out for most of us, like poetry, but not this morning.

"Baby! Please...I don't know where your watch is!"

"Bitch you know! You probably pawned the muthafucka...!"

Mya pleaded with the muscled figure over by the dresser, ransacking the drawers. The shirtless back rippled as he tore through the dresser. "You must have hid it!"

9

Mya got up from the king-size bed she lounged on and cautiously walked toward him. "Baby...let me help you..." She nervously twinged as she put her hand on his arm, still confused, trying to figure out exactly what had set him off. They had just made love. Spoke about a wonderful future together, all sweet pillow talk, but now he was having none of it. He stopped, stepped back, then suddenly pushed her up against the wood-grained dresser. She grimaced as her hip crashed against the topside, "Ughhh" she groaned. He didn't even bat an eye.

"I remember the last time you had it on..." She rummaged her hands through the roughed up clothing he tossed around, "it might have fallen in...oh! Here it is!" Mya beamed as she held up the ten carat diamond encrusted Jacob watch she gave him as a gift for his birthday. "See...you just misplaced it..."

The slap was sudden, unexpected; blood slung out the side of her mouth. "Bitch, Do you know who your fucking with, you knew where it was all along!" He grabbed her by the throat and tossed her small lithe body over to the bed. "Why you fuckin' wit me! Now I'm gonna be late! Fuck!" He turned and slowly unbuckled his belt. "This is what you want, huh? You just wanted to wake the ducking beast. Now you got em.'"

Mya trembled as she rubbed her throbbing lip. "Please...no!" She crawled back onto the bed, and pulled the sheets up over her. "The kids haven't gone to school yet...please"

"Shit! This is all the education they need." he snickered. Turning towards the door, he walked over to it and slammed it shut. "Now bend your ass over....you've been bad and big daddy's gotta punish you!"

"Please, Aziz...please..." Tears swept down the side of her face as she cringed, the closer he got. "I'm sorry...." Apologizing for what, she didn't have the slightest.

Aziz grabbed her leg hard and punched her on the thigh. "Turn your ass around now! I won't fucking tell you again bitch!" She let out a cry as he punched her again, then put her hands up for him to stop. "Okay, okay!" She turned over and raised her ass up high, reaching for a pillow in front of her.

Aziz grabbed her long silky hair and tugged her closer towards the back edge of the bed where he stood stroking himself into an erection. "Yeah, bitch...you like this shit..."

Mya said nothing as he moved towards her. She bit hard into the pillow as he forced the tip of his now throbbing cock into her ass. He spit in his hand and stroked the wet slime down the base of his dick, lubricating it, the head much too large for her tight anus. Still, he didn't care as he continued to push his way up in her. As she tensed from the pain he said, "Oh, you want to fight it, huh..." Veins popped up on Mya's forehead as he thrust himself deep into her; crying as he pounded, she felt nauseous. She could feel him all the way up into the pit of her stomach, and he laughed at her vulnerable position. "Yeeeaaahhh..."he cried out as he unmercifully started plowing his dick into her now loosened, but hurt asshole. Mya prayed through her pain that he would cum quick. She relaxed herself to let him go deeper, not wanting to excite his anger any more than it already was. She faintly let out fake moans she hoped he would enjoy. "Ohhh, baby yes fuck me, ohhh, baby....stick it to me! My sweet big dick...fuck me deeper...ohhh...ohhh!" everything she could think of to get it over with quick. She then felt his dick tensing up along its shaft, and knew it wouldn't be long more she thought, while holding the pillow tighter, digging her long manicured nails into it.

Aziz finally pulled out of her as his semen mixed with blood and shit sprayed out the tip of his head. "Ohhh, yeeeaaahhh...!" A small milky puddle pooled up on her back as he stood with his mouth opened wide, drooling with his head tilted back, hand on his hip, breathing hard. Mya waited until he went soft before she attempted to make any sudden moves. He looked down at her with his limp cock in his hand, and even though she was sore as hell, she attempted to reach up and hug him, kiss him, but he pushed her away and shouted, "I've got shit all over my dick! Clean it the fuck off!"

Mya started to get up off of the bed to go to the bathroom for a wet, warm rag to do the job. But suddenly, he grabbed her by the hand, and she thought, didn't I just go through all this-what now? "Nah...not with a rag." he said as a sneer grew across his face, "GO DOWN AND SUCK MY DICK!"

What! Was he kidding me! Mya's eyes grew wide with the thought; lick his dick with my...he's a pig! All she saw next was stars as he slapped her across the face backhanded. "Bitch...Suck It!" Mya wanted no more of the ass-kickings she received earlier in the week. No more blackened eyes. No more threats of being pistol-whipped with a gun cocked to her head. No more-hell, there were just too many to count. She stared up into the face of the madman she once, and even some ways now still loved, in his eyes, and pleaded. "Please Aziz, don't do this to me. Don't make me..." He raised his fists, and she put up her hands in submission and grimaced. "Okay...okay..."

Mya pulled him closer to the bed by the hips, took a deep breath, and closed her eyes and opened her mouth; swallowing his soft smelly cock into her mouth, and washing it gently with the salty spit of her tongue.

She loved Aziz and even reasoned with herself that this was just another one of his tests to see if she was true. She swore she'd pass them all, just to show him how much she really, truly loved him. Yes, her mind rationalized, it wouldn't be long before he would come around, see how dedicated a woman she was. Hell, she thought, after all, it takes years for couples anyway to really know each other, she reassured herself.

Aziz looked down on her as she sucked his dick back up to its peak again; then he furiously flipped, bitterly he shouted at her, "Bitch you like this, don't you! Freak! Fuckin' hoe!"

Mya gazed up at him. "What are you crazy...stupid...?" Aziz raised his fist as Mya closed her eyes, "No! No!" She took more of Aziz's cruel and unusual punishment, and actually thought for the first time that she'd been with him, that maybe, maybe she was wrong. She'd have to make a move quick, somehow, someway...someday.

Yeah, just like flowers, it's beautiful the way they bloom in the spring; like Mya even. The only thing though, Aziz doesn't have a green thumb, and he damn sure ain't no Shakespeare.

SIX DAYS LATER, ALL hell broke loose.

"Mya...put the gun down!" Aziz held his hands up as he pleaded frantically. The moon peeped conspicuously through the wide paneled window, lighting the barrel of the .44 magnum Mya had pointing at his chest; the only witness to what apparently would be a perfect homicide

"No, muthafucka! You gonna die tonight!" Mya screamed as she held the gun perfectly still, wavering not from the weight, but from the sheer anger she had built up to what seemed like now to her was years of abuse, shame and intolerance. Aziz gazed deep into her eyes, searching, trying to grasp onto something, anything, trying to convince her not to kill him. "C'mon, baby...we can talk about it..." He tiptoed slowly towards her.

"If you take one more step, Aziz, you're a dead man...don't try me..." The hammer was cocked and locked; her wide stance widened more to prepare for the recoil. She was ready, and Aziz knew from examining her closely, she was dead serious, so he backed off. "Yeah," she sneered slightly as he moved, "back da fuck up!"

Aziz retreated very cautiously towards the black leather recliner he'd just bought. "Okay, baby. I'm gonna sit down...okay." He suddenly remembered he had stashed a .25 automatic pistol underneath the seat. He didn't question why he left it there, he was just glad he did. The only thing his mind concentrated on now was whether or not the .25 had any standing power against the .44 she brandished in her hand, and if it had a clip with any bullets; he questioned if he even had a chance. Maybe he'd rush her, he thought, tackle her, then..."Sit your ass down now!' she barked, interrupting his frantically racing mind.

"Be cool, baby, c'mon now. Look...I know we had our differences, but," as he sat, he groped the arm of the recliner as he slid into the plush, leather chair, "we can work through this." Slowly, he tried to feel for the gun. No use. He had to figure just how to slip his hand underneath without being caught. "I mean, baby, we're grown. I know we need a change..." Remaining calm, he leisurely crossed his legs; and with his left hand, dug into the side of the seat. Steel. "Baby, you need to put the gun down..." He could feel the butt and gripped it. He got it, but, "C'mon, baby just sit down..." he still had to slide the chamber and put a round in; he felt for the clip. If he could just convince her to sit down, he'd have time to. "Baby, c'mon now, grab a chair and let's kick it, please," he begged.

Mya kept an eye on him, his movements, knowing how slick he was. She enjoyed it as he seemed to beg for his life. Finally, she liked his petitioning demeanor. Now, all she had to do was find out where the rest of the money was at. Make him pay, much more than he had already. "Okay, I'll grab a seat. We can....*talk*. Matter of fact, there's something I'd like to know, but," she lowered her gun down a little and then glanced over to the side of her for the foot stool that accompanied the recliner, "if you make one false move, flinch, or even blink too many times you're dead." With caution she reached for it, and pulling it closer to her, sat down in front of him, with the gun still aimed at him, a little lower though, pointing this time at his crotch. "Now muthafucka, where's the money?"

"Huh....money?" Aziz looked perplexed as he stared. "The...money..." He leaned forward, blinking rapidly as if he were just coming to his senses even after all that was going on. "What the fuck you know about that?" "What do I know- that's a hell of a question! And bitch nigga I said don't blink to many times! Slow ya'role or you're dead!" Mya took pleasure at the twisting, searching twitches on his face trying to figure out how did she know about money that he'd stashed just a couple of-"You dumb-ass! You think I would put up with all that shit you put me through all these years...for nothing!"

Aziz struggled with his emotions, but still managed to keep his hands on the .25 thinking to himself, after all this time, all the muthafuckas that were killed, all the bullshit he went through...was it this bitch? No, it couldn't have been that simple. "Bitch....it was you?" "You got one more bitch in you. Call me it again, I'll blow your limp dick right off," she said as she started to stand, her line of interrogation wasn't working; she had to go another route, be more direct, drastic even.

Aziz was pissed. The one person he'd searched for hell and high-water. He was tricked, played like a sucker, the tables were turned, but no, he figured he had one last hurrah. "You fucked up now..." he mumbled from his throat as he pulled the small caliber revolver from the side and lunged at Mya. "You gonna die, bitch!"

Wasting no time, Mya swung out of the way of his propelled body and hit the floor rolling, almost going back from her head slamming against the floor as she dived. Aziz had the slide pulled back listening to the bullet catapult into the chamber. "Got'cha ass now bitch!" He pointed and took aim.

Aziz's mind was transfixed by the events of last week. How could it all come down to this, his last thoughts were before he squeezed the trigger, and at the same time, so did Mya.

"Baaap! Baaap! Baaap!"

"Badoom! Badoom!"

Silence was the only thing stirring as the smoke started to clear.

Six days, that's all the time it took.

chapter 2

Day one.

HEADING UP THE LONG chilly avenue towards 44th Street, Mya held her head cocked to the side as the wind raced along Lexington Avenue in Manhattan. It's late October and the winds were coming off the Atlantic Ocean rather swiftly and rigidly cold. It was that time of the year in New York City, late fall.

She briefly eyeballed her reflection in a glass that mirrored her image as she turned onto 44th Street. The hat she had pinned to her hair was broken down on the side, fixed stylishly, but not intentional; she wanted to hide the dark reddened bruise along side her face. Aziz had left his mark again, and this morning he seemed more brutal than ever.

Thinking of stopping at a news stand to pick up a newspaper was out of the question. This time of the morning all her friends would be on their way to work, and she really didn't have the time or want to explain, or tell them the lie about how she had fallen into the doorway of her bedroom; for what seemed like the hundredth time already. No one was that clumsy. She figured she'd send one of the messengers out later to get one.

One more block, that was all, then she would dip into the restroom at work, quickly and quietly, and dab the foundation in her purse on her face to hide the bruises. It seemed like a plan, hell, by now she knew the routine all too well. There it was in sight, the entrance to the building: 377 East 44th Street. No one in sight. She planned on getting there early to avoid everyone, and it worked. The messengers were usually outside hanging, smoking, but strangely, there seemed to be no one around, probably because of the weather. Good, she thought, bouncing up the steps into the building, she let out a sigh of relief. Yes, she made it. Or had she?

"Hey girl. is that you?" Standing by the alleyway off the side of the building was Skyler, her girlfriend. A stunning five foot nine inch wanna be runway model. Her voluptuous figure strove for attention, and got it. Even under the three-quarter shearling mink she modeled, it showed. The long burnt auburn wavy bangs she sported, swayed as the wind gust through her hair. Her full glossed lips curled as she blew out smoke from the cigarette she puffed on. Skyler was fine as all outdoors, and she knew it.

Mya held her head down slightly as Skyler tried to peep. "Yeah girl, I dropped the kids off to school early. Figured I'd come in and get a good start...ya know...I like the hat. Who's it by, Versace?" Skyler reached for it and Mya blocked her hand. "No. Just somethin' cheap I picked up....the wind blowing and all..."

Skyler knew something was up right away. Mya, cheap? Hell no, so she didn't let up. "You got a new do or somethin'...hmmm," she picked at her, "the ends still seem kinda frayed. Maybe you should go to my beautician. I can set you up."

"No!" Mya turned away from her. "It's okay!"

"Awh man, Mya...again." Skyler covered her mouth. Whether or not she really was concerned about the marks on Mya's face didn't matter to her; she knew where it came from, and this morning it was all too shocking. "Damn, he did it again!" She too was tired of it all.

Mya took off the hat as she stepped into the elevator, hell, it didn't matter now, she thought. "Look at least let me run into the bathroom and do my face up before you go around telling, okay." Skyler moved away from her. The elevator stopped and the doors opened, she shook her head in disgust as she walked past. "Mya, it ain't about me telling. Hell, everyone already knows."

"Whaaat!" Mya rushed behind her as Skyler pulled out the keys to open the front door of the office. "Girl, you really think you can cover those bruises with foundation," she sighed "you're trippin'." Mya pushed open the door and brushed past. "Yeah, and I'm sure you don't help matters any, huh?"

Skyler was used to the sarcasm, but it still stung anyway. She shoved the keys into her purse, and stopped behind a huge gold-trimmed walnut desk that was her home for the next eight hours. She sucked her teeth as she threw it onto the cluttered paper filled workstation. "Mya, you can bullshit all you want with that smart-ass shit, but you need to lock his ass up!"

"What do you know about it, Skyler?" Mya shot back. "You like his type don't you? Money! Jewelry! Nice car..." She stomped towards the restroom, mumbling under her breath, "Fuckin' gold digger..." Skyler spun from around her desk as quickly as her stilettos would allow her, and was hot on her heels. "Shit, Mya. Maybe it's somethin' you ain't' doin'. Hell," she cut her eyes, "looks like you done fell off anyway."

Normally this would be the beginning of a perfectly good cat fight, but Mya was too badly beaten already. The only thing she could do was talk shit. Mya turned around and got up in Skyler's face and said, "You think this shit is my fault?"

"Well, Mya, for one maybe you should keep him happy. Evidently he ain't happy. And two, you're staying with him. Maybe you like it!" That one hurt. Mya stared at her then continued into the bathroom. "Yeah Skyler, maybe you're right. Huh, huh, I like getting my ass kicked in front of my kids...black eyes, swollen lips," she pulled up the side of her blouse, revealing a nasty bruise on her side, "even fractured ribs...yeah, my fault." A tear trickled down her face as she pulled out her makeup kit and scattered it all over the sink. Damn, Skyler thought as she dropped her head and reached over for the foundation. "Here..let me help you." Skyler moved close to Mya and softly dapped the brown honey powder foundation on Myas' swollen, but still pretty face. "Here ya go..."

"Thanks Skyler...ouch!" Mya said as she grimaced slightly from the stinging pain around her lips. "Hold still!" Skyler pushed back at Mya's long brown red streaked hair, admiring just how attractive Mya was. "Girl, you too fine to be going through this type of shit with anybody!" "C'mon Skyler, not the speech. I've heard it all before-"

"Well you must not be listening'!" Skyler turned Mya's face gently smoothing out the makeup she had applied. "You know I can make a call, and my brothers can take care of this."

Mya managed a smile. "Yeah, I'm sure. Your crazy brothers....I'll be alright. Besides, he's like a daddy to my girls....he doesn't do anything to the kids. Ouch!" "Sorry 'bout that."

"He wasn't always like this, Skyler...but, pressure...the hustling...it's hard."

"Hell, he ain't gotta take that shit out on you. It's not like he has too much pressure. His hustling should have y'all money put aside...don't you?"

"Yeah, I guess. He said something about a move; get out of the city, maybe Long Island...way out there."

Skyler finished and stowed away the makeup kit. "Mya, Mya, Mya. Dreams, big dreams. I understand, believe me, but being beat on ain't part of a dream... that's a nightmare and you need to wake up."

Mya acknowledged her by smiling as she put the makeup into her purse. "Maybe, but you gotta live for something. I mean, I got these girls and still living in the projects. We need a little time, that's all."

"Hopefully for you Mya, that's what you have."

"Yeah, yeah. Skyler...but, please, don't say anything to no one-"

As Skyler turned to open the door she abruptly stopped. "Mya. Like I said. Everyone knows...and I sure as hell didn't say anything, but," she turned and faced Mya and put both hands on her shoulders, "if I were you, I'd at least get paid."

"Paid?"

"You take it any way you want, but there's no way in Hell I'd go through that shit without at least getting paid-and I mean paid."

"Huh, huh. Girl, you trippin'." Mya reached out and hugged her. "But thanks, anyway."

Skyler pushed her away then grabbed her arms sternly. "I'm not trippin'!" Then she pulled her back closer and whispered, "Get paid, girl... then haul ass." She walked out.

Mya stood silently leaning against the counter of the sink, staring into the mirror as she contemplated what Skyler had just said as the door slowly closed, thinking out loud to herself, "Hmmm. Paid..." She looked at the covered-up bruises on her face and felt along her ribs, still sore. "Get paid...maybe she's right...maybe."

She grabbed her bag and headed out the door, shrugging off everything that Skyler had said. She rationalized to herself that Skyler didn't know Aziz like she did and besides, he loved her and she loved him. That's all she needed to know. That's all she needed to hear.

AZIZ EASED SLOWLY DOWN 4th Street off Avenue C looking around at the abandoned buildings, big hulls of wreckage and slab managing to somehow stay standing. Peeping inside of one, he could see the movement of the junkies that occupied the dingy tenements, they were far from empty as he watched their peering heads chirping outside the ragged doors watching him as he drove by. Someone made a half-assed attempt to wave as they saw Aziz's blue car go by, he honked and kept it moving.

This was Alphabet City, New York City's prime dope spot, or at least one of them. Dope fiends and junkies were everywhere. They walked, or slumbered on the streets during the day, looking for food or some unfortunate individual wandering too far from West 4th Street, the New York University campus, to rob. Most times that was the case, but all too many just came to cop a fix.

Aziz knew the area well; having grown up in the brownstones that sat on 8th Street, growing up and playing ball at 'The Pitt', the recreational center he was headed to, now a haven for dope dealers and hustlers.

The fiends, junkies and jack boys knew not to fuck with Aziz or his ride but still he'd pay a fiend some money or dope just to watch it. One thing about a fiend: when he needed a fix, all was fair game and Aziz knew it, but he also knew if he promised a fiend some dope, it would be protected with the fiends own life if needs be. Aziz smiled as he eyeballed Poppi running out of one of the buildings trying to catch up to the car. Poppi was a dope fiend Aziz knew from the neighborhood; he also just happened to be the fiend whose job it was to watch Aziz's car, which he handled diligently.

"Yo, Aziz!" he yelled as the car glided into a space in front of The Pitt. "Yo, man, I'm here!" He ran around the passenger side of the car and smiled, showing teeth that had been eaten away from years of heroin and cocaine. He reached for the door. "I got it!"

Aziz waved him off, "Naw...don't touch!" Aziz had a thing about fiends. He'd seen too many in his lifetime for one; many had overdosed or succumbed to the AIDS virus and too many never even thought to go to the clinic to get checked out, thinking that they would miss a good hit. Aziz was real leery about being too close; open sores and blood still oozed out of the pricks to the necks and arms, hands, wherever they could find a vein to shoot up in.

Poppi didn't take it personal, it was all in the game.

"Wassup Aziz." Poppi stepped back a little as Aziz got out of the car.

"Same way..." Aziz nodded.

"Yeah, same way." "Cool... I got it."

Aziz glanced towards the entrance of the building and saw Miles, his partner, all six foot two, muscular upper body and Latino facial features that put one in the mind of a gigolo if you really never saw one, standing outside the door staring down at his watch. *Damn*, Aziz thought, he knew better than to be late for these meetings, especially when the big man came downtown from Harlem. Of course, he'd have an excuse, but he knew it wouldn't be good enough; he shot a glance back at Poppi. "Yo, man, wash the car and I'll put something extra to it...cool?"

"Yeah, Aziz...cool." Poppi waved his boys over that sat across the street, wishing they were in his shoes, "Yo! Get me a couple of clean rags now!" They did, knowing one thing for sure, Aziz was definitely going to bless Poppi and they all wanted to be anointed.

Aziz shook his head as he watched them scatter. He liked attention, thinking to himself that maybe one day he might become a big boy in the game. He shot another look over at the Bentley parked by the door that belonged to the big man, *yeah, one day, one day*, he thought.

"Wassup, Aziz," The tall, dark figure dressed in a sporty, tailor-made, blue denim two-piece said as he held out his closed fist and dapped him, "Damn, kinda late...again." He glanced back at his watch. "Uh yeah...traffic." Aziz tried to brush past him but was abruptly stopped by a hand on his arm. "Traffic? You kiddin' me. He let go only after Aziz shot a sneer his way. "You're only what, 4, 5, 6 blocks away or sumptin'." He blocked the doorway. "Look, either you be on time or-"

Aziz huffed up and pushed past him and shot back, "Or what, Miles! What!" Miles bit his lip as he just about reached into his waistband then his attention was caught by the man inside the doorway beckoning them to come in. Aziz laughed, "Yeah, I thought so."

"This ain't over Aziz."

"Yeah, Miles, it never is."

They were waved in while another stood guard inconspicuously by the entrance to the office. Miles nudged Aziz on his back. "Yo, man, just tighten up, alright. At least call." Aziz nodded. "A'iyht...next time."

Motioning them to go in, the man pointed to the office. Aziz stepped first, then knocked, three short raps to notify the occupants just who was at the door; it was their code. Aziz had done this all too many times before, so well rehearsed he could have closed his eyes and kicked the door and gotten the same response, "Who is it!" The same response.

"Aziz...Miles, we have a meeting."

The door opened slightly as a bald-headed figure peeped through. "We were expecting you." Aziz leaned over towards Miles and whispered, "Shit...I can't tell."

"What ya say!" the bald-headed man said as he jerked the door open.

"Nuthin' man, just nuthin'." Aziz shot back.

"Thought so."

The opened door revealed a mid-sized office once used for the staff that worked there, file cabinets were lined up against the wall; a window encased trophy cabinet on the opposite side of the room showcased rows of trophies from years gone by. Off to the side was a brother Aziz recognized from the streets growing up; he stood motionless, trembling as they stepped towards him. "Yo, wassup, man?"

The high-backed leather chair behind the desk was turned around and the person sitting in it squirmed and shifted from side to side. An ashtray was posted to his right as he flicked ashes from a cigar. Aziz tried to peep around him to see what was going on but was pulled away suddenly by the bald-headed man.

"Step back! He'll be with you in a minute...or so." Miles stared at Aziz with a look on his face that read, What the hell is going on?

Then a woman rose up from in front of the chair wiping her mouth with the back of her hand, embarrassed as she looked at Aziz and Miles; she recognized them and they recognized her. Her name was India. Her brother was the one standing off to the side of the desk. Damn, Aziz thought, what the hell did he do now?

"Aziz...Miles...ahhhh." The voice in the chair waved the woman off and he spun around towards them straightening up his pants pulling up his zipper and said, "Fella's, good of you to make it."

India stood next to her brother, and as the bald-headed man approached they quivered. The man in the chair relit his cigar and took a puff, then blew the smoke their way. "You see, Aziz, Miles. I tried to work with him." Him, being Peanut, Aziz and Miles homeboy. The last time they heard anything about him, he tried to set up shop over on Avenue D and Houston Street; it seemed harmless enough. He never bought any weight from them, but it was so small-time it didn't matter anyway, he was no threat. At least, to them.

"But, he tried to get over on me." This time he gestured the bald-headed man over and whispered in his ear. The bald-headed man smiled as he looked up at the woman then Peanut. Peanut looked over at Aziz and his eyes read save me, but Aziz was a spectator only, plus, he knew to make a deal with Joker was literally making a deal with the devil, especially when he didn't know what Peanut had done anyway.

"I gave him the money, the dope, everything to hold down a spot for me. No big thing. Hell, I'm doing him a fuckin' favor." Damn, Aziz frowned, Peanut messed around and got fronted by Joker. "And what does he do."

The bald-headed man grabbed his sister by the arm and marched her over towards the door; tears welled up in her eyes as she turned her head when she bypassed Aziz and Miles. "He sells my dope...doesn't pay...tricks my dope on hoes!" Joker got up and stalked towards Peanut, then dumped ashes on his head from his cigar straight up playin' him. "Then he tries to duck me...tsk, tsk, tsk."

The bald-headed man came back in and nodded his head towards Joker and he stepped slightly away from Peanut, then savagely punched him in the stomach doubling him over as the bald-headed man held his arms pinned behind his hack, bending him over on a desk. "He fucked me! So-I..." Joker, though small in stature, was strong as a bull, he pulled out a switchblade and cut Peanut's pants; a hole from around his ass, then he continued to punch him brutally in his kidneys. "I fuck him! This unappreciative, thieving, black bastard!" The bald headed man stood back and watched, making a move towards Peanut's exposed ass, as Joker wrestled him down. His next move took Aziz and Miles by surprise. Peanut cried out loud as he was held down. Aziz and Miles couldn't take no more, they got up to go to the door and Joker stopped them. "No! Watch! This is what happens when I get fucked! This is what happens to him...and anybody else!"

Aziz cringed at the thought. Peanut lived with his mom, his sister and her two young sons. "I fuck the whole family!" Joker yelled out. He could only sit with his head held towards the ground as Peanut screamed; a scream he would soon never forget, or hopefully hear again.

The bald-headed man squealed like a fat pig as he plunged the pool stick deeper into Peanut's ass as Joker laughed. Rule one, don't mess over Joker, cause he's fuckin' nuts.

After Peanut had been thrown out into the street by the bald-headed man, whose name was known as Bezo. Aziz and Miles settled back into their chairs waiting for Joker to hold court.

"Gentlemen, gentlemen..." He kicked his feet up on the desk. "I hated for you to have witnessed such...uh, what can we call it..."

Miles glanced over at Aziz as if to say; Is this guy kidding me or what? A man was just brutally sodomized, his sister made to perform oral sex, and the man that orchestrated the whole thing sat in front of them leisurely, as if nothing had happened. Couldn't even come up with a name for the horror that he'd just inflicted. Couldn't even let the words come out of his mouth. "Dis...Dis...Disgrace. You think so?"

Miles eyeballed him, thinking of the right thing to say before he answered, "Uh, yeah, I guess you could call it that." Aziz shook his head and said, "What's gonna happen to him next?"

Joker reached into the pocket of the suede shirt he wore, just off the rack. "He still has to pay me my money."

"After all that," Aziz responded, "do you really think he'll do it?"

Joker lit a cigar he pulled from the humidor that sat on the desk; after taking a long pull of the Cuban-rolled cigar, he blew a thick cloud of blue smoke into the air.

"Hmmm, well, in case he doesn't..." He put his feet down off the desk and leaned forward toward them, "we still know where his mother lives; believe me...somebody will pay me my money!"

His face stood motionless, serious, and then he blurted out in a raspy laugh, "Hell, I hear she's got bigger lips than her daughter!"

Miles faked the laugh along with him while Aziz, repulsed by the whole thing, just sneered. If Joker's intent was to put the tim down on them, it had worked, at least with Miles. Aziz took it as a threat. If Joker was to ever try that on him, he knew he would have to kill him, and as he sat next to Miles he glanced over and thought, Yeah, him too.

The look on Peanut's face as he was dragged out and tossed into the street was a look Aziz swore he'd never have, at least he'd have to die before that would ever be the case. "Fuck Joker." he grumbled.

"Alright gentlemen, the reason I called you here was not for what you just witnessed, but because I need two good men."

Aziz eased up in the chair; Miles had damn near raised his hand up like a school kid or something. Me boss, me boss, pick me boss. Aziz was hating, but he held his head even though he knew that to become one of Jokers' main made men, they would be in. No more running, no more small-timing, no more projects; but he was still resentful because Miles was up on his game much better than he was. "Yeah, what's up, boss. What's the deal." Aziz responded. Miles damn near wiped slob coming out of Aziz's mouth. "Yeah...what's up." he said.

Joker had them where he wanted them, and he knew it. He eased back in his seat. "I've got a major player coming in tomorrow...wants to invest some money, check things out...know what I mean?"

"So you want us to..." Miles queried.

"I want you both to help me show him around. Make sure he sees what he needs to see." Aziz rubbed the lines on his forehead; it seemed like one big babysitting job, a headache. "If we do that...then who's gonna run the operation while we're with him?" "Yeah." Miles chimed in; "Hell, if I ain't there at least three or four times a day...damn!"

Joker took another drag off the cigar and dumped the ashes in the ashtray. "Well gentlemen. That's your problem. All I know is the count better be right...muthafuckin' money straight!" Bezo had stepped in the office and silently closed the door, peering down on Miles, who felt his glare on his neck, and it made him uncomfortable as hell.

Joker also stared their way, waiting for a response. Aziz chuckled a little and stood up and walked over to the door where Bezo was and sized him up. Bezo was a big dude, but he knew he could handle him, if needed; already he'd shown a weakness, dokey love. "Don't worry, everything will be a'iyht." He motioned to Miles to come on and he jumped up, nodded to Joker and ducked around Aziz dipping out the back door. "I'll make sure things are cool, but just in case-"

"I'll call you in a few hours, look...you're in charge, ya hear! Don't let me down. I know I'm making a good decision...right?"

Aziz turned towards Bezo and looked him in his eyes, causing Bezo to avert his. "You can trust me. I ain't no ones boy! I don't fuck people over;" he brushed past him, bumping him slightly and said, "and believe me, ain't nobody fuckin' me, either!" then slammed the door shut.

Joker leaned back grinning. "Bezo...I think he likes you, huh..."

Bezo snickered, trying to respond in broken English.

"Yeah, boss, but I no like him."

"Me neither Bezo, me neither. Keep an eye on him."

chapter 3

"OKAY, YES MA'AM. THE order is on the way. Yes ma'am.-I'll make sure the messenger arrives before-yes, ma'am.-He won't be late.-Yes, ma'am-no, you don't have to worry..." Mya glanced over at a room towards the far side of the office. "Yes, ma'am-I'll make sure of it!" Shaking her head as she angrily hung up the phone, she pressed the extension button buzzing Skyler. "Did the messenger going to West 12th Street leave yet?"

Skyler looked around, checking the lobby, then paused knowing the answer she was about to give Mya wasn't the one she was probing for.

"No...At least he didn't come this way. You want to check-"

"No. No, I got it...thanks." Her response was hasty and dry as she got up from her desk and stomped towards the messengers' office.

Daystar Graphics, her place of employment, had their own in-house messengers, a way to expedite deliveries to and from clients quickly, at least that was the plan. The messengers were retired older gentlemen, mostly all part-time, and the buzz of high school kids in the afternoon made up for the rest. But there were still a handful of experienced bike messengers that were always depended on for the bulk of their deliveries as well as the rush dispatches. Daystar paid them well, more than average for bike messengers in the city, and they knew it and took advantage when they could.

Mya was in charge of making sure the messengers got from point A to point B without any setbacks, making sure whatever they needed to get picked up or delivered they got. She took her job very seriously because she was the one that had to put up with the crap when they weren't on time, didn't want to wait around, or were just hanging out in the streets around Times Square hawking hookers and tourists. Art News on 12th Street bit straight into her ass, and this wasn't the first time.

Steve Jackson, the ladies man with swag, the kind of guy who felt like he was God's gift to the world, self-centered, he was the fastest courier Mya had. She dealt with him gently with kid gloves as a result, but today, as far as she was concerned he'd plain ole fucked up.

"Steve!"-And she was fed up with it.

"Yeah, what's up?" Steve answered; he was just wheeling his bike out of the office.

"I'm on my way out right now-"

"It's about damn time!" Mya stood in front of him blocking the way, determined to confront him about his tardiness; she shoved her watch up in his face. "You were supposed to be gone a half hour ago! Art News has been calling me and calling me! I told them you should have been there, and here you are...ain't even leave the damn office yet!"

Steve stepped back a little, her demeanor was out of character for her. One of the retired messengers, Vito Lasosa, stood up in an attempt to defend him, "Ms. Mya, he had to take care of-" but was cut short.

"No disrespect, but, you need to mind your business, right now. Matter of fact, don't you have somewhere to go? I mean, that's what we pay you to do...go!"

"Oh hell no..." Steve said as he placed his bike alongside a wall.

"You don't have to talk to him like that!" "You're right! You're the one fuckin' up!"

Steve threw up his hands in submission.

"The hell with this!" Mya backed up and cowered slightly then spat back, "What! You wanna hit me!"

"Hey look you crazy ass mutha-my bike caught a flat! A'iyht...I bent the rim! I had to fix it. I was on the way-you know good and damn well I can make that run in no time, but not with a bad rim and a flat!" Mya looked down at the tire, inspecting it, then said, "Looks good now...you still here!"

Steve scratched his head trippin'. "You know, for a fine-ass chick like yourself...you're seriously crazy." He grabbed his bike and maneuvered around her. "And no...I don't hit women; maybe the asshole you call your man should take notes, huh." Stunned, Mya wasn't expecting that and turned towards him, shouting at him from down the hall, "Well, all y'all...assholes, are the same!" She was too upset to notice the bruises she tried to cover up earlier with foundation had smudged. "All of y'all!" She screamed out.

Steve stormed past Skyler's desk and glanced back, then dashed into the elevator and took one last look at Mya before the door closed, mouthing the words, "Not all of us."

Mya stood motionless, silently leaning against the wall as her co-workers glanced at her from out their cubicles. Holding her hands up to her face, she ran into the bathroom. Skyler was right behind her yelling at one of the receptionists. "Deena...catch these calls for me. I'll be right back!" "Go 'head, Skyler...talk to her!"

Mr. Vito quietly made his way out the doorway picking up his destination slip; he reached into the brown leather satchel he always carried, and pulled out a store-bought silk flower. "Deena...give her this, please. Tell her that we're there for her... if she needs us...even Steve."

Mya was leaning against a sink crying as Skyler rushed in. "C'mon Mya..." She hugged her.

"Skyler, I was wrong! I shouldn't have done that!"

"True...but, shit happens."

"Steve ain't that bad a guy. I didn't listen to him and-"

"Calm down, calm down. It'll be okay." She pulled some tissue out from its holder and gently wiped around her eyes. "But, you really need to handle this problem, it's affecting things around here."

Mya looked up at her and said. "Everyone knows, huh."

"Funny thing...we all understand. Don't like it-but, you need to do something, soon."

"You think the boss knows?"

"Not sure, but I know one thing for sure."

"What's that?"

"His wife knows and she damn sure doesn't like it. Told Deena she was gonna have a talk with you."

"Damn...could lose my job behind this shit."

"Don't think so.

Just wants to talk.

You might want to kick it with her anyway, she has friends, Mya."

"All Cops."

Skyler tossed the tissue in the stall then made an attempt to straighten up Mya's makeup. "Maybe that's what you need,"

"I ain't no snitch, Skyler. I can't do that....come on now."

Skyler held her hand walking to the door and said, "I feel you. I really don't know what else to tell you." She opened the door and walked to her desk. Deena gave her the flower Mr. Vito had left and she handed it to her. "Here you go girl. Now, you know you owe Mr. Vito an apology....Steve too." Mya took the flower and sniffed it, then smiled. "I'll take care of it, promise." "Damn...me and Steve go way back, too." She turned towards Skyler as she strutted back to her desk. "And...Thanks, girlfriend."

Skyler beamed and said. "Humph. Don't know what y'all do without me around here." A voice came from the messengers' office snickering, "Don't know either hell...don't know where we'd watch a ass that fat shake...for free. Damn, don't quit now!" Skyler picked up some paper and balled it up, throwing it towards the doorway. "I need to start charging you horny-ass old men."

"How much?"

Mya giggled and shook her head as she listened, then thinking about her impending conversation with the boss's wife, she made it back to her office and plopped down in her chair, thinking. What did she really know? How much did she know? And, why did she even care?

AZIZ AND MILES STROLLED around the side of the rec-center. Aziz stopped and sat on one of the benches overlooking the playground and asked the question, "Wonder what Joker's got planned?"

"Dun'no...always got something up his sleeve." Miles said.

"Thought he was making good money. Wonder why he needs to go in with someone else?"

Miles sat next to him with his eyes fixed on one of the abandoned buildings down the block, noticing some of the activity that appeared to be stirring. "Maybe, he's trying to get the whole Alphabet-"

"No one's ever took over Alphabet City...no one."

"True. But it's primed and ready to go, kna'mean." Miles stood up and pointed towards the FDR Highway. "The projects are filled to the brim with dope fiends. They walk from 3rd Street, 2nd, even as far as Hampton Square Houses just to cop dope."

"It can be done, maybe...think so?"

"I muthafuckin' no so. Just never had the kind of loot to do it my damn self."

Aziz glanced over at his car being wiped down and changed the subject. "Nice ride, huh." he said.

"Meant to tell you that...yeah. What is it...Audi, G5?"

"Know you shit, Miles...paid for, too."

Miles averted his attention away from the building and walked towards the car and bent over, checking out the shiny 22's Aziz had just put on. "Nice wheels..."

"Got them in Brooklyn. Forged metal, Mark Levinson's.

He opened the door. "Check out inside."

"Okay, okay...Italian leather...wood grain...I feel you."

"And check out the system." Aziz walked around to the driver's side and opened the door wide, then took out his keys and cranked it up. He leaned towards the radio then waved for Miles to get in, but Miles was focused once again up the street. He'd spotted a black, four-door, Crown Victoria. "Yo, Aziz...up the street. Look like five-o."

"Damn, you're right." Aziz said as he looked, "Wonder what's up with that?" He gestured Poppi over to the passenger side window.

"Know anything 'bout that?" Poppi stood up and looked.

"Naw, don't know. That's new to me...ain't been there earlier that's for sure."

Aziz closed the car door and said, "I'm out. Miles...you riding or what?"

"Naw..." He'd already surveyed the building, looking for spots to dip in, just in case he needed to. "I'm dirty...you? Aziz thought about the bundle he had in his pocket. "Damn...hell yeah."

Poppi reached into the vehicle, not about to let this opportunity slip by and said. "Yo...I got it. I'll just take what I need-"

"But...if you get busted."

"Yeah well, better me than you, huh." That bought a grin to Aziz's face; he slipped him the package. "Take what you need. I'll catch up with you later." Poppi grabbed the bundle and stuffed it into his jacket, then took off running up the street, disappearing into an abandoned building.

"That's a good man, Aziz. We need to work with him a little more. He's been down for a minute...real thorough, old skool. You know, now that we're like, lieutenants, we can make calls like that."

"Damn right-oh shit!" Miles noticed the car he was checking out starting up. "I gotta dip." He stuffed his pockets with the dope bags he had on him, then transferred his, 9mm. Glock from his waist into his jacket, in case he needed to bust one.

"Here they come...Miles, if they stop, I'm a haul ass up the street. Might have to ditch the car, damn!"

"Be cool...'sides, I ain't going back to prison." Aziz knew he was dead serious. Miles had just not too long gotten out from under an eight year bid, little over three years now. He caught hell in Sing Sing and swore he'd never go back to prison again. Aziz had a lot to lose himself and he wasn't going out like a sucker. Even though he knew if he ever got popped, Joker would put up the money to get him and Miles out, his best pushers but why chance it anyway, he thought.

The unmarked car cruised by them and slowed down, long enough for them to spot two males; one black, one white, and they knew they had to be cops. They kept their eyes fixed on the dark, tinted windows until they reached the corner and turned off. "Miles...something ain't right. Let's get the fuck outta here while we still can. Miles jumped in the car as Aziz sped off up the block and turned opposite the other vehicle going towards 14th Street. "Think it got something to do with Joker?" Aziz chuckled, "It's got everything to do with Joker!"

After riding a few blocks in silence, Aziz turned down the radio of the Bose system he had bumpin', breaking the rhythm of the nod Miles had going. "Yo...check it; we do good to manage the spots we have without too much bullshit. But, really, how we gonna keep in check," he pointed out the window to the neighborhood as he drove, "damn near a whole...hell, a whole city"

Miles looked around, then nodded his head.

"I thought about that too. But, I guess it's like what you just said...manage."

"Like doing business, huh."

"Shit, like a whole muthafuckin' corporation."

Aziz pulled up to a stoplight and leaned over on the driver's side door glancing at Miles. "Corporation? That's big boy talk, huh."

Miles grinned. "Let me tell you something. When you locked the fuck up, you get plenty of time to read...and, that's what I did."

"I hear you. You never cease to amaze me..."

Miles glanced over at him and said, "Good." Aziz let out a laugh as the light changed, then his cell phone rang. "Wonder who this is...might be Mya." He pulled the phone out from inside his jacket pocket and answered it, ignoring the numbers that had appeared on the screen. "Mya. I'll be there to pick you up-"

A sultry, sensuous voice came through from the other end and said, "Hello, baby." Aziz pulled the phone back from his ear and shook his head then answered, "Wassup...I ain't expect to hear from you."

"Don't worry, baby, after a while, you will."

"Heard that before."

"So...Mya. I see I'm gonna have to make her a thing of the past."

"Might prove to be difficult..."

"Never been a problem...before."

Miles glanced over at Aziz; he couldn't believe he had a chick on the side. He spoke up and Aziz started frowning up. "Humph...Cheating on Mya...fine-ass Mya. Know this hoe better be bad..." Aziz threw another frown his way and whispered. "Shhh, keep your voice down."

"So," Miles continued, "she ever finds out," he pointed at his chest, "Pow! It's your ass." Aziz had enough, he pulled the car over. "A'iyht, 12th Street and Avenue B. How 'bout you go to the pool-room or sumptin'. Know your ass got things to do." Miles reached for the door handle and said, "That's a'iyht, got pick-ups anyway." He slipped his head back through the window after he slammed the door. "Remember...you kicked me out for some pussy. Don't get shit fucked up, use the goddamn brain in your head-" Aziz revved the gas and threw the car in gear; Miles snatched his head out as he pulled off. He stared at the car as it sped away, giving him the finger, and mumbling to himself, "Always a stupid muthafucka' gotta think with his dick!"

"Miles!" A short, bald-headed, young boy, looking to be about middle school, called from in front of the poolroom. "You're early. Everything a'iyht? You here to do the count... right?"

Miles kept his eyes on the car as it slowly faded out of view up Avenue B, still in thought about Aziz's dis. "Yeah...yeah...count."

Aziz pulled over by the library on Avenue A and 9th Street, Tompkins Square Park, to finish his conversation. "Yo...I don't know if I can get up with you tonight."

"Why'? I know you ain't trying to put that bitch in front of me!"

"Damn...You sayin' that. You know I live with her...and I keep dipping out. She's gonna know sumptin'!"

"I don't give a flyin' fuck what she knows! You need to tell her anyway, 'bout me-"

"No!"

"Why?"

"Time ain't right...not yet."

"Well," the voice on the other end of the line got incensed, then uncontrollable babbling was the only thing Aziz heard next, "When! When! You just can't be leading me on like this!" He rubbed his hand across his face; the wrinkles on his forehead showed lines of stress, the kinda shit he didn't need. "Okay! Okay I'll...try-"

"Now baby...that's better." The voice turned down a notch to a soothing lullaby. "Look, come over. I'll rub your back like you like. Massage your chest like you like; then, I'll go down and kiss that thing like you like, too...baby." Aziz squirmed trying to redress the hard on between his legs, but it was useless. "I'll be there, but I got to handle some business, okay."

"Okay, sweetie. I'll meet you at the studio...might even take pictures this time."

"Pictures? Oh, hell no."

"One day, one day. Bye, bye."

"Yeah...bye." The voice on the other line blew a kiss as the receiver went dead. Aziz cut the phone off; he knew to expect a call from Mya shortly after and he damn sure didn't feel like having to explain to her that he would be home late or not at all. "Damn!" He said as he glanced at his watch then the bulge in his pants. "I need to handle this shit better than this".

MYA CALLED AZIZ'S PHONE and it was answered by voicemail, again, then waited a little while longer and tried again. This time, the same thing, she knew he had it turned off. It was already 5:15 PM and the last messenger had come back in early, so now she could finally leave for the day. The only other thing she had to do was drop off a couple of FedEx packages at Grand Central Station on the way home, then catch the LL subway train and it was a wrap; the weekend was about to begin.

She was hoping to spend some quality time with Aziz alone, wanting to discuss ways of ending their fighting, maybe counseling might help. It was a long shot, but she had already made the calls and even discussed it with enough people to make a move on it. Tired of the beatings, but not tired of Aziz, she thought it might just be worth it.

Dropping off the packages she dialed Aziz and it was the same thing. Maybe, she thought to herself, that he was doing pickups. After all, it was Friday and the first of the month; plenty of money on the street. He'd be busy and tired; she smiled as she started thinking about the hot pink lingerie she'd picked up earlier on in the week, just waiting to spring it on him. All he needed was some real good lovin, she rationalized, but unfortunately for her, other plans were being made without her knowledge, or consent.

POPPI HOPPED THE STEPS, two, three at a time inside the abandoned building he dipped into; slowly creeping past doorways of apartments used for junkies shooting up. The whole building was used as a shooting gallery, but enough apartments made space for literally, crawling room only shooting arenas. The building had lookouts with guns posted on top and the inside, making sure five-o, TNT-Tactical Narcotics Team, or jackboys didn't get the ups on them. Most times a lookout would also patrol the building making sure fiends didn't try to hole up in another apartment and steal.

The windows were boarded shut except for a few exceptions and even those had steel bar coverings. Joker had taken over the majority of the abandoned buildings in the area and crafted them all in categories: shooting galleries and mills, where the dope was cut up and bagged. Joker never kept both in the same building. His cop houses were also separate; if a runner was caught selling in a shooting gallery he would definitely pay, sometimes with his life; but most of the time a beatdown would suffice.

Runners did the moving of the product and usually they were all kids. Joker strapped them with AK's and made sure all the I's are dotted and the T's were crossed, but still Aziz and Miles had their hands full.

Poppi was a former runner for Joker when he had just started. He knew the drug game, but got caught up in getting high with Joker's supply and not his. Joker found out quickly and he was eliminated from his staff. He tried to make up for it, to get back in, he steered, hustled, ran, even picked up a gun, shooting at jackboys when needed. So, Joker let him hang around.

He crept into the backroom of a dingy, piss-smelling apartment and sat on an old sofa. "Gotta get a hit before I get back up with Aziz..." His hawk-like eyes darted around the apartment like flying sparrows as he scanned the room. A nauseous feeling began to invade his gut as he quickly opened up a package from the bundle he'd gotten; he swallowed, fighting back the sickness. His head jerked as he heard the sound of a rat making its rounds through the building. His eyes looked at the floor where small pools of blood lay from where fiends had tried to get a hit, but the works got stopped up from pulling the needle out and letting blood spurt all over, leaving a trail of gory, dirty toilet tissue.

He sprinkled a little of the white powder into a large bottle top and slowly cooked it, almost burning his hand when it became too hot to hold, but not enough to make him drop it. Slowly, he rolled up a piece of cotton he pulled out of his pocket along with his works and dropped it inside the cooker, drawing the heroin up through it as his fingers delicately worked; he pushed the other bundles up under the sofa out of sight.

He felt for the vein on his arm and hit it hard, causing it to swell. Then, he took the needle he had and stuck it; the dropper filled with blood. Removing the dropper from the needle and leaving it still in his arm, he squirted the water out, drawing up some heroin that was in the top. Gently, he placed the dropper into the needle that protruded from his arm, waiting until the blood flowed in the dropper again before releasing the dope slowly. Waiting for the re-flow of blood was the only way of knowing if the works had stopped while he changed the dropper.

Twice more, Poppi refilled then ran the dope, picked up the top and wriggled the dropper around and sucked up the last bit of dope in it. When he pulled the needle out, blood ran down his arm as he lay out on the sofa. He managed to pull out some tissue and wipe it before he-"Daaaammmmnnnn, this shiiit is gooood..."-passed da' fuck out.

Poppi didn't hear the footsteps as they approached. Still high and sluggish from the dope cruising through his mind and scratching at his worn out tracks, he did manage to mutter, "Wha-wha..." then nodded back out.

The mysterious figure slowly crept towards him. Stepping closer to the sofa, the figure moved over towards the window and pulled back the worn, hole infested curtains, making sure all was clear. The lookout had already made his walk.

Searching underneath the sofa and spotting the bundle, the figure bent over and deliberately reached for it. "Hey!" Poppi grabbed at the hand and with his other, swung, catching all air. The silent thief stepped back as smooth as a cat and reached into the short, leather jacket and pulled out a snub-nosed .357 with a silencer attached. Poppi stood with his hands up. "Whoa! What you want! I mean...I ain't got no money!"

The figure pointed the gun towards the dope; Poppi looked down. "This shit belongs to the man!" The figure pointed once more, but this time pulled the hammer back.

"Damn...just what the fuck I don't need!" Poppi kneeled down to pick up the dope and said, "Just don't shoot me!" then cut his eyes up towards the shadow that stood in front of him. The curtain opened slightly from a breeze that blew allowing him to catch a quick, slighting glimpse of the face standing over him. No one he recognized, a ski mask covered everything up, but there was something that still wasn't right.

He knew he'd have to explain this shit to Aziz and it wasn't going to be good, an ass-kicking at best, one he couldn't take. Tired of them now, he was just too old; hell, he figured, if Joker hadn't forgiven him by now-he jumped.

The figure side-stepped him easily. Poppi was still sluggish from the high and he crashed to the floor, hard. The next thing he knew the cold steel tip of the silencer pressed into his forehead and Poppi begged for his life. "Please...no...Don't kill me. Please!"

The mysterious figure slowly peeled up the bottom of the ski mask and said. "Fuck you..." then pumped two slugs into Poppi's brain. Smoke and blood oozed out of the small holes as Poppi's eyes fixed frozen forever.

Bending over and picking up the package, the now cautious figure, knowing that the lookout would be back through at any moment, stuffed the bundle into the jacket of the rugged, cowhide bomber jacket; looked back down at Poppi and spit, then shot him once more. "Fuck Joker...and Aziz."

The lifeless body of Poppi moved only once more, after the rat that moved through the room bit his body making sure he was dead, then scurried away quickly to notify the others of the find.

chapter 4

MILES GAZED AT THE customers walking in and out of the Chinese restaurant all the while reading the menu special on the window: fried egg rolls, chicken wings and shrimp fried rice; it made his stomach rumble. He hadn't eaten all day and it was coming to a close rapidly, already 5:45 PM. He waited on the young boy that had called him, ran upstairs to get his partner, his brother, Pancho. Miles took them both in, after all they were pretty thorough for runners, even though they were young.

They didn't go to school half the time and he would find them at drug spots hustling his customers, hell, Miles figured it would be better for them to work for him than against him; besides he'd show them the real business, and at the same time, keep an eye on them. Maybe one day make them partners so he could retire from all the bullshit. It was getting old for him.

Pancho came running out in front; his brother Big E was right on his heels. "Miles! Got bad news!" Miles turned and asked, "What's up? What's wrong now?" He walked towards them and reached into his jacket for the gun thinking there might have been trouble upstairs. "It's all good inside." Pancho said as he frowned at his brother. "He ain't been gamblin'...lately."

Big E had been prone to gambling on the pool table and even though he had game; he'd catch hell making the older runners pay him his money, but, a couple of pistol whippings later from Miles resolved that problem quickly. Not only would they pay him, they even bought his big overweight ass something to eat. Miles now stood in front of them with his arms crossed, scolding them. "Didn't I tell you two not to make any moves without me. I know I did-"

"There was a shooting at the spot over on 4th Street." Pancho blurted out.

"4th Street...the Pitt?"

"Naw...a shooting gallery, right up the block from it."

Miles looked over at the restaurant and sighed, then shook his head; Chinese food would have to wait. He had to go see what had happened; the spot was Joker's and it was too close to the boss's headquarters. "A'iyht, let's go get the truck..."

He drove a Range Rover Evoque fitted out with Sabini, Z-9 chrome 24's he'd copped from a car show in Brooklyn. They were the only ones in New York and he had to have them. Miles was hung as well as Aziz, but he was built different. He stayed in the hood close to his community of junkies, hustlers and runners, maintaining a close relationship, knowing all the comings and goings the ins and the outs. With no kids and no steady woman in his life, figuring that would only hinder him in his quest for the larger-than-life status, he endeavored to achieve ghetto greatness.

His heroin-addicted mother died of an overdose when he was just eight and his father was killed in prison somewhere in Florida, at least that's what he was told. He was raised by his sister, not too much older than himself. As he grew older she resorted to turning tricks on the street so they could eat, keep a roof over their head and wear decent clothes. When he was introduced to the game, he swore he'd pay her back, get her off the streets; but she was murdered by a crazed serial killer who migrated into the city from the Midwest, Wisconsin somewhere, so he was told later by Detectives. She was strangled by him and left in the street, leaving Miles bitter and on his own. It was he who would avenge his sister's death; his revenge resulted in an eight-year bid upstate for manslaughter.

Joker at the time was a small time pusher working his way up when he heard what Miles had done, saving him hundreds in sales from scared customers around the area. If the killer had continued to hang out in Alphabet City any longer, more bodies would have been found instead of the seven he was credited with. Joker took care of Miles' books upstate but he still had to fend for himself.

The fellas walked across the avenue to PS-7 where he'd parked his truck. He tried to keep it inconspicuous until needed, this way the cops wouldn't have him pegged; unlike Aziz, who showboated his car and himself around the hood. He would stay low-key until the time would come for him to show his face and when he did, it wasn't good.

"Who the hell would have the balls to fuck with one of our spots?"

"Don't know. Ain't nobody...different been in the hood, right Pancho!" Big E said.

"No one! Least, none that we know about, and we usually know what's going on!"

Miles looked at his two loyal soldiers and grinned. They were picking and choosing their words carefully, understanding that the last person that came in the hood unnoticed killed his sister. "Good...well, we'll have to see what's up. Make our run from there."

"Work our way from Houston on back?" Big E asked.

"Til we make it to Hampton Square."

"A'iyht...we're ready."

The truck was parked in a lot reserved for the teachers to the school. Miles pulled out a small remote no bigger than the palm of his hand and opened the doors before he got in, then waved up towards the second floor across from the school at a pretty, blond-haired woman smiling down at him. "That's some good pussy..." he said as he winked while Pancho and Big E gushed. "Boys, boys...take notes." Miles had another name, one that the local Latino woman gave him, one that stuck: hombre de damas-ladies man. That was him.

Miles decided to make his way over via Avenue B, swing down by Tompkins Square Park and see if the suits coming in from work and the professors coming over from NYU-New York University, had started making their daily hiatus to buy heroin. Looking down the street towards the 5th Precinct, he saw no unusual activity. Usually if there wasn't a big buy and bust or a shoot-out, the cops didn't bother to rush over, unless of course, they wanted to get paid off.

He pulled up to the corner and The Pitt was closed. Strange, he thought, Joker's ride was still parked in front. Getting a better look, he spotted someone looking out the door, probably Bezo. Turning his head he looked up the street; EMS was already there, and to his surprise so were the cops. He turned right and pulled up in front of the basketball courts a little ways down from The Pitt facing the crowd that had formed. "A'iyht, fellas...this is the deal," he said as he kept his eyes on the building where the cops were already interviewing whatever witnesses they could muster up. "Go find out what's going on, but be quick...we still got work to do." Pancho and Big E jumped out; Miles rolled the windows down and called out, "Y'all clean, right?"

"We straight." Pancho answered.

"A'iyht then, be quick! Pancho!"

"Yeah, Miles...we heard you."

"Look in the back and grab the basketball."

"Basketball?"

"Just do it...okay."

"Whatever you say."

Pancho popped the lock on the hatch causing it to rise upward and Big E snatched up the ball that sat off on the side. "Be careful," Miles said as they bounced up the street; his cell phone vibrated and he checked the caller ID, nothing, but he had a good idea of who it was. "Miles, good to see you...sent your boys in, huh. Smart move." It was Joker

"Need to find out what happened. Know anything?"

"Naw...hell, cops just rolled up, then EMS. Figured some muthafucka must have overdosed, but they went in with their guns out."

"Guns drawn, huh..."

"I told Bezo to put everyone out, close up shop, least 'till I find out what's up."

"That's what's up, but that's one of Aziz's territories. Miles said.

"Yeah, true. I called him and his fuckin cell is off! Where the hell is he? He's the one that needs to be handling this shit!" Miles knew Aziz had gone on a pussy hunt and turned the cell off to keep Mya from tracking him down. It was after six and normally he'd be picking her up from the train station; he didn't have a clue to his whereabouts, but still he covered for him. "I think he got sick or sumptin'. Told me he'd meet me at the mill."

"He looked good a lil' while ago. A'iyht, but he'd better be there!"

"He will." Miles's attention turned back to Pancho and Big E as they ran back up the street towards him. "Hey, uh, look boss...I'll call you back."

"Let me know what you find out."

"A'iyht."

"And Miles. You know I thought about makin' you my top dog...don't let me down, huh." That put a smile on Miles's face. That's what he wanted, for now. He knew he was worthy of it, but still he'd go about it like a man, not like Aziz, he'd earn it. The fellas made it back to the car and hopped in. "You ain't gonna like this."

"Wassup!"

"That muthafucka Poppi, Aziz's dope fiend runner-"

"Be steering muthafucka's for a hit!" Bug Tiny butted in.

"I got it!" Pancho shot an eye at him. "Yeah, that muthafucka...got himself killed. Two shots to the brain."

".357!" Big E added.

Miles leaned back and thought about the package Aziz had slipped him; maybe Poppi had gotten robbed. "Did anybody see anything?"

"Naw...that was strange. Muthafucka's ain't even hear no shots bust. No one!" Miles knew that was dangerous. A sure sign; whoever killed Poppi had a silencer. It was a planned hit. Jackboys don't work like that, then just Poppi. If it was jackboys they would have robbed the whole spot. Shoot it up at best. "Did they find any dope?"

"Nope. The houseman told me to tell you he stashed everything: money, dope, said when things clear up, and Aziz comes by, he'd give him the take."

"Ain't really worryin' about that. I meant Poppi's dope. Sumthin' ain't right...sumthin." He pressed the brakes, signaling to Joker, whom he knew was watching his every move, to call, and sure enough, his phone rang. "Hey...I need to meet with you some time tomorrow."

"Wassup...don't sound good."

"Ain't figure it out yet, but it ain't been no jackboys."

"Figured that much. Hell, everyone knew I was in here, my Bentleys' right out front. Nobody don't want that type of drama, naw, especially right in front of me."

"Sounds like a hit, but who were they tryin' to get at? Damn! Maybe I need to switch routes for a minute."

"True, might want to do that. Look, Miles, I'm out, it's gettin' late. We'll get up tomorrow."

"Yeah, tomorrow."

Before Miles could hang up Joker yelled out, "Hey! The money's straight...right!"

"That's what I heard."

"I'll meet you at the stash house tomorrow then...be careful."

Miles closed up the phone and stuck it back in the console and turned hack to Pancho and Big E. "A'iyht fellas, lets dip. We got work to do." He cruised up the block past the building where Poppi was killed. The junkies stood out in front as the police tried to ask questions, but they knew better than to say anything. Being labeled a snitch would fuck them and their high up for while. They started walking off as Poppi's body was loaded up in an old, black van from the Coroner's office. A beat up van used only for junkies suspected of having the virus, and Poppi wasn't just a suspect but the goddamned poster boy. What a way to go, Miles pondered as he stared.

Towards the upper left window on the 5th floor of the building, a scraggly old curtain opened slightly, unnoticeably; someone else was watching also. As the mysterious figure watched Miles drive by, the mumbling that came from the voice was littered with rasp and hate. "I'ma get your ass...you'll see. " The curtain gradually eased back, closed.

SKYLER WALKED PAST the turnstiles leading down into the subway LL train. Already missing the 5:30 PM to Eighth Avenue after stopping in a few boutiques along the way. Skyler's thing was shopping; she dove through fashion magazines like a bee to honey, but just like the pollen that the bee's got to have to make the honey, in her case, money, she just didn't have it like that, so she window shopped half the time. She was about to sit and wait on the train and spotted Steve a little ways down.

"Hey Steve!" she called out. Steve looked up waving her over, "Yo wassup!" he said. "Damn. You made it back already? That was quick...fast..."

"I know the shortcuts." He smiled, then shook his head as he thought back to his earlier beef with Mya. Skyler sensed it and stroked his back reassuringly. "She didn't mean what she said. She's got issues going on."

Steve turned his head toward the tunnel slightly as he heard the roar of the oncoming train, and backed up with Skyler, then responded. "Issues...yeah...getting beat up, huh."

"I mean...that's what she seems to want. I don't know, it's crazy, though." Skyler said as she turned her head from the wind that came in hard; the graffiti stained locomotive blazed into the station, causing her to cover her face and cough from the dust and stench that lurched along with it.

"Crazy, you think. Insane is more like it." Steve said.

They stepped aside as the passengers moved out and almost got swept away in the swarm that seemed to appear out of nowhere. It was the third train after rush hour, less congested, but still overcrowded. "Damn..." Steve said as he tried to navigate his bike through the throng, "should waited on the next one."

Skyler wriggled around him, then glanced around at the doors looking for any signs of dirt and dust. "It's the weekend, that's why it's so crowded, but forget about that, uh, y'all grew up together, right?"

Steve pulled out a rag from his bag and wiped down the doorway for her. "Yeah, we did..."

"Lower East Side...right?"

"Alphabet City." Steve leaned back and reflected. "We went to school together, PS-7...and Junior High. I had a crazy crush on her, she was fine as hell;" he grinned "still is, but school fine is different, ya know."

"Okay...you liked her."

"She was all I thought about." His eyes lit up as he drew deeper into the memory, then just as quickly, his eyes turned downcast. "But, she didn't want me."

"Whaaat? I mean," Skyler eyeballed the lean, swimmers frame of a body Steve had and admired it, "you're a good-looking guy."

"Wasn't about the looks." He eased his bike over as someone stepped in between them going into the next car. "It was about the money." He collected his thoughts. "That's how she met Aziz anyway."

"Aziz, who's that?"

"Aziz."

"Oh, okay, but...didn't she have some kids...before him, though."

"Destiny and Hope. What's up with that?"

"They almost grown and Mya ain't that goddamn old."

"You right," Steve chuckled, "she's not. She had the oldest, Hope, in Junior High. I remember that shit well, broke my muthafuckin' heart when I found out she was pregnant."

Skyler licked at her lips and played with her makeup staring off into the window, catching glimpses of her reflection. "Broke your heart, huh...maybe because it wasn't yours." Steve's eyes met her in the image and he said, "Yeah....that....and, maybe, I found out she was fuckin' and not fuckin' me."

Skyler turned away, knowing she'd hit a sore spot, but still, she probed deeper anyway. "Did you know the father?"

"Actually...yeah, I did. Dude I grew up with. Played ball wit' him."

"What happened...with him?"

"Well, I mean. He was one of the baddest ballers out there. Muthafucka' was nice. I mean, he was all that."

"C'mon now, fuck that. What happened to him? She never told me nuthin', always ducked the issue."

Steve looked out the window on the platform as the train glided to a stop at the Sixth Avenue station. "Maybe, she doesn't want you to know. Ever thought about that."

"Don't be like that," Skyler frowned, "you know I won't say-"

"Yeah, right...get the fuck outta here!"

"Why everybody thinks I tell everything!"

"Because, you do! But...I'ma tell your ass anyway." Skyler pointed towards an empty seat and pulled at his arm. "Let's sit down."

"You'll be off next stop."

"So...I wanna hear this. 'Sides, my feet hurt." He looked down at her feet and she blushed. "Damn stilettos."

Steve's smile, a full set of whites, seemed to hypnotize Skyler, pulling her in as he continued the story. "His name was Dante Roberts. He played ball....but he also hustled...dope. He was a runner for a dude down my way named Joker. New to the hood, trying to set up shop; hell, don't know where he got all the money and dope from, he just like...blew in." He adjusted his bike and paused, then smirked. "Anyway, Dante hooked up with him after he met him at a game. Joker used to bet crazy money on him; won too. Next thing you know they're kickin' it, like they knew each other for years and shit. I tried to talk to him, tell him he was fuckin' up, but he wouldn't listen. All he saw was the money, cars, jewelry, all that... not a broke ass muthafucka' like me...his words, not mine."

Skyler sensed the bitterness in his voice and asked, "Why didn't you go for the life, too?"

Steve stretched his long, slender legs out and said, "That's another story..." The train came to a sudden stop and the lights blinked. "Now what." Skyler said as she turned her head around. "Don't worry, happens all the time," Steve said. "Anyway, it'll give me a chance to finish tellin' you what happened."

"I'm listening."

"Dante was large and getting larger by the minute, then, he saw Mya. Damn...that was it. Actually...it was my fault they hooked up."

"Your fault...why?"

"She'd come to the Pitt, a rec center down there, and watch me play ball with him...I would invite her."

"That's where she met him."

"He went after her hard. Gave her jewelry, money...next thing I know, pregnant again."

Skyler shook her head as she imagined the chain of events Steve laid out before her. "What ever happened to him...prison?"

"Naw, he got killed. Shot point blank...in the face, right in front of her."

"Oh hell, no!" She hadn't expected that, she was shocked and stood motionless as the train started to move again, slowly creeping into the station. They got up and made their way to the doors and Skyler asked. "Did they ever find the guy that-"

Steve walked towards the exit steps and hesitated then turned and stared as she stood at the entrance of a stairway marked, D Train-Bronx. "Funny thing...they say it was Aziz." "Aziz, the guy she's with now!"

"And the fucked up thing about it...I believe it, I do."

Steve waved goodbye as he picked up his bike on his broad shoulders and hiked up the steps out of the subway. Skyler stood there thinking about what he told her as he disappeared out of view, she said to herself, Mya...what's really going on?

THE DRAB, DISMAL APARTMENT building seemed to stick out as it was approached. Yellowish brown and gray with dulled colors highlighted years of urban plight, too much decay in a neighborhood meant for better things perhaps like living. The damp sprays from the cross winds coming off the East River stripped it of its shine and grandiosity many decades ago. What was left of 110 8th Street were the memories of productive families struggling to survive in age-old New York; but instead, the reality of vacant, rat infested apartments occupied by dope fiends, whores or steel mailbox panels pulled apart by addicts desperate for a fix, was all that was left.

As the black, rusted metal front door of the apartment building opened, the black and white checkered tile, creaked against its weight. Abruptly, doors opened halfway and heads peeped out, tenants looking for a way to escape from this hell-hole or even junkies looking for their next vic. The steps shined colors of orange and glistening yellow piss, heroin vomit muddled up in the corners, stanched the already disfigured landscape.

The third floor was cooled by a shattered hallway window inviting in the crisp, biting air that chased chills through your bones. Apartment 3C, a one bedroom flat with a separate bathroom and kitchen. A steal at a market price of six hundred a month. The door was shut and locked only after a quick survey of the surroundings were taken. No break-ins today, but only because of the five locks that were affixed to the door to hinder any more such attempts; so far, so good.

Walking down the short foyer revealed three openings; to the left, the kitchen which connected to the dining room, and the other was the bedroom. Across from the door of the kitchen was the bathroom, an old porcelain sink and tub that still held remnants of copper plumbing, all intact. The whole place seemed to overflow with an opaque murkiness, leaving the kitchen odorless and flat.

The refrigerator door was opened. Beer cans, flat sodas and containers of old Chinese food showed signs of a green rot growing along the lids. A dingy sheet separated the living room as the Smith & Wesson .357 Revolver, blue steel handgun was placed gently on a table in contrast to the ambiance.

In the bedroom, on top of the dresser above a small, black and white, 13 inch television was a small pocket sized map of the Lower East Side of Manhattan; red ink traced a route along Alphabet City. Clothes were tossed about on the floor as a closet door was opened, revealing a row of steel-toe, black leather boots lined up neatly next to an old pair of WalMart slippers. At the foot of the bed, white undergarments replaced the leather jacket and scruffy jeans worn earlier as they were discarded in an off-white laundry hamper.

The bathroom had crisp white towels stacked next to the tub, all stolen from a Motel 6. The water ran hot as it was turned on and steam rushed up into the air, misting up the tightly built bathroom; a quickly raised window eliminated the problem any further.

Lighting up a cigarette and sliding into the tub, the ranting would begin like always. "Fuckin' dope fiend...dumb muthafucka...gonna try me like that! Shit! Shit! Shit!" The water splashed violently up over the tub as the tantrum continued. "I hate them dope fiend muthafucka's!" Violent laughter, hideous and sinister, until the coughing from the cigarette smoke silenced it to a whimper. "I'ma get you, too, Joker! Fuckin' flunky ass!"

No robe or towel came between the body and wet floor as the map was stared at as the voice said, "All you muthafucka's gonna die!" Sliding back into the tub and lighting up another cigarette caused the tensed body to relax. "Need to kill..." Another pull from the Newport was enough to coast deeper into the soothing waters.

"I'ma get them...I swear..." After one last look at the map and it was tossed on the floor and the voice became mute and silenced to a snore, and tears mixed with the steamy hot water soothed a mind only occupied, with revenge.

chapter 5

LEAVING THE LOWER EAST Side the money green, smooth riding Bentley made its way up the FDR Drive towards Harlem, 145th Street. Joker had just inhaled deeply on the chocolate, brown cigar he'd just lit then pulling it away from his mouth and eyeballing it, he said, "Damn, good smoke." as he slid deeper into the plush, leather interior of the back seat. The rich, green weed he'd stuffed it with earlier started to take its toll as he tripped on how opportunity had turned his fortunes upward.

He remembered back to a time when he once sold dope for a pusher by the name of Akbar. Akbar made a bad move, a move that would eventually cost him time in the Fed; 240 months-20 years. Joker took over his connects, and no one, not even Akbar knew who snitched him out, except for Bezo. "That muthafuckin' weed connect out of Queens was the best fuckin' thing that pussy-ass Akbar ever did." Joker talked shit as he took another deep pull and blew the thick, purplish haze of smoke upwards towards Bezo and laughed. "Too bad that muthafucka did more talkin' than he did smokin' or I'd never knew how to set 'em up. Right Bezo!" It was a bad move on Akbar's part, trusting Bezo.

Akbar trusted him with his life because he thought he was loyal, but mostly because he thought he was slow and figured he could handle him anyway he wanted. But, he wasn't slow enough to make a move on Akbar when Joker hit him up with the plan to get at him. Joker set Akbar up, and the next thing he knew, he was locked up and all of what had belonged to him, now belonged to Joker.

That put him high up in the game. A fish in a big pond called Manhattan. He greased all the hands he needed to, but one in particular wanted more than his fair share. Dude wanted it all and was willing to pay the cost. Joker was ready to get out of the game anyway; he had enough money put back to retire, go down to Cancun, Mexico, smoke weed and play on the beach. When the transaction came his way he was ready to deal, but he only bargained with Alphabet City; the spots he had in Harlem were much too lucrative for him. It was the type of deal he'd been wanting for a long time.

'Bzzzzzz'! 'Bzzzzzz'! 'Bzzzzzz'! His cell phone vibrated, disturbing the sedated mood he was enjoying. "Who the fuck is this..." The face of the phone lit up and his eyes grew wide once he recognized the number. "Damn...shit! This muthafucka!" He straightened up and motioned to Bezo to roll the windows down; get the smoke that had built up inside, out. Bezo didn't smoke weed, but still he might as well have; he'd caught enough second-hand highs to be considered a junky for the green his damn self. "Dis Joker...what up!"

The voice that came through the line was high pitched and irritated him every time he heard it, and it made him grit his teeth. "What's uh, up with you, Joker?"

"Hey, look, Mr-"

He cut him short. "Now, now, Joker. You know we don't do the name thing over the phone...or did you forget?" -

"Uh...naw..." Joker shook his head knowing full well he did and the weed didn't help at all. "Sorry 'bout that." he said.

"Accepted. Now, do you have things in order for my little...tour?"

"No problem...tomorrow, right?"

"Joker, Joker. I don't know how you made it this far being so careless, and I really don't care, but when it comes to me...got to be more careful."

The car slowed down as they approached the exit to 125th Street. They'd caught up with the traffic coming in from midtown and had to sit a minute. Normally, this would be Joker's cue to light up another blunt, but the conversation he had now called for him to be sharp or money could be lost. "I've got things handled and in order. What time to expect-"

The voice laughed then said, "Whenever I get there," then he hung up. His laugh lingered around in Joker's head, fuckin' up his high and he threw the phone on the floor. "Muthafucka! Who the hell does he think he is?"

"Everything a'iyht, boss?" Bezo asked as he looked through the rearview mirror. "Trouble?" Joker stared his cold, conniving eyes back at him and said, "No, no trouble...not yet." He lit the blunt he had clipped back up and looked out the window towards the river. "Just hope Aziz and Miles got their shit together. Don't need no fuckups."

"Maybe, you should call-"

"Call who, Bezo?"

"Aziz, make sure he's on it."

Joker grinned when he heard that, thinking about the game he was setting up. "Naw...that's a'iyht, Bezo. Everything's gonna work out just fine...trust me"

"Whatever you say, boss." Traffic picked back up again as Bezo switched lanes going on to the off ramp heading into Harlem, laughing all the way to the bank.

MYA GOT OFF THE TRAIN at 14th Street and 1st Avenue and pulled out the small, demure Samsung smart phone from out her purse checking for a signal, walking over to the side of a building to get away from the draft coming off the East River, she speed dialed Aziz and this time he answered. "What's up, Mya."

She smiled when she heard his voice and said, "Hey, baby, been tryin' to call since I got off work. Where ya been?"

"Been makin' my runs," he said as he pulled the car over out of traffic. "You okay?"

"Yeah, I'm okay. I thought maybe we could do something tonight..." A pause came over the phone as he looked around through the rearview mirror for any signs of five-o. "Well...I'm kinda busy right now."

Mya was used to him being busy and figured out ways to work around it. "Not now, a little later on, tonight. Maybe, shoot over to Coyote Ugly or something...a few drinks..." Aziz thought about it. He did have enough sense to realize he'd been an asshole lately, plus he needed to talk to her about the headaches he'd been having lately. "What about the kids?" he asked.

"That's no problem...I can make arrangements."

"Well...uh, it's gonna be late. Gotta make some pickups."

Mya leaned against the side of the building, a feeling of consolation came over her, maybe this was the one time they'd get it right. "I'm on my way home now."

"A'iyht." Aziz said as he threw the phone into the glove compartment. An old tattered photo caught his eye and he reached in and pulled it out. A citywide basketball team photo: him, Miles and Dante; Mya's two daughters' father, posing in front of the Pitt. He tossed it back in the glove compartment and slammed it shut, then slid deep into the seat. His mind racing, going back to a place where he didn't want to be. His head started to pound, gently, another headache. Not again, he grabbed the steering wheel and hoisted himself up and banged it with both fists. "Damn!" he yelled out, "Will it ever end!"

MYA WALKED TO THE TRANSIT terminal to catch the M15 bus going down 14th Street to Ave D, then stopped in her tracks. "Oh shit..." She glanced at her watch and saw that she had a little time before the next bus arrived, but she needed to call her girls. She pulled out her phone and dialed.

"Hello, Hope."

"Ma! Where you at? Been waitin' for you to call." Her daughter voicing concern about her whereabouts made her feel good; Hope was the older and more responsible of her two girls. "Hey baby, worked a little late...sorry 'bout that, shoulda called."

"Yeah, Ma...you should have. You know how I worry."

"Worry? Sweetheart, I'm grown." She thought back to the fight she had with Aziz last night, hearing Hope's muffled cries as she turned up the TV loudly in her room to keep from hearing her mother cry out, made her take a deep breath and sigh loudly into the phone. "Baby, there's gonna be changes. We'll talk later-"

"Ma, he ain't never gonna change! He crazy!"

"Hope don't start!"

"But, Ma...he does it all the time-"

"Hope!" Mya raised her voice this time and said, "Let's not start this! I said, we'll talk about it later...I promise baby."

She'd heard that a thousand times before and blew into the phone. "Okay, Ma, whatever." They never had the talks.

"I was thinking maybe you and Destiny can order Chinese tonight-"

"And what, leave us here by ourselves? Hell no!"

"Stop that cursing. Didn't I tell you about that?"

"Yes, ma'am," Hope sarcastically sang into the phone.

"Now, me and Aziz are going out tonight and we won't be back home 'til late."

"You sure!"

"Of course, I'm sure...you sound just like my mother."

"Yeah...well, maybe-"

"Don't even start. Where's Destiny?" Hope walked over to the window and looked out in front, then frowned. "Outside. Trying to be cute... in front of all those boys-"

"Boys!" Mya looked around and glimpsed an old lady staring in her face, ear-hustling, then politely turned her back to her. "You tell Destiny she better have her ass upstairs by the time I get there...you hear!"

Hope smirked and said. "I'll tell her."

"Boys...you wait until-" She gathered herself once she checked her watch and realized she had to go. "Okay, okay, I'm gonna pick up some things from C-Town and I'll see you in about a half hour or so."

"Okay, Ma. See you then." Hope hung up the phone and ran to the window. "Destiny!" she hollered, "Mama said to get your hot ass upstairs!"

"Shut up, Hope!" Destiny said as she rolled her eyes and looked upstairs.

"A'iyht. Stay your fast ass down there then!"

Destiny knew her mother was on her way in and it would be in her best interest to be upstairs by the time she got there. She said her goodbyes and walked off, acting cute, swishing her neophyte, pubescent ass to the door of the building. As she glanced upstairs, mean-mugging her sister, she gave her the finger. The young boys giggled. She turned and winked at them and said, "Like what you see, huh?"

THE EVENING SUN WAS setting, retreating to a place west, soon to rise to the start of a new day somewhere east as Miles made the last of his rounds, finishing his day off. Fourth Street, Avenue A, B and C: the Avenue D bodega: Houston Street Projects; that's where they spotted Destiny. "Damn, Miles. She's fine as a muthafucka," Pancho said as he scoped her out.

"Who are all those boys?" Miles asked as he looked over.

"Bunch of wanna-bees."

"Wann-what?"

"Wann-bee in our shoes." Big E laughed as he reached over and dapped him. Miles managed a chuckle but added, "I hear you, but I'll tell you this," Big E leaned his head over and asked, "What?"

"You fuck with Mya's daughters and believe me, you may wann-bee somewhere else. Feel me."

"Ain't like that Miles. We ain't tryin' to like, force her to be with us and shit." Pancho pulled down the zipper of his jacket and pulled out the shiny gold serpentine chain he'd just gotten. "All they like anyway is the floss."

Big E reached into his pocket, coming out with a good, three inch folded stack, and added, "Yeah, and the loot, too!" Miles smiled as he watched his young partners shine. "I hear you. I was like that at one time...just like that." He pointed over towards Destiny as she walked into the building. "But...leave her alone. That's trouble, just like her mother was...trouble." Big E and Pancho shook their heads as they listened. "You right; 'sides, that's Aziz's people anyway."

"Hell." Miles said as he pulled up to a stoplight, "It ain't Aziz that's the problem...just watch yourself. a'iyht."

They both nodded their heads yes, but continued to watch Destiny as she walked through the door of the building she lived in; Miles traced their stares and said nothing more. He knew eventually the boys would have to find out the hard way, just like he did. Goes with the territory and the game.

He pulled up to the corner of 9th Street and Tompkins Square Park and parked; both boys jumped out of the truck. The big park was home to the dope fiends, the pushers and undercover five-o and they knew they had to be cautious. Joker had control of most of the work in the pack and even though he wanted to give it up because it was too hot, Aziz opted to keep it because of the side money that came through. Miles never liked coming through to pick up any money, but he had to get it before his pushers got 'got'; too much shit was going on. He'd already had to kick some ass and pull out his gun more than once from muthafucka's tryin' him, shortin' him; the spot to him was one big headache.

Miles's eyes darted in and out throughout the park like a sniper, zooming in on any unusual activity and checking out all who might even be watching him; taking mental snapshots and storing them in his memory bank. He kept up with the boys as they dipped in and out stuffing their jackets with bundles of money; sticking and moving. He liked the way they maneuvered, steady, watching each other's back.

Finally, when they had finished; Pancho walked opposite Miles, giving him the signal that he was finished. Head back to the truck is what it meant. Big E posted up and angled himself in a way so that if someone rolled; he'd get a good shot off. That was the plan, rehearsed.

Miles drove up 9th Street and made a right on Avenue A, slowed a little ways up the block and after looking around a couple of times, Pancho jumped in. He picked up Big E waiting on the steps of the Library on 10th Street, the last stop. It was time to go in and count the take; a good night, money was made and no one was hurt, or caught, so far.

They pulled up to a poolroom and Pancho hopped out and ran in. Two men came back out with him and Big E passed out satchels from the truck to them; they were Joker's ghetto accountants, Gutter and Smack. It was their job to make sure that the money that came in was straight. Miles got out of the truck as another one of his workers jumped in on the drivers side and said, "Same place, Miles"

"Same spot, Tonio."

Tonio pulled off to the parking location set up for Miles around back; wiping down the seats and steering wheel for anything, prints, evidence, clues, anything.

Someone darted out from the shadows in front of Miles, a jackboy he thought, had reached for his gun and so did Pancho; Smack and Gutter already had theirs out and up to the intruders head. He raised his arms up high, very slowly and said, "It's me, Miles! Me!"

Miles stepped back a little into the light trying to make out his face. A scraggly, shrunken-faced, thin man, he finally recognized. "You almost got yourself killed!"

He lowered his arms wearily and extended his hand towards him. "Yo man...I-I need a favor." Miles looked him up and down like he was crazy. If he really knew him, he'd know that he didn't do favors; he knew he was a dope fiend and said, "You better talk, quick."

"Yeah man, quick." He grinned, showing teeth that had been stained, yellowed and barely held on to the gums they were attached to. "Man, I need a fix...I'm hungry, real hungry, ya know..." He started scratching the side of his neck.

Miles never gave out dope; obviously this man didn't know that, and if he did, he was trying to play him, but he must have felt that he and Miles must have been cool enough for him to ask anyway. He motioned to his boys to pat him down, looking for a wire in case the police had sent him. "For you to even approach me like this ain't cool." he said as Pancho motioned to him that he was clean. Miles moved swiftly into the lobby ignoring him; he followed behind him protesting. "C'mon Miles, brother. We did time together. Remember...I looked out for you."

That stopped Miles dead in his tracks and he turned. He remembered him now, they did do time together. Elmira, upstate, gladiator school. No one looked out for him except himself. Time was hard on him. He had some, but not a lot. He didn't ask for shit and no one gave him shit. He turned towards him, his eyes narrowed to a slit and he said real low-like. "You never gave me a muthafuckin' thing!"

"Man, Miles...if you would have asked..."

Miles thought about that for a moment then a twisted grin came across his face. "Yeah, ask...I did, once."

The man smiled, thinking he'd hit pay dirt. "Yeah, yeah..."

Miles grabbed him by the collar and shoved him hard against the wall and took out his gun. "Remember, when I asked you for that hot dog!"

"H-h-hot dog?" Evidently, he forgot, but Miles didn't; he fucked up.

"Yeah, muthafucka! I wanted that hot dog! We was working on the road crew...hot as hell. Just like you, I was hungry as hell!" Miles put the gun up to his temple. "But, naw...you said you wanted to take them, all fuckin' six back to the dorm...sell them. Got slick with the mouth and er'thing!" He snarled as he stared into his eyes. "Y-y-yo man...it was just hot dogs..." he said as he quivered under his grip.

Miles raised his gun up over his head and slammed it down on his head; blood splattered against the walls. "Yeah...a hot dog, but muthafucka, just like you...I was hungry!" Miles hit him with the butt of the pistol repeatedly, causing Pancho and Big E to look away. He glanced over and yelled at them. "Naw...y'all watch this shit!" He kicked and stomped him in his ribs, his head and his hands. "This is what I do to muthafuckas who shit on me! You see, the same muthafuckas that step on you on the way up," he pulled back the hammer of the gun and pointed at him, "the same muthafuckas that see you on the way down." He shoved the barrel of the gun in his mouth. "You still hungry now! How does this shit taste!"

"No, Miles. Not here!" Smack eased over to him. "Joker wouldn't like it...too much heat."

Miles's hand shook as the anger and venom coursed through his body, causing it to tremble and said, "You're right...not here."

The broken, bloody body fell to the floor as Miles kicked him one more time in the stomach. Vomit spewed out of his mouth, but still he managed to utter, "Man...I'm sorry."

Miles straightened out his clothes and looked over himself for any traces of blood, then turned to walk up the steps to the pool room and said, "Too late for that now." He motioned to Gutter and Big E at the door. "Get his ass out of here...and uh, give him a dime bag."

Struggling to pick up his body by bracing against the wall; he spit blood on the floor. His hands had curled and was visually deformed; they were probably broken. Grimacing from the pain that shot through his ribs as he moved, he staggered towards the street. Gutter shook his head as he peeped out the doorway and said. "Coast is clear." Then, rummaged into his pocket pulling out a dime sack and handed it to him. "Here ya go. Now, get the fuck outta here before your dumb ass remembers somethin' else...stupid muthafucka'. Get the fuck on!" He laughed, "First muthafucka' I know that ever got his ass whipped over a fuckin' hot dog. What kinda shit is that?"

He staggered out the doorway then looked over his shoulder and sneered. "Won't be eating no hot dogs for a while." Gutter nodded as he reached to turn on a spigot to toss water on the floor. The fresh, cool water turned red at first then cleared up as the muck seeped into the gutter, including the man's teeth. It was over with.

Miles walked up the steps to a door; a gray steel door that slammed loudly when the wind got behind it, almost taking a few fingers with it. Thick, nearly three and a half inches wide in case the Police got the notion to roll with battering rams, it'd take a minute to get through; enough time for anything to get stashed quickly and, most of all, efficiently. The huge coiled springs that sat atop the door kept it from being too heavy to open until they were removed, then it was hard as hell. That was the job of the doorman and lookout, Dominique, or Blu as he was called. "Yo, yo, what-up, Miles."

Miles dapped him as he walked through then playfully jabbed at him as Blu countered, "Gettin' swift on me, huh." He felt his bicep and said, "Liftin' weights or sumptin'?"

Blu flexed into a pose; his jacket opened revealing his 40. cal. and two sixteen shot clips stuffed into his waistband. "Little sumptin', sumptin.'"

Miles nodded. "Damn...you sure look good since you stopped drinking." Then made his way towards the bar where he met eyes with the bartender. He'd been trying to get some of that ass for a while now, but she had an angle that he couldn't quite figure out. "Hey, Tempest, wassup, baby."

"Hey Miles." she sang as she turned around. Miles scanned her firm, bouncing ass as she moved about, even slightly. She looked at him and said, "Now Miles...you know better...we talked about that shit."

Miles burst out in a laugh; he'd been busted and it wasn't the first time. "Damn, girl. Least I could do is look."

She walked over to the bar where he sat and leaned over. "I don't mind, you know that." She pointed towards the men that played pool who stopped and gawked every chance they got. "But...then, everyone'll do it; then I'd have to kill one of these poor slobs if one of them tried me wouldn't I."

He stared around the room and chuckled, he got the picture then got up as he watched the last of the satchels go through the back door and said to her, "Got a point there, besides, ain't tryin' to go to Rikers Island to see you. Don't give a damn how fine your ass is."

"You're crazy." Tempest grinned. "'Sides, you got too many anyway. I'd just get lost in the mix."

He cocked his eyebrow when he heard that and was about to turn around then caught Pancho waving at him from across the room. "I doubt it, Tempest."

"They waitin', Miles!" Pancho yelled out from the doorway.

He winked at her as he made his way over then glanced around at the pool tables looking for new faces, strangers, and there were none. Just the same ole, same ole. The doorman who was set up by the hallway motioned him through then shut the door back and locked it. The hallway had a long corridor that had three other doors leading to different rooms. One, a stash room, where guns were bought in before making their way to dope spots and the serial numbers shaved clean. Two, the count room, where the money that the dope had made was counted. And Three, a room used mostly for storage, liquor, and where Joker would come to hide out. A room that Miles thought about converting into an office momentarily. He felt he deserved it; he'd been putting in most of the work lately anyway.

He walked into the count room and money was neatly stacked on tables, separated in denominations of 1's, 5's, 10's, 20's, and some 50's, 100's. Mostly small change that was got from dope fiends.

Smack and Gutter were already doing their thing, counting. Miles nodded at them. "I'ma call Aziz to finish out the night. Y'all cool with that?"

Gutter emerged partly from the stacks and said, "We a'iyht wit it. Just make sure one of y'all is here...don't want no shit."

"Yeah," Smack added, "you know the drill. Where the fuck is Aziz anyway? Wasn't it his day to make runs, and damn, ain't all this money from his spots?"

"Yeah, yeah...he got caught up..."

"Miles, fuck that! You need to let him know this is business!" Smack yelled at him.

"Hell yeah!" Gutter chimed in. "If Joker knew he wasn't here. Yo man, this is fucked up! If the money comes up short, it's on you."

"I know." Miles walked towards the door and pulled out his cell phone and dialed Aziz." It's me, Aziz, Miles."

"What up..."

"You need to be here to do the count; after all, it was your run and you were the one that was supposed to be here, not me-"

Aziz's dick was deep down the throat of the caller who'd called earlier, looking at busting his first nut, when the cell phone buzzed; his companion begged him not to answer it, in between gulps, but Aziz recognized the number as Miles's, figuring it was important and picked up anyway. "Yeah...I—I'm on the way."

"Oh yeah, one of your runners is dead, too."

Aziz raised an eyebrow when he heard that and asked, "Runners? Who?"

"That fiend...Poppi."

"What! Get the fuck outta here!" He raised up from off the bed; his dick slid out as he pushed the mouth off letting out a cum spray. "Whoa, baby...slow down!" he hollered out.

"Damn," Miles chuckled; "that shit got your attention, huh."

"What happened to him? He got robbed?"

"Look, I don't know...just make it over here. We'll talk about that when you get here, cool."

"On the way now..." he said as he clicked the phone off then looked down at the fingers that still played with his now limp dick, trying to bring it back up; he pushed them away gently and said, "Yo...another time, I got to go."

Miles hung up the phone and waved over to Gutter and said. "Yeah he's on the way now."

Gutter reached into his shirt pocket and pulled out some big black, but sleek glasses and stared at the sheets of paper in his hand. "Hey, Miles, y'all went to all the spots, right?"

"Yeah." Miles said as he walked towards him. "Something wrong?"

"Not sure yet." He glanced at him then Smack and said, "But, uh, stick around until he comes, cool."

"Damn!" Miles said as he pulled up a chair and sat. "If it ain't one thing-" "It's another!" Big E finished his sentence as him and his brother pulled up some chairs to a table pulling out a deck of cards. "Don't forget about that spot where that dude Poppi was killed. It's bound to be short, remember."

"Oh yeah," Miles said as he banged his hand into his palm, "That's right. Dude said he was going to give his take to Aziz when he got there, so it's gonna be a little short."

Gutter looked up from the stacks. "That sounds 'bout right, but we'll see what's up. But yo, Miles."

"What?"

"I wouldn't sweat it. You'll be alright."

Miles turned facing Pancho and Big E, watching them as they played cards, and thought about what Joker had done earlier, "I hope so...don't need the bullshit." he said.

chapter 6

AZIZ PULLED IN FRONT of the pool room and slid the 9mm that was stashed in the console into his jacket; he'd always been prone to never roll without it, too many confrontations to name. He checked the rear-view mirror and primed up his face before he stepped out of the car. The young man from earlier, Tonio, came running towards him. "Park the car 'round back, Aziz?" He reached into his pocket and pulled out a crisp fifty and handed it to him. "Yeah...do that."

Aziz let him park the car around back even though he didn't have plans on staying long, but he'd break that to Miles later. He hopped up the narrow stairway and tapped on the door; a narrow 2-X 6-inch eyelet slid open. "Who is it-oh, it's you, Aziz..." Blu opened the door and let him in, "Yo, wassup. They're in the back." Aziz attempted to put his hand out to dap him, but

Blu turned his back and slammed the door shut, ignoring the gesture. Aziz paid it no mind. He glanced over at Tempest at the bar and he smiled; she smiled back. Blu and Tempest had dealings at one time, but she'd pulled back ever since his confrontation with Aziz, the fight they had tore whatever friendship they had drastically apart; she let it roll off her back. Blu wasn't worth the jealous, violent tantrums he would portray. Just too unpredictable she reasoned, not worth the trouble. But as Aziz headed towards the back she couldn't help but eyeball the tall, handsome build he swaggered. Aziz dapped the doorman and before he stepped through he turned and met Tempest's gaze, then grinned as she averted hers quickly. He knew he could possess her regardless of Blu's brow-beating.

Miles heard the door and stuck his head out and waved him to the room, "C'mon in..." Aziz stepped through the door. Smack and Gutter were in the middle of the count; Pancho and Big E were wrapping up money when he came in. "Miles...why they handling the money?"

Miles stood casually with his hands folded; his stomach still grumbled from not eating. He caught Aziz's remark and it rattled him. "Hold up..." it pissed him off; "You bring your late ass up in here! You didn't even do the pickup, didn't even call!" He turned towards Smack, "Hell, I called him...and now you come in here with some bullshit about why they handling-" He reached into his jacket; Aziz stepped back with his hands opened, palms up. He knew Miles's temper and didn't want any part of his vicious, Dominican anger any more than the dope fiend that confronted him earlier. "I'm just saying, Miles...If something gets missing, it's my ass."

Miles paused then pulled out a small notebook. "Damn, you're fucking crazy!" He threw the book at him. "This is a recount! Hell, shit is missing, anyway!" Miles walked over to him as he flipped open the book and reached over and pointed at an entry. "You see, right there! Where your boy got killed...somehow the shit is short."

"How much?"

Miles calmed down a little. "Six grand."

"Damn...that's a chunk."

"You damn right." Miles walked back over to the table. "Like I said this is the second count. Pancho and Big E are baggin' up the money, that's all."

Aziz walked over to the table. "Sorry 'bout that fellas. What's up Smack, you know which spot?"

Smack leaned back from the money counter and reached into his pocket and pulled out some Newport's; he took out one and tossed the pack on the table, put it to his lips and lit it. He pulled deeply and blew out a thick, blue cloud that escalated slowly towards the ceiling before he rubbed his forehead. "I believe it's the second spot, Miles said." He picked up two satchels and threw them over at him. "From out these bags..."

Miles stepped forward. "The houseman did say that because of the cops being there he'd give you some money later. Now, I don't know if he has more or if; well, I don't know, he said he'd deal with you."

"Aziz, man, this shit needs to be handled quickly. You know we got to give Joker his count," Smack added. Gutter looked up. "Hell yeah, and this shit ain't corning out our pockets...hell, you muthafucka's already owe us a couple of hundred already."

"Whoa, hold the fuck up, Gutter!" Miles protested. "My shit never comes up short and if it did," he looked over towards Big E and Pancho, "it would get taken care of...quickly." Big E and Pancho shook their heads in agreement. Aziz looked over the table then at Miles. "Yo man, I need a favor..."

"Damn...figure you did."

"I mean, I need-"

"Pancho! Go get the cash and bring it over, you know where to go." He threw him the keys, "And fucking take Blu with you, just in case there's trouble, cool." Pancho took the keys and was out the door. Miles looked back at Aziz who had a shit-eating grin on his face. "Now what!"

"Yo man...I gotta dip-"

"What-dip!" Miles exclaimed, "I made your pick-ups and you come up short, then...I straighten you out and now you tell me some shit like you got to go! What the fuck are you on, dope!" Aziz moved towards him. "Naw, man. I made a promise to Mya."

"C'mon Aziz, this is business; hell, Mya knows the business." Gutter yelled out, "You can't be pulling this shit!"

"C'mon man, this one time."

"One time," Smack chuckled, one, two, three hundred times." He stood up from the table, "Aziz, take my advice." He walked towards him after grabbing his coat and glanced towards Gutter and Miles, "Yo, I'm gonna pick up the Chinese food we ordered." He opened the door and shook his head as he walked past Aziz, "Tighten up!" and slammed the door shut.

Miles sat down and picked up the bundles of cash stacked on the table and hurled them into a black duffle bag as Gutter gazed up. "That's it." He looked at the numbers in front of him. "30 k...that's with the six grand added in." He tossed the receipt to Aziz. And oh yeah...and an extra two hundred added in...Right."

Aziz nodded his head yes; that was the cost of doing business. Miles looked up at him. "Go on, man. You owe me!" Aziz reached out and dapped him; Miles waved him off. "Tell Mya I said wassup, ya hear."

Aziz opened the door. "I will...thanks man, I owe you." He walked out into the pool area and stepped towards the door. Tempest called him over to the bar. "You, uh, leaving out early?"

"Yeah, gotta hot date...how 'bout yourself?"

She rolled her eyes flirtatiously, looking him up and down. "I guess...I'll be alright, huh." Aziz chuckled as he heard that; he walked over to the door as it was opened and stepped through, not before he looked back at Tempest "You'll be just fine," he said as he glanced over at the back room door at Miles who had his head sticking out, watching her every move.

Pancho crossed the street; Blu was right on his heels. They dipped into a tight, narrow, alleyway that led behind the Boys and Girls Club next to PS-7. Pancho dipped into a playground through a hole cut open in the fence and found himself on the backside of the old school building.

Blu kept pace with him and his hand on his gun. "Yo, Pancho...I ain't in ya business, but where you goin'?" Pancho turned, then pointed to a small window located on the lower bottom half of the building. It had a padlock attached that kept it closed. Blu gawked, "What? I know that ain't where y'all keep money."

Pancho smiled, "Why not? It's out of the way...low key, and if you look around, it's dark as hell, but in the day, it's bright like a muthafucka and that's everywhere." Blu turned and scanned the area then thought to himself, he's got a point; the cops patrolled the area all the time and it does have its own alarm system. "I hear you, but why trust me?"

"Well," Pancho squatted down towards the lock and pulled out a key, a key that Miles only gave to him and someone else-he didn't know who, and he didn't ask-then unlocked it. "I think Miles wants you off the door at the poolroom, not sure but I believe he's got other plans for you and it's got something to do with money." Blu grinned, thinking to himself that he finally caught the attention of one of Joker's lieutenants; he could be a big player in the game now. "Good lookin' out, man."

Pancho pointed towards the street. "Oh, yeah..." Blu said as he hurried back towards the Street with his pistol drawn, "I got your back."

"Good." Pancho said as he pulled the window out and there was just enough space for him to crawl through, quickly. Blu looked back and he was gone; he leaned against the building inconspicuously and stuffed his gun in his jacket pocket and pondered on what Pancho had just told him. Now, he could impress Tempest like he wanted. She'd respect him; buy better clothes, take her out to nice places. "Blu!" his thoughts were interrupted by someone calling out his name. He looked around; it was Smack crossing the street. "What the fuck you doing over here?" He looked around, "You with someone?"

"I'm just handling some business...I'm alright." He stood up straight blocking his view. "I'll uh, see you when I get back..."

Smack tried to look over his shoulder; Blu took his gun out of his jacket and looked both ways up the street before saying, "Yo, man...I said I'm alright. I'm handlin' some business...for Miles...cool!"

"Cool..." Smack backed up. "I hear you. I was just askin', that's all." He turned around and threw up his fist, "See ya later, peace. I need to bring this food back before it gets cold anyway." And continued walking around the block to the poolroom.

Blu spit then put the gun back into his pocket. "Damn....nosy-ass muthafucka." He heard a sound behind him, but kept his eyes fixed on the street. "Yo, Pancho...the coast is clear." He waited for a response, but didn't get any. He turned. There was no one; the small opening was still ajar. "Damn...what the fuck." He shrugged it off and turned his attention back towards the street.

Located on the rooftop directly above him was a shadow and extending over the ledge was the long, sleek barrel of a rifle. Along the top was affixed a scope and the figure aimed it directly towards the top of Blu's head, who was oblivious to anything as he focused on traffic. The lone figure took aim and snickered, "...I'ma take your dumb ass out-"

Blu was tapped on the shoulder; he jumped. It was Pancho, "You ready." He turned and Pancho had a leather bank bag stuffed in his pants, covering it up with his shirt. Blu shook his head, "Yeah...let's go." They walked across the street, but not before Pancho turned around to make sure that no one had seen them; Blu turned also. "Yo man...did you come out earlier or something?" he asked.

"Naw."

"Damn...I thought I heard you creep up behind me."

"Hell, D...when I did...I locked the door and everything, you didn't even hear me."

"You're right. Must be my nerves."

"Yeah, probably nerves." Pancho said as they walked off; he hoped Blu didn't pick up drinking again. With all that Miles had planned for him, he needed to be straight.

The lone figure pulled back the rifle and cursed as they walked off, then looked over the railing at the orifice Pancho had come out of and stared. "Hmmmm."

MYA LEANED OUT OF THE way of the traffic as people scattered to make their way home, thinking about her next call. She auto-dialed the number already stored in her cell and waited, but not too long.

"Hello?"

"What's up, girlfriend?"

"Hey, Skyler, I just wanted to thank you again for, uh, helping me through. "C'mon, girl...that's what I'm here for."

"So...what's up?"

Skyler had just gotten off the train on 174th street in the Bronx; 2 blocks over to the east was where she stayed; Echo Park Towers.

"I just got off the train. I'll probably stop by the store and pick up a meal."

"Pick up a meal. You don't cook?" Mya chuckled.

"Why? It's just me and when I eat good usually someone is taking me out."

"I hear you. I'm going out tonight myself."

"What..."

"Me and Aziz-"

"I know you're not going out with him after all you went through." Skyler stopped and sighed, "Did you not learn anything, Mya?"

"We're going out to talk...get things right!" Mya's voice cracked as she tried to convince Skyler of something she herself wasn't sure of.

"He said he would-"

"How many times!"

"But...it's different," Mya asserted.

Skyler walked into her building, catching the elevator, and pressed eight. "Listen Mya, it's part of his sickness. He did it before and said he would stop, then it just gets worse, trust me." She got off the elevator pulled out her keys to her apartment, and as she walked in she tossed her purse on the couch and plopped down. "He's sick, Mya. You've got to get away...before you get caught up in his madness."

"He ain't sick!" Mya pouted. "We gonna work through this, that's what couples do! I mean, just because you don't have no one yourself-don't be jealous of me!"

That hurt Skyler; Mya was a good friend she confided in, now she wished she hadn't because what Mya said stung. "Look. You do what you want, but as much as you say things that hurt, I'll still be there for you, okay." She was just about to hang up but added, "But, if I were you, I'd at least get paid." "Paid...you said that earlier. What do you mean by paid?"

Skyler paused. "When you're ready, just give me a call. I gotta go."

"Skyler, c'mon...I'm sorry-"

"Yeah, well...I gotta go." She cut the call short and threw the cell phone on the table, still a little upset by Mya's remarks. She stretched out her legs and thought about Aziz, the money he made for Joker. She grinned as she thought about her plan, wishing Mya had enough sense to jump on it, but she shrugged it off, kicking off her shoes she headed towards the bathroom for a nice long bath.

Mya still had the phone in her hand when she heard the horn from Aziz's car. "Hey cutie!!" She looked up and smiled. "How you doin' handsome," she said, then opened the door and jumped in. He kissed her warmly on the lips as Mya got comfortable in the padded, leather seats. Aziz looked at her with a smile and said, "You look good. Yeah, you're right, we do need to talk and maybe..." he slid his hand over to hers and squeezed it, "Get ourselves right, cool."

Mya stared off into his eyes; maybe, she thought, this was the right time for a change. "Okay..." she cooed.

They took showers, changed clothing and sent the girls out for Chinese food, then sat waiting on them to come back before they would step out for the evening. "Damn...where did those girls go...China?" Aziz asked.

"No." Mya chuckled and got up and looked out the window, "they should be back in a little while-"

"They know we were going out!" Aziz's voice got incensed and Mya picked up on it. "Relax." She walked over to him and sat, massaging his neck trying to soothe him. "Let's talk..." Aziz twisted his head around. "Yeah, sure, sounds good. Hey, you seen my pills?"

"No...Probably in the medicine cabinet."

"Okay...what do you want to talk about?"

"You still having those headaches, Aziz?"

"Every now and then, like now."

Mya got up and walked to the bathroom and opened the medicine cabinet, searching for his pills. "Did you get it checked out?" She found them then closed it back; he was standing behind her. "Naw...not really," he said, then rubbed his groin against her ass, getting a hard-on; she moaned as she felt his dick rise against her. "Much as I want it, baby, the kids will be back anytime." He reached under her skirt fondling her clit then reached down, pulling at his zipper. "C'mon...I want to fuck."

"C'mon now Aziz, I just took a shower...after we get back." He then reached back down between her legs and ripped her thong off. "No...Now!" He had his dick out in his hand and with the other shoved her in the back, bending her over on the sink. She protested, but it was useless. "Aziz...not like this..."

He spit into his hand, lubricating his dick, then rammed into her asshole; she grimaced. He started to grunt as he grinded into her unmercifully. "You like..." Mya bit down on her lip as his dick tightened up and plunged deeper. She met his strokes, trying to get it over with quickly, as she felt him tense up inside of her; he was ready to cum. Then she heard the front door open; it was the girls. "Ma!"

"Aziz...stop, they're here..." Aziz continued to grind and push her down; she squirmed and he pushed harder. She could hear the girls walking towards the open bathroom calling out her name; she couldn't let them see her like this. She struggled to position herself, turning and fighting to get his dick out of her ass; the pain was excruciating. As she did he groaned; his dick exploded out as cum shot in the direction of the girls as they stood motionless and in shock at the door. Aziz held his dick in his hand as it leaked onto the floor. Mya pulled her dress down and rushed the girls. "Y'all, get away from the door!" Aziz leaned against the sink breathing heavy. "Hell...it ain't nothing I'm sure they ain't never seen before." He caught Destiny's glimpse and winked; Mya saw it. "Oh, hell no!"

she turned. "You don't do no shit like that!" Aziz raised his hand and slapped her. "Shut the fuck up!" She fell back against the shower wall and cringed in pain; Hope grabbed her and ran for her room locking the door behind them.

Aziz laughed as he pulled up his pants; he looked over at the pills that lay on the sink and the food that the girls had dropped all over the floor. "Somebody better get this shit up!" He reached for the pills and stuffed them in his pocket then headed for the door shouting, "Fuck you bitch...I'll take someone else out!" He slammed the door behind him.

Mya lie on the floor cowering in fear as Hope bitterly ranted, "You see, ma...he ain't gonna change." She was right, Mya knew it, but she had to get away from him, now. She crawled over to her purse and pulled out her phone and dialed.

Skyler picked up the phone as she relaxed on her bed watching cable; Mya ran down the whole incident. "Damn girl..." she reached over and grabbed a pack of cigarettes and her lighter. "This is what has to go down." Then grabbed her notepad from off her desk and an ashtray.

Mya peeped out the window at Aziz's car as he sped off into the street and replied, "Yeah...I'm ready, what's the plan?"

"OKAY...THIS IS IT." Smack got up from the table and stretched. "It's all accounted for except for...no, no...That was handled already." Gutter reached over and scrolled through a list of numbers then threw it back on the table. "It's straight." Gutter said, "So...you want us to keep this quiet until when, Miles?"

Miles was feeding his face with fried rice. "I'll get it back from Aziz. That money covers everything."

"A'iyht," Gutter said as he walked over to the coat rack, grabbing his jacket. "I'm out, see y'all later." Smack followed behind him. "Yeah, me too. See y'all tonight." He glanced down at the bag filled with money. "Oh, yeah...you found a new stash man or what?" He grabbed at Gutter. "Or you want us to..."

"Naw. Miles waved them off. "I got it...y'all can go 'head." They glanced over at Pancho and Big E. "I know you're not-"

"No, no...I said I got it."

Gutter wiped his hands. "It's on you." Then walked out behind Smack. The man who held the door down stuck his head in. "Yo, Miles...I got to lock it down."

"Yeah, of course." He got up, wiping his hands with some napkins. "Just give me a minute." The door closed. "Hey, fellas, wake up...time to go." Pancho and Big E got up groggily, grabbing at the bags of food that had put them to sleep in the first place. "Okay..." Miles smiled. "Hurry up. We can finish up the food at the crib...get the duffle bag."

"Alright!"

Smack and Gutter walked out towards the bar. "Hey, Tempest....before you lock down, let me get two rounds..."

"Sure...what 'cha drinking?"

"Beer...two pitchers." He glanced back at Smack.

"Yeah, that's cool." He looked around towards the door at Miles and them as they came through; Miles escorted Blu to the office behind the bar. Tempest came back with the drinks. "Here you go." She glanced over at the doorway. "I hope everything's okay..."

Smack looked. "Everything's alright...trust me." Tempest smiled, then walked back to the cash register, counting the take for the night; Smack leaned over. "Yo man, I saw something strange tonight."

"What's up?" Gutter asked as he swigged the beer down.

I saw that dude Pancho and Blu in an alleyway behind the back of PS-7. I approached that dude, Blu." He took out some cigarettes and lit one up. "Yo...he acted real funny."

Yeah, yeah...Miles sent that young boy out to pick up the money...the six grand."

Smack puffed from the cigarette. "Damn...you think that's a stash spot back there?"

"Hell, sounds like it. Did you see exactly where he went?"

"Naw...not really, but damn, there's only so many places he could have gone. Hell, I went to school there and there's nothing over by the playground. All the windows are up high-"

"Whoa-wait up. I went to school there, too." Gutter paused and took another swig. "The only thing over there is the boiler room."

"In the basement?"

"Remember when we were little and we would play..."

"Yeah, yeah...so what."

"So what? Stupid, the window! The fuckin' window."

Smack almost choked on his cigarette. "Hell yeah. The little windows that lead to the basement, but I thought they were gated up or something."

"They are...iron bars."

Smack leaned back. "Yeah, that must be the spot." Tempest came back over. "Is that all fellas?" Gutter reached in his pocket and threw her a twenty. "That's it."

She grabbed at it. "Damn, y'all throwing big boy money around like this is a strip joint, y'all hit the lotto or something."

Smack glanced over at Gutter. "I think so," and they both started laughing. Tempest walked off looking at them. "I appreciate the money, but y'all crazy as hell."

Miles sat the egg roll he was eating on the mahogany-laced table over by the desk opposite the door. He opened a drawer and searched for some papers. "...Now where the hell..." Blu sat opposite him watching him rummage through the desk, he glanced periodically over at Big E and Pancho, amazed at how mature and on point these young boys were in this business; the way they had Miles's back was powerful to him, the loyalty alone. He had heard stories about how Miles got up with them, how he adopted them, about how it was said that their mother was a strung-out junkie and she sold her babies to Joker for more dope, but it was all just rumors.

Tempest came over to them and asked, "Y'all need something before I close the bar?" Miles stuck his head up. "Naw...I'm alright." Then he glanced around. "Don't know about anyone else, though." She looked over at Blu, "Naw...I'm straight." Big E and Pancho shook their heads no; they were still digging through bags of now cold Chinese food scrambling for anything at best, edible.

Blu quickly glimpsed Tempest as she left, thinking about maybe her being serious with him now. Miles hadn't said what he wanted him for or even to do, but with the heads-up he got earlier, he knew it was serious and he wanted some more responsibility anyway, he also wanted the recognition, and Tempest.

"Okay...Blu." Miles sat back in the large, leather chair studying him. "You alright?"

"Yeah..." Blu responded, shaken, wondering just how long Miles had been staring at him, he straightened up. "So...uh, what's up?"

Miles turned towards the boys. "Okay fellas, I'll meet y'all downstairs in a little while. Why don't y'all go get the truck...cool?" Big E and Pancho got up and headed towards the door then Pancho doubled back and turned. "You, uh, want us to get the bag..." he pointed to the large duffle bag full of money. "Naw..." Miles said, "It'll be handled..."

Pancho shook his head. "Alright...see ya later." Miles got up and walked to the door. "Tempest...be out in a minute." He waved towards the doorman to the back room who shook his head and came over to the office. "Blu...I know you've seen each other; hell, you both work here."

Blu got up. "Yeah...seen dude around. He doesn't talk much." Miles grinned. "Yeah...that's how I like my people." He walked back over to the desk and sat down. "What we do don't require a lot of talkin.'" The doorman took a seat opposite Blu. "His name is Chino." The tall, big-built, dark-skinned man smiled and put his hand out toward Blu. "Wassup."

Blu couldn't help but notice how neat he was; he'd never been that close to him before. His haircut was tapered just right, mustache groomed, but what caught his eye was the smile; his perfect white teeth gleamed against the dark background of his near perfect skin. "Yo...wassup."

Blu shook his hand then sat down; they turned their attention towards Miles.

"Let's get straight to the point." He waved them closer. "Joker is looking at revamping camp, so there's going to be some changes. Me, personally, I'm making them on this level. Joker made me and Aziz lieutenants, so I won't be doing no more pickups, and I need good people I can trust to replace me. And believe me, that's y'all." They both smiled. "I want y'all to make the pick-ups starting tomorrow."

"Cool," Chino said, "but, what about Aziz?" Miles leaned back in his chair and pondered. "Don't worry 'bout him I'll handle that. Hell, he doesn't do much anyway."

"You gonna take care of him, huh." Blu smirked. Miles gave him a stern look. "Blu...we don't talk like that...understand!" Blu's smile disappeared as he got serious. "...Sure."

Miles pointed towards the duffle bag. "You need to know where the stash houses are so you can drop off the cash. Tonight, I'll take you to one and then we'll get up early tomorrow and we'll make the rounds, cool."

"That's cool...'bout what time." Chino checked his watch; Miles reached into his pocket and took out two small Motorola's and tossed them at them. "From now on, I'll call y'all...just be there. Pretty soon it'll be like clockwork and you won't need a watch," he pulled up his sleeve and profiled the Jacob on his arm, "except for show." He got up and pointed to the bag. "Let's go so Tempest can close up."

"Who's gonna replace us," Chino asked. Miles snatched up the paperwork he'd dug up and stuffed it in his jacket pocket. "Pancho and Big E." Chino nodded. "Cool...real cool."

Blu tossed the bag over his shoulder then glanced at Chino. "You got the other?" Miles grabbed them instead. "I got it." Blu shook his head; now he was confused. "But, I thought..."

"It's cool, but you see, being that you're large, strong and the bags really don't weigh much, well that's your gig to get the money, physically...but, I like your presence... your persona is large!"

Blu stopped and stared at the satchels then Chino. "Well...what's his job?" Miles smirked then waved over at Chino and he popped open his coat revealing two sleek butcher knives that hung from the inside of his coat like gun holsters. He snatched one out and flashed it in front of Blu. The glare from the shined, polished chrome made him squint. He reached for his gun but it was too late; the razor-sharp blade was already to his throat, all it took was one deep breath from him and his throat would be cleanly slit without any movement from Chino at all. He quickly pulled it back and stashed it stealthily into its holster; Blu shook his head in amazement. "Damn!"

"Hell yeah...damn. That's why he's your partner...the man that watches your back...you cool with that?" Blu rubbed across his neck, then looked at Chino. "Just remember one thing...we fuckin' partners!"

Chino and Miles laughed as he picked up the satchels and walked out of the room; Tempest was posted up by the door. "Y'all finally ready?" Blu opened the door for her as she gazed at the duffel bag across his shoulder. "Yeah...one day this is gonna be me and yours." She smiled at him then turned and looked at Miles. "You better take care of him." Miles was about to say something but Chino put his finger to his lips hushing him; he picked up on it. Chino had already seen the play between him and Tempest, and he knew if Miles said something now, it would upset the balance of things. Chino also knew that the only reason Miles put Blu down with him was so he could get him out of the way, and Tempest would be wide open for his advances. It was a dirty game, and Chino knew it, but to mention it now would only create problems; it would be better to let him shine, and Miles knew it. "Yeah, Tempest...I'll take good care of him." He glanced at Chino; he knew he'd made a good choice. "Real good care."

chapter 7

DAY TWO.

"Yo, Miles...where they at?" Big E checked his watch and looked up and down the street. "They shoulda been here by now!" Miles sat in the truck with his long legs kicked up on the dash, still a little sleepy from the night before, and rubbed his eyes. "They should be on the way-" Before he could finish his sentence Big E blurted out, "There they go!" He pointed to Blu and Chino as they bopped up the street crossing Avenue D from 4th Street.

Blu spotted them. "Wassup, fella-" Big E jumped in his face. "Yo, man, wassup? 'Y'all need to be on time, that's wassup!"

Blu backed up and peeped over at Miles. "Cuz, you need to talk to your kid!" He eyeballed him. Big E was big, but Blu was built and swift with his hands; he also had him by about ten years. He respected Miles's cronies, even stood up for Big E at the pool room when he owed money on the tables; he wasn't feeling the disrespect thing right about now. "This is wassup, man! You need to back da fuck up!"

Miles waved Big E off only after watching Pancho creep up behind Blu. Miles knew Pancho would easily defend his brother and it wouldn't be pretty. He snickered as he watched them; he had a pretty tough strong team, a crew he could easily build to a point where they could take on a spot as big as the Alphabet; but that was later, Miles thought to himself, but not too much longer. "C'mon, Big E, back up off the man."

"But, they're late! When y'all come late, you throw everything off! Everything has to be on point...it's that serious!"

Miles moved over towards them as Blu stood listening with his arms folded; Chino stepped forward. "You right. This is business." He held his hand out to Big E. "It won't happen again." He looked over at Blu, "least not for me. How 'bout you D? "

Blu looked over at Miles and then Big E, then pushed him aside. "I feel you young bro, but next time handle me a little better, ya hear."

"I hear you, Blu, and no disrespect, but you know how I feel about the business. I may be young and I shouldn't have raised my voice, but you down with us now and we real serious about this thing." Pancho rubbed up next to him, feeling out his weapon. "This shit can get real ugly...quick." He mean-mugged him and Blu threw his hands up. "A'iyht...point made."

"C'mon, fellas... they're waiting on us," Miles said and pointed to a bodega across the street. He led the way as they walked into the store and greeted the heavy Spanish man sitting behind the counter. Then they walked towards the back through an archway that revealed three armed young boys, who nodded to another door that led down to a basement. Miles knocked. "It's me...Miles!" An eye slit came open and closed, then the door slowly opened. "Come in..." They all, walked through and Blu gasped. "Oh, shit..." The man that opened the door locked it back behind them and walked towards a table and pointed two other young boys with A-K's towards them. "Who are these guys, Miles? No one told me about this shit. Is it legit...or what?" Miles walked ever to the young boys and lowered their weapons aimed at Chino and Blu. He glanced over at Chino inching his hand readily towards his blade, and stopped him. "You know...I would never bring nothing bad into the den. He stared over at the man who ran the mill, Flaco. "Be cool...but, I appreciate your caution, I really do." He walked over to him and shook his hand. "We're expanding, just like I told you. These are my new runners, Chino and Blu.

Flaco looked them up and down then waved the young boys off. "You can never be too sure in this business." They walked over to the curtain that separated them from the other side and stopped and turned, then walked over to Chino. "I hope you're good with whatever you are concealing." Chino nodded yes then he glanced at Blu. "I remember you from the pool room." Blu tried to recall. "Trust me, I remember you. Hell, I picked you out." He smiled at Miles turned, then opened up the curtain and moved aside. "This, my friends...is the business."

The windows were sealed and the fluorescent lights that shined overhead shone directly on the bags of crystalline, white powder that was spread out on two long bingo tables. The faces that gawked up were all masked and clad only in loose fitting boxers. Chino walked in first and glanced over the bags of heroin, this wasn't the first time he'd been in or seen a milling house, but this was the first time he was actually responsible for one. He was a runner now. He was in, finally; and all this was his domain and he liked it. Blu was all teeth as he looked around and locked eyes on the tablet. "Yeah... this is what's up." Flaco stepped up behind him real close, "It is what it is, but remember, you're responsible for this...no slip-ups." Miles nodded, then pointed him towards the tables. "Flaco...tell them how this works." He slipped into the background with Big E and Pancho and watched as Flaco explained.

"Listen to me...listen to me, real fuckin' good, because I will not repeat myself." He looked over at Miles then closed the curtains. "There are ten people who actually do work here. All tota's. So how many does that make?" He pointed to Chino. "Uh, ten-" "No!" "Fourteen." Blu said, "Ten tota's plus..." he pointed to the curtains, "two guns, Flaco and of course...a doorman."

Flaco smiled and caught the frown on Chino's face as he looked down. "No...Don't do that! You just need to know where everyone is at all times, and exactly how many people you have! Know your environment and if something is out of place, investigate it. If it doesn't belong...eliminate it at all cost!" He glanced back at Miles then added, "Or it's your ass. You understand!" Chino nodded his head in agreement, Flaco barked at him, "What was that!" "Yes...I understand!"

"Come...let's finish." He guided them to the table. "You will have to know your people and being that this is your house now, you need to know them soon. Those two running back and forth around the tables getting bags, their names are Miguel and Guillermo. Miguel runs the side making half bags. Ivan and Angel spoon the bags, then they're slid down to Jose who tapes them and stamps a label on them. Then there's the quarter bag table right behind us, over here. The same routine."

"Do the bags already come quartered?" Blu asked.

"Good question. No...They're ripped in half from the half bags. The tota's have to be more precise with that, Juan and Pedro have that task and once that's finished, it goes down to Carlos who tapes the bag just like the others."

"Okay, I see. But, how do the bags stay separated?

"That's your job. Since you're eventually responsible for the money, then you separate them. If you notice at the end of the table, a box-"

"Looks like a business card box or something..."

"It's called a matt. That's where they're stacked up, like little business cards. The matts hold 100 bags apiece. Four bundles..."

Miles got up and walked over and picked up an already filled order. "Yeah...you're responsible for this. You know why?" They both shook their heads, no. "A bundle is twenty-five bags. Each bundle is worth 250 dollars." He held a bag to the light and observed it. "I let them go at about 175, wholesale... that's if I like you or you're a good pusher. My runners collect the difference from 150 dollars. That's a little hustle for you... incentive."

Blu smiled then did the math mentally. "Damn... that's pretty good. When do we collect that?"

Miles cut his slanted eyes to a glint, then stared off. "After I get mine...that's why you're responsible. Remember that."

Flaco stepped towards the far end of the table pointing to small batches of heroin that was being swept into a stainless steel bowl. Anything else that was left over got scrambled with quinine into bags of p-funk; Blu smirked, "That's the cheap shit...huh."

"Ain't none of it cheap. Everything gets sold. Hell, bags of p-funk go for ten dollars a pop." A tota came through with a small dust broom and scooped up specks of dope on the floor into a pile along with some dirt that lay there; Flaco shook his head. "Everything!"

"Okay..." Miles got up and stretched. "Lesson one...over." He motioned to Pancho and Big E. "It's time to go."

"It's been a pleasure, Miles." Flaco embraced him; Miles smiled as he hugged his mentor and looked him over. He looked older, more than his age of fifty. The short, stocky figure showed signs of spunk but was still bent over from wear, his hair grayed from stress and though he was well groomed and his clothes fit well, his eyes had begun to sink from age.

Joker knew it was time to let him go and retire gracefully, but he also needed him to train and that was a problem. They went through enough people already; either the dope would lure them to their doom in this case, the East River-or it was the money which resulted in the same demise. "Flaco, these two should work out."

"I hope so, Miles. I'm getting older you know."

"I know, I know."

"If not," he glanced over at Pancho and Big E, "your sons will have to-"

"No! I got bigger plans for them!"

Flaco threw up his hands "Okay, okay, don't bite my head off!" He embraced him again and walked towards the curtain. "Grab the matts, boys...and get the fuck outta here!"

Pancho showed Blu and Chino where the matt's were. They cuffed them and followed the boys to a door off to the side of the door they came through; the armed boys went along with them. Miles walked back up the steps into the store.

Miles dapped the fat man behind the counter, snatched up a pack of Skittles and dipped out the door. He cranked up the car and let it idle, checking his environment as well as the lookouts that were posted. Once he got the signal, he drove up the alley behind the bodega heading towards Houston Street; he could see Pancho as he showed himself outside the door where he slowed down. The two young boys with A-K's came out behind him and posted themselves opposite the door. Big E opened the truck door and Chino and Blu climbed in.

Miles gave the young boys the signal and they ran back inside and slammed the door back. He punched the gas and skidded out of the alley towards the avenue.

Miles didn't say anything as he made the right on 3rd Street and circled the block going towards 4th Street, the first dope spot across from the Pitt. "A'iyht, this is the lick...pay attention!" Blu and Chino leaned forward, Miles pointed to the satchels that lay in the back, Big E passed them forward. "We go to the Pitt and package up."

"How do we split up the matts?"

"Good question, Blu...you're on it." He looked at Chino through his rearview. "This is where you earn your keep. You have to always watch Blu's back...you have to! There's too much shit that can happen!"

"I got you!" "Cool."

He pulled up in front of the Pitt and Joker's goons were already there, but no sign of him. "Let's go." They jumped out, and the door to the Pitt was opened by two of Joker's men who pointed Miles to a room in the hall that was bright and well lit. An older gray-haired man stood at the door. "I've been waiting." Miles nodded, "I'm training..." "I heard...good luck."

Miles ordered Blu and Chino to put the matts on the table and the older man grabbed them and opened one up. "Okay...good." He held a couple of bags to the light and inspected them, then he pulled out a small pen knife and cut into it, then spooned some into a small capsule along with some chemicals and mixed it. "Yeah...this is good shit..." he mumbled to himself as he watched the browning of the chemical as it fused then pointed to the satchels. Big E lined them up on the table by the numbers and opened them all up. Blu whispered to Miles, "What's that shit he's got in his hand?"

The man overheard him and looked up. "To make sure that the dope is pure enough for the spots, or, if it's too pure." Miles leaned against the doorway. "He's also the man that makes sure the right amount of dope goes to the right spots."

"I thought you did that," Blu said.

"He does…" the gray-haired man said; "I just make sure it's right every now and then… like an audit of sorts"

"Damn…Joker don't trust you yet, Miles."

The man smiled at Miles then pointed to a small, hidden camera that watched overhead. "Joker don't trust no one."

The satchels were filled and closed one by one, the gray-haired man nodded and Miles opened the door and they all dipped back into the truck. "Okay, this is it, fellas." He pointed to an abandoned building up the street. Big E passed up the satchel for the building to Pancho; "We're doing Aziz's spot's too." He pulled off and rode a little ways then parked in front and looked around. Pancho nodded and jumped out of the truck with Big E, then turned towards Blu; "Come on."

"You lay back, Chino," Miles said. They all bounced up the steps with the satchel, knocked with the code, and were let in. A head protruded back out and nodded at Miles then the door closed. "What do I do now, Miles?" Chino asked.

Miles looked through his mirrors and outside the window, looking for anything unusual; he didn't turn away as he responded, "Watch…watch your surroundings…"

Chino understood his job now. He played a big role in the game, looking out the windows he scanned the area, doing what Miles had said, and the paranoia seemed like a natural fit for him; "Yeah…my surroundings."

Not too much later they came back out and got back into the truck. Pancho reached into his jacket and pulled out a stuffed envelope and handed it to Miles. "The house man told me to give you this." Miles opened it up and looked through; he had a good idea of what it was; it was eight grand. Miles remembered from last night that he only needed six grand. The house man must have given him the extra money out of his pocket to make up for the confusion from yesterday, figuring he'd take the hit himself so that Joker wouldn't think the whole thing was his fault, or his idea. That was good, Miles pondered to himself, but he didn't need the extra loot so he reached in and pulled out two grand then handed it to Chino. "Split it up, you and Blu. Pocket change." "Good looking...Blu said. Pancho smiled and reached for another satchel as Miles pulled off. "Welcome to the team."

SKYLER STOOD OVER MYA with her arms crossed, nervously tapping her feet. She turned towards the girls who were in the kitchen making breakfast and motioned to Hope to get her some coffee; turning her attention back to Mya she yelled at her, "Mya...you see!" she was pissed off, but very much concerned. Mya had made it uptown about an hour ago with the girls in tow and a few bags full of clothes. Skyler paid for the cab she got by calling in a favor from a friend, but that wasn't a problem; the girls felt safe and she knew they would be, at least for now. Eventually Aziz would figure they were there and he would come looking. "So...what are you gonna say! I told you so!" Mya barked back.

"Hell, yeah...he did the same bullshit...whip your ass!" Skyler picked up her cigarettes and lit one up, then stared at her. Mya solemnly looked up from the floor. "He didn't beat me..." Hope came into the living room, passing Skyler her coffee, and sat next to her mother. "Mom...he did...he slapped you..."

"It was just...a slap, Hope."

Skyler frowned then leaned up in the chair. "He's beat you so much you think a slap...is a small thing." Skyler laid the cigarette down in the ashtray and Mya picked it up and puffed a couple of times before she said, "You're right..." her eyes still perplexed, in shock and shaking her head in disgust, she gasped, "You're fuckin' right."

Skyler sighed and grasped her hand. "Look...he's the fucked-up one, sweetie." Destiny came in and stood on the other side of her mother, hugging her.

"Look, we all love you. It's time for this shit to come to an end, Mya, for real." Mya looked into her eyes. "But...how?" The girls also looked at her for an answer, direction. "Okay, okay...let's look at this. What did you do?" She plopped down in the chair across from her. Mya slammed the cigarette into the ashtray. "Nothing! I didn't do anything, he just snapped!"

"Something had to happen...think!" Skyler pleaded with her. Mya leaned back on the sofa and crossed her legs and thought out loud, "Let's see...hold up, he did say something about some pills..." "What kinda pills?" Skyler asked.

Hope jumped in. "Yeah, I remember seeing them too, in the medicine cabinet. I would remind him to take them and he would just shrug it off."

"Damn!" Mya jumped up. "Yeah....those pills. Every time he would fly into a rage...he would ask about the pills, but I thought they were for seizures."

"Well," Skyler said, "that's a start. We need to find out about those pills. That might be why he's going crazy." "Maybe-" "No!" Destiny yelled out. "Hell no! Just because he on some fucking pills don't give him no right to beat you...or anyone else!" Mya cocked her head. "I'm sorry mom, but no disrespect...it's not your fault! It's his!"

"It's true, mom..." Hope said. Mya looked over at Destiny then Hope; the look on her face was stern, causing both girls to cringe slightly, then quickly turned glum. "You're right..." She hugged Destiny. "You're absolutely right." She sat back down between them. "Skyler, what about that plan you had?" Skyler lit up another cigarette and pulled the ashtray closer to her. "It's about time you asked. Now, we can talk...but, are you really down or what?"

"What you talking about?" Mya asked. Skyler leaned forward. "All of you, the girls and all, have to be down..." She looked at them all and they shook their heads in agreement. "First...what happened to Dante?"

Mya shook her head. "What does that have to do with-?"

"Every goddamn thing, Mya...now spit it out! What the fuck happened?"

"But.

"But, nothing! Aziz's rages and him beating you has got something to do with these girls' daddy. Besides...they need to know the truth, so if you wanna get out of this shit, start fucking talking." Mya's jaw dropped; she knew Skyler was right and the girls needed to know what happened anyway. "Okay..." she got up and walked towards the window and stared out. "It was really...all my fault..."

"He was so fine...and so easy to love." Mya walked back towards the couch and gently rubbed Destiny's tender, smooth skin. "You favor him, so much..." Destiny smiled. Skyler crossed her legs "Steve told me-"

"Steve...I knew it!"

"Girl, quit with the dramatics. You know I would have asked him...besides, to what I understand, you and him were an item anyway."

Mya cocked her hips to the side and put her hands on them. "Humph...yeah, yeah." She turned on her heels, pushing her long swaying hair away from her face, giving attitude much to the delight of her two daughters and even managing a chuckle from Skyler herself. "Anyway! Like I said, he was tall, handsome, the finest thing in Alphabet City and he had eyes for me. Yeah, granted, I would go with Steve to his games and I know he liked me, but believe me, it was all about Dante." She turned and walked over to the coffee table and picked up Skyler's pack of cigarettes; Skyler slapped her hand. "Leave my cigarette's alone...you don't smoke!" Mya ignored her and lit one up. "I'll admit, I was in love with him and the money, the gifts. I mean he would take me places and buy me all sorts of things...mostly jewelry, but hell, I was young. Jewelry was the big thing especially back then...medallions...rope..."

"What you talkin' 'bout..." Skyler laughed; "Hell, a good gold rope and bam...he can get it!" They both laughed and high fived each other then turned towards the girls. Hope shook her head in distaste but Destiny was intrigued, caught up and she asked, "Well...is it wrong to do it now..."

Mya put up her finger and scolded her, "Let me find out you taking some jewelry from boys and I'll-" "Mya, Mya...get back to the story!"

She cut her eyes as Destiny sucked her teeth. "Yeah, you can suck your teeth, I'll knock them out. Just like your daddy," she snickered. "When I would get on him about the drugs, carrying them around, he would do the same thing...suck his teeth." She reached out and stroked Destiny's hair. "I stayed around him all the time...he was fun to be with then. Joker eventually made him a runner and was looking towards giving him his own territory in the City; I mean, that was pretty large. He recruited some of his friends...one of them was Aziz. He played ball with him too, but Aziz seemed to be more of a loner. He would stare at Dante all the time; Dante never thought nothing of it. He knew a lot of guys wanted to be like him...hang out with him, be around him. He never flirted with me or nothing...if anything that damn Miles, hell, he was something else. Damn, I couldn't keep that boy's hands off my ass!" she giggled. "We were all in junior high then, that's how it was. Me and Dante started sneaking off from school...next thing you know," she pointed to her stomach, "Hope...kept doing it and bam, Destiny. He loved his girls; he would shower money on them like nothing. Joker gave him a spot as a gift."

She turned and walked over to the table and Skyler handed her an ashtray. "But he still played ball at West 4th Street park; some scouts even offered him a deal. Man, but when Joker got word of it...he showered him with more money and another spot, that's when Miles got on. Him and Aziz ran Dante's two spots while Dante did pick-ups for Joker; he was about to be his right hand man. We were looking at condos in midtown Manhattan, that's how much money he was making for Joker."

"Dag, Ma...what happened?" Destiny asked; Hope slid in the chair next to her. "Yeah, ma...what?"

Mya walked over and squeezed in between them and kissed them both. "It all happened so quick." She looked up at Skyler. "I remember...he didn't want me to go, but I insisted anyway. I had just gotten a full-length fur, and I guess I just wanted to show it off; we were going to the Roxy or something. I rode with him to do a pickup, he was doing a route for Aziz...they couldn't find him or something; no one could get in touch. All Dante had to do was pick up the money and bring it to the mill; Joker said he'd handle it from there, it was supposed to be a favor, that's all."

"What happened Mya, damn...don't be stopping and going and shit-"

"Skyler, hush!" She rolled her eyes. "We pulled up in front of the spot, it was cool, Dante went inside. About 15 minutes passed and I got impatient, also hot, hell I didn't take the coat off. Anyway, I went inside to see what was up. I thought I would be alright; he left me with a gun, a .38. I got out the car and walked up the steps, pushed the door and it opened. I didn't see no one, but I heard some voices. I walked towards the sounds I heard and right before I got there, I heard shots. I saw the flashes from the muzzle and I ran towards it thinking about Dante. I get around the corner and blood was all over the place and there was Dante, hunched over on the floor...Aziz was standing over him with a gun...smoke coming out the barrel."

She picked up the cigarettes again this time Mya lit one for her. "I reached for my gun and he turned towards me...he put his gun down and walked slowly towards me saying he didn't mean it...that it was a accident. He told me that there was a robbery, he begged me not to shoot him. I didn't, I was scared...confused. I walked over to Dante and tried to wake him up, get him up out of there...to a hospital. The siren from the cops was all I heard when Aziz pulled me up and told me we had to go. I asked why. He said if the cops find all the dope here, the money and guns, we would be blamed and go to prison for life and that wouldn't be good for me or the girls." She sat down on the carpet sitting in an Indian cross-legged position, staring off into her memory, and took quick puffs on the cigarette before she continued. "I left with him, I was scared. Later on that night we met up with Joker and Aziz and I talked. Joker was pissed, he mean-mugged me, said Dante was stealing from him, told me to get out of town or he'd take his revenge out on me." Tears streamed from her eyes. "Aziz stepped forward and told him he would take care of me...and the girls, Joker let it go..." She held her head up and looked towards the ceiling. "That's how we hooked up..."

"Whoa...whoa, hold up." Skyler leaned forward in her seat. "Who shot Dante?" "I want to say Aziz, but all I saw was the gun in his hand but..." she broke down. Hope rushed over and embraced her. "I was scared...I felt like I owed him..."

Skyler got up and gently reached down and eased her over to the couch, "Hush now...it's gonna be alright." She walked over to the kitchen table and picked up a pad and opened it. "Okay...we need to get the money."

"Money...what money?"

Skyler turned. "Every goddamn dime." She held up her fingers counting. "From Joker...Aziz....even that fine-ass, fuckin' Miles. Payback...every cent that's owed to Dante!"

Mya looked over at Destiny. "That's owed to my daughters."

Hope gazed over at Skyler and asked, "But how, Ms. Skyler...how do we get hold to all that money?"

Skyler stepped over to her and caressed her face. "Remember when I told y'all, I needed all of you...well, my darling, that's how. By using all of us...all of us."

"Girl, we can get killed...I hope you got a good plan."

Skyler smiled. "A plan...yeah, I got a plan...a good fucking plan."

GUTTER STOOD ACROSS from the playground watching parents keep an eye on their kids; it was early morning and he sipped on a bitter cup of coffee. Looking at the old school building he remembered his days as a child; school was a haven from a drug addicted mother and father, an escape for him and his two brothers. He would have never thought he'd actually be selling the same wares that eventually killed both parents; coming in from school and watching the body of his mother O-D'ing, her eyes flushed, opened wide, glazed from the heroin she injected into her small undernourished body. After watching her shoot up all the dope she could get her hands on, death must have been a heaven of sorts for her, he figured. After witnessing that he still chose this direction, but certainly glad his brothers didn't even though they didn't speak to him at all anymore; but everybody has a choice to make in life and this was his.

He smiled as a child waved at him and his mother looked over and returned the grin, not knowing that behind the stare was the cunning demeanor of a stone cold predator waiting to pounce at any moment; the only thing he cared about was whether she needed any dugee, just like his own mother.

His crude thoughts were disturbed as Smack came into view, making his way towards him. Smack had the glide of a panther; his movements weren't swift, but he always seemed to cover a lot of ground as he flowed, like a liquid, his alias, one that stuck, Smack. His slender frame appeared much larger than the oversized outfits he favored; besides chain smoking cigarettes he constantly kept one hand on his waist, pulling up his pants like a child needing a belt. "Wassup..." He tossed the butt he had in his hand to the sidewalk. "I see you made it." he said.

"Yeah, man...so, what's up. It's a little early for this shit." Gutter folded his arms impatiently as Smack waited until the last of the kids ran into the schoolyard. "Give it a second. I don't want everybody in our business..."

"Hell, ain't nothing but school kids out here...we're in their business."

He pointed to a window facing the parking lot adjacent towards the back. "Up there...you see! She just stuck her head out!"

Gutter squinted; he wore Coke-bottle glasses that were thick as hell and he would only put them on in desperate situations, avoiding the howls of laughter that came with it, but this was one of those circumstances. He reached into his pocket. "Oh yeah...who's that chick?" He traced her line of sight. "Damn...she can see the front of the pool room from there...who is it...5-0?"

Smack walked across the street to the side of the playground, Gutter right on his heels and leaned against the side of the fence. "Miles's lookout..."

"That muthafucka got everybody working for him, huh..."

"I'll say one thing about him, he's smart. He's got that broad so in love with him, she stares out the window looking for his ass-"

"And she don't even know she's playing the role of a fuckin' lookout. If anything goes down I bet she's right on the phone, too-"

"Yep...calling his ass." Smack lit up another cigarette as Gutter fist dapped him. "He's a smart muthafucka!"

Gutter looked around on the walls! "So...where's the spot?"

Smack pointed towards a window located on the bottom, lower side of the building right where he described, barely in view. "Right there."

"Oh yeah...I see. It is a tight spot, but damn, that's straight to the boiler room."

"Yeah, we need to get in and case it out so we know what to hit and what to bring with us."

"You're right, but are you sure that's the spot?"

"Well, let's put it this way. How quick did it take for Pancho to bring back six grand?"

Gutter leaned back and thought, "Not long...not long...15-20 minutes." "Well..."

"Okay, okay...I'm sold, but how we gonna get in the building?" Smack snickered and gawked at him. "Damn, you must be drinking too much of that nasty ass coffee. Hell, this is Alphabet City, the biggest drug nest in the city, damn near the world." He pointed to a window that overlooked the school.

"Look, right up there...the window overlooking the front."

"That's the Principal's office...right?" Gutter caught on. "Oh shit that muthafucka on dope, too?" Smack threw his butt into the street. "Everybody here is on dope. All we gotta do is get to him...get the keys..."

"Hell yeah-" Gutter turned abruptly as he spotted Miles's truck turning up the street. "Damn, there's Miles." He threw up his hand to wave and Smack snatched it back down. "I don't think he saw us..." he said.

Smack frowned. "What are you, stupid! Naw...I'm sure he did, your waving and shit-but right now he doesn't see the plan in motion; we better hit it fast before he does."

"Damn, cuz...you sound like we might have to-"

"What, take him out?" He pulled at his pants. "That's life...you think if he found out he wouldn't do us, think! Let's get the fuck outta here."

"Yeah...you're right." Gutter and Smack walked up the street away from the school heading towards the poolroom. Gutter turned back and glimpsed the small, padlocked opening. "Man gotta do what a man fuckin' gotta do..."

chapter 8

"OOOOO, YEAH BABY...." Aziz cooed as he laid back coming out of his deep slumber feeling the sweet, wetness on the shaft of his dick being massaged by the hotness of a wet tongue. His toes curled as his ass stiffened by the tingles that ran up his back and down his spine; mews were the only sounds he could muster out of his mouth only after he managed to open his eyes and gaze upwards towards the ceiling, shutting them back tightly after his dick was engulfed and thrust slowly into the mouth using sultry lips as a guide that went along with the delight, stroking hungrily on his dick. He squirmed and used his hands to caress the back of the head that mastered the treat he was receiving, then clasped them around the neck and pushed until he yelled out more perceptible words, "Yeah...it's sooo good...don't stop, Mya..."

Abruptly without warning the next thing he felt was the stinging on his face from the hand that slapped it, apparently he let out the wrong, audible words. He couldn't fathom how his mind was at once engulfed in erotic pleasure and then unforeseen by him he was now seeing stars and deep red, he yelled out, "What the fuck!" But, somewhere deep inside of him and not too far, he liked how both of the emotions intermingled and his dick responded by exploding the cum he held in his loins; he hollered as he was met with another slap. But this time more deliberate; it felt like a punch more than anything and along with it came shouts. "Muthafucka... Mya, my ass"

Aziz was fully awoke now as he glanced down and saw his dick going limp with cum oozing from out of it, "What the fuck?"

"What the fuck my ass!"

"How the hell did I get here?" he said as he looked around at the apartment of his already vexed lover who now sat on the side of the bed lighting up a blunt. "How you gonna call that bitch's name out, Aziz, and you here with me?" A tear ran down from the side of his lover's face as Aziz slid off to the side of the bed. "How long was I here...I don't remember-"

"You don't remember what, Aziz!" His lover's name was Peaches, and Peaches now looked into his face wiping the tears asking why, but Aziz still couldn't and didn't understand how he got to Peaches' apartment in the first place, so the question remained unanswered. Peaches lived on the west side past Broadway in a loft overlooking the pier and he couldn't fathom why he couldn't recall how he'd gotten all the way over here. "When did I get here-"

Peaches gaped seeing that he was thoroughly confused, "You mean to tell me, you don't remember your coming here last night."

"No...I don't..."

Peaches reached down and picked up a bag from off the floor on the back end of the bed, "Oh, shit. Aziz, you came by here last night with some of this Chinese food, cursing Mya out and swearing to God you wanted to kill her ass and I let you in..."

"Damn..."

"Damn? Now what!" Peaches hollered, "You don't want to be here!"

"No, it's not that, baby..." he reached over and stroked Peaches' face, "I must have been drinking cause I don't remember anything, that's all." He leaned forward, "Really."

"I hear you baby..." Peaches grabbed his dick and stroked it until it got hard again, "but...I didn't smell any alcohol on your breath."

Aziz shook his head in discord, then gently slid Peaches' hand away and mumbled, "No...Alcohol..."

"That's what I said...I should know, you fucked the shit out of me. You don't remember that...damn..." Peaches turned over, "raw...right in my ass."

Aziz looked down at his dick then sniffed at his fingers, "I need to wash..."

"No, not yet baby."

He glanced over at his cell phone, "Oh shit...it's eight in the morning. I gotta call Miles, damn! I missed my runs, he's gonna be mad as hell!" He speed dialed the number as Peaches continued stroking on his dick, "C'mon, Miles...pick up..."

"Wassup...Aziz!"

"What up, Miles...hey look, I'm on my way over in a few-"

"Whoa-hold up, brother. You should have already been here for one, and two...I already looked out for your ass last night, remember...partner." Miles pulled a right hand turn onto traffic on Ave C barely missing a pedestrian, "I mean...hell, you ain't never here and shit, I gotta do what I gotta do...you know."

Aziz eased up as Peaches swallowed down on the tip of his dick causing him to stutter, "You...uh, damn, you...already makin' the runs ...sssss, damn..." Miles pulled the phone away from his ear and goggled at it, "Muthafucka! I know your ass ain't fuckin' right now, not while I'm talkin' to you!" He made a left and the truck swerved as it zoomed up 8th Avenue with Pancho protesting in vain, he hollered back on the phone, "I've been out here bustin' my ass...you didn't hear Joker when he said he was bringing someone in town today, or what!"

"Aw, man, Miles...lighten up. Hell, you need to get you some..." he grinded his ass into Peaches' face as he felt his dick tense up, "So...yo...where you want...me to meet-"

"Meet!" Miles's truck came to a screeching halt as he stomped on the brakes on the corner of 8th Street and 1st Avenue, "There's been changes!" He looked in the rear at Chino and Blu, "Chino and Blu are making the pick ups from now on!"

"Blu...from the pool room?"

"Seems like he's more on point...since you got other shit going on." He made a right on 9th Street cruising down the block slowly past Tompkins Square park to make sure his pushers were in place. Pancho glanced over at him motioning for him to slow down but Miles was already pissed, he wasn't hearing anything, "Yeah...you might be replaced."

Aziz couldn't believe what he'd just heard, Miles was trying to cut his throat or so it seemed. "What...you trying to cross me, Miles!" His anger was aroused and it seemed to sensitize him even more as Peaches ran his dick around the lips of a mouth that was ready to receive, "Ahhhh, shit....I told you I, ahhhh, had some things going on, ahhhh." He couldn't help but moan as he felt the cum rise. Miles was pissed now; Aziz didn't have the respect for him to at least hold off what he was doing, "Even now you don't give a fuck...you too busy getting your dick sucked or something...damn!" He stomped the brake and the big bodied truck shook as it stopped, almost sending his passengers through the windshield. Pancho and Big E screamed, but he still didn't pay them no mind. Chino shook his head and Blu finally spoke up, "C'mon Miles, we too fuckin' hot for you to be driving crazy and shit!"

"What! Who the fuck-" he turned, "You talkin' to me!"

Blu reached into his jacket, "Yeah...I'm talkin' to you! You and Aziz need to get y'all shit together!" Chino saw that the situation was heated and he intervened, "Look, Miles! He's right! I understand you got some shit going on, but damn, we got a truck full of dope and you drivin' crazy and shit, tighten up! I ain't going to prison on no fuckin' humbug!"

"Hell, yeah...I mean, c'mon man, pull over and talk!" Blu said as he eased his hand out of his jacket, "Look man...better safe than sorry."

Miles looked at Blu and then the others, realizing they were right. Aziz had pulled him off his square, "Damn...sorry 'bout that. Y'all right...damn!" He pulled the truck over towards the back side of St. Christopher's Church, "Look, Aziz...you fuckin' up and Joker's the one that needs to be handling this shit. You work for him...not me. I'm doing what I need to do!"

"Ahhhh...sssss..." Aziz's dick caught a spasm as cum shot off into Peaches' mouth and was hungrily gobbled down, he grabbed his dick and squeezed the last of the cum out and exhaled then blew, "Oh, so...you gonna snitch-"

"Snitch! You calling me a fuckin snitch! I should kick your ass! Here it is, you're not here making the pick ups or drops, somewhere getting your dick sucked. You do this shit all the time and I cover for you...that it's for me, let Joker handle this shit! I'm through with it!" Miles watched the traffic as Pancho and Big E got out along with Blu. Chino leaned back on the side of the hood watching as they scrambled through the park, "Look, don't bother coming through this morning...it's being handled. You need to get in touch with Joker, okay."

Aziz realized he'd made a real bad move and now he had to deal with Joker and he really didn't want that, "Hey, Miles...sorry, man...just been going through a lot of shit, man. Sorry 'bout things, we can work this shit out ourselves. I just need time to sort things out..."

Miles watched Pancho and Big E take Blu through the ropes, swelling up his pushers, passing out the bundles, Chino was on point scanning, looking out for the Police and jack boys; he smiled, he knew the time was right to get rid of Aziz, the whole territory could be his alone. No more splitting of the paper, Joker would be glad he made the move with Chino and Blu. Hell, he thought, he had him in his pocket, right where he wanted him. Aziz would have to go through him because Joker sure as hell didn't want to deal with this bullshit, if he did, it would be ugly, at best. "Yeah...sure Aziz...call me back later." He shut his phone off then knocked on the window at Chino, "Yo cuz...you doing a good job."

"Everything cool?"

"Yeah, everything's cool...trust me."

"Yeah...I will." Chino said.

Aziz threw the phone on the bed as it went dead in his ear, Peaches came out of the bathroom and cuddled up next to him and asked, "Is everything alright, baby?"

"I can tell it's gonna be one of those days...one of those fuckin days." He stared off from Peaches at the pistol he carried in his jacket, "Shit goin' down..." He pushed Peaches out the way and headed to the shower, "Yo...I gotta go..."

THE EAST RIVER WAS calm for a soothing, balmy morning; traffic seemed relatively smooth as the car shifted gradually, in and out cruising the highway. Joker looked across the water at Rikers Island and smiled, reminiscent of his youthful days of folly; remembering how his stepfather, Earnest came to see him; he'd just gotten busted for shoplifting in Macy's midtown store for the umpteenth time. Normally he'd be given a fine, a slap on the wrist, but things were different; Judge Cathey. She swore she'd teach him a lesson, one that he couldn't worm out from under, he snickered as he recalled her exact words. His step-dad pleaded with her to not send him upstate, but the Judge had heard that song more than once from him before, she swore he'd have to pay the big boy price. Joker didn't bat an eye as the Judge sent him upstate on a 1 to 3 felony, shoplifting. He didn't even flinch, he'd just turned seventeen and he felt he was ready for it.

Joker had inherited his father's frame of a bruiser. He was somewhat of a brute, the mannerisms of a charmer he'd gotten from his mother; dead now, struck by syphilis, that finally took its toll on her mind and her body. His father was also dead, an overdose of drugs soon after took his life; the cataclysm of events leading Joker down the coarse road of capriciousness, rebellion and oppression, his young soul already tormented based on the heartbreak scourging New York City.

His stepfather was the only relative he had after coming off his bid, he lived in a studio apartment on the Lowest East Side of Manhattan, Delancey Street. But there were too many discrepancies that Joker would not be privy too; namely Earnest's homosexuality. So, Joker turned away from that side of Broadway and his step-dad and back into his father's haunts across town in Alphabet City; which was being controlled by a host of drugs coming into the once Irish neighborhood, now more frequented by Puerto Ricans and Italians, most of them heroin addicts. He observed the dealers, the hustlers, the tricks and even the users, who taught him how to shoot people up for a profit, and watched the drugs deal death and poison to the once thriving community. By this time his step-dad had contracted a virus not known by AID's at the time, and he left all of what he had to Joker. When he died, thinking his legacy would have some viability to it; Joker sold everything. He took the money from the sale of his property and invested in two things; a .38 snub nosed revolver and a kilo of heroin.

At first he bumped his head, took loses, but learned through connections he made in the business of drug trafficking, namely Akbar. He was taught that it was cheaper in the long run to polish off the greedy that were constantly holding their hands out and kill off all the other competition. He instilled fear, a planned persona of terror on his allies. His diabolical scheme served him well and pretty soon Joker easily took control of a six block radius in Alphabet City and kicked his mentor, Akbar, to the curb.

He slid back in the seat and reached into his vest pocket for a cigar, sniffing the aroma he licked the back end and reached for a lighter, looked in the rear view mirror and caught the attention of Bezo and leaned forward, "Yo...uh, Bezo..." He motioned for a light and Bezo pushed in the cigarette lighter. Soon after it popped out, Joker reached, then was met with a clearing of the throat from the other passenger that rode with them. "Are you seriously going to light that up in this stuffy ass car?"

"Yeah..." Joker looked, "It's just a cigar...you do smoke them..."

"When, the environment calls for it and right now it doesn't." The male figure that sat across from him merely sat back not even turning to glance at Joker as he made the next suggestion, "Matter of fact, just wait...we'll be there soon, okay."

Joker was ready to protest but he knew he had to kiss the ass of his arrogant occupant, "Sure...okay." He mean mugged him as he stuffed the cigar back into his vest then looked over and smirked. His passenger was the man and Joker didn't want to disappoint, he wanted to secure his favor with him. This was part of his retirement, to sell off his holdings in Alphabet City, call it quits. He'd been there too long and things were changing, much more business, more grimy and not looking to get any better. This guy was a longtime acquaintance of his stepfather and had a lot of money, perhaps he was his lover at one time. Joker didn't care about that right now, when he was approached and offered the opportunity to let his drug trafficking routes change hands, he went for it. He thought about looking out for his people that were loyal to him by keeping them working. It was better than actually cutting them in on any of the profit.

Joker was greedy and most people knew it, so many expected nothing from him. Miles and Aziz had been with him the longest, longer than anyone and even they weren't privy to any extra, apart from what they made for themselves. Joker knew whatever hustles they made his money would always be straight and even then he still didn't trust them well enough, because they didn't trust him either.

He was ready to get out of the game and this man was his ticket; he took a lot of shit from him and his attitude but to Joker it was worth it. He heard about the man's reputation in regard to business and he was ready to refine his taste and be a legitimate entrepreneur instead of being dubbed a thug, the two bit gangster that he was. He turned slightly towards him and pondered on his question before he asked it, "So, what's with you anyway?"

The gentlemen turned towards Joker and cocked his head curiously, trying to figure out the angle Joker was heading. He licked his lips surreptitiously, feminine in a way that made Joker uncomfortable. His stare made him advert his eyes downward somewhat, he now had complete control of the environment therefore making the atmosphere totally his. "What is with me...hmmm, what do you mean, what's with me?" A question answered by a question, a technique used by one who wished to be concealing asked, "What is with you...Joker?" Joker looked and his beady eyes closed to a slit, he tried to zero in on the validity of the question. What does he really mean? What is he really saying? The man now seemed to enjoy the game that was being parlayed between them; nothing given, nothing received. But Joker's limited mentality could take no more, it seemed like too much pressure to be able to reason, rationalize, so he did what he did best, react. "You trying to trick me, muthafucka! Look, man..." he leaned forward and rapped on the driver's seat, "Bezo, pull the fuck over...now! I'm tired of his shit!"

"But...boss, we're almost there!" Bezo protested as he glanced around for a place to pull the car over, "The next exit..."

The man knew Joker's pedigree, and was thoroughly prepared for whatever he bought, he chuckled a little and calmly leaned back. "Joker, Joker...that shit may play well with your little fuckin' friends in your little fuckin' circles, but....I promise you, one, if you pull this car over the deal will be off and two, if you pull this car over and raise, just raise your hand to me ever so slight in any way shape, form or fashion, even to cover your mouth from a fuckin' sneeze..." The sun reflecting off the steel of the Brooklyn Bridge mirrored the barrel of the 9mm directed at Joker's chest and as he squinted and shielded his eyes from the glare the man in front of him nonchalantly spoke, "I'll kill you...understand."

Joker uttered a curse, the glimmer still blinded him enough temporarily not allowing him to go for his gun which was buried deep in his jacket; he had no wins and the man on the other end knew it, so Joker conceded, "Yeah..."

"Muthafucka! Did you fuckin' hear me!" he hollered and Joker cringed. The pistol was cocked, a bullet already in the chamber; Joker knew from experience, his own, that he had no wins, "Yeah, yeah...I hear you!"

"Good!" Slowly the gun was holstered back into his coat as his demeanor abated to a tentative but delicate stop, then he responded, "Look, Joker, you show me around your routes, I'll check them out to make sure that they are actually viable, lucrative, and then I go. If I like what I see, the checks in the mail, literally. You go your way and

I go mine, that's what's with me...that's all. You don't have to like me, just like what we're trying to do...make a lot of money, okay."

Joker had made a bad move and he knew it, the man was right, it was all about money, business and he had to learn to play the game much better, keep a cooler head. "You're right....I apologize." He looked up front, "Bezo...keep going-"

"I never stopped, Boss...I never stopped." Bezo said as he glanced through the rear view mirror, even he knew Joker pulled the wrong card from the deck. The man looked over at his shaken counterpart and rolled down his window, reached deep and long into his inner jacket pocket slowly as Joker watched carefully, not knowing what to expect this time, nervous. He pulled out two long cigars, looking to be Cubans and handed one to him, "Hey...it's on me. Go ahead...light up." Joker smiled, he thought maybe this guy was okay after all, it was his ways he wasn't used to. He'd never been around someone like him before, except for, perhaps, his stepfather.

The gentleman across from him puffed on the smooth pulling chocolate cigar. He browsed around at the buildings as Bezo came down the ramp off the highway, staring off for a while looking at the windows of the old tenements for traces of the memories of people from his past. He was back in his old neighborhood trying to regain what his father had lost or stolen, he still wasn't quite sure. His father, Henre Cannessa, was a French man who at one time controlled the properties that housed most of the drug dens that now belonged to Joker. The plan was to get them back and rent out the high dollar property, still allow for the profitable drug trade to prosper but more civil, no more drug dens, but instead highly sophisticated, drug resorts. The era of the Joker's was over and Gustavo Alvaro Cannessa was the new age of dope pusher. The same property that Joker sold so easily, given to him by his stepfather was in all actual the same properties Gustavo wanted, property worth millions, much more than the dope Joker actually peddled. Greed had not worked in Joker's favor at all; then or now and Gustavo would take full advantage of that.

The car pulled into traffic on Houston Street and made a right on Ave C. Bezo looked through the rear view mirror at Joker and asked, "Uh, boss...you need to make any stops?"

Joker nodded his head no, "Straight to the Pitt, Bezo." The car continued up Ave C as Gustavo checked out the surroundings, noticing the full potential of the old neighborhood; it was prime property and he was ready to benefit from it. They made a left on 4th Street and the change was drastic, junkies were all over hanging out on corners bent over; heads turned as they noticed Joker's car, and Gustavo wasn't comfortable with that at all. "It's not good that everyone should recognize you..."

Joker knew he was right, too many people had his car pegged the minute it came into Alphabet City, the Police and even someone waiting to make a move on him, so far it hadn't happened yet, but he felt enough of the paranoia that he kept armed men. One of those armed men strolled to the curb as the car pulled in front of the Pitt, startling Gustavo, "Who is this, Joker?"

"My people." He said as he straightened up his clothes. The young man opened Bezo's door and Bezo then opened the back door letting Joker get out; Gustavo was right behind him and glanced at the doors of the gym where he saw two other men. He casually stuffed his hands into his jacket feeling for his gun as he walked behind Joker to the building. The older man from earlier approached him as he went into his office, "Miles came by...the product is good, but I suggest you make a few calls, seems like it's been stepped on a little."

"Maybe you think from the mill house."

"No...no...I checked it out myself," he looked around at Gustavo and asked, "Who is this guy?"

Gustavo walked up next to Joker and put his hand out, "This is the gentleman I told you about...the man." Joker said.

"Oh yeah ...the man." He shook his hand, "Good to meet you...Eduardo." Joker opened the office door and ushered them both in, "He's been with me for a while, Gustavo, he makes sure the product is pure, at least to the point where it can be marketed for a profit."

Gustavo shifted his piece into his pocket, took off his coat and handed it to Bezo, "I see. So, you have a system in place that allows you to check the product...is that before or after the initial purchase?"

Joker turned and smiled, "You know your stuff I see." Eduardo spoke up, "Before and after...we buy, and of course in bulk so I check out the product for purity then we stay with the distributor until that funnel runs its course."

"We buy from different sources, too." Joker added.

"Of course...one source being perhaps, France." Gustavo said.

"Oh yeah, France. It's the best merchandise we can get...mostly Middle Eastern."

"That's right...but not direct from that source, it has to come through other hands, government gets jumpy...things are different, drugs are becoming more global now. Not like before when you could buy kee's coming off the boat at Fulton Street, heh, Eduardo."

"The good old days, Joker."

Gustavo crossed his legs and Joker handed him a drink of Hennessey on ice, he took a sip then said, "You seem to have it together Joker and that's good, but I need to see the operation and your main people then like I said, if I like, we can start business immediately."

"Let's toast!" Joker raised his glass, "To success and money!"

"Success and money!" Gustavo said as he raised his glass to meet Joker's, "So...is this your, uh, headquarters?"

Joker sat down at his desk looking around, "This is my main spot, but you have to make other arrangements. I don't think you'd be able to do business here after we leave."

"No problem...I won't be coming down here too much, anyway. I have a place of my own."

Joker put the drink down and reached for his phone, he dialed Miles's number, "Miles.....it's me. Where you at?"

Miles had just pulled up in front of the library on 11th Street, "Just came back from Tompkins' Park...getting ready to go through Hampton Square Houses...what's up?"

"I got the man here, remember."

"I remember, but also remember I told you I needed to break in some new people...I'll be there but it'll be in a while."

"Where's Aziz? Isn't this his day to do the rounds...I don't understand..."

"Hey boss...you need to call him, like I said, I'm doing the rounds."

"Hmmm, I hear you. Okay, call me when you get a chance, cool"

"That's cool." Miles hung up the phone and looked over at Pancho, "Aziz's on his own."

Joker dialed Aziz's number after gesturing to Bezo to refill Gustavo's glass. Eduardo explained to him the system he used to test the quality of the dope, he seemed intrigued. Aziz answered the phone, "Yo...Joker, what's up!"

"You, Aziz. Why you not doing your rounds?"

"I'm right around the corner...getting ready to pull up to the spot now...we'll talk."

Joker pulled back the curtain and Aziz's truck had pulled up. He grinned, "Here's my guy coming in now."

"Miles?" Eduardo asked. "No...Aziz."

Gustavo raised an eyebrow, he'd heard that name before. Aziz came in and shook Bezo's hand, putting on a show of it, "Gentlemen, how are you?

Joker...good to see you!" He shook Joker's hand and turned around, "Eduardo! And you sir..."

Gustavo put out his hand, "Gustavo." He squeezed Aziz's slightly causing him to jerk it back, "Sorry 'bout that."

"So, uh, why is Miles making the rounds?" Joker asked. Aziz knew he would have called Miles so he had to get his lie together. "Well...I had to take care of Mya."

"Mya...how is she? Is she alright?"

"Yeah, yeah, sure...dumb bitch. She fucked around and got drunk last night," he poured himself a drink then turned towards Gustavo, "Had to put her ass in check...know what I mean."

Damn, Joker thought, he couldn't believe Aziz would go in this direction, he knew he was arrogant but not stupid. Evidently Eduardo did, and excused himself seeing that Aziz was about to put his foot in his mouth and he didn't want to be a party to it. "Joker...I gotta go." He shook Gustavo's hand, "Nice to meet you and I look forward to seeing you again. Aziz...later."

Joker waved at him as Bezo closed the door, leaving out behind him. Gustavo was already checking Aziz out and traced his movements carefully as he sat down next to him, "So, you are Joker's, lieutenant?"

"Yeah...his right hand man." "I see." He sipped solemnly on his drink, "Now, I'm curious...what exactly do you mean by putting someone in check?"

"Oh, okay." Joker cut his eyes at Aziz intending him not to go there but Aziz's contemptuous attitude ignored him, "You know women, they're stupid. You gotta put them in check, like you do a dog."

"Oh...I see. So you put people in check, then."

"No...just her. I own her."

"Okay...you own someone-"

Joker saw where this was going and tried to redirect. "Gustavo...maybe we could ride around a little."

Gustavo put up his hand, "Sure...later. Right now, uh, Aziz seems to interest me." Joker couldn't stop it, like Miles had said, he was on his own. "So...Aziz...you beat your woman..."

"When she needs it..."

Gustavo put his drink down and leaned in towards him, "So...who beats you when you fuck up...like now."

Aziz jumped up. "No one ...no one! I ain't no one's bitch!"

Gustavo leaned back and crossed his legs again. "Well...once you work for me," he peeped up at Aziz then over at Joker, "that will change...right. Joker..." he chuckled. Aziz was incensed as well as embarrassed and stood over Gustavo then leaned into his face, "You try it and I'll bust your faggot ass!" Joker got up and zoomed in pushing Aziz to the side after watching Gustavo reach for his gun. "Leave that shit alone, Aziz!"

"You heard this muthafucka! This faggot muthafucka!" he yelled. All Joker could do was bite his bottom lip at this point. Aziz was about to get shot, if not killed, but he'd rather deal with Gustavo as opposed to the wrath he was mustering up right now.

chapter 9

GUSTAVO STARED OUT the window, it was up in the day and he was well behind his schedule. For all practical purposes he was supposed to come here to see the cash flow of things, then be on his merry way to Kennedy Airport for a flight to Miami to give a report to his cohorts; it seemed simple enough.

This disarray was the last thing on his mind, he loathed dealing on this level, but this was a favor called in from a long time accomplice. He took the job totally on that premise, now, as it stands he was going to have to kill this muthafucka standing behind him, Aziz. He couldn't believe it, bad enough Joker tried him, but now this punk. He tried to reason with himself why he shouldn't just shoot him in the head and be done with it; but he needed to know at what point did they lose the respect, or did they ever have any for him at all.

It bothered him, these were savages in comparison to his normal circle of associates he dealt with, they were ignorant and wanted to be big time not even comprehending the power he exerted. Gustavo had a highly advanced sense; he ventured into this business fervently, the dope was only a way to an end. He had at his disposal an empire, so he took shit personal. Alphabet City was playing itself out, eventually it would be green lighted and twisted to fit an ever growing upper middle class community, west of New York University; it was inevitable, even Joker knew. Gustavo was ordered by his people to secure the dilapidated area and the property. Drugs would still be of benefit but only to a distinguished echelon of users. Namely, rich overseas nationals, marketed exclusively through power brokers, the new age of drug dealers. For Gustavo, this was his time, but he had to take care of the grunt work before it could be set in motion, and this was the task to be put forth.

He turned around measurably, and leaned against the frame of the window and turned slightly Joker's way avoiding Aziz's glare, then slowly and lethargically got up and walked towards Joker, who sat at his desk mean mugging Aziz. "Let's go. We have business and we're late." He didn't even face Aziz's way as he strolled by, he was much too aggravated.

Aziz himself had calmed down long enough to come to his senses realizing that he'd fucked up. Gustavo kept his cool and that was different, it kept him at bay, he didn't coax a reaction. He seemed composed, level headed. There was nothing about him that showed temperament, emotion, unlike Joker, who was clearly predictable. He didn't know how to reciprocate, he made an attempt at reconciliation, "Hey, uh, I'm sorry. I didn't mean to-"

Gustavo coldly put up his hand and walked towards Bezo who had come in after hearing the commotion, "My coat, please."

Joker sighed, he knew he'd lost some money somehow as a result of this outburst and would have to put the damage control on it, he didn't say a word as he slumbered past Aziz, who held out his hands pleading, "C'mon now...I didn't' mean to-"

Gustavo had had enough of Aziz, he had just insulted and threatened him and now he cowered. He was flimsy, he didn't have the balls needed for the operational direction he wanted to go, and besides he didn't like men who preyed on the weak. The business of dope dealing is highly predatory and he seemed like a scavenger, he turned his direction to Joker, he made his decision. "He's a liability; I have no need of him." then walked through the door, "I'll be outside...you do what you do."

Joker exhaled, he didn't want to go there but he needed the money and if Aziz was going to interfere with that he'd have to go, "Yeah..." He turned back around and motioned Aziz to have a seat, Bezo stood off to the side. Aziz backed off a little and reached for his gun and it wasn't there, he realized he'd left it in the truck and that might be a mistake, he eyeballed Bezo, "Oh, I see what this is..."

Joker shook his head and stared, "Aziz...what's going on with you? The outburst, your attitude...what the fuck is up? You were my right hand..."

Aziz turned towards Joker and gazed into his face long and hard. Joker was right, he's been going through a lot lately and couldn't explain any of it, he pointed towards Bezo, "Back him off first."

"He's not the factor." Aziz sat cautiously as Joker lit up a fresh cigar and leaned back in his chair, "You disrespected the wrong man. He wants you-"

"I know you ain't gonna-"

Joker banged the top of the desk, "You see, Nutt! You don't fuckin' listen!" Bezo lunged, "Boss...fuck this, let me handle him!"

"No!" He waved him off and yelled at Aziz, "This is it...our affairs are over..."

"But-"

"Look...you know me! The only reason you're still breathin' is because we're a'iyht! So..." he spun around towards the window, "I'll make sure you're taken care of before you go your way..."

Aziz knew one day that this hand would be played so he kept a secret, he calmly looked up at Bezo, "You need to back off. I ain't going nowhere!"

"What!" Joker spun around, "What the fuck you mean-" he stood up, he was outraged and Aziz Just smirked, "You fuck with me and you're through. I still got dibs on you. You think I'm gonna go out like a sucka! I got all the information on Dante! Yeah, remember Dante, cause, I sure as hell do!" It stopped Joker in his tracks, he hadn't heard that name in a while, "You don't have nothing..." he said.

"Yeah, fuckin' try me." They stood eye to eye. Bezo waited for Joker to say the word, he'd rip Aziz to shreds, then feed him to the fish in the Hudson River. But Joker yielded, "Okay...you got this one, but remember this, from this point on, you watch yourself." He walked past him and grabbed his coat, "Let's go, Bezo." He turned one last time and looked at the cheese eating grin on Aziz's face, he had to find out what he knew, and the minute Gustavo left he would procure the truth and he'd better have something. "I hope you know what you're doing..." He stepped in front of Bezo and the door was slammed shut, hard enough to be heard echoing from outside.

Aziz watched them go to the car and thought about what he had, enough information to send him away for a long time, for life; but questioned whether he should have played the card this early on. He knew Joker would be checking him out now, so he had to come up with something to even the playing field and that something was Mya.

Inside the car Joker's mood was ice cold as they drove to the Bodega, the mill house. Gustavo was escorted inside and allowed to observe the packaging up of the product while it was illustrated to him, the process of getting the junk to the dope house; he liked the system that was in place but knew it would have to be tweaked. Joker at last warmed up a little but was still leery from earlier, he hoped to get in on Gustavo's good side and so far he was doing all right. His phone buzzed, he checked the number and it was Miles. "Yeah, Miles...what's going on?"

"I'm on my way to the pool room. You think you can meet up with me there and we can rap."

"I'll be there."

Miles was no Aziz, and he felt a whole lot better introducing Gustavo to him, "We're going to another spot...a place where we can talk. I'd also like you to meet another one of my lieutenants."

"I hope he isn't like the other one." Gustavo said as he shook his head, "I mean, how many of these men do you have anyway? The area doesn't look that big."

He was right, Joker thought, the person for the job would have been Aziz but lately he was dropping the ball, and Miles was the one running the touchdowns. Somehow he'd have to get rid of Aziz and that was difficult, he remembered Aziz's threat and he needed to know how grave it really was. He was going to tell Miles about it, get his opinion, even though he knew what it was going to be.

Joker's car pulled in front of the pool room and Bezo got out first as always, he peeped inside the doorway and came back out with the young man that normally parked cars, he whispered in his ear and pulled out a roll and put it in his hand, then Bezo came back and opened the door for Joker. The young man got out of the way and hopped in the drivers' seat.

"He's going to stay in the car until we get back, make sure no one fuck's with it...or it's his ass." Bezo said.

Gustavo snickered, he couldn't grasp how primitive they were, things would have to change before he'd set up. They walked up the steps and the door was opened. Nothing was happening; no dope or money was being moved, not yet. During the day it served as a hang out that catered mostly to old men pool sharks, and other shady inhabitants who frequented the dark and seedy place.

Gustavo was ushered to a seat by the back side of the bar overlooking the pool tables, the air was dry and dusty. Tempest came from out the back room behind the bar, "Joker, Bezo...long time no see." She wiped the table off and asked Gustavo if he'd like something to drink, he shook his head no, commenting on how attractive Tempest was, she cut her eyes, "Oh, yeah, she's fine." Joker smirked, Tempest sneered at their candor, turned on her heels then disappeared into the back room; Miles came out soon after, "Gentlemen..." He walked over towards Joker and shook his hand, "Boss..." then gestured at Bezo. He didn't make any sudden moves towards Gustavo, he didn't know him, therefore he didn't trust him, but instead waited for Joker to introduce them, after all it was his people.

Joker knew Miles's pedigree and respected that, he was different from Aziz, more poised. "Miles...this is Gustavo, he's the gentleman I've been telling you about." Miles walked over to the table, observing as he sat, he held out his hand and grasped Gustavo's, noticing how gentle a handshake it was, firm, rough around the fingertips like someone that hadn't done any hard work except to handle a gun. The powder burns caused calloused wells of charred skin under his manicured nails, his hands told stories that Miles didn't want to be a part of. "Please to meet you." They sat back, both keeping their eyes on each other looking for an opening, a kink in each other's armor so to speak. Miles called out to Tempest, "Could you get me a club soda, please...and you?" Joker and Bezo waited in anticipation to the response from Gustavo, he was trying him; he figured any man that started drinking hard liquor this early into the day trying to conduct business was unwise and could be easily compromised in due time, bad habits weren't good in this business.

"Club soda, also... thank you." He leaned back and crossed his legs, "Now, let's get down to business." Miles nodded his head and told Tempest to keep the glasses full.

Chino and Blu came from out the back of the count room and Miles called them over, "Joker, you know these fellas. "Joker nodded his head, "Of course, Chino... Blu, wassup."

"Well, Chino been...uh, posting lookout for me, and Blu been helping me with the routes."

"Okay...how's it going?"

"It's good, real good. I'm thinking of putting them on their own, moving them to the streets, I mean, of course with your blessing. What do you think?"

"That sounds good...we might be needing that soon. Real soon, but who's gonna replace them in here?."

"Well, uh, I'm thinking Pancho and Big E, they know enough to handle business. What's up with Aziz anyway?"

Gustavo squirmed when he heard the name and Miles caught it. "Things don' t look good for Aziz, Miles...Look, I'm okay with Pancho and Big E, but no fuckin' gambling!" Joker said.

"Got it...talk to me about Aziz." Blu and Chino stepped over to the bar out of ear shot. "I don't like him, period, he's not about business, he doesn't know me, then he called me a faggot! Normally he'd be dead, and this wouldn't be an issue." Gustavo said.

Miles knew he was right, Aziz definitely fucked up but still he needed him for the moment then he himself would dispose of him, properly. "I understand, but still he knows too much."

Gustavo's eyebrows raised as he stared at Miles, he liked that, he was thinking, "What do you suggest?"

"I suggest we wait him out, until I can see all that he knows, and well, I believe you know the outcome from there."

Joker rubbed his chin, "That's cool, but he says he can blackmail me.

"Blackmail? Naw, don't worry...I got it"

"Just come up with a plan and by the end of the day we'll know what's what."

"Sounds good." Tempest came back out with another round of drinks and Gustavo continued to be enticed by her beauty, "She's bewitching...gorgeous." he whispered to Joker.

Miles smiled and watched Blu trace the eyesight of Gustavo back to Tempest's ass, "She has...another admirer..." Joker said, Gustavo looked up and met Blu's gaze. "Sorry. No disrespect..."

Miles chuckled, "Oh, uh, none taken." Gustavo glanced around at Miles, "Okay...okay...I hear you." He picked up his glass and looked over at Joker, "Now this is what's up! I like this guy!" Gustavo was about to make Miles the man in Alphabet City. Blu and Chino pulled up some chairs and Bezo played the door. Pancho and Big E came out the back room behind the bar. At first Gustavo felt leery from all the movement, but he didn't question Miles at all, the way he moved so far prompted credence. Pancho pulled out a map of Alphabet City and spread it on a pool table, they all got up and surrounded it. Miles asked Joker if he could explain the rest of the operation to Gustavo, so he complied. "Do you.." Gustavo nodded, he was in better spirits now; Miles laid out a plan he had for a new Alphabet City, a better one, so he took heed. Alphabet City would be a crutch to a mind like Miles, he thought, he'd like to introduce him to some of his associates, set him up somewhere where his talents could be better appreciated.

Joker watched closely as Gustavo checked him out, he didn't want Miles to end up cutting his throat like Aziz. He scanned the room and his observation was met with a long hard stare from Bezo who seemed to contemplate on the same thing and he nodded, Joker had that same glare before and nodded back, he had a bad premonition.

"I DON'T KNOW...IT'S risky."

Skyler was coming out of the kitchen with a fresh pot of decaf, Hope picked up her mother's cup and moved it towards her. "What? C'mon, now, Mya...stop being a little pussy." She tipped the steaming, glass bowl over and poured, "I never said it would be easy." Hope placed it down then reached for Skyler's. "Suppose it doesn't work?" Mya asked.

"Well...then, what's the most you got to lose, then?" Skyler responded cynically. "Shit...our lives, girl."

Skyler snickered as she turned and walked back into the kitchen shaking her head, she replaced the globed kettle back to its setting and beckoned over towards Hope, "Want some Kool-Aid or something..." Hope shook her head no, "I really could have used some of that coffee." Skyler looked over at Mya who shrugged her shoulders, "My bad, Hope...I didn't know..."

Hope smiled, "That's alright Ms. Skyler..."

Skyler reached into the cupboard and poured Hope a cup then walked back into the living room, "Here you go." She sat across from Mya who stared aimlessly out the window past the hanging ferns, "Let's go over it again, this time...slowly, okay." she said, Mya turned around to face her, "Alright..."

"Everyone knows that dope pushers keep a stash. I mean, it's common practice; someone could rob them or they may need money for a lawyer or something and they can never come short with the bosses money because the dope is always C-O-D"

"C-O-D," Hope asked, "What's that?"

"Cash on delivery." Mya answered, "Dope is always credited so at the end of the day, the money for the dope needs to be there."

"That's right." Skyler added, "That's why they keep stashes." She reached over and picked up her cigarettes and slid an ashtray close to her; she lit up a Newport and leaned back taking a swig of her now cooled liquid, "You see, Aziz has a stash and being that he's been in the game awhile, it's probably pretty large and-"

"But," Mya interrupted, "you're assuming that it's not in a bank or something."

"Girl, give me a break. Aziz's a fuckin' dope pusher...he ain't got no kind of credentials. I'll bet my life on it. His stash is somewhere near where the money is counted..."

"Ms. Skyler...you know a lot." Hope said as she sat entranced by Skyler's swagger.

"Not by choice, Hope, don't get it twisted. After dealing with all these guys who push dope, their M-O is all the same, believe me. When they need money...dinner or something, a hotel!," she humphed and muttered under her breath, "I make them spend. Anyway, they disappear for a while and then come back strapped, always with cash, twenties, fifties and hundreds. Sometimes, I time them and it's always between fifteen to twenty minutes, after thirty, I'm out"

"So, what does that have to do with anything?"

Skyler inhaled on the cigarette and blew smoke into the air before she answered, she couldn't believe that Mya was so naive to this game and realized why she had been dragged this long. "Ask yourself these questions Mya, you work at a business." She turned slightly towards her then crossed her long shapely legs and ran the manicured tips of her fingers through her hair, Mya admired how good Skyler looked and took notice, "Listen up, banks put out money that's either old or new. ATM's, the same thing. But, here it is...new money, old money, crinkled money...dirty money. It ain't been laundered yet, girl!"

"Okay...I hear you and see your point but how do we find out where Aziz's stash is?"

"That's where I need you to set him up...make him go to it then we watch him...like a rat in a trap."

"Hopefully a big trap." Hope giggled.

"Shhh. Hope! But, what would make him go to his stash, Skyler?" "That's simple. What do dope dealers fear the most?" Mya's face crossed up, looking perplexed, she then hunched her shoulders, "What?" Skyler uncrossed her legs and put out her cigarette in the ashtray, her patience tried, "C'mon now, Mya. I can't think for you, too." She leaned up and turned towards Hope and asked sarcastically, "What do you think? Cause, your momma's crazy as hell." "Uh...from what I see...the police."

Skyler burst out laughing then reached over and hugged her, "Now, please tell your mother. Mya...the police! We have to convince him that the cops are gonna be on his ass and he needs to have some money available. Trust me, he's gonna leave the cash with you because he knows...or thinks...you'll go to the police, so he'll pay you off first."

Mya leaned back pondering at what she was hearing, disappointed with herself but she knew Skyler was right, he would do exactly that and she sneered, "Yeah...his good bitch, ass!"

"Ma!"

"No...no, let her vent. It's finally sinking in."

"Yeah...we need to crank this shit up." she grumbled bitterly.

"We will, as soon as I hear from-" Skyler suddenly looked around and noticed Destiny was missing. Looking along the floor at the telephone wire she followed it to her bedroom and opened the shut door, "Girl...who you on the phone with?"

"Destiny giggled as she playfully rolled over on Skyler's California, king sized bed, almost engulfing her diminutive frame, "My boyfriend."

"Your boyfriend..." Skyler smirked, "What kinda boyfriend you got?" She smiled and rolled her eyes and was about to close the door behind her, "Mya...you better watch that girl-" she stopped in mid-sentence as she stared in Hope's, frantic face, her mouth had dropped and her eyes were wide open. "What, Hope...what's wrong?"

Mya looked over at her, then got up and rushed her, "What's wrong Hope...you alright?" Hope's eyes had terror written all in them as she stared at Skyler's room, then she stammered, "Destiny's...b-boyfriend"

"Spit it out child!" Mya said as she shook her." Skyler swung open the room door, she'd figured it out, "Who's your boyfriend Destiny!" she yelled.

Destiny was startled as Skyler rushed into the room, dropping the phone, Skyler dived for it, and yelled into the receiver, "Who the fuck is this!" There was silence before the reception went dead, "Damn girl...you done fucked us up!"

Destiny sat on the bed scared and in shock as her mother rushed into the room, "Your boyfriend...what's his name!"

"Lonzo!" Hope screamed out as she staggered towards the door, "His name is Lonzo...he a runner who works for Aziz and them!" "I told her not to mess with those boys!" Destiny started to quaver as she crawled away from her mother who now looked at her with venom; Skyler stepped in front of her as she balled her fist, "No, don't, she didn't know." Skyler nudged her to the side and dashed into the living room and looked out the window towards the street, there he was, Aziz's truck, pulling up the block. She ran back into the bedroom "C'mon y'all...pack a bag, quick!" she called out.

"What!" Mya yelled, "What happened!"

"Momma. I didn't know. He just wanted to come see me. Bring me something to eat..." Destiny quivered.

"What did you do-" Mya hollered.

"C'mon now, Mya! It's too late for that shit, now! Her boyfriend called Aziz and told him where I lived, okay! Just get a bag and pack some clothes. We got to get the fuck outta here, quick!"

"Where we gonna go!" Mya asked as Hope scrambled grabbing at the bags Skyler tossed out the closet; Destiny ran into the bathroom gagging. "Where you going now, Destiny, I should kick your ass!" she screamed. Skyler stopped and grabbed hold of Mya. "Calm down look at me!" She shook her and Mya looked in her eyes. "You know who you sound like? Think about it, deal with her later, you hear me. Right now, get some things together into a bag. We got to move quick, you understand." Mya shook her head slowly, dazed and in shock, "Now do it..."

Skyler grabbed her cell phone and dialed some numbers at the same time shoving hygienic stuff into a shoulder bag. The phone on the other end rang briefly then someone picked up. She stopped in her tracks relieved, "God, I'm so glad you answered."

"What up!" The voice blurted out on the other side.

Skyler ran back out into the living room and watched as Aziz's vehicle sought out a space to park, "I don't have much time, I'll have to explain later..."

"What's wrong, Skyler!"

"Steve, I need your help, baby!"

AZIZ'S, JET BLACK, Range Rover Evoque dipped the corner off the Grand Concourse down Tremont Avenue. He kept his eyes peeled for the address he had written down in front of him on the dashboard; the numbers he'd gotten from Lonzo, his runner. All he had to do was put the word out, a little money and he'd find out where they were, this time, thanks to Destiny.

He didn't know the Bronx that well and he felt uncomfortable in what seemed to him to be a strange environment, it was outside his level of comfort; here he wasn't the man, but he was hell bent on going after Mya. He had it made up in his mind, an inclination that was now filled with anxiety and phobia that she was the root of his ruin. He never did see why Dante spent so much time with her anyway, why he just didn't do her like all the rest then dump her? What was it about her? He couldn't figure it out. They'd been close, now it was all about Mya, his kids. No more good times, spending money like they use to; no more, and all because of this bitch, he rationalized.

Unconsciously he banged the steering wheel and the horn abruptly blew, it startled him as his thoughts faded and he pulled to a stop sign on Park Avenue across from the building where Skyler lived.

The 20-story building stood apart and distinct from the neighborhood that borderlines the South Bronx. It's new look construction made it stand out in this once thriving neighborhood located on the pulse of a one-time prosperous thruway.

Aziz looked up the street for a parking space close to the doorway just in case he needed a quick getaway. He spotted a parking lot located off to the side but it was locked and there appeared to be a security officer of some sort inside the lobby; he crept by casing the area. Driving up Park Avenue about two blocks he made a U-turn, he had developed a plan; get Destiny to come downstairs, snatch her up and bait Mya back to the projects. He jeered, he knew he should have picked up Lonzo, but the call came to him too soon, by the time he caught up with him he was already hustling. Rather than answer questions about what was going on, he paid him off quickly, got the address and shot uptown.

He had to move quick, he remembered Joker's threat and took it seriously, he needed to make a stop and pick up a manila envelope he had stashed at Penn Station in Manhattan; a small locker he'd kept for years, stowing information: names, places, routes, everything he needed to back Joker up off of him. He still had to deal with Miles, he hated that, but he should have taken him out years ago when he had the chance, never let him in, but it all was Dante's idea. And now Dante was dead and gone and he was left holding the remnants of the pieces of someone else's dreams. He played the game well, but that's exactly what it all was, one big game and he was losing fast, everything was now about to be uncovered.

Maybe that's the way it should go down, Aziz reasoned with himself. Maybe he would just blackmail Joker, collect the money, maybe rob the mill house and haul ass out of town with Peaches, who understood him best, find new life in Atlanta, Georgia. Peaches talked about it all the time; he just needed the money and he knew where he could get it. It all made sense now, but he had to do something with Mya, sew up the loose ends, put the memory of Dante behind him, right now there seemed to be no other way. He closed the door of the truck and stood off to the side covering the .45 he masked. He'd just put in a clip and pulled back the slide jetting one in the chamber. He reached for the silencer he had in his inner pocket and screwed it on the muzzle, then placed it gently in his jacket, straightening up his clothes. He checked his face and turned towards the entrance of the building; the security guard stood as he approached the entrance way.

He was just about to open the door. Aziz grasped the butt of his gun, but instead he motioned for him to turn around. Aziz's lights were still on and rather than bring about any suspicion, he politely smiled, walked back to the truck and got in. The security guard opened the door and beckoned him, Aziz rolled the windows down.

"Everything alright, son? You live here?"

"Oh...no sir...I just noticed, it's the wrong address..." he put on the best shit eating grin he could muster and replied, "Sorry...it must be another building, I guess."

The security officer walked out a little ways and glanced up Park Avenue and waved at the patrol car that turned onto Webster Avenue going towards the back of the building, "Well...okay..." he walked back towards the building then turned around, "Oh, yeah...you can't stay here too long...it's a no parking zone."

Aziz looked up at the sign then waved at the officer, "Sure...no problem." He cranked up the vehicle and pulled off around the corner towards Webster Avenue, paused, then recognized a small diner a little ways past 183rd Street and figured he'd go there, invent a better plan than the one he had now.

Oblivious of the eyes that watched him go by; Skyler stayed low. If it wasn't for his lights being left on they would have run right into him as they got off the elevator. She hustled the girls towards the back door leading to the parking lot. They hurriedly tossed the bags in the trunk and was about to crank up the car when a light shone through the window. They gasped. Skyler jumped as she held up her arm and squinted through the glare, damn, she thought, Aziz, I thought he left. It was the security officer making his rounds, "Hello, Ms. Skyler...sorry about the light. He looked suspiciously into the car, "Everything alright?"

"Yeah...Mr. Wright. I'm fine, just uh...running my girlfriend and her kids home. Everything okay with you."

"Yes, ma'am...okay, I'll see you around." he slumbered back towards the building. Now all she needed to do was ease out to make sure Aziz wouldn't see them, he may have turned back around. She moved cautiously then spotted the patrol car as it came back through. It was her chance, she batted her eyes flirtatiously as it came by. The young, now entranced officer stopped, she licked her lips seductively and he let her in front. She drove up Tremont Avenue towards the Grand Concourse as the patrol car rode shotgun behind her. Winking at the cop she turned off then exhaled, "Girrrl...it made it a lot easier being that he was cute."

Mya smiled as she looked at her then glanced at her daughters in the back seat, half sleep, she moved her hand over and grabbed Skyler's and mouthed the words, thank you. Skyler smiled back but deep down she was scared as all hell.

After not finding a diner open; Aziz made the u-turn on Fordham Road. It was Saturday anyway, he thought, nothing much, the only thing on the streets were dope fiends looking to re-up. He had his mind made up to kidnap the girls and hold them until Mya spit out what she knew about Joker and his stash from Dante. She had to know something, that had to be why Joker didn't do her in that night, it had something to do with money.

The building came into full view as he passed the PAL on 183rd Street. He readjusted his gun as he observed a parking space in back. This time he checked his lights before he walked into the lobby. The security guard stood up behind his desk and slowly eyeballed him up and down. He remembered him from earlier, something didn't seem right. As he came from around the metal desk, "Apparently, this was the right building after all. I'm looking for Skyler." Aziz said.

"Skyler...who? I'm not at liberty to tell you who all live here. You know her last name, I might have-"

"Uh...we're old friends. We work together. I knew she lived in the neighborhood and I figured I'd surprise her, you know."

"Well, she's not here. She left-" innocently slipped out the guard's mouth.

"Left! When! Was anyone with her!"

"Whoa, hold up, young man. I thought you just said you were in the neighborhood and wanted to stop by."

"Look! I'll ask the questions! Now, was there anyone with her, old man?" He reached into his jacket, he might have to take him out, "Talk!"

Cautiously, the old security guard back pedaled towards the front door,

Aziz knew he had to do whatever he was going to do quick.

"Hold it right there..." he reached into his jacket pocket.

The old man turned, weighing out his options; should he make a run for it and yell, maybe one of the tenants would hear him. He glanced over his shoulder and out the corner of his eye he could see the routine patrol car creep up the side of Park Avenue. He knew they would be making their last rounds momentarily and he was sure as hell glad they did. Aziz had to rethink the situation.

"Old man...if you try anything, it's going to be a real bad night." he looked over his shoulder as the car came to a halt, "For all of us."

The old man started to turn and haul ass, Aziz reached further into his pocket, he remembered he had a small stash of money in his inside collar slit. As one of the officers got out he quickly reached for the money he'd collected from Lonzo earlier. The old man was now swinging the door open as the cop started walking up the sidewalk. Aziz flashed the stack of twenties and some fifty's. The old man looked at Aziz then the officer, "Hey, old man...what's up." the cop asked.

The guard leaned back against the door jab and stared at Aziz who stuffed his hands in his pockets, "Everything alright."

Aziz's hand searched out the trigger and he held it firm, the security guard looked too nervous but he did manage to nod and mumble, "Naw officer, everything's alright..."

"Oh...okay." He scanned Aziz up and down, he didn't recognize him as a threat so he turned his attention back to the old man, "Say...who was the chick that, uh, came out of here about a half hour or so ago. She was fine as hell."

"About an hour ago...uh..." he didn't want to divulge Skyler, at least not until he had the money from Aziz in his hand but he had no choice, "Young girl, lives in the building...yeah."

"Damn, she was fine! Think she said she was taking her sister back downtown or something. Say, when she comes back, put in the good word for a brother, okay."

That's all Aziz needed to hear, Mya and the kids were there and they were on their way back downtown, he started backing up out of view. The officer walked out the door with the security guard as he rushed him away trying to get back at Aziz then he turned and saw the truck crank up and it raced down Webster Avenue. The guard rushed back to his desk as the cops left and picked up the phone, he needed to make the call to some of his old buddies at the Precinct, pull some strings, kick some ass he thought as he frantically tore through his desk drawer for the number. No one fucks him over he mumbled as he glanced over at something sticking underneath his newspaper, a lump of some sort, it was out of place. He looked, and it was a stack of money; twenties, fifties and not too many tens. He counted it out and it came up to two grand. He turned and looked at the spot where Aziz was parked and he thought about it. He paid no mind to the thumbs up that Aziz brandished as he sped off.

He hung up the phone. He knew what he was doing was wrong, but as he stuffed the money into his pocket, he spied around to make sure no one was watching, perhaps he was putting a young girls life in jeopardy, he shrugged his shoulders and thought; her problem, not his. After all, he had enough money now to buy the pussy he wanted anyway, fuck it, he thought, mind his business.

Aziz zoomed down Webster Avenue hell bent on catching up with Skyler. He figured he'd go to the apartment and lay. He didn't think Mya would go back that way, but he sure as hell knew Destiny would try to sneak over there to be with Lonzo. That, he knew for sure.

chapter 10

DAY THREE.

Steve's apartment sat adjacent to the projects where Mya lived on the other side of Avenue D. The small one bedroom walkup was a hole in the wall situated in a six story apartment dwelling. It was cramped but a lot of life was hung on the walls, pictures of scantily clad women and phone numbers scribbled on torn paper and napkins collected from his travels throughout the city as a bike messenger; he was a playa.

He now sat reposed on the ledge of his kitchen window sipping on hot cocoa while Skyler buzzed around scratching up a meal for her and the girls. He watched as she sashayed around in the tight fitting nylon cat suit she donned, and kept his eyes glued to her shapely physique as he shadowed her every move. Maybe one day he mused, he would add her to his compilation. Mya smiled as she caught his gaze, there seemed to be something between them so she dared asked the question, "Steve, what's up..." as she nudged toward Skyler. He was reticent, with an effaceable demeanor. Skyler in turn noticed the innuendo, navigating her way around the tight squeeze of a sink cupboard, she wriggled her curvaceous ass in his face, and then muttered, "Steve don't want none of this..."

Steve turned quickly toward the window, embarrassed, concealing the hard on he'd worked up in his pants, "Look, girl...me and you don't get down like that, alright" He put in as much harshness in his voice as he could muster, even though if the chance arose he'd fuck the shit out of her. She stood and turned on the faucet to the sink and murmured as she looked over at Mya, "Like I said...he don't want none..."

Mya shook her head, "Y'all got too much drama, this shit is crazy!" Steve turned back around and motioned for the girls, Hope and Destiny to close the door to his room, it was time they discussed a plan. "Okay...so, how we gonna get to Aziz's stash?" he asked.

Skyler passed around some salad she tossed together and plopped on a small, tattered love seat, "Well, we really don't know where his stash is..."

"I got an idea, but I'm not sure." Steve glanced over at Mya, "You know anything?"

Mya picked through her plate and reflected before answering the very serious query. "If I had to say...it's got to be the poolroom."

"That's what I thought! I see them sometimes coming out the back room with duffle bags. Everyone tries to act like they don't see anything, like nothing is going on, but hell, it's either cash or dope." Steve added.

"True...either or. There's also a room behind the bar where they go and make plans and shit. Usually it's just Joker, Miles and Aziz that go in...I hang out front with Tempest at the bar."

"Oh yeah...my girl, Tempest..." Steve said, Skyler looked over and threw a fork his way, "Girl...what the fuck!" he yelled as he ducked.

"What the fuck my ass! Pay attention!" she stood to pick up the fork, and inadvertently maneuvered in front of his face as she bent over; Steve could see nothing but thong inching into the crack of her ass cutting deep into a pussy that bloated. She turned and watched as she hypnotized him with the stout, swell of her cunt as it bulged through. "Tempest who, Steve..." she cooed. Mya reached over and smacked her hard on her ass cheek, "C'mon now, sit your horny ass down and get serious!" Skyler pouted her lips, "We ain't got time for that bullshit! Now, the pool room, how the hell are we gonna get in and out pass the goons with the money? If there's any in there at all!"

Steve leaned back against the window ledge, she was right. This was not a well thought out plan, spur of the moment at best, and if they didn't get it together, they could all end up dead, very quick, "I got to call my cousin."

"Your cousin? Hell no! That's too many people in our business. How do you know we can trust him? Who is he?" Skyler questioned.

Steve picked up his cell phone and started to climb onto the fire escape, "Trust me...it's alright. Somebody on the inside that's been thinking the same shit as us, for a while."

For a while, Mya thought, damn, all this time, people were all around her planning and scheming. This had to be the time to split from Aziz, she twinged as she could only imagine how many other enemies he made that where after him, but they would all have to wait, she'd have to get him first. Skyler eased closer to her snapping her out of her daze, "You know I've been here before." she said as she stared over at Steve.

"Yeah, I can see that. Why don't y'all just hook up?"

"Because all he wants to do is fuck something, I want more than that Mya, much more than that." she said thrusting out her lips.

"I hope so, Skyler, cause right now that's all I see between y'all. Put it aside...we've got much bigger things going on!

PAPERS WERE STREWN about the floor and a table tossed. The damage inflicted by Joker's anger seemed somewhat nominal in regard to his normal wrath, perhaps because Gustavo was across from him shaking his head in disdain taste at his trivial, trifling tantrum. "Get Miles on the phone...now!" he hollered at Bezo.

Gustavo couldn't believe Joker's rage but more and more he came to understand it, and him; he dangled as many responsibilities and welled as much power as a head of state for a small third world country. One false move could cause an empire such as Alphabet City to come crumbling down. He had to rule with an iron fist of a cruel, unyielding dictator and he played the role well.

Joker had picked up Gustavo early this morning from Starbucks over on 5th Avenue by Washington Square Park. He didn't ask where he was staying, he really didn't care, after all he wasn't footing the bill. Gustavo didn't want him in his business anyway, but he wasn't far from Alphabet City staying across the other side by the piers. Last night he managed to make it to Nanny's, the infamous, pink gay club on 7th Avenue, checking out some old acquaintances he knew from Miami. He inquired about Joker and pretty much was hit with the same responses. Joker's crazy, but his dope is the best in the city. Gustavo grinned as he watched Joker pace up and down restlessly waiting on Miles to call him, "Joker...Joker. Sit down, relax he'll call."

Joker stared at him, his mind couldn't comprehend the calmness of Gustavo but deep down it soothed him, "Uh..." he sat down laboriously. "He better call!" he said as he banged the top of his desk. Gustavo reached into his plaid, fashionably panache, linen jacket and pulled out a Cuban corona, and sniffed it, "Hmmm, chocolate..." he tossed it over to him. Joker was for the moment pacified, and leaned back hunting in his jacket for a lighter. That was the image Gustavo was left with as his mind picked up the tracks to the prior night.

He asked questions about Aziz and as he thought, he remembered most just blew him off saying he was alright, but he never did get any real answers. It seemed as though they were covering up something, it was strange, he knew something about Aziz wasn't right but he just couldn't put his finger on it.

"Joker...Joker! I left Miles a voice message, but...Smack and Gutter just walked in!" Bezo said as he bust through the door.

Joker's eyes bulged as he heard their names. He needed to see them anyway because they were the one's who counted the money, and as he checked through the books trying to impress Gustavo with the numbers; he was six grand short and he wanted to know where the hell his money was or at least, who was stealing from him, "Send them in!"

Gustavo leaned back now, he knew he was about to witness some real serious grilling, but hell, he didn't blame Joker from getting to the bottom of it. Nip it in the bud quick because if you let it go, six grand could easily become 60 grand and so on and so on. Someone needed to be made an example of, at least that's how he would handle the business and pretty soon the business would be his.

Bezo escorted them in. They sat down in front of Joker who leaned forward. Smack and Gutter knew what it was about, money. Joker blew long thick curls of smoke over the top of their heads in silence then he spun his chair around and sat, leaving them to wonder at what he was thinking, or planning next. Gustavo loved the melodrama; he crossed his legs and stared at them also, for the effect. In no time they broke, "Yo, Joker I don't know nothing about no money! All I know is, we count the money and when it comes up short, we tell Miles, right Gutter!"

Gutter looked over at Smack with a smirk, ready to smack his snitch ass. He couldn't believe this was the son of a bitch he wanted to do a job with. "Damn, Smack...he didn't even say shit..."

Joker had them now, the attack was on, he spun the chair around and stood up and slammed his fist down on the desk, "One of you muthafucka's stealing from me, right!"

Smack trembled a little as Gutter looked off to avoid eye contact, "Man, Joker...we ain't did nothing, but-"

"But, muthafuckin' what! I go to check the books and I'm six fuckin' grand short!" Gutter and Smack gawked at each other, finally figuring out what exactly was going on. "I don't give a fuck about the hundred dollars or so you muthafuckas skim off me, fuck that! But...six...fuckin'...grand! That's a whole fucking spot, am I right!"

"Ye-ye-yes sir. You're right..." Smack said as Gutter mean mugged him, "Fuck that, I'd take a hit for Miles any day but that fuckin' Aziz, he ain't shit and you know it!"

"Aziz?" Joker was puzzled. He plopped in his seat, "Damn...now what..." Gustavo also leaned forward, once again Aziz dropped another ball in Joker's court. There had to be something between them cause his ass should have been dead yesterday, or at least let go. He watched as Joker listened.

Gutter hunched his shoulders and blew, "Fuck it...go head, but you tell him, cause I ain't no fuckin' snitch..." he turned and scowled at Smack. "Naw, man, it ain't about that. But, shit, he's been fuckin us up! Why you think Miles put Chino and that fat ass Blu on the runs, because he sees that we soft! Always let Aziz come up short, then coverin' for him. Fuck that! He works for you, Joker, you handle it! Me and Gutter doing what we paid to do and yeah...his shit is short...sir."

Joker pulled softly off the cigar and leaned forward and reached out, Gutter and Smack twinged a little as Bezo lingered over them, he reached for the ashtray and pulled it towards him then outed the cigar and as he rubbed the burnt ambers out he said, "Okay...I got it. Y'all get on through." Smack and Gutter damn near left behind their shadow peeling out the room, Joker hollered out to them, "Don't mention this to Aziz. You can hold that...right..."

"Yeah...sure, it's between us!" Gutter said as he turned back around. Bezo closed the door behind them and asked Joker, "You want me to find Aziz?"

"No, no...I got it. Just make sure Miles gets here...now!"

"Okay, boss..." Bezo turned and left out as Gustavo got up and walked over to the window looking out, "So...where do you go from here?"

"It's a funny thing...just when you think you know someone."

"Well, maybe you should have known him better...maybe."

"Maybe. But, I damn near grew up with this guy; hell, how much time you need to know a man?" He got up and pulled the curtain back a little and pointed towards the projects on Houston Street, "Our first spot was over there, by the projects...him and that fuckin' Dante!"

"Dante?"

"Yeah...got killed years back. Can't shake him, though..."

"Hmmm, Dante...rings a bell..." Gustavo stepped away from the window towards the door, "Hey, I gotta make a quick run, I'll be back in about an hour or so, that'll give you enough time to clean up this...mess, okay."

"Yeah, sure," Joker said as he stared out the window as Miles's truck pulled up, "Soon as I clean it up...I'll call you, then we can finish the tour."

"Later." He walked out the Pitt and spoke briefly to Miles as he walked by, telling him he'd see him later. He finally had an idea where he knew Aziz from, but he needed to confirm it and he knew just the place and the person. He'd have to get up with Joker a little later on but as he turned around and looked at Miles walk through the door, time was what was needed anyway, because it was going to be even uglier if his hunch was right.

Joker's eyes caught the stirrings of a small mouse across from him creeping ever so slowly along the baseboard of the checkered, tile floor; whiskers twitching, unobtrusively trying not to be noticed. With eyes beaded and grinning, Joker figured he could possibly pull his gun and catch the small rodent broad side across its frame, all in one shot. The mouse caught him staring and instinctively stood still trying not to be noticed but it was all too late; the cat and mouse game was set in motion. Perfect. Joker thought. He slowly and meticulously started to reach for his gun but was startled by the sudden hissing of the radiator next to him. The mouse was given just enough time to dip underneath the doorway and escape the perilous fate that had awaited it. How it managed to flatten out it's body that thin as it disappeared behind the burst of vapory steam that shot into the air, was a mystery. Joker's wonder gave way to curiosity.

His mind was brought back to attention from his straying when he heard the curtains tapping lightly against the window. A draft he thought, from the air that moved briskly at the foot of the door from which he now heard discordant raps coming off the backside of it. It was Bezo. He stuck his head in and said, "Boss...it's Miles."

"Send him in..." Joker said as he mentally pulled himself together. The familiar scenario that just played out in front of him he likened to the drama that's been unfolding around him lately; the positions his opponents played. He adjusted his shirt and straightened up in his chair against his side, propping himself up for the visual effect he wanted to orchestrate.

The door was opened and Miles strode in. He cautiously looked around the office space and his eyes came to rest on Joker's stern face. He sat down across from him not taking his eyes off of him and asked, "So...what's up." He leaned back slightly, but not enough to reach for his 9mm. if need be; Joker was unpredictable and his gorilla, Bezo would die for him at the snap of a finger, but hopefully this wouldn't be the case today.

Joker smiled slightly and leaned forward slowly, "Well...let's get straight to the bullshit...cause that's what it is...bullshit, huh."

Okay, Miles thought, he knew at least it wasn't about him, he wasn't about bullshit but he knew who was.

"Why is my money short?"

"Money...short...when?"

"It doesn't matter. The books say my money's short."

"Whoa...hold up, Joker." Miles leaned forward, the brows on his forehead had met and it was easily seen that he was peeved, "It does matter what day, so I can pinpoint when, or whoever stole from me, cause I don't come up short, Joker"

"Yeah, yeah, yeah. Fuck the muthafuckin' speech, Miles," he reached into his top drawer and pulled out a legal pad and tossed it to him. The cover had dates that were coded. Miles knew the codes and the day in question was yesterday. "I'm six grand short according to that..."

Miles thought then smiled and leaned back, "Naw...it's all good. I handled that."

"Handled what! The books say I'm six grand short and you say it's handled!" He leaned back and reached into his desk drawer and pulled out a leather burgundy cigar humidor. He opened it up after he gently placed it on the table and pulled out a dark brown corona, "Explain this shit to me...please."

Miles didn't feel comfortable with what he asked but he knew if he were to account for the money it would implement Aziz and he wasn't no snitch, but he had to cover his own ass, "Look...I forgot to notate it, that's all. The money's there and accounted for!"

"But...you don't do the counting, Miles. How come the money's short...on the books? What happened Miles, that's all I want to know? Look, if you fucked up-"

Miles leaned forward, "I ain't a fuck up! My money is always straight. You're asking questions to the wrong person. Like I told you, Joker...I handled it. The books say that you're short, but trust me! You're not...okay!"

Joker lit up the cigar and blew the smoke out and savored it before he spoke, "Tell me...it was Aziz, right? He fucked up huh."

Miles stared, he couldn't believe Joker was playing him like this. "Joker didn't I just tell you..." He shook his head and stood up, "You got me fucked up. No disrespect, but I gotta go. You need to talk to Aziz...bottom line. Once you do that, then start making some decisions, I ain't trying to hear this shit!"

"You walking out on me!"

"Yeah...I ain't got no beef with you." He opened the door and turned towards him, "And you ain't got no beef with me." Then stepped through it and slammed it shut.

"Miles!" Joker's voice thundered throughout the building and the door opened again; this time Bezo stepped through first and pushed the door wider revealing Miles in his clutches. Joker pointed his finger in his direction, "Don't you ever fuckin' walk out on me, again, you hear!"

Bezo nudged him, "Yeah...alright...boss..." Miles mumbled sarcastically.

Joker folded his arms, "Look, this is what you do. Find Aziz and take care of this...problem. Find out what he knows...whatever, but just fuckin' handle it. I'm tired of this shit already!"

Miles nodded his head robotically as Joker walked up to him and extended his hand in a truce, "There's a lot of shit going on, but you've been handlin' yourself real fuckin' well, better than I expected." He put his arm around Miles's shoulder, "You take care of this...problem, and according to Gustavo...the man. You'll be set up well after I leave. You got my word."

Miles looked down at Joker's hand then gazed deep into his eyes, "Joker, once again, no disrespect, but you know I don't play."

Joker grasped his hand firmly and shook it then held on and returned the gaze, "I know Miles, I know." he said as he looked over to the window. Looking down at the doorway he shook his head and grinned; he'd finally realized who played the role of the mouse. "Just find Aziz and handle the problem...okay."

"YO, TINY...WHAT'S HE talking about?"

Big E had the sleek, shiny black, cell phone to his ear keenly listening to the voice on the other end of the receiver. "Lonzo...You serious...no shit..."

Pancho stood off to the side of him trying to ear hustle the conversation and Big E was paying him no mind, "C'mon Big E...what's up?" Big E turned away from him, but that action only agitated him. This time he reacted and snatched the phone from his hand, "What the hell is up with you!" Big E screamed in protest.

"Fuck being ignored! I asked you what the fuck was up and why are you grinning so goddamned much!" Pancho put the phone to his ear but Lonzo had already hung up. "It was Lonzo, man."

"Yeah...and-hold up, ain't that one of Aziz's runners from across town."

"Yeah...that's him."

"Can't stand that muthafuckin' snitch ass-"

"Anyway...check this out."

Big E and Pancho had got a call a little while ago from Miles who told them to meet him down the street from the Pitt while he made a quick call to Chino and Blu. It was now late in the day and no Miles in sight, or Blu or Chino. They figured they'd hang out on the corner of 3rd Street across from a Mexican restaurant watching slow games of chess being played by old school cats with low tucked, brim hats across the brows of their eyes and wait. "Lonzo was telling me that Aziz paid him some money to find his old lady..."

"What the hell does Lonzo have to do with his old lady? What the fuck is he now, a private eye type of nigga or what?" Pancho chuckled. Big E only smirked then continued, "No man...listen. Her daughter; that chick Destiny, Lonzo was trying to hit that, you know he's got her on smash. So, when Aziz's old lady took off on him, he found out about it and went to Lonzo-"

"He snitched her out. Told you that muthafucka wasn't no good."

"But, hold on, bro. Come to find out that she went to the Bronx and Aziz went up that way trying to catch but she got away. Now he thinks she's back in the Alphabet."

"Hold up. Why'd they leave anyway?"

"C'mon man. You know Aziz's on some ole crazy abuse shit."

"True."

"So now, Lonzo got his phone on speed dial and posted up near the projects waiting for Destiny to call him so Aziz can kidnap her and she can lead him to her mom. Shit is crazy!"

Pancho got off of the bench and walked off a little ways rubbing his chin in thought. "Miles know about this..."

"Don't know, but if he knew he'd be pissed."

Pancho turned and handed Big E back his phone, "And you said Miles told us to wait here for him, huh."

"Yeah."

"Well, bro...I think he knows something. What...I'm not sure." He looked up the street to the spot and spied dope fiends scrambling in and out in swarms and oddly enough, the door was wide open, "What's going on up there? Where's the door man Hector?" he said.

Big E got up and checked also, "Don't know...haven't heard from Hector since the other day."

"Let's go see what's up."

Big E and Pancho hastened up the street towards the broken down building watching dope fiend activity in and around the spot. A few recognized them as Joker's people and hurried past out the door trying not to make eye contact. "Something ain't right..." Big E said. Pancho grabbed a fiend coming out of the building and asked, "Yo, man...what the fuck is up? Where's my people?"

The dope fiend's face was sunken in from years of wear and as Big E got closer to him, his breath stunk of cheap 40's and brown, enamel stains were glued to his already cracked teeth, but Big E stomached it long enough to receive an answer, "The place is wide open."

"Wide open!" Pancho said. "What the hell you mean...wide open!"

"Been like that since yesterday evening. Don't know where those guys are that work there."

"What! So the dope is-"

"Naw, the dope spots are still pumping, but there's no type of security. People shooting up in the hall and shit...turning tricks..."

"Oh hell no!" Pancho said as he breezed up the steps two at a time, "We ain't going for this shit!" Big E was right behind him as they burst through the door. Sure enough, just like the dope fiend had said; there was shooting up in the hallway, and undressed, scantily clad strung out women turning tricks. As Big E and Pancho came in they weren't even noticed around all the activity. "Man...Where the fuck is Hector?" He looked down the long corridor to the back and yelled out, "Yo, Hector!" No answer. They checked upstairs and didn't see any sign of the young boy, a sentinel Joker kept in place. "Something ain't right. Let's go upstairs." Big E said. Pancho agreed and was right behind him.

The spots seemed to be putting out like the fiend said but Pancho kneeled down and scanned the empty bags on the floor and knew it was old dope. "Didn't we do pick ups here...yesterday?"

"Damn right. You-Me-Chino...Blu."

"I'ma call Miles." Big E said as he dipped into an abandoned apartment to get some reception while Pancho sprinted around the building knocking on doors of the apartments that sold dope. All he got was silence. But, in one he did manage to hear the sounds of movement on the other side, and the creaking whine of a window being opened. "Oh hell no!" He kicked at the door and it burst open. It was a front. The apartments had been taken over by dope fiends. As he bust through, two or three were already jumping out the window. He grabbed hold of one and pulled him back in as the frame shattered, causing Pancho to cover his eyes from the glass that sprayed in his face. "What the fuck!" He wrestled down to the floor what appeared at first to be a man but was instead a woman. He pinned her arms back as she wriggled furiously and only calmed down after running out of breath.

"Who the hell are you!" Pancho screamed at her.

Her eyes were wide with fright and she started to thrash wildly again. Pancho thought of smacking her but he didn't want to chance getting scratched, he didn't know her status, whether she was positive or not, so he shook her, hard. It calmed her down briefly then he asked the question again, "Who are you?"

This time she replied, "I just wanted to get a fix! My old man and me found the door open and the dope all over the floor...so, we picked up everything and just ran a hustle." She turned her face towards the door, "Everyone else in the building was doing it!"

Damn, Pancho thought, they'd taken over the dope spots, but still that didn't solve the first dilemma, "Where the hell was Hector!"

She squirmed around trying to free herself and Pancho shook her once more to test, to see if she was lying. "That's all I know! I don't know nuthin else! It was like this when we got here! I swear!" Pancho scanned the apartment briefly and everything seemed to be intact like it was when he'd delivered the dope yesterday. He let her up and she took off for the window, but before she crawled through she glanced back, "But, I will tell you this..." Pancho looked up at her, "there's a hell of a smell running through this place. It smells like..." she twisted her nose up, turned and jetted down the fire escape.

Pancho sniffed at the air, she was right. He hadn't noticed it before but there seemed to be a stench in the air. He followed the foul, smelling odor and it led upstairs to the roof. The door was half way ajar. He pushed at it and it was jammed. He backed up a little and rammed the door with his shoulder and it opened a little, still ever so slightly. He grimaced from the pain in his arm but he managed to squeeze through then he saw what had made the door jam. He couldn't believe his eyes, "Oh damn!" He started to vomit, nauseated he reeled back. "What the hell happened!" he said as he spit up on himself.

chapter 11

THE BODIES OF HECTOR and two others had been behind the door; the weight of their bloated corpses against the backside had been responsible for the impediment. Pancho covered his nose from the reeky stench, then pulled himself together and walked closer to get a better look. Hector had been shot twice in the head, and so were the others. One looking to be no older than him had his neck twisted so bad it shredded the skin from around his shoulders. It was a horrible sight he thought, who could have possibly done this brutal slaughter...mayhem.

He had to tell Miles. The building. The bodies. Everything. He squeezed back through the door but suddenly stopped in his tracks getting goosebumps as he felt eyes staring his way. He turned but saw no one, he continued to move, cautiously, slowly away from the door feeling at his waist for his gun. He didn't have it on him; he'd left it in the poolroom thinking he didn't need it, being that Blu and Chino did the runs now. All he could think of now was how wrong he was.

He backed away measurably from the door to the stairway, hearing another sound but this time it was down below. His brother... his mind raced to Big E in the apartment underneath him. He jumped over the banister and rushed down the stairs and into the apartment where he'd left him. No one. He peered around the darkened, gray apartment and faintly heard sounds coming from an adjacent room, he ran in and that's when he saw him; Big E.

Pancho yelled out to him, "Damn! No! No!" Pancho looked down at Big E, and could see the sterling silver tip of the machete's blade slowly protruding from his stomach. His legs tingled as the blade cracked apart his vertebrae. Big E felt the warmth of the blood rushing up through his mouth and out the sides as he gurgled. He wanted to move so bad but the blade had ripped through his spinal cord, paralyzing him. He opened his mouth and grit his teeth as the piercing blade penetrated his diaphragm, ripping into his spleen, cutting into his arteries and finally taking his breath away as he gasped for air. He stood slumped over mercifully, as the blood pooled around his feet. His shattered anatomy fell to the floor, as Pancho jumped backward out the way.

He couldn't believe his baby brother was dead, murdered. He cried, he was angry. He mustered up the nerve and reached for the phone still in Big E's grasp, and took it out his hands. He called Miles and his phone was busy; he got his voice mail instead, "Miles! Come to Aziz's spot on 3rd street...up from the Pitt! It ain't good! I need you, man! Something's happened and Big E is-"

The lone blue jean, leather jacket wearing figure now stood in front of him with a wide legged stance and picked up his head looking into his face mocking him. Pancho now saw the face of his killer. A face he didn't recognize, but nevertheless the same face of the murderer who killed his brother; darkness started to overtake him as he strained to look over at him. Tears ran down his eyes as the last thoughts he fathomed were of Miles, how he let him down. What would he do without him. He was viciously kicked in his chest and his body fell over violently backwards towards his brother as the person that was responsible for this carnage stood over him. He wrapped a cord around Pancho's neck and began strangling him. Pancho fought to unloosen the cord, desperately trying to pull away the hands of his attacker. But his grip was too strong. His face was turning red, as he gasped for his last breath of air. Pancho looked up, and saw a thick, white glob of spit come crashing down into his eyes blinding him, but he was dead before the words "Miles...is next!" venomously came out the killer's mouth.

MILES SLOWLY DROVE the full bodied SUV through the streets of the front end of Hampton Square Houses; the complex where Aziz lived with Mya. It was getting late and he had to meet Pancho and Big E over by the Pitt to start the pickups for the day. He didn't get a chance at all to call Blu or Chino yet, so much had been going on. He damn sure didn't like having his ass chewed out by Joker about some shit that didn't have anything to do with him. He couldn't wait to get up with Aziz and jump dead in his ass and return the favor.

He pulled up near the building where Mya lived and looked up. The curtains were drawn closed and the windows shut. He wondered where she was at; it was Sunday and she was known to stay around the house. Even the girls were nowhere in sight. Her and Aziz must have gotten into one of their skirmishes and she hauled ass somewhere. He came across a group of Aziz's runners hanging out by the park and slowed down. They recognized him, but no one came towards the truck. He pulled in front of a supermarket and took out his cell phone and dialed Aziz's number. The phone rang a few times and was picked up, "Yo...wassup."

"Yo, wassup, man. Where the hell are you!"

"Takin' care of some business..."

"You need to be takin' care of the business you gettin' paid for. Man, Joker's looking for you! He jumped on my ass-"

"Whoa! Hold up! I'll get with Joker...after I take care of some things." Miles didn't like the sound of that or the tone in his voice when he said it.

He knew Aziz's pedigree and he figured somehow a scheme was involved. Joker told him that he'd threatened him earlier, but Miles needed to know his angle; he was holding back on something. Miles got straight to the point. "Look...you know what it is, Joker's looking for you, and he said you threatened him. What's up...talk to me."

Aziz paused. He knew Miles, direct, no beating around the bush, but he also knew that of all people Joker would send him. Miles was the only one who knew his haunts, hangouts and knew more about him than most. He had to be careful. He slouched down a little behind the steering wheel as he peeped across the dash at the back of Miles's truck. He was parked in the parking lot of the Associated grocery store Miles pulled in front of. He'd been there for the better part of the morning in lay for Mya or the girls. He posted Lonzo in front as a lookout. Miles had passed by Lonzo several times, but thought nothing of it; just a runner. Aziz knew he had to get Mya before he could concentrate on Joker. Get the stash, flee the city with Peaches in tow, least that was the plan but right now he needed to buy some time, get Miles off his ass. "Look, I know Joker wants me taken out, but like I told him, if he lays a finger on me....his ass will see time."

"Damn, Aziz...what's up with you? You mean to tell me, you'd snitch. I mean, that'll fuck me up, too."

"Gotta do what I gotta do."

"Naw, not like this. Hey Joker just wants to know what's going on with you, that's all...me too."

"I'm alright-"

"No, you're not alright. You've been acting strange lately. Hey, wasn't you on some pills or something. Mental type of-"

"No!" Aziz banged the steering wheel of his car and the horn honked loudly. Miles heard it and turned. He scanned around the area into the lot looking for the source, then someone tapped lightly on the window and startled him, "What the fuck..." It was a well-dressed man of thirty that Miles recognized from the Pitt. He was also a dope addict, but he couldn't figure for the life of him what he wanted now. He rolled the window down, "Yeah...what's up!"

Aziz had ducked his head down and looked back up and saw that someone had distracted him. That's all the time he needed to crank up and dip out the lot unnoticed, "Uh, look, Miles...I gotta go. I'll see you later."

"Whoa...hold up. Where are you going? You gonna do the pick ups or what? Talk to me, damn-it!" The phone went blank as Aziz cut it off. Miles banged the dash, "I had him!" The man stood off a little way from him reaching into his jacket and Miles reached for his gun. He put up his hands, "No...Hold up. I got something to show you, that's all." "Show me.. .what the fuck you got to show me?"

He pulled out a money clip and handed it to him, "Man...you know I don't carry no drugs on me. I can't do nuthin' for you." Miles said as he looked around for an undercover van thinking it may be a setup. He was about to crank up and handed it back to him, but the man stopped him, "No. I found it."

"Found it?" Miles looked at it closely again. It was a 14kt gold money clip. He'd seen it before, then it came to him, it had belonged to Aziz, "Yeah...I know who this is. How'd you get it?"

"I found it at the spot over on 4th street..."

"By the Pitt."

"Yeah. I went in and found it near the stairs. I knew it was big time; figured it might belong to one of you. Know it didn't come from a fiend."

"Okay. Why didn't you just give it to my people posted inside?" he asked. He looked at him inquisitively, then squinted his eyes, "You mean to tell me, you don't know."

"Know what?"

"Damn...the spot's been taken over by dope fiends. It's wide open. They're shooting dope up in there and everything."

Miles reached out and grabbed him by the collar pulling him forcibly towards the truck, hard, "What! What the fuck you talking about!"

He panicked, "L-L-Look man. I just thought I'd bring it to you or that dude Aziz..."

"What happened to the spot!" he hollered at him.

"I don't know. Ain't been there since last night. The place is wide open though. Thought I'd tell Aziz." He pointed to a space behind him and Miles turned. "He was right behind you sitting in the parking lot before you pulled up. Hell, he just took off!" Damn, he thought, Aziz was watching him all the time. Now he knew something was up, he was hiding. He had to let Joker know to put the word out, Aziz had to go, but first he needed to find out about the spot. He let the guy go and told him to wait while he pulled out his phone. He noticed the blinking red light on the screen letting him know he had a message. He pulled it up and listened. His eyes widened and his jaw dropped. The man hunched back a little from the reaction as Miles stared off and cranked the truck up, "Yo man...you clean!"

"Clean?"

"You ain't got no works on you!"

"Naw.

"Get in the truck!" The man scrambled around to the passenger side and climbed in. Miles punched the gas heading towards the Pitt. He was cautious and composed as he stopped at the stop lights not wanting to draw any unnecessary heat towards him but inside he was pissed. He glanced at the money clip in his hand and read the inscription on the back, "In God we trust." He mumbled as he looked over at the man beside him, "You did good. I got you when we get there a'iyht."

"Yeah...sure." he smiled.

Miles didn't know what to expect once he got there. Poncho's message had been cut short and what he heard he didn't like. But one thing he was sure about was that Aziz had lost his mind running behind Mya or was there more to that. Did he know about this? He wanted to get up with Mya before Aziz did and ask her some questions; maybe she knew what was going on. He reached into his glove for the 9mm and the two 13 shot clips and stuffed them in his jacket.

"Yo, Miles...if it's going down, I'm with you." the man across from him said. Miles looked over at him and said, "I hear you, but if it's going down, you might not want to be nowhere around."

Joker was finally enjoying a good smoke, it'd been two days and some futile attempts, but here he was at last kicked back on a bench in the walkway of West 4th Street park watching the pigeons with a nice fat corona between his lips. Bezo sat next to him reading a newspaper and he exhaled, finally, thinking, peace. Bezo picked his head up long enough to pose the question, "Are you sure he'll show up?"

Joker looked over at him and blew smoke back towards the park, not wanting to disturb the tranquil mood and responded, "He'll be here when he gets here, Bezo...just enjoy, be cool."

"Sure boss whatever you say." He plunged his head back into the newspaper while Joker reflected back to earlier on what Aziz had said about the alleged information he'd had on him. He searched back through the years and the only thing he could figure was the time he'd spent with Dante, other than that nothing, he'd been careful.

The night Dante was killed there was money missing, he remembered that. Money that Aziz couldn't account for. He blamed it on Dante's girl, Mya; said she'd stolen it.

He did think it strange that he wanted to be with the girl after Dante had died, but he didn't think it would last anyway, just a pussy thing. But, they persevered, raised the babies and stuck it out. After seeing that, Joker thought maybe things could be good with Aziz and he'd make him his right hand man, bring him in on business, a partner. Now look at him, a little pressure and he was ready to turn snitch, he couldn't believe it, his bitch ass, but then it was what it was. Aziz had to die, it was that simple. More than likely Miles would be the one to do him in, but he needed to know what Aziz had on him. Maybe he needed to question the girl Mya. She would have to know something but she seemed way too smart, Joker figured, to get involved with any of Aziz's bullshit; Dante taught her better than that. Still something just wasn't right. Aziz kept beating on her and for what, he never did understand it, but he knew it had something to do with Dante. Maybe it was money that Dante had stashed, or for that matter, she stashed. That had to be it. Joker's cigar had burnt down a ways, and he looked at it and frowned, having enjoyed the smoke. He watched as Bezo reached for the cell phone that buzzed on his side and answered it. He handed it over to him, "It's Miles, boss...says it's important." That was it, it was over. No telling what Miles had to say. He'd just left him not too long ago so it couldn't be good. He tossed the cigar to the ground and the pigeons attacked it thinking it to be food and he laughed at them, how they fought over anything thrown to the ground. He looked over at Bezo, maybe that's what he should call his people from now on, crumbs, "What's up, Miles." he said.

"Yo, Joker...it ain't good."

"Kinda figured that. Now what?"

"The spot up the street from the Pitt. Something's wrong. Don't quite know what, but I'm on my way over there now."

"Damn...that's where that guy got shot the other day?"

"Naw, the one closer towards the corner. Aziz's spot...well, the other one was Aziz's too, but-"

"What's up with that muthafucka! Where's he at!"

"He's hiding from me. Need to get him though...put the word out."

"No problem. You got an idea what's going on?"

Miles looked over at his passenger. "To what I understand...dope fiends took over-hell, Pancho just called me from there and he said something was wrong."

"Okay, okay, look, I'll met you there-" he looked up and saw Gustavo walking towards them, "Damn...fucking Gustavo's here. Really don't need this shit."

"Don't bring him..."

"Yeah right...sure. Hey, look, I'm on the way. Don't bring any heat, okay."

"You got it."

Joker handed the phone back to Bezo and stood as Gustavo had just approached him, "So...you ready for another ride?" Gustavo nodded his head. Bezo got up also and they walked towards the car. "I know that guy, uh...Aziz. I know him from somewhere else." Gustavo said.

Joker looked over at him, his face didn't look good, "Everything alright." he asked.

"To be honest Joker... I don't know. Tell me what you know about this guy."

"No problem. I'll tell you on the ride over."

"Where are we going?" Gustavo asked.

"Miles's gonna meet us at one of my houses. Say's there's a problem that needs to be handled."

"On your level...must be a big problem."

Joker ducked into the car and scooted over with Gustavo right behind him. Bezo closed the door and he leaned back and blew, "Yeah...must be."

Miles pulled up the street and just like the fiend had said, traffic was flowing in and out the building and people were hanging out in front like flies to shit. He shook his head displeasing and pulled over in front of the Pitt and waited for Joker, but not too long; Bezo had just turned the corner and was pulling up behind him. They drove slowly towards the building and pulled up in front. Recognizing both vehicles, people started to scatter. Miles jumped out the car and grabbed one of them. "What's happening in there?"

The person he snatched was high and he swayed the dope fiend swagger. He scratched at his arm and answered, "Maaaan, sheeet. Them muthafucka's partyin' up in there. Don't know where they got the dope but," he sniffed at his nose and opened his eyes up long enough to recognize Miles, "Awww, sheet. You the big dope man!" he tried to pull free and Miles pulled him back. "Where's my people?"

"Man, I don't know nuthin'..."

"Muthafucka! Where's my people!" He shook him and Joker waved at him from the car to let him go. He walked over to the window, "I need to go in, Joker. Something ain't right. I can feel it!"

"Yeah," Joker said as he put the pistol he had in his jacket, "Me too."

Bezo opened the door and they got out. Miles walked back to the truck and grabbed his gun. They walked up the steps and Bezo pushed opened the door and they gasped at what they were seeing. "Man, what the fuck!" Joker hollered. "This shit is crazy!"

Bezo had already started running people out as Miles looked towards the back of the building. The door was wide open and they ran out into the alley. He pulled out his gun and crept slowly towards the narrow passageway. Joker and Gustavo looked around the floor at the discarded, empty bags of dope. "Has to be at least a hundred," Gustavo said. Joker nodded his head in agreement then heard Miles call out and they ran towards him. He was bent over the bodies of the doormen, both dead, holding his nose from the stench. "What the hell happened here?" Joker said.

"Don't know, but I'm heading upstairs..." Bezo was right behind him. Joker looked at Gustavo, "Damn...don't know how this could have happened."

"Looks like somebody robbed the place, but..." he looked back into the lobby on the floor at the packets of dugee strewn about and said, "they didn't take any dope, so...where's the money?"

Joker nodded, "Damn...you're right! Upstairs...let's go!" Before they got to the stairs their bodies shivered as they heard Miles's ear splitting shrill coming from above them. "Noooooooo!"

Bezo made it through the door first and deliberately, immediately backed out. Joker and Gustavo was right behind him. Bezo turned and put his hand out, "Boss, hold on. It doesn't look good..." Joker stared at Bezo in horror, he'd never seen the big, burly, 6 foot 9 bruiser broken like he was now. All Joker could hear as he glanced past him into the apartment were the sobs of Miles, his wailing now simmering down to a whimper.

Gustavo stepped around Bezo, popped in, then disappeared into a back room and stepped back out grasping at his stomach, "Aw, shitl" he stumbled towards a window and gagged. Joker knew whatever it was had to be serious. He hesitantly stepped around Bezo and lurched into the back room. His eyes focused in on shiny, dried up blood; thick, saturating deep into the wood grained floor. He groaned as he recognized the pale, motionless faces. Big E was damn near gutted in half, his eyes bulged open as he laid sprawled out on the floor in front of his brother. Pancho hovered over him, lifeless, on his knees; eyes protruding out it's sockets. It was a sickening sight to see, but Joker managed to stay focused and scanned the surroundings. He looked over at the window and saw that it had been cracked. A slight breeze moved through swaying the curtains. "I opened them...couldn't stand the smell..." Joker was startled and turned suddenly. It was Miles.

"What the fuck happened..." Bezo managed to say.

"I don't know...don't know." He moved around in front of the bodies and crashed against the side of the wall, tears still streaming down his face. Joker walked towards him, "I know you don't want to hear it, but get hold of yourself."

"They...w-w-were li-like brothers..."

Joker beckoned for Bezo to come through the door, "Look...we'll find out who did this, but right now we got bigger problems."

"W-w-what...now..." Miles managed to utter, he was still choked up. Joker looked at Bezo and he pointed towards the window, "Open it...all the way." He looked back at Miles, "We gotta clean this up. We don't need the police here investigating nothing. It could lead a trail straight to us and believe me-"

"You'd get blamed for the bodies." Gustavo added. He'd composed himself long enough to step into the room still wiping throw up from the corners of his mouth, "We got to clean this up and it ain't gonna be good."

"But how..." Miles walked towards the bodies, "I need to move them-"

"No!" Joker interjected, "I'm sorry...but we can't."

Miles looked at Joker, his eyes glared, "What do you mean, no!" He lunged towards Joker and Bezo stepped between them. Joker shook his head a second, he could see the distress in his eyes but he knew they couldn't get involved with moving any bodies. "Look, this whole place was just overrun by a bunch of junkies. Pretty soon the word will be out and it'll get to the police-"

"But...we got them on the payroll..."

"Yeah, we do, but not for no murders."

"He's right Miles. You still got bodies downstairs and who knows where else. They'd pin everything on us...in a heartbeat. We gotta come up with something." Gustavo said.

Joker turned towards the window and looked out through the curtains at the alleyway and adjacent buildings, all unoccupied, gutted out. He looked past at the next building towards his other spot surveying and spotting the lookout's posted up top then turned back towards them, "Burn it."

"What?" Miles asked.

"We got to burn the building down. This way we could cover up-"

"Burn it!" Miles hollered. "Right now...what about Big E and Pancho? No! I need to bury them!"

For the first time in a long while Joker felt an emotional lump in his throat as he looked in Miles's face. He knew it was a hard pill to swallow but it had to be done. If he torched the building it would look to the police like another abandoned building set on fire by squatters. The bodies would be chalked up as transients, they wouldn't pursue it. If he let Miles take the bodies out, there would be too many questions asked. Someone was bound to see them and he couldn't risk that, "Burn it...I said."

"These were my partners! We just can't leave them here...no!" Miles screamed out.

Gustavo put his arm around his shoulders to soothe him. "Miles...hear him out. He's right. We just can't pull the body's like that. Too much blood. And even if a funeral director were to see these type of wounds believe me he's gonna call the police. Too many questions asked, and even if you paid all of them off...it would cost...way too much-"

"I'll pay for it!" He jerked away from Gustavo and walked over towards Joker getting in his face with his hands out, pleading. "I'll pay it all myself. They deserve better than this! C'mon...Joker...do it...for me..." Joker leaned against the window feeling Miles put his hand on his arm. "please..."

"Enough!" Joker hollered out, and spun around, looking him in his eyes. "You know what I'm saying is right. I'm sorry about what happened to them, believe me! We'll put the word out. We'll get whoever did this, but this is the business where in! It's ugly at best, but it is what it is. Bezo! Get some gas"

"I need a hand, boss." Joker looked around him and spotted the dope fiend that had come in with Miles, "You...you work for me, right."

"Ye-ye-yeah."

"Okay, give Bezo a hand." He waved Gustavo over, "You got to get your hands dirty too...you good."

"I understand...I'm cool with it."

"Okay...we need to pull the other bodies from upstairs inside and separate them around the building best we can. Then when Bezo gets back, we'll break the gas lines and sprinkle gas on the bodies inside the apartments." He walked towards Miles, "I need you to understand..."

Miles took a deep breath then looked up at him. He knew Joker was right. He straightened up and took another glance over at Pancho, Big E and then stepped around the blood to a clear spot and shoved him toppling him over onto his brother. The blow was nauseating as Miles then turned towards Joker, "Give me a minute, okay."

Joker led everyone out the room. Miles stood over the bodies and closed his eyes, "I promise I'll find out who did this to you...I promise." He got up and turned to walk out of the room and stopped, "You never let me down...and I won't let you down either."

He caught up with Joker and pointed towards the upstairs stairwell. They walked up and it was the same thing. More bodies; the look-outs, and his workers.

"Joker...this is a problem." Gustavo said.

It reminded Joker of years ago when the serial killer was loose in Alphabet City. The carnage...the mutilated bodies that were discovered, same scenario. Miles looked at the holes in the middle of their foreheads and he thought the same thing; and of his sister.

Bezo had called, he'd started checking the apartments looking for more people, dope, so far that was it, nothing more showed up. Joker had him make sure the windows and doors were opened so that the fire would burn rapidly and stay contained to the building, once they were downstairs.

Miles knew he had to get to the money stash spot in the building; the basement, where the boiler room was. He scrambled downstairs and opened the old, Harris boiler and nothing, it was cleaned out, "Damn! We was robbed too!"

Joker, clearly pissed off, stomped down the steps cursing the day among other things. The dope fiend that had went with Bezo stepped towards Miles and pointed to the outside of the basement door, "Hey man, this is where I found the clip..."

"What!" Joker had heard, "What clip? What's he talking about, Miles?"

Miles reached into his pocket and pulled out the money clip and showed it to Joker. "He found this earlier. He showed it to me when I went looking for Nut-Nutt."

"Whose is it?" he asked.

"It belongs to Aziz." Miles said.

Joker looked upstairs, then back down to the boiler room and thought back to

Aziz's threat, "Find that muthafucka! Find him! Put a price on his head... the first muthafucka to find him gets ten grand!"

Gustavo heard it loud and clear. Aziz was fair game and he wanted the easy money also. Besides, he thought to himself, it was all, sport anyway. Miles stuffed the clip back into his pocket, thought about Big E and Pancho one more time; Aziz would have to pay, no doubt.

"Bezo!" Joker called out, "Let's burn this muthafucka...and get the fuck outta here, quickly!"

Joker stood in solitude as they scurried around with the gas cans sprinkling the flammable vapors throughout the tenement. He looked down on the checkered, marble floor at a dope package and picked it up. He squashed it in his hand and thought out loud to himself, "Somebody's gonna pay for this...somebody." He took out his lighter and lit it, then tossed it to the ground sending the trail of flames zooming into the gloomed, murkiness of the upstairs loft.

The once thriving dope peddling enterprise, was instantly turned into a morbid crematory.

chapter 12

SKYLER PONDERED AS she stared out aimlessly overlooking the traffic coming round the FDR Highway. Looking beyond, she drifted towards the far end stretches of the East River across the water into Brooklyn. The question that had aroused her awareness was one that Mya had asked: suppose the money isn't there. She was right, Skyler thought, suppose the stash wasn't in the pool hall, then what would they do? Would they still rob it? They could easily get themselves killed if things didn't go right.

She turned back around, finally having a response, though she herself wasn't too sure, but nevertheless it was what it was. "Everyone in there would have to die." she said.

"Die? You mean just kill everyone?"

Skyler reached towards her pack of cigarettes and lit one up, then turned back around looking out the window again, "Yeah...everyone."

"But, why?" Mya asked. Sitting back in the recliner still waiting for the call back from earlier, Steve said, "She's crazy...that's all."

"Crazy..." Skyler turned quickly, "You think I'm crazy, do you!" She stepped towards Steve and standing over him said, "Okay, let's see. One...we don't know for a fact if there is a stash there or not and-"

"I told you I would know for sure once I get this call." Steve snapped.

"Okay...okay..." Skyler found an ashtray and put out the cigarette. "So, we're supposed to find that out from a source that none of us know except you. I'll live with that...for now, yeah right." Steve rolled his eyes.

"Then...we are, I mean, us...you, me and little miss prissy over here, supposed to roll up in there and just take the money even though we do know for a fact that it's heavily armed."

"We'll be 'heavily armed too." Mya said.

"Oh yeah...couple of handguns...right."

"Hell, you're the one that's talking about killing-" Mya remarked snidely. Skyler reached over and grabbed her by the collar, "Look, bitch! Because of your scared fuckin' ass, we're in this shit, you hear! So keep the smart ass shit to yourself!" She let her loose and Mya cowered back, never seeing her girlfriend like that before. "You damn right we kill them. Go in there blazing, because if we give them the upper hand then, believe me, they're gonna kill us." She looked at Mya, "After they call Joker and his goons and they rape us...you know they gonna do that!" "And you," she pointed at Steve, "To what I understand...ain't no exception!"

"Yeah, right...one of them muthafuckas touch me-"

"Shut up! It's not that good a plan for now. We need more help. Steve, we talked about this before, we might have to go with the plan that we had earlier."

Steve eased up uncomfortably on the couch, "Damn...was hoping not. We in too deep...not like before."

"Yeah, well...gotta be some sacrifices."

"What are you two talking about?" Mya asked.

"It's not important right now-oh shit, he's calling me." Steve got up and stepped into the kitchen closer towards the window for a better reception and privacy, "Yeah...it 's me, Steve. What's up?"

"You tell me....you called." the voice from the other side answered. "Remember that deal you was telling me about before..."

"What? Spit it out."

"The pool hall thing...stash..."

"Damn...you remembered that?" The voice on the other end went silent, "We was drunk. Thought maybe you'd forgotten."

"Naw...I remembered and I'm still down, but we may have to do it...soon."

"Hold up. Now you're moving too fast. Me and my people still working out the bugs. Then, we have to case the joint."

"I already did that...me and my partner-"

"Partner! Damn...you told someone. What the fuck are you, stupid?!"

"Look, man, she's down."

"Aw, hell...and a bitch. What the fuck is the matter with you!"

"You met her before...Skyler.

"That gold digging ass, psycho bitch. What's up, the dope boy market went bad and shit?"

"Look, we also got a inside."

"Inside...how much more inside can you get?"

"Believe me...deep."

"Who the fuck is it, already? You already got one crazy ass chick. Who the fuck is this"

"Aziz's girl...Mya."

The voice went silent again, "Yo...you still there or what?"

"Yeah...I'm here. I 'm on my way over...now."

"Alright...I'm at the Hamp' on 14th and C Apt. 6-B.

"Got you...I'm on the way."

The phone went dead and Steve looked over at Skyler and Mya, "It's a done deal. He's on the way over. I think he's down."

Skyler walked towards the window and stared out, "I hope so...or we're dead as hell."

Gutter folded up his phone and stuck it in his jacket pocket and hollered at Smack, "Yo, man. I gotta make a quick run."

"Quick run? Smack hollered back, "Where?"

"Gotta go see my cousin cross town."

"Cousin...what cousin?"

"Steve."

"Oh yeah, Steve...tell him I said what's up."

"No problem." Gutter reached into his drawer and pulled out the 9mm and extra clip and loaded the gun, "Yeah...I sure will."

Gutter stood at the doorway of the tiny apartment reassessing the situation. Here it was: a childhood cousin, Steve, his mommas' sisters' son; a girl he'd always known as a gold digger for as long as he could remember, Skyler; and his drug boss lieutenants' girlfriend, Mya. Just great he thought. They wanted to be part of something-the wrong thing, a robbery. He pondered their scheme, actually trying to figure out just which one of them came up with the idea. It was bold, but at best, foolish.

He hated that he mentioned anything to Steve. He was drunk that night, spending money at Coyote Ugly's and talking that big wily talk. No harm done, no one even took him serious, at least so he thought. Steve had been there also but never paid him no mind before when it came to him running his mouth.

Steve was the good guy, he didn't go around any trouble, or get into any trouble.

But somehow, now, he had organized a plan with this motley crew of sorts to rob one of Joker's stash houses. Pure imbroglio, but they were dead serious and he needed to know just how sincere they were. He also needed to know if Mya would talk. She was Aziz's woman and in all actuality they would be robbing his spot. A spot that Aziz was supposed to have full control over as well as safeguard it.

"Okay...run down the plan." Gutter said. He stepped around Mya to a spot on the couch of the tiny undersized room and sat. He shifted his body weight from the 9mm that had poked his backside. Steve stood up, "Like I was telling you, cuz, I...uh, we were thinking of robbing a stash house, the poolroom and-"

"Well, how do you know that the poolroom is a stash house?" Gutter interrupted.

Steve shifted his eyes over towards Skyler. It was a good question he thought, because they really didn't know for sure. He was stumped and Gutter knew it, they didn't have nothing. That was quick. Now he needed to figure out why Mya was here with them and was this something that Aziz knew about, maybe it was a setup. Skyler stood up and tried to cosign Steve's bullshit, "You right...but, I'll tell you what, if it's not, there's gonna be a lot of muthafuckas talkin' and spittin' out money...or some dead muthafuckas who'd wished they had known where the stash was." She folded her arms, "And I mean that shit."

She was daring, dauntless arid right now, stupid, Gutter told himself, but all that didn't make for a good plan and that's what they lacked. He put it all on the line. "Okay...I hear you. But hear me. For one. We don't have to go through those changes, because the muthafuckas you talkin' 'bout being bodied might just be us."

Mya blew a sigh of relief when she heard the word, us, hopefully he was down. "And next...for the money that you talkin' 'bout taking muthafuckas out for, well, there won't be no one else there except the money counters." He turned towards Steve, "And that's usually...us."

"Okay..." Skyler sat next to him, "Well, it sounds like you're okay with us, but you're just leery because we don't have a good plan and if we go the way we're thinking...somebody could get killed, namely you- "

"Or you...sweetie." Gutter said, "Look...evidently we want the same thing...and we can get it." He looked Steve's way again then at Mya, "But...to be straight up and it looks like we are straight up. Why is she here? Damn, the muthafucka we stealing from is her man."

They all looked her way. Mya pushed her straight, auburn hair away from her pretty face and Gutter grimaced at the sight of the black-n-blue bruise that still showed itself from the night before, "This good enough for you? Or, do you want me to go on?"

"I heard some things but I never-"

"Yeah, well, what you heard was true. He kicks my ass on a regular basis and I want him to pay for that. You understand."

"I had to ask."

"It's okay...you had to know. I don't give a fuck about him and if given the chance, I'd kill him."

"Damn." Steve said.

"Yeah, damn, but only after I get my hands on some of his money...Joker's...or even Miles for all I care."

Gutter stared off as she spoke, remembering how his momma would get the same treatment by some of the tricks that came by the house. She had that same look, that same bitter, determination, even spoke the same shit she did, except this woman in front of him was no junkie and had no other vices that could stop her except for her two daughters. "What about your kids? If they found out you had something to do with this, they'll be coming after you. Me, personally, if it goes down like that, I don't know you muthafuckas, and I ain't no fuckin snitch; but if you snitch on me I got a back up and his name..." He reached into the small of his back and pulled out the 9mm he had and pulled back the slide and as it snapped, Mya flinched, "is nine fuckin' millimeter. You feel me."

Skyler looked at his arrogance, "Yeah, I hear you, but remember this shit... Shakespeare...hell hath no fury like a woman scorned."

"What? What the fuck are you talkin' about?"

Skyler got up and walked past him going towards the kitchen table and picked up her cigarettes and just as casually lit one up, then blew out a mouth full of smoke his way, "Trust me...you don't want to know."

"Alright, alright...all that shit sounds cool, but what's up?" Steve asked.

Gutter leaned forward and beckoned for the notebook pad Mya had placed in front of her, "Okay...here's a simple layout of the place. You need to study it. Know the spot. Me and another partner, who will remain nameless for now, is casing the joint and we think it can go down in another 2 weeks-"

"2 weeks! Oh, hell no!" Skyler turned, "Tomorrow!"

"Tomorrow...are you crazy!"

"Yes...I am. It's tomorrow or it's a no go. Shit, I ain't got time to case no joint. I'm out. My fuckin lease is up and I'm expected somewhere else."

"Somewhere else...where?" Mya asked."

"Don't worry about it, but far from here, believe that."

"Yo Steve. What the fuck." Gutter stood up and put his gun back in his waist, "Is she kiddin' me or what. I thought y'all was serious. Man, y'all wastin' my fuckin time." He stepped towards the door, "I tell you what. You go in there without a plan and I guarantee you, you'll be coming out in a body bag."

"Whoa...hold up, Gutter!" Steve interjected. "He's right Skyler. We need to case the joint at least. See what's going on."

Skyler sucked her teeth then thought, "Okay, okay, but it doesn't take but a couple of days. I mean, hell...the first of the month is Wednesday and that's when most of the dope fiend money is spent. So that should be a good day...right." She looked at Gutter, "I can give it until then."

Gutter took a deep breath, "Damn!" He walked up to Skyler and got in her face looking her shapely body up and down, sizing her up then stepped around and pushed up on her ass and brushed aside her hair away from her ear and said, "We can ride like that, but I'll say this; we make this lick, and me and you got other business before you leave town." She could feel his hard on as it rose up in the crack of her ass, she was a freak, she liked it, it even made her wet but she couldn't show that she had a weakness especially between her legs, and she shoved him away, "Yeah...we'll see...youngen." He walked over to the door and waved at Steve, "I'll be in touch."

"When!"

"Soon..." He looked back over at Skyler and winked, then at Mya, "Real soon." then opened the door and left out.

Steve walked over and closed it then turned towards them, "Well...it's going down. Make plans to haul ass because he's right about one thing. If they find out who's involved..." he walked over to Skyler, "Then...when they finish with you," reaching down he pinched her ass, "you'd wish you had more cushion on this sweet ass of yours, cause they gonna fuck you from now till next-."

"I'll be alright!" she snapped.

"Yeah...well, Skyler," Mya said, "I ain't trying to go out like that." She took out her phone.

"Who are you calling?"

"My girls. We need to make plans..."

"Plans?"

"Yeah. Plans to get the fuck out of dodge."

Smack and Gutter stood talking in front of the poolroom waiting for Tempest to open up the poolroom to start the nightly count for the take this evening. Smack stood off to the side of the building looking up towards 4th Street watching a huge ball of thick, black smoke balloon high above the buildings. "Damn...wonder what the hell is going on over there?" he said.

Gutter looked up also, "Don't know. Probably one of those abandoned buildings got caught on fire or something."

"Maybe so...but whatever it is, it's pretty large."

"Somebody will be over in a little while telling us what happened."

"Yeah." He packed the back of the cigarette he had in his hand and put it to his lips and lit it up. He pulled in a deep drag and let it out then took a swig of the hot cup of coffee he had in his hand, "So...what happened..." he asked.

"Happened...what do you mean-"

"With your cousin!"

"Oh, yeah. It was a trip." Gutter directed him towards the street and they sat on the side of a car, "I think it could work in our favor."

"Favor? What the hell is up, Gutter?" Smack took another swig.

"They thinking about robbing the poolroom."

"The poolroom. For what?"

"They got wind of it being a stash spot and they want to stick it up."

Smack got up off the car and threw his butt in the street, "But, that's us. Man, what did you tell them?"

Gutter grinned watching his friend get agitated at the notion, but he had a plan schemed up. "Fuck it...let them."

"Let them...what are you crazy?"

"No...hear me out." He guided him back towards the car, "Remember we got a plan, too. They don't know nothing about that. What they want is the count money. So, fuck it, we stage it like a robbery. Set it up so that they come in and, well, rob the muthafucka."

"Hold up...who are they?"

"Oh yeah, that's the kicker. My cousin Steve...that girl from uptown he's always around...the gold digger chick-"

"Redbone girl...yeah I know who you talkin' about."

"Skyler! That's her name."

"Yeah...Skyler. Damn, that fine ass robbing shit...thought muthafuckas was giving her money."

"Huh...never know them 'til you know them. And check this out...Mya. Aziz's old lady."

Smack staggered back, "Oh shit! You kidding me! Why the fuck is she down with..."

"Hell, I don't blame her. Aziz's smacking her up and shit. He doesn't appreciate her so she's gonna get hers, probably wants to haul ass with the kids somewhere."

"True."

"But, anyway...we set it up so that it looks like a robbery, but in all actuality we let them in and take the shit and-"

"Then we meet up later for a split? But suppose Joker catches one of them. You know he can make them talk and then it'll come back to us."

"That's why we tell him to be there so that they can get snuffed. We only let Steve get away, but the two broads...get taken out. Make it look like Mya tried to get even with Aziz or something."

"Damn...that's fucked up, but hell....I'm down. But, yo, Gutter, what about the stash spot at the school?"

"Shit, that's easy. We can get that spot too. That's where we tell Steve to hide the money. He doesn't know anything about it and when he comes in...*bammm!*"

Smack backed up away from the car and folded his arms, gawked at Gutter then shook his head. "Damn...you's a dirty muthafucka."

Gutter kicked back and crossed his legs, "Yeah...I know."

Smack laughed at his deviousness and reached over and dapped him, "But...it's a plan as far as I'm concerned. When is it going down?"

"Wednesday-"

"Wednesday! That's two days from now!"

"First of the month...good money. Fuck it."

"Yeah you got a point. Okay...I'm down."

Gutter noticed Tempest's car pulling up into the alley. "There's Tempest...let's go upstairs."

"Yeah, we need to get shit together."

Tempest came from around the back and waved them over to the stairs, "Damn, y'all heard about the fire and shit?"

"Naw...we just seen the smoke..."

She fumbled in her purse for the keys and continued, "There's a big fire over on 3rd Street across from the Pitt."

"Yeah, and..."

"And...shit! It's one of Joker's spots! I heard someone say that bodies were found and everything."

Oh shit..." Gutter held his hand to his mouth, "Damn...wonder what the fuck happened now?"

"Don't know all the details, but you better believe they'll be over here, soon." She finally got the keys out and they walked up the stairs, "So...I got a feeling when they come in there's gonna be an ass of money around. Plus, all the money that's still needs to be collected for the night. Yeah, we gotta have our shit in order, ya hear."

Gutter looked over at Smack and winked, "Yeah...we hear you loud and clear."

Tempest turned around suddenly, "What the fuck you two got going on. Some old secret shit, I saw you wink!"

"Gutter squinted his eyes, damn, she busted us. Her long, pouting face quickly turned into a smile, "Y'all need to stop staring at my ass! Perverts!" The door was opened and as she walked behind the bar she yelled out, "Call Blu and Chino, too. I gotta feeling we gonna need extra security!"

"No problem." Gutter and Smack made their way towards the back, thinking that this couldn't have been a better time for the plan they had in motion. It was all about timing and the timing was right or they were about to be fucked.

"AW SHIT!"

"Now what's up!" Skyler asked as she turned and glanced at Mya. "All you did was send those girls to the store. Damn, I know that girl didn't hook up with that boy again!" She walked over towards her and reached for the phone. Mya showed her the numbers that appeared on the screen, "It's Aziz..."

Skyler pulled her hand back, "Damn...what he want?"

"Shit, you know what he wants." Mya stared at the numbers then sighed. Steve overheard them, "Answer it, Mya."

"What! Why...hell, he wants to kill me!"

Steve came over to the sofa she sat on and stroked her back, comforting her, "Look...I'm here with you. I ain't gonna let nothing happen, ya hear. Besides, we need to know what he knows. We play our cards right, we might be able to have him meet us at the poolroom Wednesday and let the chips fall where they may."

"You mean...use him to..."

"Right! I got it..." Skyler crossed her arms, "Let him be seen there so Joker will think it was him...or something like that." She looked over at Steve.

"Hell yeah." Steve said, "Kill two birds with one stone, ya feel me." Mya picked the phone up to her ear, "Hello?"

Aziz was somewhat surprised she even answered, he'd expected to get voice mail as usual, "Mya? It's you..."

"C'mon, Aziz, you know it's me. Now, what do you want?"

"Aw, baby. I just want to talk. I miss you-"

"Miss me! You tried to kill me, fool! Then, you followed me and the girls uptown. Probably trying to kill us up there, too, huh."

Aziz paused, he needed her to hear him out, but she needed to vent, "I'm sorry about the other night..."

"Aziz, you always sorry! You know what!"

"What!"

"I'm sorry of your sorry shit! What is it that you want?"

"Just forgive me..."

"No!"

"I was wrong. I don't know what got into me..."

Mya held the phone away from her ear and shook her head, "He just don't get it!"

"Hell, find out what he knows about the poolroom...the stash." Skyler whispered.

"Mya! Mya, you still there!"

"Yeah...I'm here. Look...what is it that you want from me? You want to kill me?"

"No...not that. I'm just going through some changes. Miles and Joker been trying to kill me, baby. They want me dead."

"Dead? For what?"

"I think Miles wants to out me so he can take over Alphabet City once Joker leaves."

"Joker leave...where's he going?"

"He about to sell the business...get out the game."

This was the first Mya had heard of it, but still, what does that have to do with her, she thought, "I mean...what about the spots. You use to collect his money. What about that? I mean...you know a lot about him."

"That's why I think he wants me out. I know too much." Aziz paused, he needed to take a second before he formulated his next thought, "Just like...Dante."

"Dante ain't got shit to do with this!" Mya screamed, "He's dead!"

"Right, Mya...but, I think that Joker wants to know if he had a stash spot or something."

"Stash...spot..."

"Yeah, a stash spot. Did Dante have one?" His tongue was dripping honey as Mya listened, "You believe that! They think that Dante had a stash spot. Picture that, I mean...if that was the case you would have told me, right?" Aziz put it out there then waited for it to come back.

"Aziz, think about this...and think real hard. If Dante had a stash spot, one, why would I tell you and two, do you think I would have stayed with you this long and three, would I have even messed around with you? I mean, damn..."

This wasn't the response he was wanting and it pissed him off. His temper flared up, "Damn-it...I looked out for your ass!"

"Yeah, you did. But, I don't need you anymore. Hell...you asking about Dante's stash, shit, you need to be looking at Joker's stashes."

"What! Look, I know you know where Dante's money is at!"

"No baby..." this time she threw out her own bait, "Maybe...it's at the poolroom where Joker's money is." She giggled knowing it would make him even angrier.

"That's Joker's money! He's trying to frame me now for some missing money!"

"What missing money, Aziz?" she asked.

"The other night we were up there counting and some money came up short...bout six gee."

"Well...y'all need to find the money or something-"

"The money's there! I think it's Miles that's trying to fuck me up. All that damn money and they worrying about six fuckin gee!" Mya could hear the outrage in his voice. It was just a matter of time before he went completely mad, "Where you at! I need to see you!"

"No, Aziz...not now. Have you been taking your medicine lately?"

Aziz was gasping. Maybe the medicine might be a way in. "No...I need my medicine. Do you have it? Maybe you could bring it to me.."

"No, Nut t-Nutt. I don't have it." She rubbed the side of her face and the bruise still stung. "Maybe you left it back in the apartment that night..."

"Yeah, maybe you could meet me-"

"No, Aziz. I ain't getting beat up...no fuckin' more! Now, good fuckin' bye!" She cut him off. Skyler was there with tissue as she reached for one and dabbed at her tears, "That muthafucka! I hate him!" she sobbed.

"Why did you stay with him so long?" Skyler asked.

Mya looked up at her, "Because...I was a fuckin' gold digger, too...that's why."

Skyler pulled her closer, "It's gonna be alright. Shit, Wednesday...us...gold diggers gonna have their day."

Aziz snarled as she hung up the phone. Maybe he was wrong about Mya she might not know about the stash. That was all good, he figured, but still, he had to get rid of her anyway. She knew too much, way too much about Dante's death. It was time to pull back. He'd get up with Mya later. Right now he needed to go by the apartment and collect some things. Call Peaches and make plans to leave New York.

He knew Miles would be right on his ass, even if he didn't know exactly why; six grand was no money to Joker. So, he knew it had to be something else, and he thought more about the day he sat with him. It had to be when he told Joker about his package. From that point on, he should have known he was a marked man.

chapter 13

MILES SAT ON THE BENCHES opposite the basketball court overlooking the backside of the Pitt, staring at the huge globe of smoke rising high above the building and exploding. The scene was frantic as fire engines gathered from all over trying to bring the blazing fury under control. Buildings next to it had to be evacuated from the intense heat that escaped from it, twisted steel and metal. People were standing in the street watching as fire engulfed the once habitable tenement.

He looked down at the phone in his hand as it buzzed. It was Joker, probably ready to move the rest of the money they had collected from the other spots up the street. For the first time since when the area was ravaged by the serial killer, did Joker ever shut down any of his spots.

The serial killer was something serious; Miles flinched as he thought back to those days. Those days stuck in his mind as the neighborhood woke up to bodies scattered in the street, mutilated, cut to pieces. His sister was a victim of the terrible carnage.

He hated the memory of her telling him just that very morning she decided to turn over a new leaf, stop tricking and go straight. She'd saved up enough money to find a place in Brooklyn and she could attend school at night. Learn nursing she figured or better yet, counsel to those less fortunate. Her dream, he smiled as he thought back; the tip of his lips nudging his cheeks causing the welled up tears to run down freely off the side of his face.

He never did grieve, there was no time. The killer moved quickly. Miles recalled how the blood still ran out her mouth as he found her sprawled out in a stairwell aside a guttered brownstone; panties down below her gapped open legs. He remembered that her hand seemed to point in the direction of the boiler room and he acted. It came out of him, the beast that the killer turned him into as he cornered him. The poker that was used to push the burnt ambers seemed to whistle in the air as Miles raised it over and over, down into his skull. He stopped only when the luminous shadows that stood behind him grabbed him; the police. He was convicted of manslaughter and sent away; Sing-Sing.

Joker had been looking for the killer also. He'd already taken out some of his pushers, customers and costing him so far in total, thousands.

Joker put up the money to bury Miles's sister, he also put up a lawyer to cushion his time, got it cut down from fifteen to eight on good behavior.

When Miles got out he put him in a place of his own, checked on him and set him up in the highly lucrative dope trade in Alphabet City so that he could fend for himself. Miles owed him.

The neighborhood was in return grateful for what he did, a hero of sorts. Miles looked out for his people; the prostitutes, hustlers, and panhandlers, they were his family. The dysfunctional actions of it didn't even make it seem out of place when a young teenage girl was found od'ed in her apartment with two kids playing over her body. The streets took the children in, but it was Miles who did what Joker had done for him. He introduced them to the world of hustling dope money, giving them all he had and they were loyal to him as they grew, looked toward him as a father of sorts. When Miles would think of leaving the hood, perhaps pursue his sister's dream, they would be right there with him. But now, they were gone, dead. Just like his sister. There was no one for him to look after anymore.

He got up off the bench and reached into his jacket pocket and pulled out the money clip that was found earlier. He snarled as he glared at it. He never did take to Aziz since way back. It seemed like he was always better than everyone else, like he harbored some sort of secret. He stuffed it back in his pocket and stalked towards his truck. He answered the phone, "Yeah, Joker...what's up!"

"Hey...I'm gonna take all the money to the pool room. I want you to meet me there-"

"Look, Joker...I'm busy!"

"Busy! What do you-"

"You know what it is!" He stopped and sighed, "Look, man. No disrespect, but it's been a bad fuckin' day. I need...some space..."

Joker paused. He understood. It was a difficult day for them both and he had a good idea of what floated in his mind. Revenge. "Alright, but Miles."

"Yeah..."

"Be careful."

"I'll be there later on tonight. Just call Blu and Chino-"

"I got it. You just watch your back!"

"I got you." Miles continued to walk towards his truck and stopped only once more. The firemen had started to bring out the bodies. He couldn't make any of them out, but he didn't have to, he didn't really want to.

He opened the door to the truck, cranked up then quickly glanced in the back seat. Pancho's book bag. He noticed a small blue, velvet box in the side satchel. He reached for it and curiously started opening it. Maybe he thought, it was for one of those little, young ass, gold digging wannabe's they flirted with. It was a watch case. He was taken aback by its contents. An all gold Rolex watch. On top was attached a card. He opened it:

Yo, Miles. This watch will look good on your arm when you retire down south and you learn how to play golf. (lol, smiley face). Signed; Tariq and Malik (Big E and Pancho).

That did it, that's all it took. He gripped the steering wheel and with his head down, the tears flowed like a faucet into his lap. After he finished and in between sniffles he put on the watch and turned the truck around making it over to Hampton Square Houses looking for Aziz with a vengeance. He reached in the glove compartment for his gun and put it in his jacket. This time he wouldn't get away he thought, and he had better have the right words, if not, he was a dead man.

'*SWOOOSH!*'-"Why are you-'*gurgle-gulp!*'-doing this to me!"

'*Swooosh!*'-"Why don't you just-'*gurgle-gulp!*'-leave me alone!"

'*Swooosh!*'-"Stop, it's-it's-'*gurgle-gurgle-gulp!*'-too much!"

'*Swooosh!*'-"I can't breathe! Let me breathe!" Gustavo stood mean mugging over the figure bent to the knees gasping for air reapplying his grip as he grasped the back of the neck as water gushed over the floor, "Now...you gonna tell me where Aziz is! Or do you want to go for another swim!"

"I don't know! I swear, I don't know!"

Once again, the wrong answer. He shoved the wet, drenched head into the toilet bowl and flushed again, *'Swooosh!'* Holding the head down this time a little longer then pulling it back up again, he hollered, "I can do this all day...Peaches!"

"Please...no more. I can call him! Please..."

Gustavo pulled the head up out the commode and tossed Peaches' dripping, sopping body to the side of the black and white, checkered, bathroom floor. He pulled a towel from off the rack and wiped his hands, "Now...you call him." He threw it down to the floor and Peaches quivered. Gustavo walked around the small, photo studio observing the dangling snapshots draped along the walls, "Hmmm...you do good work..." Totally oblivious to the fact that he almost killed him, "How did you come to know Aziz anyway?" he asked. Peaches was out the bathroom and crawling along the floor sloshing around water that was spit up, "What business is it of yours!"

Gustavo looked around and grinned, "Oh, I see you still want to play in the water, huh."

"No...no..."

"Then answer the fucking question...smart ass!"

Peaches cringed as Gustavo yelled, "Okay...okay." Peaches plopped down on a seat by a light table and pulled out some photos, "Years back when I was going to school at New York University, I did a thesis on photography...wanted to do a portfolio on street life of sorts. Pictures of the hood and what goes on kinda thing. Anyway, I was hanging out down by the Pitt taking shots of the dope fiends coming in and out the dope spots and this guy rolls up on me. He grabbed the camera and threatened to kick my ass. I told him I was just a student and wanted some pictures; he thought I was the police doing surveillance. After explaining to him that I wasn't, he let me go. I invited him to my showing at a gallery and we sort of hit it off from there."

Gustavo walked over to Peaches, unmoved. He stroked the long, dark hair that flowed down Peaches' back, then unexpectedly grabbed a handful and snatched, pulling out tracks of weave, "Did you bother to tell him you was a fucking man!" He threw it on the floor as Peaches covered up the patch in his head, "Or did he know!"

He dove for the floor and picked up the hair piece and put it back on his head as best he could, "It doesn't matter. We love each other!"

"Love? You don't know what love is." He pulled up a chair and sat in front of Peaches and reached for his chin, forcing his head up. "You are deceiving him. That's not love. Tell me, be honest. Does he know you are a transsexual?"

Peaches looked off and Gustavo pulled his face back looking him in his eyes, "No. He thinks I'm a woman." he said.

"But...how?" Gustavo looked him up and down bizarrely. "You've been together for sometime. How does he not know?"

Peaches reached into his desk and pulled out another array of pictures, some new, some old. "Look! I lived my life as a woman since I was fourteen. I know the mannerisms better than most women."

"I knew who you were...Pete."

"Fuck you!"

"No, it wasn't me that was fucking you, it was-"

"Your father! A fuckin' pig! It's his fault." Peaches lit up a cigarette. "He raped me!"

"To what I understand...you wanted it." Gustavo shot back.

"Wanted it! I was twelve! How could a twelve year old want some man shoving his dick down his throat?" Gustavo looked away. "Oh yeah...and when that wasn't enough, he fucked me in the ass!" Peaches walked over to Gustavo and this time grabbed his arm, "So when you ask why Aziz never thought-I look just like a woman! And check this out, when he wants to fuck!..." He took off the robe he had on, turned, dropped his boxers and bent his ass over, spreading his cheeks, revealing half healed scars from whips and belts, "Your old man made sure my ass hole was as big as a pussy!" Gustavo pushed him away. "No, muthafucka! You wanted to know." He put back on his robe and turned. "Yeah...he thinks he's fuckin' one big pussy. And you know what else, muthafucka?" He kneeled in Gustavo's face puffing on the cigarette, "And when he does asks questions, like why don't you turn on the light, I take his dick in my mouth and-"

"Enough!" Gustavo angrily stood up, "That's enough! I don't want to hear about that shit!"

"Oh, I'm sure you don't." Peaches walked back into the bathroom, "As much as you may not like it, Gustavo..." He peeped out into the foyer, "I am you. Your father couldn't do what he wanted to do to you, so he picked me."

Gustavo looked out the window, reflecting on those dark days he suppressed; Peaches was right.

They were once friends. It was him he was coming to see when his father attacked Pete. Soon after, once his family got wind of it, they sent him to Florida sparing him his fathers' mental illness and bouts and dysfunctional cruelty; leaving a childhood Pete in New York to fend for himself.

However, he managed to stay in touch...remembering how Peaches bragged about a dope dealer he was doing when he saw him at the club the other night. It wasn't too long before he figured in on Aziz.

Peaches knew enough about Aziz. He also would have had to know enough about the money that Aziz collected. Gustavo reasoned, maybe this could work in his favor after all, "Look, Pete-"

"Don't call me that, Peaches!"

"Whatever...we could stand to make a lot of money-"

"Money! Remember, the muthafucka that I'm fuckin' is a dope dealer and believe me, he puts out da cash, baby." Gustavo stomped toward the bathroom door, "Oh yeah, he puts out, huh. Listen to me and listen well, if you cooperate you could get much more than the pocket change he's throwing at you! Now, think about it. He may just as well know you are a trans and he may be playing you!" Peaches stalked out the bathroom past him, "Picture that!"

"Yeah, picture that. He never left Mya for you, did he?" "He was...sooner or later." Peaches pouted.

Gustavo leaned back against the wall and said jeeringly, "He don't know what he's fuckin...well, I can't tell. He's still with the real pussy!"

Peaches threw the towel that he used at Gustavo, "Fuck you! You're just jealous. Trying to confuse me, that's all."

Gustavo picked up the towel, rung it out and popped Peaches with it, "Naw...not jealous, trust me. Now look, he told you things...didn't he."

"That's personal."

Gustavo's tolerance had reached its limit, he reached into his jacket and pulled out his gun and slid a round into the chamber, "Let's get real. Now, I don't want to kill you, but I need you to tell me some things or..."

"It-it-it's that serious, Gustavo?"

"Yes. It's that serious."

Peaches sat down and looked up at Gustavo, "Put that away. You won't need that. I'll tell you what I know but Gustavo...it better be worth it."

Gustavo put his gun away, then pulled up his seat and sat closer. "Believe me...it is."

"So, do you think he'd go for that..."

"Peaches, Peaches..." Gustavo sat back on the stool and crossed his legs; a wispy smile grew across his lips, "Why do you doubt me? Why?"

"Well, it's not that. It's just...the double crossing type of thing, that's all."

He put his legs down and leaned forward. He was agitated now, "Double cross? Wait are you kiddin' me! Let's go over this again!"

"No...no...I got it."

"But, will you do it?" he said as his patience grew short.

"I said I would-" Peaches' attention was taken away by the sound of his cell phone on the table. He picked up the small phone and checked the number. It was Aziz. "Okay...here we go, but you better have my back-"

"Just answer the fuckin' phone!" Gustavo barked.

"Hello...Aziz, baby." Peaches' voice had changed to resemble a feminine intonation, "I'm glad you called me."

"Oh yeah..." Aziz answered, "I was thinking of coming over."

"Really. You don't have to be with her?" Gustavo shook his head in satisfaction, he egged him on to stick with the plan, "I mean...I'd hate for you to just come, then go, if you know what I mean." Peaches giggled. Gustavo still tripped on the fact how Aziz didn't know that this was a man, damn, but better him than me he mocked.

"I need to talk to you about some things." Aziz said.

"Things...like what?"

"Bout...you and *me*."

Peaches crossed his legs and adjusted the hairpiece on his head, "It's about time, baby. But, uh, you know if we make a move, we gonna need some serious money."

"I have that covered."

"Okay, baby...you got it covered, well, all right then," Peaches snapped his fingers. "Let's do the damn thing, baby." Gustavo nodded his head then motioned for Peaches to tell him to come over later on in the evening, "What time can you be here...tonight, maybe." "As soon as I go by the house and pick up some things. Probably will be later on this evening."

"See you then." he cooed seductively.

"Alright."

Peaches kissed the phone in Aziz's ear as he hung up, then turned towards Gustavo, "Okay...now what?"

Gustavo grinned, "We wait...that's what. When he gets here you find out where the money he's stashing is..."

Peaches lit up a cigarette and gazed towards the pictures he had of Aziz on the wall as Gustavo looked over his shoulder, "Then we kill him."

Peaches winced and said, "Just like that?"

Gustavo took his gun out and stroked it gently across Peaches' face causing him to tense up and said, "Yeah... *Pow*! Just like that."

Peaches flinched and turned abruptly searching Gustavo's solemn eyes for the boy he grew up with or the same young man he knew that would spend the summers here in Alphabet City. There was something different about him now, more sinister. What happened, he pondered. "Gustavo...please, just don't drag it out. Make it quick."

Gustavo peeled his eyes away and turned, "Yeah...sure." Once he found out where the stash was and cleaned it out, he'd give Aziz's lifeless body to Joker for the reward money and then- "We still gonna split the money?" Peaches asked, interrupting his thoughts.

"Oh...sure...split the money." Like he was thinking; give the body to Joker, come back and take Peaches out on a nice long drive. A drive up the West Side Highway along the river. A good secluded place to dump a body; Peaches'. He chuckled.

"What are you laughing at?" Peaches asked as he walked into the back of the studio where he kept a small closet and dresser drawer with clothes. He looked through the closet shuffling outfits, and spotted a frock, "Okay...here we go..."

Gustavo got up and walked towards the window looking out, reminiscing back to his childhood days with Pete and thinking, thinking hard. It was time he took him out of his misery for his old man's sake, "Nothing, nothing much." he answered back.

BEZO PULLED UP TO TOMPKINS Square Park and opened the door allowing Blu and Chino to hop out. Joker leaned back in the glove, leather seat and surveyed the area still in thought about losing one of his dope houses, 30 grand a week hard money he figured. It was a sizable chunk from his cash flow and he swore to himself he'd find the man responsible for the slaughter that took place inside. It had cost him considerably.

He continued to scan the half empty park, watching Blu's back as he darted in and dashed out retrieving the money from the militant but keen runners that hustled for his team. It was late in the evening approaching twilight and most of the inhabitants were already making their way out. Tompkins Square Park had its fair share of police that frequented the area but after hours it could still be very harrowing. Most would rather not chance the experience, and opted instead for the lights and eateries running up along 6th Avenue instead. Joker shook his head in contemplation, he still had money missing from his stash inside the building and the only individuals who had any inkling of where the spot was, were accounted for except for one, and that was Aziz.

It made him cower thinking about Aziz, after all these years, why would he double cross him like this? Hell, it was only just two days ago he spoke to him about making him his main man in Alphabet City. It's like someone had put a hex on him or something; maybe someone had, Joker mused, the way things were going lately.

Blu jumped back inside the car first as Chino came around the drivers side. Bezo cranked up the car, looked around cautiously then sped off.

"The take wasn't that good tonight, Joker." Blu said as he counted the dollars in his hands. Joker interrupted him, then snatched the money from him.

"Don't ever count inside my car, especially after you've collected!"

Blu's eyebrows crossed in bewilderment and semi vexation. Joker caught it and clarified the matter. "If the man was watching, and he could just as well be watching; the minute you jump in and they roll up and see you counting this much money, then what?"

"25 to 30 years in the Feds...that's what." Bezo said.

"Damn right!" Joker chimed in. "You see, you never got the time to spend with Pancho and Big E. They would have schooled you-"

"Man, Joker, man. We didn't know-" Chino started to protest.

"No-No, don't worry. It's alright. You see, the money is straight. Believe me, if it's not, when we get to the count room, we'll know where it came from and we get it right. So, don't worry."

Bezo stopped at a light and peered through the rear view mirror, "But...it never happens."

Joker snickered, "Never...especially once they see my car, they don't bullshit, but just so you know, next time okay."

Blu grinned, relieved, "*Yeah... I got it.*"

Joker gestured to Bezo, "Let's go do the count and call Miles, tell him where we're at, then call it a night. It's been a hell of a day."

MILES'S GRIND WAS RHYTHMIC and steady as he embraced his arms tightly around the woman he laid on top of. Deliberate yet forceful he moaned in ecstasy as she met him stroke for stroke. He needed every drop of satisfaction he could get. Too much went on today and he wanted to forget so he sort out solace in Mariah Santiago, his vivacious blond, Dominican look-out.

He stopped by to divulge to her that Big E and Pancho were dead and he needed her to claim their remains at the morgue. She'd front it off as the grieving mother. He told her he'd pay but she refused it, instead she took him to her bed where he broke down again.

Like a baby she pulled his head down to her plump, perked nipples and he sucked gently until she gritted her teeth in pleasure. In return she raked her nails ravishingly up the middle of his back causing his hard penis to spew clear liquid, oozing down to his balls. She lifted up her legs and wrapped them around his waist and pulled him closer. His dick so hard it was near numb as he felt the euphoria coursing through his body.

Driven he pulled up his head and dove his tongue deep into her mouth and flipped her on top of him. She rode wildly on top with her hands running through her long, golden mane and Miles braced his legs back then pushed his hard dick up into her until she couldn't take it. She cursed in Spanish at her passion, "Ay, si, si. Mas! Mas!"

Miles slowly pumped his dick in and out of her curled, sparkled lustrous pussy and she bent over him opening up her clit as she ravenously sat on it, exhaling deeply as his dick explored into her cavity searching for a home to empty the sperm that now raced to it's dripping tip. Miles stroked and she could stand no more. Ready, he swelled; she could feel it and grabbed his shaft, and squeezed and plunged one more time before he grimaced. He couldn't hold it in anymore. He let loose of the fire in his loins and his white creamed cum exploded inside of her, causing her to answer back in spasms of orgasms. "Tómelo see todo! Mi amor!" she screamed out as he laid there, paralyzed in rapture. Collapsing on top of him, she curled up into a ball onto his sprawled out drained body rubbing his chest soothingly.

There was nothing said between them. It was simple. He needed her, she needed him; a naive, uncomplicated language of love shared. He laid back with her in his arms as his mind drifted toward a peaceful slumber. Recognizing it, she caressed the back of his neck as he cooed blissfully to sleep.

"Miles! Miles! Wake up!"

Miles woke up to Mariah shaking him out his sleep, "Wha! What!-" His eyes barely open, he sprung to his feet and immediately reached for his jacket. Mariah was brushed to the side as he took out the 9mm he had, brandishing it towards the door, pointed. Mariah stepped back in fear as he flashed the gun and cowered, "No! No..."

Miles was fully awake and focused in on her, "What's the fuck is up!" he said as he lowered the gun and eased towards her, still keeping his eyes fixed on the door. She reached out grabbing his arm and pulled him towards the window overlooking the pool room. He started to turn on the light but she jerked him close towards him, "No!" She stayed low beneath the ledge and cautiously looked over; he did the same as she pointed towards a shadowy figure that paced over near the entrance of the poolroom by the alleyway. He rubbed at his eyes then squinted, "Oh shit, Aziz!"

He glanced over at Mariah and smiled then mouthed the words, "Thanks!" He had told her that he thought Aziz was responsible for the deaths of Pancho and Big E and was looking for him; he all but gave up his search by the time he got to Mariah's house, and figured on picking up the tracks tomorrow. Now, here he was right in front of him, and he needed to act fast before he disappeared. Staying low he reached over to the bed for his clothes, Mariah was already straightening them out and handing him his shoes. He slipped into the next room got dressed then eased back out, "Mariah," he whispered, "I'll see you later. I'll take you over to the morgue-" She put two fingers gently to his lips and hushed him silently then smiled, "No worry. I got it covered. Just go." He kissed her softly on the lips and headed for the door.

"Be careful...please." she said silently as the door shut. Sliding back over to the window she ducked down keeping a vigilant eye on Aziz.

Aziz paced nervously about as he thought of what he would say to Joker. He spotted his car on his way to the apartment and figured he'd stop through. He knew it was count, and he himself wasn't available, and that would be a beef with him, but why would Joker do the run and not Miles? What had happened to Miles? Suddenly he flinched, then cautiously started to turn around, "Uh, uh...don't! Ease into the alleyway, nice and slowly." Aziz hesitated then the blunted object was shoved harder into the pit of his back, "C'mon...you know the drill!" He complied, and slowly walked into the darkened narrow passageway.

"Who the fuck is this! Do you know who I am? Man, this shit'll cost you!" he protested angrily, but to deaf ears, "Shut the fuck up!"

This time he recognized the voice. "Aw...c'mon, Miles! What's up, man?" He started to put his hands down but Miles nudged him not to, "No...keep them up." He pushed him against the wall and made him bend slightly so that he could search for the gun he normally kept in his waistband. He found it then stuffed it into his jacket, searching his legs up and down he took a couple of steps back and said, "Okay...now turn around."

"Miles...what the hell is going on?" Aziz asked.

"What the hell is going on with you?" he answered back.

"What do you mean?"

Miles motioned for him to keep his hands up while he reached into his jacket pocket and pulled out the money clip. "This yours..."

Aziz looked down at it. He recognized it as a gift he'd gotten from Dante back in the day, "Yeah, it's mine. How'd you end up with it?"

"Somebody found it."

Aziz was about to reach for it when Miles pointed the gun chest high and said, "No. It's not that easy. Where were you earlier today?"

"I had to take care of business!"

"What business!"

Aziz lowered his hands, "Fuck it! If you gonna shoot, shoot! This shit is crazy. Get to the point Miles!"

"Alright then..." Miles turned slightly then recoiled with the butt of the gun connecting with Aziz's jaw. He fell to his knees spitting blood on the ground, "What the fuck!"

"Muthafucka!" Miles held the gun pointed to his skull and hollered, "Pancho and Big E are both dead! And this shit," he held the shiny, gold money clip to his face, "was found near the bodies!"

Aziz fell back against the wall, putting it all together in his mind, it clicked,, "Hold up...you think I-"

Miles struck him again, "I don't think, muthafucka! I believe so! Now...fess up!"

Aziz rubbed his throbbing jaw and looked up at Miles. The anger in his eyes made them bloodshot red. "Miles..." choosing his words carefully, he spoke lethargically, "Man, I'm sorry about your boys, man, but I ain't have nothing to do with that. You've got to believe me."

Miles stood back and looked at him then the gun. "Tell me why I shouldn't kill you, now!"

"C'mon, Miles. Why would I kill them? For what?"

Miles bent over slightly and glared in his face, "The money...that's why."

"The money? Hold up...where did they get killed?"

"The second trap house-"

"Over near the Pitt?"

"Yeah, you know where, muthafucka!" Miles held the gun up over his head ready to swing again. Aziz put up his hands, "Hold up, hold up! I wasn't no where near there-"

"Then where were you!"

Aziz couldn't tell him that he was ducking him all day putting together a plan to get at Mya, at least until he found out where she was at, but he had to say something to get up out of this, "Man, I was with Mya! If you don't believe me, then you can call her! Call her!" He threw his hand out there hoping Miles would play the card, even play a mean poker face for the whole show.

Miles pulled back a little. He couldn't tell if Aziz was telling the truth or not, but one thing he knew for sure, he didn't have anything to lose on a phone call. He reached into his pocket, "Yeah, I'll call her then." and called his bluff.

Beads of sweat permeated on Aziz's face. If he called and she picked up, he would know he was lying once he spoke to her and Miles would probably kill him or even worse, yell upstairs for Joker. He had to think, buy some time.

Miles turned slightly away from him then dialed the numbers when suddenly he was struck from the side. He fell to his knees as he tried to turn, and let off a shot, but he was walloped again and dropped this time. He was laid out. Aziz looked up at the figure that stood in front of him. He shivered a little as he waited for the pistol that was aimed at him to explode, he had no wins. He held up his hands and pleaded, "No..." Then as quickly as the shadow appeared, it vanished into the darkness of the alley. Aziz stood up and looked over at Miles to see if he was still breathing. He was, but he was groggy and started to shake it off. He didn't have time to waste, he dipped outside the alleyway to his car and sped off.

Miles got up dazed rubbing the back of his neck then looked around for his gun. He spotted it on the ground and picked it up and swirled. He didn't see no one, specifically Aziz. He staggered outside the alley and looked up at Mariah. He saw her head above the ledge. He waved and she didn't move. He jetted to the building and up the stairs to her apartment. Easing open the already cracked door he called out her name, "Mariah! Mariah!" She was still over by the window, unmoving, on her knees, still unclothed. Her hands dangled off to the side. Miles walked over cautiously. He could see the blood now trickling down from underneath a small hole behind her ear. Looking at her from the front, he could see her eyes were still open. She was dead.

He gasped and shook his head. What the fuck happened? Then he thought back to the alleyway with Aziz and instinctively he just knew some how he'd struck again. He looked around the apartment and picked up a rag and wiped down where he'd touched, then slowly with dexterity eased back out the door. He knew he'd have to call 911 but not after he'd got up with Joker for an alibi. He looked both ways discreetly as he left the building then crossed the street and slipped into the entrance way to the pool room, cursing Aziz's name under his breath.

chapter 14

DAY FOUR.

"Where're you gonna park?" Mya asked over and over as Skyler continued circling the block around 3rd Avenue, "The only place I can think of is over on the east side but that's where the United Nations building is at so-"

"Mya! Mya!"

"What?"

"Shut the Fuck up!" Skyler shouted as she pulled over into a bus stop and took out her cell phone dialing some numbers. "You think I'd drive into the city and actually look for a parking space. You must be kidding me! I know good and damn well there ain't no parking spaces in the city this time of day-" The person on the other end picked up the phone, "Yes...I'd like to speak to Mr. Pierre, please." She glanced over at Mya winked and smiled, "I got this, trust me-yes...hello, baby..."

Mya slid deep into the seat and grumped. "Whatever you doing better work."

After helping Skyler back the car up in a space at a parking lot over on 41st Street west of the Heliport, Mya waited impatiently for her to put on her makeup. "Girl, you are something else!"

Skyler gave the keys to the attendant then they were escorted over to a 4 door, black, Mercedes Benz. The driver waited patiently with the door open. "I told you I had this...didn't I." she said as she got in behind Mya and sat back in the plush leather seating.

"How did you meet him?" Mya asked.

"Oh...it's how did you meet him now? What happened to gold digging ass-?"

"Shut up...you know you're my girl." Skyler grinned as she pulled playfully at her sleeve. Skyler looked out the window as the car turned up 44th street taking them to work and said, "I'm your girl with a Benz, damn, suppose it was a beat up hoop-tee. Would I still be your girl?"

Mya thought about what she said and realized she'd touched a nerve, then playfully smirked, "No...you're right. You'd be that slut, bitch." They both laughed as the car pulled up in front of the building. The messengers were out in front in full force. Steve sat on his bike over near the front and waved Skyler over towards him; Mya was right behind her. "Everything all right?" he asked as he looked back over their shoulders at the chauffeured Benz they pulled up in, "I mean...what happened to the car?

"Parked at a friend's parking space over near the Heliport. His boss offered us a ride-"

"Hold up, hold up." Steve said. "What the fuck did I miss? His boss? I mean, Skyler...I still don't know where you got the other car.

Remember, the last time we talked you had needed a car..." he turned towards Mya. "Heliport, chauffeur...what the fuck."

Mya grinned at his candor then turned around looking up the street searching for any suspicious cars or any trace of Aziz. She was still very much paranoid and rightly so. The girls were at school, they had dropped them off, and they were being watched closely by school security after Mya explained to them her and Aziz had a fight. It wasn't difficult, especially after she showed some of the bruises he'd left, so they knew to call the police the minute he showed up. Mya figured he'd try to make a move on the girls, he was just that sick. She resolved that she'd only have to deal with it just two more days if that long, before they made a move on the pool room like they'd planned.

After seeing nothing, she made some small talk and dipped into the building on her way upstairs to the office. Once she got to her desk, Skyler picked up a note attached to her phone. "Mya...the boss's wife wants to see you."

"Look, don't worry. Just tell her what he did to you and see what happens."

"But, that's all!"

"Of course, but hey...she might help you out."

"With the robbery or what?" she slighted.

"Yeah, right." Skyler chuckled. "Something good will come out of it...believe me."

She walked with her to the conference room and opened the door. The boss's wife sat at the long, oblong table and waved her in. Mya stepped in and closed the door behind her leaving Skyler in the hall with her ear pressed against the door. Skyler hoped everything would turn out good for Mya. Maybe the boss's wife would offer her another opportunity, a better one, and then she wouldn't have to deal with the poolroom situation they'd planned. If not, she thought, it would be a bad day for somebody and she wanted to make sure that that somebody wasn't her.

THE VIGOROUS, TIRELESS school kids were tucked safely in their classes after creating havoc on the walls, halls and stairways, of the old red brick school building after the bell had rung. Remnants of paper and juvenile art work littered the halls as it quieted down to a tranquil hush. Gutter unnoticeably slipped out of one of the closets, and eased towards the stairway downstairs towards an entrance way in the back and opened the exit door.

The light poured into the dimly lit stairwell and Smack right along with it, puffing on a cigarette. "Put that out!" Gutter said, "That'll draw the heat to us!"

"What! It's only a cigarette." Smack protested.

Gutter walked over and snatched the burning amber from out his mouth and threw it out the door, "Little kids don't smoke, stupid."

"Hell...I did..." Smack said as he walked closely behind Gutter up the stairway.

They then maneuvered their way past the classroom towards the offices unsuspected; no one had paid them any mind. Gutter did make mention to Smack last night that it would be better for them to dress the part of custodians and it worked, they stirred around unnoticed. Once inside the offices, they spotted the principal's workroom and proceeded towards the door, pulling trash bags out the bins as they moved. The principal's office was located towards the rear and out front was his secretary. An older woman of 50 or so, who seemed at one time to be quite alluring in her day. Her eyes locked on to a handsome, youthful Smack and he took full advantage. After some hard earned rap, he finally convinced her to step outside to smoke a cigarette with him. It worked, as Gutter opened the door and promptly stepped inside the office. The principal sat at his desk and didn't even raise his head as he picked up the trash bin and shoved it his way. Gutter raised it up and emptied its contents on his worktop getting his attention real quick, "What the fuck!"

"Yeah...what the fuck. Now, just do what I say and no one gets hurt, ya hear."

He stood up abruptly, very indignant, "Gets hurt...do you know who I am, young man?" he shouted. Gutter smiled. "Do I."

"You can't just come in here! I'll call security-" he stepped around the desk pointing his finger at Gutter who in return, reeled back and then back handed him and said, "Don't piss me off!"

The principal staggered back feeling his face, now sore from the slap and reached for the phone, "I'm going to call the police-"

Gutter back handed him again, this time twice, getting his attention. Smack came through the door and he glanced back, "Where's the chick?" he asked.

"I gave her a couple of bills and told her to go pick up some Chinese food...said we were good friends of the principal, didn't hurt either, come to find out she shoots up," Smack grinned.

Gutter turned his concentration back to the principal, "I'm gonna make this real simple! I want the keys to the boiler room!"

"No-I can't do that!" he protested. He had to know it was a stash spot and he'd rather deal with what he was dealing with right now than Miles later, "What do you want them for!"

Gutter could tell by how agitated he was that they'd hit the jackpot. He smacked him again, "Give me the keys!" "Or I will continue this shit until later on this evening!" He smacked him two more times. The principal gave in, he could take no more, "In the desk drawer!" he hollered, quivering out his shoes then Gutter let him go and he crashed to the floor on his knees. He searched the drawers and found them, then motioned for him to get up,

"C'mon...you're going with us. And...if you make any fucked up moves," he flashed the gun in his waist, "I'll kill you. You understand." His eyes bulged open at the sight, "Yeah...yeah..." he stuttered in fear.

Smack stuck his head out the door giving Gutter the okay, they eased out with trash bags playing off small talk with the principal walking in between them. Making their way towards the back end of the school building where the boiler room was, they came across the doorway marked boilers and Gutter tried the keys. It opened easily. Once inside the dark clammy, roach infested room, they found the lights flicked them on and scouted around. They caught the outline of a small, outdated, grubby old boiler located towards the back. Overhead was the window they'd spotted from outside; small steps were built to accommodate anyone coming in or out.

Gutters' eyes traced the steps to the floor, and he could make out some vague footprints in the dust and traced them to a portal on the hull, pointing Smack towards it. A lock had been built into its sides and it appeared to be pretty clean like it had just been swept off. "Yeah...this must be it." Smack said as he inserted the silver key and it clicked open. He looked in, slowly and cautiously; sure enough, bundles of money were exposed. Gutter squinted and stuck his hand in and pulled out small stacks of fifty's and some hundreds. He looked around inside, and he could see what appeared to be a book of sorts; a black and red ledger tucked off to the side. He pulled it out, knocked off the dust and opened it, "Damn!"

Smack looked also and couldn't believe it, "Damn...this shit is deep!" All these names...councilmen, police chiefs, and right here." He pointed to a line written in red ink, "Payoffs!" They both looked over at the principal, "Shit...hell if I know. If I'd known this was here then-" he said as Gutter closed up the book and tucked it firmly under his arm.

He cheesed, they'd hit the big time. Extortion was now the name of the game, to hell with stealing; everything would be given to them on a silver platter. Gutter shoved the principal against the boiler and pointed his cocked gun to his head. "Please...I won't say anything...don't kill me." he beseechingly said.

"You damn right you won't say anything..." Gutter was about to pull the trigger when Smack stopped him, "No...we might not have to." He turned towards the principal, "When do they normally get the keys from you?"

"They have their own keys-but..." Something was strange. He pondered for a split second, "A woman. A light skinned woman...might have been black. She came in and dropped me a package...dope. I didn't think too much about it. I gave her the keys and she comes back, drops them off and she's gone, just like that. A couple of days ago."

"What was so strange about that?" Smack asked. "I'd never seen her before...then...ever."

"What did she look like again?" Gutter asked.

"Black, yeah, black girl...I really didn't get a good-"

"That wasn't the one Miles said Aziz killed last night?"

"His look out!" He glanced over at the principal. "The school teacher!"

"What-school teacher. Who?"

"Blond, Spanish...good looking..."

"No. Not here. Maybe you mean someone else." he answered.

"Hmmm. Damn, then the chick that watched the stash wasn't a school teacher. That's strange. Wonder who the hell she was."

"Hell, the way Miles carried on last night when he came in, you'd thought it was his mother or something."

"For real. Anyway-"

"Someone was killed last night?"

"Yeah...Last night.

"Killed...hmmm" the principal said, "Please, I don't know about all this."

"I'll tell you what. I'll let you live for now. Just keep this shit to yourself, ya hear!" He pointed the gun to his temple. "I promise...I will!"

Gutter turned to Smack, "You better have a good ass plan."

"I do. We still need to get all this shit out of here. We have to come back and we don't want to arouse any suspicion. "Hell," he eased Gutter back out of the principal's ear range. "We can always give him some bad dope and let that do him in. That's all he really wants anyway...understand."

The deviousness on Gutter's mind was evident on his face as he responded, "You're right...cool." He stuffed his gun back into his waist and turned, "Okay...we'll be back and bring you some real good shit."

"How do I know you're coming back?"

Gutter reached into the boiler and pulled out a bundle of fifty's and threw it at him, "Trust us." He tossed it back at him, "Just bring back the dope."

Smack smiled at Gutter and winked, "I told you so." he said as they made their way towards the stairs back up into the building.

It was already past noon and he'd done the rounds: lunch room, class inspections, stopping hyped up children on Kool-Aid from running the halls at a bat out of hell frenzied pace. Now he sat back in his office, his palms sweating and arms were itching as he waited for his package to arrive. They couldn't have been lying to him, he thought, too much was on the line. Beads of sweat popped up and seemed to dance on his forehead as he got up and paced the floor in exasperation.

He stepped over to the window and lifted it up pulling out a pack of Kool's and bent over. He was just about to light up when he heard a knock at the door, it was his secretary, "Sir...a package just arrived." she said as she stepped into the room. It was the dope. A ravenous sneer came across his face as he threw the cigarette out the window and rushed over to her. He grabbed and she jerked back, closing the door behind her, "C'mon, now...really." He looked at her peculiarly and caught his balance. He was already highly agitated and he really didn't have time for any foolishness especially hers.

"What the hell is wrong with you? You better give me that package!" he said as he walked up on her.

The secretary stepped back a little and responded, "Smack told me you're supposed to share."

That's what it was, he thought she wanted some. Hell, he didn't have a problem with that. He eyeballed the size of the package and it was more than enough, "That's all...no problem."

He peeped over her shoulder and opened the door, "We have to do it somewhere where we can be in private..." He softly closed the door and turned, catching a glimpse of her full, vivacious figure, figuring he might be able to negotiate this just right; a piece of ass wouldn't hurt right about now. "He calmly walked over to his desk, "I mean, things are alright around here, quiet. We can...maybe slip off to a hotel and...you know."

She knew where he was going and normally she would go for it, but she'd made plans already. She had Smack's number and she'd get off better with a nice young piece of meat. It's not like the principal was a bad deal in so far as her career was concerned, but good dick was always a winner and hard to come by at her age. She put the package on the table and bent over so that he could see her titties as they juggled in his face giving him something to work with later. He smiled as his dick started to rise up, she reached out with her long, manicured nails and caressed the side of his face causing him to tingle. He needed a hit now, "Some other time. I've got something to do." She stood up, "Just give me my cut-"

"Your cut!"

"Yes...my cut." She reached for the phone, "Not unless there's a problem. I mean...we can call Smack-"

"No-No." he said as he slid her hand away, "That won't be necessary. Of course...your cut." He opened the pack and in a small, match box sized package, was 10 small quarters of heroin. He opened one up and dipped his pinky finger in and tasted it. "Damn...yeah...this is it..." he squirmed. He gave her five and she stuffed them in her bra and turned to walk out the door. He called out, "Sure you don't want to change your mind."

She turned and adjusted her cleavage and hair giving him a full view and turned, then glanced back, "I'm sure."

He locked up his desk got up and grabbed his coat. He turned the light off and rushed out the door, his secretary still there sitting at the desk on the phone. She waved him on, "Don't be late for your meeting sir." playing it off for the other employees to see and hear.

"Uh...yeah...I'm on my way now." he said as he made his way out the door. His secretary was still on the phone as he left, talking to Smack, "Yeah, baby...he just left out."

"Cool...he took the dope, right."

"He's on his way to shoot up, now. So, uh, will I see you later on?"

Smack paused as he thought, but not too long, after all, she seemed like a good piece of ass, "Yeah, we can do that. Find a hotel-"

"I got one in mind already."

Call me after you get off then...cool."

"No problem. Bye, baby."

Smack hung up the phone and glanced over at Gutter, "Okay...it's a go. He got the dope."

"Good. He should be dead by this evening."

"Hell yeah...that much bad shit should fuck him up quickly-"

"And quietly."

The principal's secretary stepped into the restroom and took out the packages she'd stuffed and opened one up, "Damn, this shit sure looks good." She turned and looked under the stalls to make sure she was alone," Maybe I should-"

The door opened suddenly, startling her, she poured the powder down the sink, turned on the faucet, flushing the heroin and frowning as she watched it's toasted sepia, chalky hue rinse into the sewer. She shook her head side to side and thought about it, oh well, I still got four more packs. I'll wait until I get with Smack to do the rest of it. She adjusted her makeup in the mirror as she primped. Hell, if I put it on him just right I won't have to worry about shit like this anyway. She checked herself, turned and strutted out of the bathroom.

A toilet flushed behind her as the door shut. The figure that had come in stepped out on the sly, out of the stall, and with a sneer, stalked her back outside the bathroom until she sat at her desk. Spying over her head and noticing the principal wasn't at his desk, and the office darkened; she laughed with a raspy cough. The mysterious shape disappeared into the lack luster, obscure dimness down the stairway into the awaiting basement.

Aziz didn't really want to be there but the call sounded too important, urgent. He was awakened by a phone call; the principal babbling something about a stash spot, getting slapped. Only after he'd finished whining, did he realize it wasn't Miles he was speaking with. Haphazardly he told Aziz about what had happened. He didn't know names but went into detail about the stash that was found in the basement as well as the ledger.

Aziz had searched the car as well as his apartment and didn't find it; the ledger was his. Trying to figure out who took it immediately led him to blame Mya thinking she had planted it there. 'Just how?' He rationalized in his wayward thinking that he would figure it out along the way. The boiler would provide him the clues. He wasted no time getting to the school.

Now here he was sneaking into the building. No one had seemed to notice as he crept towards the stairway marked basement and slinked down the steps. The door was half way ajar. Remembering last night's exchange with Miles made him creep slowly towards the door with his hand on his gun. Looking around every turn he planted his steps firmly as to not arouse anyone he came up on. Ducking behind a corner, he quickly snuck in, and then sighed as his body relaxed once he saw the principal sprawled out on the floor. He eyeballed the surroundings before stepping to him and it seemed safe enough. He kneeled over. The principal still had the syringe in his hands as Aziz picked up his head, his eyes dilated. Aziz smacked him and as he did his mouth spewed out some white froth and he coughed up blood then looked up at Aziz and said, "This shit is no good..." and clutched at his shirt.

Aziz looked at the package on the floor that was torn open and its contents emptied. It belonged to Joker, but the color inside was off, it had been tainted. He tasted the residue then spit it out. It was rat poison. The principal had shot poison into his blood.

"How long have you been here!"

He could barely breathe as he looked up at Aziz trying to respond, "They...was...supposed to bring...me...good shit..."

"They! They who!" Aziz picked his head up trying to get him to breathe and to tell him who was responsible for this, "C'mon, man...talk!"

It was too late as his eyeballs started to flutter and roll back in his head. Aziz laid him back down on the dirty grubby floor, and was about to get up when he noticed the other bags in his shirt pocket. He pulled them out and it was more of Joker's dope. Aziz couldn't make heads or tails of it, Joker's dope was checked before it hit the street. There was no way it would be tainted. No one in his organization would even think much less try it.

He held the bag to a ray of light coming into the room through the small windows and noticed that it had been tampered with, re-taped. Someone had opened the bag and put the poison in. He turned towards the principal who still tried to grasp at the needle as his body had a spasm; crazily enough he still wanted to get high. Aziz shook his head as he watched, it was pathetic. Whoever did this to him knew exactly what they were doing. It couldn't have been Miles he thought. He was trying to call him, but still, the ledger. He scooted back down towards the principal and grabbed him by the collar, "Where's the book!"

"B-b-book...what...b-b-b-book..."

"The ledger! The one you said you found!" Aziz grabbed the needle from him and threw it away. It took every bone in his now ebbing muscles, the strength oozing out of him slowly, but he actually tried crawling towards it. Aziz jerked him back, took out his gun and pointed it to his head, "Tell me where it is or I'll kill you!"

He looked at Aziz as the breath started to ease out of his dying body, twitching and convulsing as the deadly poison made its way to his heart. It was just a matter of time. "I'm already dead..." He tried in vain to grab at the needle.

Aziz knew it was a losing cause and let him go. He got up and walked over to it and kicked it back. The principal grabbed it with every bit of power he could muster. He wrapped his exposed arm and filled the dropper, ready to prick his vein again. He glanced at his suit, filthy from crawling all over the floor, his black, leather shoes scuffed, the silk tie he wore was the tourniquet he used on his arm, he tried to dust himself off. "I got to make it back to work..." Aziz watched over him, he waited, "There was two of them... "He said as he jammed the needle into one of the mangled veins in his arms. He jerked, then yelled and started raving from the mouth like he'd just been possessed. The poison had finished its run, his heart was about to burst as Aziz could only watch in horror. The needle broke in his arm as he convulsed and blood squirted onto the floor. The principal grimaced in pain, sobbing, he cried as he yelled out what would be his last words, "They said...it...would be...good shit..." then his chest imploded and he collapsed.

Aziz rolled his body over on its side as he made his way to the boiler. The door was still open and he spotted footprints on the outside of the boiler's hull. Two different types of boots. There was two different people here with him. He opened the small portal door and looked in. The money was still there. He didn't know anything about this stash. It was kept secret from him but from seeing the size of the money, it had to be Joker's. He reached in and grabbed a couple of bundles and stuffed them in his pocket for good measure. He knew he would need them if his plan was to come together. He'd have to rent a car, pick up Peaches and come back and get the rest. He'd have to take out Mya, she probably had the ledger, even though it didn't make sense to him, but now he didn't care. He grabbed the money and closed the door. He glanced down at the now dead body and stepped over it then backed away towards the door eyeballing the small windows above him. He didn't have keys, so he knew he had to come back today while the school was still open. It was still early and he had some time. He eased back out the door when suddenly he was snuffed from behind.

His mind spiraled as he spun to the ground. A sharp pain on the back of his neck made him grit his teeth as he hit the floor face first. He tried to look up even though the pain made it difficult, and his mind started going blank rapidly, but his hearing was still intact. The words were dreamy, fading away as he strained to pay attention, "Is he dead?"

"Naw...just out cold." Gutter said as he reached into his jacket and pulled back out the money, "He a fuckin' thief." Smack spit on him and smirked, "Yeah, wait until Miles hears about this."

"For real..." Gutter said off handily as they stepped over his unconscious body towards the boiler with a large duffle bag and started to take the rest of the money out.

Once they'd finished, Gutter took out his phone, then paused. He looked down at Aziz's phone and grabbed it, "I'ma call Miles."

"Naw..." Smack grabbed his arm, "Just dial the numbers."

"Why?"

"His caller ID will flash Aziz, and he'll probably want to track his ass down. Let G-P-S do the rest."

"Then when he comes here and sees this shit. Okay, I see now...a perfect fuckin' set up."

"Come on, man. I gotta hot date." Smack said as he stuffed the money in the bag.

"Damn...you seriously gonna fuck that old broad?"

Smack kicked Aziz's body closer to the boiler and Gutter threw the keys to the ground then they eased back towards the door retracing their steps out the boiler room and Smack happened to glance over at a six foot standing fan in the back, "Hold up...this'll work." He pulled it over and pointed it towards the bodies and looked around for a socket, "Over there..." Gutter said as Smack plugged it in.

Dust blew all over the place erasing all traces of the boots and handprints. They backed out and closed the door then snuck up the stairs outside, unseen.

chapter 15

MILES'S HEAD HUNG DOWN low to his knees in a somber reflective, mood as he thought about the cards he'd been dealt lately. Joker could only watch in unspoken, commiseration as no words were exchanged between them.

It had been a taxing night for the both of them. Joker had made the pick ups and helped count money at the pool room which put him in an ambivalent position to confide in Chino, and stash the money revealing to him where one of his spots were. It didn't matter he figured, at this stage of the game, he was getting out anyway. Tired of it all, the running, the scheming and conniving had all taken its toll on the now graying, late thirties hustler. He'd made money and then some. It was time to retire, get a place in Florida. He had everything set in motion: Gustavo. His ambition to sell him the business was enthusiastic but the way things were happening lately he questioned if he was even interested anymore. He sighed loudly to himself and as he did, Miles picked his head up and asked, "Is everything alright?"

Joker smiled, "I should be asking you that question."

They'd made it into the Pitt early that morning after a gloomy, nonchalant night considering the event that had taken place with Aziz.

"I'm a'iyht."

Joker repositioned himself in his chair and leaned forward on his desk. He felt for Miles, it was a hard blow for him. He had lost the people closest to him. Miles's world was for the most part private, he kept to himself but those he did let in, he was faithful to. He had started to let Aziz in. Even after all the years they'd held down Alphabet city together, it was only now did he really start to confide in him, but he'd fucked that up. Joker wondered if he even trusted him, "You don't seem okay. Maybe you'd better go to the house. Get yourself together-"

"I said, I'm alright!" Miles said irritably, more from lack of rest than anything else.

"Are you going by the hospital then?"

Miles rubbed his fingers through the curls of his hair feeling the bump on the base of his skull, "If I have the time."

"Well, you might want to think about it." Changing directions Joker added, "You might also want to consider having the bodies cremated."

"I thought so, too."

"I mean...not that money is an issue, but it's relatively cheap. I don't mean to sound..." Joker trailed his words off, not wanting to sound too insensitive. Miles nodded his head, he knew he didn't mean anything, but was just trying to be helpful in a bad situation "Huh...maybe spread the ashes over the river or something." Miles smirked.

"That's a thought." Joker mused, "Wouldn't do nothing but make their way back here anyway."

"For real." They both shared a laugh, then it was all too quiet again until Joker broke the ice, "Now, uh...the girl? What are we going to do about that?"

Miles straightened up in his chair, it was a very serious, tense situation. If the wrong things were said, the wrong witness statements; he could very well be implicated for murder. He had asked Joker last night if he could be his alibi. He obliged with no hesitation, "Well...stick to the plan. I was with you all last night and we hung out at the pool room later on...right."

"Damn right! Don't know anything else." Joker leaned back in his chair and swiveled around looking out the window, "Well you can expect the cops to come calling, so just be prepared okay."

"I'll be clean."

"Yeah, and don't do no pickups with Chino and Blu until after this blows over. Did the girl have any family?" he asked as he reached for a cigar.

Miles got up stretching his legs and walked over to the window and looked out also, "She had some people in Brooklyn. She was from Panama-"

"Panamanian...yeah, some of my people!" Joker exclaimed as he lit the big boy, Cuban blunt up.

"I didn't know you were from South America."

"My mother...she came to New York and met the old man here. He was from Harlem. Oh yeah...I gotta a little Spanish blood in me."

"Maybe that's why you are a...Toro." Miles laughed. Joker grinned back at him, "yeah...I am a...bull at times, I guess." He blew the smoke off into the ceiling. "One day after I kick this to the curb...I change, huh."

Miles headed towards the door after putting on his coat, "Maybe..."

"Hey...where are you going?"

"Well, you said I needed to be low profile for a minute, right."

"Yeah...I mean you can hang out with me for a while. We can go eat lunch. Get dinner. You know, get to know each other."

"Oh, I see...you mean like bond."

Joker leaned forward, "Yeah...that's it...bond..." He pulled the cigar from his mouth and a long grin appeared.

Miles cocked his head ever so slightly. He couldn't believe where Joker was going with this bullshit. He wasn't trying to feel none of it, "Naw...I don't do the bond thing." he said dryly. "I'm gonna swing into Brooklyn and see if I can find some of her people. Somewhere in East Flatbush, I think. Catch you later." He opened the door and Joker called out, "Hey Miles!"

"Wassup!"

"I mean...if you didn't have anything to do, would you have..."

Miles smiled and cut him off "Yeah...sure. Who knows Joker...maybe..." then left out. Joker watched closely as he walked to his truck, cranked up and pulled off up the street, and then he closed the curtains and turned back around throwing his feet up on the desk. It was time, he thought, the game was losing its luster, it's shine. He didn't have any friends, no seed, at least none he knew of. The only so called friend he had was Bezo, and it was more of an arrangement than anything; but still, he had to make the best of what he had. "Bezo!" Bezo stuck his head in, "Yeah, boss. Any trouble?" he gestured as he rushed into the room.

"No, Bezo...no trouble. I was just thinking, maybe we can go uptown and get some of that soul food stuff you like, huh...Sylvia 's."

Bezo's eyes frowned as they narrowed to a slit rubbing his chin thinking where Joker was going with this, "Just...me and you, huh?" It was out of character for him.

"Yeah...me and you. Get a bite to eat-"

"Boss!" Bezo walked closer remembering the times when Joker did put on a friendly facade, "I no take no money! I don't do nothing wrong! I swear! You now have to kill me!" he started to cop deuces.

"Bezo!"

"Yes...Yes..."

Joker's smile went south into a frown as he plopped back into his chair and flipped him off, "Just go, Bezo...just go..."

"You sure-"

"Bezo! Just go!" Bezo backed up out the door and as he closed it shut, Joker couldn't help but feel the pain from the incident that just took place. It was as obvious as the nose on the face. He had no friends and no one in their right mind even wanted to be his acquaintance. He was all alone. Raising his eyebrows and grinning, it finally dawned on him now, he could see why Miles was the way he was, and had the utmost respect for his younger consort and he mumbled to himself, "I ain't mad at him..." then blew smoke on the window fogging it up, dimming his view of the street and slipped back into a quiet repose.

Miles turned the corner on Avenue C and stomped the pedal hard in the SUV as he headed down towards Houston Street. He glided to a light and leaned, turning up the volume on the radio. Glancing into the console pocket, he noticed his phone buzzed intermittently; someone was trying to call him. Wondering who it was he picked up the phone and hit voicemail; Aziz's name appeared first on the screen, "What the hell could he possibly want!" The light turned green and a few cars behind honked to get his attention. He was already on the ramp way going on the FDR and he couldn't turn around now. Tossing the phone on the seat next to him, he made a mental note to get with it later. Right now he had to handle the business at hand, and the next time he dealt with Aziz he'd have all the time in the world, and it would be on his own terms. He raced up the incline into traffic and browsed over to his right at the phone, "Oh yeah...I'll see you soon enough..." he said as he rubbed the back of his head where the bump he'd picked up from last night's encounter sorely ached. "This time I'll return the favor."

Gutter and Smack chilled out underneath the overpass going to the basketball courts near the Pitt when they spotted Miles jumped in his truck and take off. They smiled at each other, hoping that he'd taken the bait, then watched the car as it headed towards the corner, but turned right going across town away from the school.

It didn't make sense. If he was going by the school to get Aziz, he would have had to have taken a left turn. Any other way would make him go all the way around Alphabet City taking too much time. Something was up or either, wrong.

"Yo, Gutter...you think he's going around..."

"Naw, it would be pointless..."

"What do you want to do, then?"

"Well," Gutter got up from off the bench looking over at the window of the rec building noticing the curtains were half opened suspecting that they were being watched, "We might want to go investigate. Make sure Aziz is still there."

Smack got up towards the street, "I can get us a ride." "Yeah...that'll work. Let's make it on over to the school, huh." Smack waved at a junkie that sat on the stoops of an abandoned building and he came over to them. He recognized him as a neighborhood runner from back in the day. He was good for rides and look-outs, and kept his car clean, his head level, but he had a monkey for the love of sniffing dugee. "Yo, I need a ride cross town." Smack said.

"No problem. I'm parked right up the block."

"Cool," Smack waved at Gutter who still eyeballed the window, "c'mon man, let's go!" he hollered as he turned towards the junkie reaching into his pocket, but he stopped him.

Suffering from paranoid delusions at times, he looked around over his shoulder and said, "No...not here. I'll get it later." "Alright."

Smack said as he followed him up the street with Gutter right behind them, then turned back around suddenly running back to the benches they'd sat on picking up the duffle bag from earlier, "Damn...almost forgot!"

Joker leaned forward in his chair watching as Gutter and Smack followed the dope fiend to his car "Hmmm. I wonder what the hell those two are up to?" he pondered as he checked his watch, "I know they on some shit! I'll ask tonight when I see them." He lifted his big body up reaching for the curtains then stopped short and plopped back down in his chair, then snickered, devilishly and yelled out, "Bezo!"

"Yes, boss!"

"How 'bout closing these curtains for me!"

Smack got out the car first with his hands in his pants pocket pulling out two clips of dugee and handed it over to the driver and dapped him, "Good looking"

He held the dugee up to the light and asked, "Is this that good shit?"

Smack stopped dead in his tracks and spun around and leaned back into the car and grabbed the bag then held it up, "No!" Remembering the bad dope they'd given the principal he reached for the other one and the driver snatched it back, "Naw...this is that good shit! It's mine!" Smack was about to explain but Gutter stopped him, "Man...just give it to him."

Smack didn't object as he tossed the bag back into the car and hunched his shoulders. The driver nodded and was about to take off then said, "I knew it was that good shit! I'll be back later...bring customers...hook me up!" and sped off.

Gutter just smirked as he took off and Smack mean mugged him, "What! He wanted it!' he said as he put his hands up.

Everything seemed to be all intact as they made their way over but no Miles and no signs of his truck. They figured they'd wait, he might be on the way. They hung out across the street at the Chinese restaurant then after a good hour, bag of wings and two egg rolls, and no trace of Miles; they figured they should at least check the spot to make sure everything was still good, thinking maybe the cell phone lost reception or went dead.

On the way downstairs they heard sounds from inside the boiler room. They opened the door and looked in warily. The principal's body had been moved. He was now propped over by the door of the old boiler.

Rushing in they saw no one. Gutter looked around and saw Aziz's body was gone also. The next thing he knew the door slammed shut behind them, and he whirled around and was suddenly met with a crushing blow in between his eyes.

Gutter reeled back in agony; stars and flashes of bright psychedelic light, was all he saw as the warm wet fluid gushed from his now twisted nose. He was bleeding heavily.

As he tried to gather his senses he was met yet again by another blow, this time to his mouth. The pain was all too much to bear this time as he spit out teeth, his knees buckled and he fell to the floor. He tried steadying himself up with his hands and at the same time blinked rapidly, trying to keep the blood from clotting in his eyes and distorting his view. Catching a glint of light he looked up at the shadow as it crossed in front of him and vanished into obscurity. All he heard next was Smack hollering out his name, "Gutter! Gutter!" He put out his hand trying to feel for anything around him to help lift him up, he was confused, lethargic and his face throbbed as he regained some of the sight in his right eye. Smack stood in front of him, bending over trying to prop him up, asking him if he was alright, but it was too late to warn him of the impending danger that lurked closely behind.

Gutter put up his hand to warn him in vain as Smack's skull split open as the aluminum bat came crashing down upon him. His eyes curled up in his head as he fell down on top of Gutter. Gutter scanned around the room again and the figure scurried once more into the darkness of the room and he saw no one. With all he had, he mustered enough strength to climb to his feet and back up against the wall. His eyes darted around looking for the next attack, as pangs of pain shot throughout his body.

He caught the sun from outside peeling into the window and the shadows of people moving about. He figured he could make a mad dash for the window, bust it and get somebody to call the police, or some help. To hell with the money, he'd explain that shit later, right now it was life or death, and neither him nor Smack were dead, yet.

He wasn't sure who this person was, might have even been Aziz he thought, so he put it out there, "Aziz...I know it's you! Look! We can split the money! Don't be a fool and try something stupid!" he yelled out into the abyss. No response.

Fuck it, he might as well make a break to the window. He glanced down at Smack and his body continued to convulse, his eyes managed to peer over at Gutter and he mouthed the words, "Help...me..." Gutter knew he had to do something quick, Smack was his partner and he needed help, now.

He wiped the blood out of his eyes with his shirt, collected himself, took a deep breath and ran for the steps leading up to the window. He made it. Looking out he saw school kids in the park. It must have been recess. He banged frantically on the window and caught the attention of one. A bright eyed young boy cautiously came towards him.

"Yo, kid!" he screamed out, "Get help! You understand! Get help!"

The small child looked curiously at Gutter then gazed past him. Gutter didn't understand his actions at first then it came to him; he turned quickly as the bat came crashing down on his shoulder. It was excruciating and overcame him but he spun back around at the window and banged, furiously, "Help! Help!" The bat this time met the mark it was aiming for-the top of his cranium, repeatedly, until it was just soft, pulpy tissue instead of bone.

The little child backed up in horror and stared until Gutter's lifeless body was drug down into the black, dim room and then frightened, he ran off.

Smack tried in a pointless attempt to gain control of his muscles as the murderous figure skulked over him wiping down the blood off the barrel of the aluminum bat. The duffel bag was picked up and tossed to the side by the door. Smack finally managed to move his body voluntarily and tried to lift himself up. The figure calmly, meticulously, stepped softly over to Smack as he struggled trying to get up.

Smack tried to defend the blows with his arm but it was effortless and of no avail as the figure lifted the bat up high and came crashing down. He laid on the ground, sprawled out, groaning, his arm broken in two and as the bat was lifted up high again, he closed his eyes. Repeatedly and repeatedly the bat whistled and echoed in the air until all that was left was a bloody mass of mangled skin and brain matter that oozed from the broken particles of bone sticking out his neck.

The figure took a neatly folded, black, plastic jumpsuit from out of the corner and donned it. On the back it read, 'Ray's Exterminators' and walked out carrying a duffel bag and a container of bug spray. The bag was opened and the ledger stuck out, but was jammed back in along with the bundles of money and zipped closed.

By the time the mysterious killer made it up the stairs, the same little child from earlier came running in with a school teacher in tow, pointing to the stairs leading to the boiler room, nearly running the now cloaked figure over, "Excuse me! Is the boiler room open downstairs?" she asked.

Dawdling, the figure turned and gaped at the child then responded to the teacher's question and answered, "No...well, at least it was. I had to exterminate some...uh, bugs. It's closed now."

The teacher looked at the canister and the uniform and turned towards the little boy, "You see...it was nothing except the exterminator, that's all."

The child peeped up at the figure remembering Gutter's face that was shoved against the window and shuddered, even more so when the figure glared in his eyes, "Y-y-yes mam. Can we go now..." The teacher jerked him by the arm and scolded him all the way down the hall only after what seemed to be a hundred apologies offered to the figure in black.

The duffel bag was laboriously touted as the door opened up. The canister was dropped by the dumpster, and the door to the school slammed shut. Outside, the figure took off the rubber boots and kicked them by the trash bin, and dipped into the street unnoticed. The only traces left were the bloody footprints glistening through the hallway. Down the stairs from the boiler room, were the voices of little children patiently waiting for the bell to ring, to change classes. One child remained stunned from a gory scene that would forever stay fixed in his mind; sending chills up his spine, every time he saw crimson red, in his nightmares.

THE PHONE CALL CAUGHT Gustavo stepping out the shower; recognizing the numbers he immediately picked up. "Yeah, wassup!"

"You tell me." It was Joker's former associate and nemesis, Akbar. "Still working on it..."

"Working on it! You should be finished with it by now!" He was the so called Miami, Florida associate and contact doing business from a 9 x 12 lock up behind the wall in a Federal pen using a jack.

"Things came up-"

"Things? Fuck that, Gustavo!"

"Like I said, some things have come up."

"Those things need to be taken care of, quickly!" Gustavo had been contacted by Akbar to seek revenge on Joker. He'd schemed up a disingenuous, double crossing plan that would come in the guise of a ploy to buy out Alphabet City.

"I'll present it to him...probably by tomorrow. It will be done."

"That sounds about right."

"You'll be able to make parole or what?" Akbar had made a side deal with the Feds and rolled over on some key players in Harlem that had set him up. As part of his snitch, he was given early parole instead of the rest of the 20 years he was facing. He disclosed this to no one else as per the United States D-A's office: a political favor called in by a dope addicted politician.

"I should be out this week. Make sure everything's wrapped up in a nice, little bow for me, huh."

"It will be. Hey, uh, have you ever heard of a pusher by the name of Aziz?"

Becoming uncomfortable after pondering long and hard, Akbar said, "Doesn't ring a bell right now. Must be Joker's people, but if he's a problem, kill him. I got you covered."

"That's okay."

Akbar giggled under his breath, "He must be that something that came up, huh."

"You can say that."

"Okay, we can take him out and anyone else that gets in the way because when I hit the bricks I don't want no problems or any other names mentioned on the streets...except mine." he sneered.

"Things have changed-"

"Wha-What do you mean! I'm still the man!"

"Yeah, yeah...whatever. Hey, uh...call me back later on tonight, if you can."

"I can do that. I need to touch base with some people in Harlem, anyway."

"Harlem? You want me to handle something for you? I can-"

"Naw. This is personal. I need to find a plot."

"A plot. A burial plot?"

"Yeah...for that cheating bitch, Keisha that left me for Joker's pussy ass!" Akbar's laughter echoed behind him in the cell bloc as Gustavo snickered and shook his head, "Alright...later."

"Later."

Gustavo finished wiping off and caught a glimpse of himself in the full view mirror. At six foot two, he had a well-built shape. His lean, long arms were muscular, strong and his body revealed no marks at all except one, and it read, *'a maximus ad minimum'*. A brand given to an exclusive, secret society of made men, Akbar included. He kept it cloaked from Joker, fearing his cover would be compromised because he also had the same tattoo.

Fully dressed he sat down to drink some coffee in the small, laid out flat he rented off of Houston Street overlooking the Williamsburg Bridge. He thought about his plan, his time frame. He needed to be swift so that he could secure Alphabet City for his own. He only had a couple of days if that and he needed to work on it fast.

He got up and walked over to a silver, briefcase; inside sunk deeply in black, padded foam were guns: a 40 cal.; two 44 mags; and two 9mm automatic's with silencers and sight tracers. He reached for the 40 cal. and stuffed it in his shoulder holster then slipped on the fine woven, linen, jacket he had hanging concealing the bulge. He closed the case and slipped it back under the bed before scanning and checking the place out making sure it was secure before leaving. He glanced over at the mirror and pulled down the brim of his fedora over his eyes then breezed out the door. Outside while he waited for a cab, he took out his cell phone and dialed Peach's number; Aziz would be first on his to do list.

SKYLER, MYA AND STEVE all sat in the break room together at lunch putting the final touches on their scheme. Skyler figured for a Friday night, but it was shot down quickly. Friday had too much traffic going on in the pool room and also on the surrounding streets; too much was bound to go wrong. Wednesday was still the best they could come up with, but Mya wanted that to change and now Skyler was questioning her motives.

"Why, Mya, why tomorrow night!"

Mya sat in an armchair sipping on some hot coffee with her eyes perplexed from the line of questioning Skyler was drilling her with, "It doesn't make sense," she turned and looked at Steve, "right!"

Steve sighed and turned towards Mya and tried rationalizing, "She does have a point, Mya. Why are you changing now?"

Mya calmly put the coffee mug down and looked around making sure that the small room was indeed empty and that no one was on the way in and then spoke softly, bluntly, "Look. I know for a fact that Tuesdays are good money days. All of the dope spots are picked up from, and so all the money is there at one time. Joker is also there, he looks through the books to make sure the money's straight."

"Okay...and..."

"And..." she rolled her eyes at Skyler, "the place is usually empty. Just the money counters, and whatever pusher, Aziz or Miles, did the pick ups and all of them will be in the back."

"How do you know this?" Steve asked.

"Trust me, Steve...me and Aziz didn't always fight."

Skyler got up opening the refrigerator door, "Humph...hellava pillow talk. I'm surprised you were able to talk. He kept his dick-"

Mya jumped up with her fists balled up, "Fuck you, Mya! You got something you wanna say!"

Skyler slammed the door to the sound of the ringing of bottles falling over inside, "Yeah! Still, I don't see why you want to change shit up now!" she beckoned to Steve, "We have a man inside who agrees on this same thing!"

"Yeah...you're right..." Steve said not wanting to get in between this ensuing cat-fight . "But hear her out...at least."

Skyler sucked her teeth and stomped over to the coffee machine pouring some into her cup, "Okay...I'm listening. It better be good, too."

Mya shook her head and sat back down in her seat, "Like I was saying. The bar is also stocked that night. Tempest buys all her liquor and replenishes her safe for the week. So, there's lots more money."

"How do we get the drop on them?" Skyler asked, much more calmly now. She realized that Mya was right all along and what she said made sense.

Steve interjected, "We roll, hell, Gutter won't make a move-or his partner, because they know what's up, so we go for them first. Force Joker to hold his hand, then tie them up...make it look real good...dip out the back way."

"I feel you, but what about up front-"

"Shit. That's easy." Skyler added, "Once we smack up that bitch Tempest, that'll put the tim on whoever else is in there."

"They don't have any buzzer's or shit?" Mya asked.

"From what I know from Gutter...no. We just roll and do what you just said, Tuesday does sound good."

"Yeah...I'll admit that." Skyler said, "But, Steve, you heard anything from Gutter?"

"Naw..." He pulled out his phone and checked his messages, "Not yet. I'm sure he'll be in touch."

Mya stood up. "If not...we roll anyway!"

Skyler pushed back from the table spitting coffee and shrieked, "What!"

"I said we roll with or without him!"

Steve checked his watch, "We'll see. Look, I gots to get going. I got work to do." He got up and walked out leaving Mya and Skyler behind. It was quiet and somber then Skyler broke the icy mood between them. "Mya, look. I'm sorry I'm so jumpy, but I am a little nervous. But, why the push? I mean, does it have something to do with the boss's wife?"

Mya crossed her legs and took another swig of the coffee and responded, "It does. She wants me to press charges against Aziz or she's gonna fire me."

"Fire you! Fuck it, after tomorrow you can quit!"

"I can. But I didn't want to bring any more attention to myself than I already have or put any more pressure on the kids." She put the mug down to the side and leaned on the table towards Mya and whispered softly, "I want to leave. Leave New York and go somewhere where the kids and I can be safe and comfortable."

"Leave...leave New York...me..." Skyler stammered.

"You can come with us, Skyler. There's nothing here for you."

Skyler stood up, "Girl...leave New York, me! Naw, this is home, born and raised." she turned to walk out the door, "Besides all these guys in the city with money and then I got money, too. The game's changed now. I can mingle with real wealth; find a real financially stable, cash cow, oops...I mean, man. Who knows...even settle down and make a baby."

"I hear you. Maybe a child will slow your hot ass down." Mya cooed.

"Then the real money can start coming in, child support! You know what I mean!" She snapped her fingers and strutted off leaving Mya by herself, but when she got to her office and sat down thinking to herself what Mya had just said, it made her jealous. Why should she want to live happily ever after? Why does she want to be better than everyone? She figured she was the one who really deserved a man like Aziz anyway then they wouldn't be going through this shit.

Opening up her desk drawer she glanced around and found an address written on yellow, sticky paper, *'Monte's Costumes'*. She was the one assigned to find masks and figured she'd leave work early and do just that. She watched as Mya whisked back to her desk sulking and inwardly she despised her. She planned on telling Steve that she could easily be a casualty that night if need be; then her and Steve could have more money and the whole thing would be blamed on her. As she waved her way, she sneered between gritted teeth, a phony smile on her face, "Everything's gonna be alright, sweetie."

PEACHES PICKED UP THE phone after the first ring thinking it to be Nutt.-Nutt, but instead it was Gustavo. A frown washed over his face as he wished he would have checked the caller-Id first, he never would have answered.

He didn't have the answers to all his questions and he still wasn't too comfortable with the plan Gustavo had devised for Aziz. Killing him didn't sit well with the man he'd fell in love with.

Thinking, maybe he'd come out of the closet, even dreamed of the moment; playing it out well into his own mind. Help come clean with Gustavo and then they could be happy with each other in New Hampshire, California perhaps; but first he'd have to deal with-"Hello! Hello! Peaches...is that you!" Gustavo and his foolishness.

"It's me, dear."

"What! Dear! I'm not no freakin' punk! You understand! Don't ever-"

"Yes, yes...Gustavo. What is it?"

"That's better. You heard from Aziz yet or what?"

"No...I haven't, but I told you if I did-"

"Yeah, yeah, yeah. Look, I thought you'd at least look for him. Don't you have a number or something?"

Peaches had grown tired of his line of questioning, his nerves were pressed, "Gustavo! When I hear from him! I'll give you a call!"

"Don't you talk-"

"You heard what I said and that's that."

There was a long, awkward pause between them. Peaches had decided that if Gustavo pushed it then he'd hang up the phone, but instead he conceded, "Alright...I understand. It's just been a little, uh...tight lately."

"Why don't you go somewhere and relax. Things will work out. Be patient."

Peaches was right. He was uptight and needed to go somewhere and get a break. Clothes shopping or just walk around the city and enjoy the sights. It all sounded good, possibly book reservations at a play. He smiled and nodded his head. "Okay...talk to you later."

Before he made any moves, he'd have to check his itinerary; at least, he dialed some numbers on his phone. "Joker. What's up?"

"Uh...nothing. Been busy last night and I'm still tired from it."

"What happened now?"

"I had to help do pick ups and a count."

"Why...don't you have people in place for that?"

"Yeah... but shit's come up."

Gustavo thought about his anticipated scheduled evening then sighed, "Where are you at anyway?"

"The Pitt...over on 3rd Street. The gym-"

"Okay...I know the place. I'll see you in a few."

"Cool."

Gustavo stuffed the phone back into his jacket, cut if off then stepped into the street waving down a cab. Sightseeing would have to wait until another time, business was first and foremost for him in this line of work. *'No rest for the weary'* his father used to say.

chapter 16

"ALL THIS HAS HAPPENED in just two days? Damn!"

Joker hung his head down as Gustavo stood over him, then paced the floor rubbing his chin in speculation trying to digest all he'd just heard, "Where's Miles now?"

"He drove into Brooklyn trying to locate the girl's family."

Gustavo stopped in his tracks and spun around, "Why! Hell, he's damn near a suspect! Why would he want to bring heat to himself like that?

"Well, uh, we just thought..." Joker stammered. Gustavo shook his head, "Call him back! There's nothing he can do for her now...except to find the killer."

"Aziz."

"Well, Joker...do we really don't know that for sure?" Joker raised his head up, he was heated, "It has to be him! He was the one who hit Miles that night!"

"From what you told me, Miles had the drop on Aziz and was struck from behind. That being the case, how could he have done it?"

"Well...maybe..." Joker said as he stood up and turned towards the window. "Hell, that's what he told me!" He turned back around and reached into his desk opening up his humidor and pulled out a cigar, "You want one?" Gustavo reached for it then sat, "I mean, hell, he was bruised up pretty good and...well, he, uh...I don't know what the fuck is going on here!" Joker plopped back down in his chair and kicked his feet up on the desk.

Gustavo leaned back and lit up his cigar, "There's a whole lot going on here, Joker. Too much drama for my people."

Joker pulled his feet down and leaned forward, "It's just one of those things, ya know. Doesn't happen all the time! I mean...the money's here!"

"That may be the case, but it doesn't seem like you have a good grasp on things." He blew a long thick cloud of smoke into the air, "Cleaning this mess up will cost quite a bit. Don't know if it's really worth it."

"I can clean this up myself. Make it all go away." Joker said matter-of-factly.

Gustavo leaned forward and said sternly, "Joker, let's not play games. Whatever offer you may have had in mind has now gone down."

"Gone down. C'mon man, don't play like that."

"Does it look like I play?"

"It's just a little bit of trouble, bullshit trouble."

"Bullshit, trouble. One spot had to be set on fire to cover up a slew of bodies, all of them worked for you. A crazy ass, so called, right hand man, that works for you; money missing...in the thousands, that belongs to you; c'mon Joker. This shit is all fucked up."

Joker bit his lip in repulse as it was laid out in front of him. Gustavo was right. "Okay...okay..."

He knew he had him now. Reel him in, take over the spots and put Akbar back in control under his thumb. He had to offer Joker some money, but he'd get it back as soon as Akbar came to New York. Just enough to keep Joker here, "Eight million."

"Eight million...that's all."

"That's it. Take it or leave it. I have to leave soon, so I need an answer immediately."

Damn, Joker thought. Seven spots pulling in at least 10-15 gee a week. I've made eight mil 3-4 times over since I took over the spot. Alphabet City's worth much more than that, at least double digits, "Need more than that..." he said.

It was on. Gustavo leaned back and pulled off the cigar some more, "Okay, double, 16 mil. But the mill house and all that's in it...is mine..."

At 16 mil plus what he had stashed, that would make a good pay day, Joker figured, but he needed it in cash so he could leave the country as soon as possible. "Okay, then, but I need cash-"

"Cash! What are you fuckin' kiddin me or what! You don't have a off shore account? An accountant?"

"Never had time to get one...cash."

Gustavo sneered, thinking to himself that he could kill this muthafucka right now if it wasn't for Akbar. He had to play the game out, "Sure...by the end of the week-"

"Thursday. I want it by Thursday."

"You're pushing it!" Gustavo snarled, then backed down, "Okay then, Thursday. I'll stay here one more day and then leave tomorrow and come back with the cash."

"No problem." Joker leaned back and swirled his chair around towards the window, "And uh...Bezo will be going with you."

"Bezo! No fuckin' way!"

"Then, no fuckin' deal."

Gustavo reached for his gun, then backed off, "Okay...tomorrow, he better be ready." Gustavo glared at the back of Joker's head like a target. It would be his pleasure to explain all this shit to Bezo before he put a bullet in his brain. The look on his face alone would be worth it.

"And, Gustavo. No funny business because I know people, ya hear. People that know what I'm trying to do."

Gustavo chomped down on the shortened stogie and exhaled deep and blew the heavy, bluish smoke out; Joker played his hand well, but the deck still belonged to him, "I hear you." he said.

THE CUTE, SHAPELY CORRECTIONS officer slid Akbar's metal food tray underneath a flap built into the door, glimpsed both ways then shoved a yellow manila envelope right behind it. Akbar nodded his head before he made a move for it, then she left and the flap slammed shut, the process echoing repeatedly down the hall as the rest of the inmates on SSR-Substantiated Security Risk, retrieved their trays.

Akbar moved slowly towards the door, then kicked the package underneath his bunk out of sight. He peeped out the two and a half inch by three foot slit of window cut into his door and saw no one else except for the same officer. He glanced across and down the hall at the other eyeballs that where watching also; body's rocking back and forth in a trance. Her scrumptious ass had set off a secession of spontaneous masturbation. Akbar paid it no mind as he looked and there was no one else.

He picked up the tray and eased it on his table then stretched underneath the bed and retrieved the package. He opened it and inside a letter sized envelope were two playing cards; one an ace, and the other a joker. Akbar grinned remembering the names he was cruelly called on the street names that stuck. One being; black ass, joker. His features were the epitome of a skull, the two knife cuts on the opposite side of his face extending from the corners of his lips to his temple gave him a daunting demeanor. His toothless grin making him resort to the dentures that fixated a hideous smile, thus establishing a moniker that would follow him for the rest of his life. He later became Muslim in the joint and his partner and confident, Ace, soon after gave him the alias, Naim Akbar. He picked it up and ran with it.

He took the cards out and tore the envelopes up and flushed them down the toilet then sat down at his desk and started nibbling on food slapped cruelly and spitefully together in a stained cold, steel tray. Shit on the shingle it was called, literally that's what it was. He slid the two cards into the deck with the other playing cards on his desk out of sight.

A light tapping on his window caught his attention and he jerked his head around, it was the same officer who just left moments ago. She smiled seductively looking into the window, then quickly glanced down the hall both ways. She tantalizingly unbuttoned her blouse and reached in pulling her titties out her bra, pressing them hard against the window.

Akbar was at first, stunned, shocked, but went with it, he turned towards her and slyly grinned. He'd never seen her before, she must have been part of the package Ace sent to him, hopefully, he thought. She rubbed herself provocatively against the window fluttering her long, thick eyelashes. Akbar's dick rose up in his boxers quicker than a shuttle as he lumbered towards the bunk. He pulled down his jumper and snatched his now hard dick out and went to work. She wet her manicured fingers and pinched her nipples, stroking them gently. Akbar grabbed the full length of his dick and stroked slowly. She started to get aroused herself and stuffed one of her hands down her pants and grinded against the door, much to the delight of the other inmates whose moans could be heard across the darkened, dimly lit, hallway.

Akbar paid it no mind as he stroked wildly away, trying to control himself, but it was of no avail, too late. The cum made its way out in spurts, shooting a long white trail towards the door. His body trembled and shook as he convulsed then slowly sunk down into his bed breathing heavily.

She grinned as the cum trail slid down the window and then she shook also, closed her eyes then shook again. She was finished. Winking her eyes and blowing a kiss at Akbar she reached into her shirt pocket and pulled out a card, an ace of spades. She straightened herself up and disappeared, then he heard her strutting down the hallway and closed the door locking it shut behind her. It was over with.

Akbar cleaned himself up at the sink and wiped down the walls, door, and floor then sat at the table and pulled out the two cards. He picked at the side of the laminated paper and it peeled back. In the middle was the SIM card he needed. His cell was shook down last week and all of his paperwork was taken from him including the SIM card he had hid. He had connections in the prison and an order was put out and it came through. Even though he had paid people in prison he still had to go through the motions, shakedowns and shit like everyone else. But he didn't mind. Every now and then, he'd get accommodated with porno, DVD's, and whatever other appendages that he could get away with. Overall, he didn't lead a hard bid and for his other cellies on SSR, they didn't either.

Still he didn't put too many in his business, it was much too risky. He peeped back out the window then walked over to the sink and washed his hands, he reached under and pressed two clips that had been put there by maintenance, and slid it back and a pocket was revealed. Along with a small stack of hundreds, porn photos and a small vitamin capsule of heroin, was a hand held cell phone. He reached for it, flipped it open and slipped the card in. He pressed on and the phone lit up. He pushed the sink back in and backed away and crouched near the toilet like he was taking a shit. The CO'S most likely wouldn't bother him or if someone did spot him he could easily flush it. He dialed some numbers and waited patiently then a voice came over the other end, "Yo...wassup. I see you got that." It was Ace.

"Good looking out."

"I met her at bike week. She give you some pussy or what?"

"Naw...but she put on a hellava show." Akbar chuckled, "I'm straight."

"Well, in a couple of more days you won't have to worry about that shit anymore. I'll hook you up with her personally, okay."

"No problem. So, what's up, man? I got the card but the other one...the ace. I knew it had to he important."

"Hell yeah. I looked into that dude Gustavo like you asked and you're right. He is a hit man that works for the syndicate, he's legit, but it seems like he's trying to make some moves himself."

"Like what?"

"I think he's trying to get Alphabet City."

"How do you know? He seemed pretty thorough when I spoke to him and damn, he made some calls to get me out."

"I mean, he might be a'iyht, but I heard there's some bad dope on the street and people getting killed...dope spots set on fire; all types of shit happening and all this since he came. I mean, that's what I hear in the circles. Coincidence? I don't know...Joker's been acting strange...real paranoid. I heard one of his runners went renegade, there's supposed to be a contract out on him. Look, Akbar, shit is ugly out here, ya know what I mean."

Akbar leaned back, "Hmmm, okay...I'll call you back later on and we'll put something in motion, okay."

"Cool, but like I said...just watch your back with him."

"Yeah, I hear you...you be careful too. Later." Akbar put the phone up and then shoved his food tray back underneath the door. The inmate run around that came to retrieve it tapped on the window and asked, "Akbar, you okay?"

"Wassup...whatcha got?" He pushed a Styrofoam tray underneath the door and he opened it. Steak, potatoes and buttered rolls, hot and streaming. "Yeah, this'll do just fine." The trustee beamed at his approval and Akbar questioned, "2-9-0-6-8, right?" That's It. "'I'll make sure your books are straight." He sat down at the table eating in thought about what Ace had told him. He couldn't figure out for the life of him what type of game Gustavo was playing but he'd learned from Joker's backstabbing ass not to trust him or no one. He figured he'd play it all out until he hit the streets, then him, Gustavo and Joker would do a little shopping of sorts...see about some cement shoes. He laughed and his voice boomed up the hallway echoing off the gray, blocked wall as he finished wolfing down his steak.

MYA WAITED PATIENTLY for Skyler to come back from her errands. She stopped by her office earlier and briefly told her that she had to make a run, and that she'd be back to pick her up after she got off work. Mya had made arrangements herself to knock off at 3 o'clock and wanted to close out some of her accounts, then pick up the girls at school so that they could pack. She would then explain to them that they would be leaving Alphabet City and Aziz for good. She didn't have a problem with it herself, nor did she figure Hope would, but she still didn't rule out Destiny's acting up. She had a very young impressionable mind, and she hoped that she would eventually understand.

She could never tell the girls what she was actually going to do, but figured she'd get far enough away from the city so that they could soon forget it.

Smiling, she thought back to earlier and the nice talk she had with old man Vito. He knew something was going on; his prudence saw through the persona she had put up and he told her in his way, very calmly, softly, like a father would a daughter, to be careful and that if she ever needed anything, she could call on him. He then kissed her gently on the forehead and slumbered off. Unforeseen, but it also gave her the courage to push on. She knew in her heart what she was doing was wrong and that a multitude of things were liable to go amiss. One thing's for sure, she grinned, she couldn't wait to see the look on their faces when she busted in with guns blazing, going for the money. It was definitely gangsta'.

Thinking back even further, reflecting, she remembered Dante, the things they'd talked about. He wanted to leave, too. He hated the game, but it was a means to an end. He wanted out for the babies. He told her it would just be a matter of time; he had a meal ticket planned. She never got to find out what that meal ticket actually was.

She was jogged rudely out of her thoughts by the uncalled for, blaring honking of a horn. Skyler. She had the old car back. She waved wildly at her, "C'mon, girl!" Embarrassed, Mya hopped in and they sped off down Second Avenue.

"So...what did you get?" she asked.

Skyler reached in the back seat for a bag and tossed it over towards her. "Here, ya go. Check it out."

Mya dug into the bag and pulled out a rubber mask. She held it up and smirked, "Damn...you couldn't find anything better than this?"

"What..." Skyler reached over and snatched it out her hands, "It's a fuckin' monster. I mean, what did you expect?"

"Well-"

"Well, what. It's a fuckin' mask; we're supposed to not be recognized. I mean, what the fuck did you want? A fuckin' makeover or something!"

Mya frowned up then looked back in the bag at the other one, "It's the same one!"

"You kiddin' me, right. I mean, you can't be serious." Skyler skidded over and jerked the car in park then turned towards her, "Mya. These masks are so that no one can recognize us. I had to go way uptown to get this shit. Don't you think Joker is gonna call the costume places in the area once he sees this shit? C'mon now Mya...think." she said as she waved her hands in the air in dismay trying put across her point.

"I hear you, Skyler. You're right. I'm just a little-"

"Nervous. Hell, don't you think I am too!" Skyler leaned her head on the steering wheel, "So much can go wrong." She turned towards her and her eyes met Mya's and softly she spoke, "Someone could get killed. This is real serious, Mya. You have to stay focused, okay."

Mya reached over and stroked her hair, "I know. I know."

Skyler cranked the car back up and Mya asked her, "So, why do you think he wouldn't call uptown?"

"He probably will, but these masks, everyone up there are buying."

"Why?"

"To what I understand, it's a mask they use at the football games at DeWitt Clinton High School. Some ole, 'we are beast' type of shit going on. Teenage stuff." Skyler giggled.

"Oh. But damn...you went all the way up there. The Bronx."

"Better safe than sorry."

"Hell, you drove this car and it made it." She leaned over and grinned then chuckled, "I ain't mad at you."

They rode further down and Mya pointed her towards 23rd Street, "Make a left..." Skyler did so and stopped at the light, "You know the place, between 1st and 2nd Avenue."

"C'mon, now, Mya." Skyler snidely responded, "I didn't make it to class much, but damn, it was still my school."

"That's right...you did go there." Mya said sarcastically.

"Fuck you."

They pulled up in front of John Hudson Junior High School and kids were standing around in groups. School was out, but working her way through the crowd was Hope, "Hey, Ma! Hey, Ms. Skyler!" Hope got into the car and Skyler pulled off and cut a left on 19th Street and sped down to 5th Avenue, pulling in front of another school, St. Vincent's, right behind Beth Israel Hospital. "Why do you have them separated?" Skyler asked.

Mya was just about to answer when Hope spat out, "Destiny! She doesn't want me telling Ma what she's doing."

Destiny came out the door rubbing her face with a tissue then tossed it in the trash bin before she got in. Not realizing she'd missed the eye shadow on her eye lids, "You see. She had on make-up!"

Destiny jumped in the car and stuck her tongue out at her and Skyler jetted off amid Mya's scolding. Skyler shook her head, turned up the radio and made a mental note to renew her birth control pills.

In between silly young girl arguments, Destiny mentioned that she thought she had seen Aziz's car stalking the area, and Hope said the same. "Did you tell security?" Mya asked.

"Yeah, Ma, but all they did was say, they got it."

"Same here, Ma. They just said, go back to class." Hope chimed in.

"Mya, now you know if he really wanted to get in, all he had to do was give them some money."

"Yeah, Skyler but damn...somebody gotta do the right thing. He needs to be stopped."

Skyler reached over and squeezed her hand, "Something will be done, soon."

Mya knew she was right. All Aziz had to do was shell out some cash and he could easily get in the school. Probably even take them out kicking and screaming. It had to be done; tomorrow had to be a go. She was scared now, not only for herself, but for the kids as well and that made for a dangerous situation.

Skyler pulled up in front of her apartment building dropping off the kids then her and Mya drove around to the back way into an adjacent parking lot. She steered cautiously into a tight parking space and threw the gear in park before letting out a deep, weary sigh. Mya looked at her and asked, "What's wrong?"

She sighed again then reached beneath her legs under her seat and pulled a notch and it gently glided back then she leaned over, "Maybe we're in too deep. We don't really have this all planned out, ya know."

Mya glanced into the glove compartment and pulled out Skyler's cigarettes. She pushed in the lighter and rolled the window down slightly. "It's too late for that..." she said as the lighter clicked and she pulled it out. Skyler watched in a trance as the amber shine of the glow engulfed her as Mya inhaled on the cigarette. Feeling an itch intensify down inside of her loins, she was captivated as Mya's lips pulled lusciously on the Salem. Her dark, auburn, lip gloss sparkled as her puckered mouth showered seduction. She could see why Aziz was so obsessed. She was after all drop dead gorgeous, just plain ole sexy. Skyler reached for a smoke also and found herself peeking into her cleavage. She gazed unrestrictedly as Mya's blouse eased open as she moved, exposing her round, dark, areolas, circling her perked nipples. Now Skyler was wet and horny, thinking to herself, maybe she should try her. Maybe she might want to "Girl...what are you staring at?"

Skyler jerked abruptly, she had been caught off guard, but inwardly she didn't mind and slowly started to react, easing her way back. Mya giggled as she reclined into the seat, clueless. She cocked open her legs, then kicked off her heels and threw her feet up on the dash. Skyler couldn't help but stare at the bulge of pussy between her legs as she did. Continuing into her flight of fancy, she imagined, if I could just rub-"You know, Skyler...you do have a point, but," Mya pulled once more on the cigarette and her chest heaved. Her full round breasts spouted through the thin garment as Skyler continued to goggle, and unconsciously, her hand strayed slowly between her legs and she fondled herself. "I mean...this shit can only get worse, but if we wait," she turned slightly and as if on cue, a tittie popped out of her bra. Mya slowly laid the cigarette down in the ashtray and adjusted her straps in the reflection of the windshield as Skyler stared deviously through the smoke's haze, "We could miss the opportunity."

Skyler had leaned so far forward so that her next move could have easily landed her on top of her and the ensuing fantasy from there would be to kiss those desirable lips passionately, unrelenting. She couldn't help herself, they had begun to hypnotize and entrance her. Uninhibited, Mya made her oblivious to all that was going on and gaped open her legs, literally inviting her in, "So, we go now while the going is good, then split!" Skyler didn't hear a word she said, she had mustered up the courage to reach over towards her ass and then unforeseen a knock came at the door. Skyler yanked her hand back and swirled around quickly. It was security, the old man, Mr. Wright. "Yes!" she said.

Intrusively looking inside the car he rambled on asking questions as he snooped," Is everything alright? Just checking to make sure. Especially after the other night." Mya had straightened up her clothes and closed her legs sitting up straight, much to Skyler's chagrin. He stared off into her face, she was pissed off and pouted up, "Is everything..." he glanced down and caught a glimpse of the wet spot between her legs, "...alright?"

Skyler traced his eyes down to her crouch, "Everything's fine!" she spat, "We were just getting out. Her face had reddened as she shooed the old man away from the door then turned her attention back towards Mya, "We'll talk about this upstairs."

"I know that's right." the old man said as he slumbered off. Mya grabbed Skyler by the arm, "Wait up..."

Skyler melted like butter as she felt her touch, hoping she was feeling the same thing. Hoping one day she would eagerly oblige her, "Yes." she cooed. Her eyes wide in anticipation.

"There's nothing to talk about. We go tomorrow night...okay!"

With a disappointing tone in her voice she said, "Sure...whatever.

"No! Not whatever. We do this! Tomorrow nite." she reached over and hugged her, "We'll be alright, baby."

Skyler creamed in her pants as she gently rubbed her thinking to herself that the feelings she had were what they were, lust. Damn, this was a mess, she wailed. There was no way in hell she could pull the double cross now. "You okay?" Mya asked.

Skyler swiftly jumped out the car, "Yeah...I'm alright. We need to call Steve. He's got the guns."

"Then, that's what we do, but I got to talk to the girls. I really do." They walked up the curved, steps leading to the elevator in the lobby past the security guard who was on the phone. He waved as they passed by, not paying them any mind. He was peeved, he'd just gotten voice mail for the third time, "Hey, man, Aziz...this is me. The security guard in the Bronx, remember. You told me to call you when the girls got back. Well, they're back, okay. Don't forget me now. You know where I'll be." He hung the phone up and watched as the arrow on the elevator pointed to the floor where Skyler's apartment was, then he picked up the phone again and dialed some more numbers, different. "Baby. It's me...Joe. Remember, I told you about going to Vegas. Well, I think the weekend sounds good for me." He glanced back up and smiled, "Real good."

Steve had just gotten into his apartment from work and checked his answering machine. No messages. He hadn't heard from Gutter all day and he was puzzled, not knowing what was going on. No one had seen or heard from him. He didn't want to just show up unexpectedly at the poolroom unannounced, but figured he might have to. He pulled out the satchel from atop the closet out a hole he'd made, and tossed it on the bed then plopped down beside it and zipped open the bag. He pulled out four boxes of bullets first, then opened wider revealing two 9 millimeter handguns and a 45 caliber, semi-automatic, then reached deeper and grabbed a 9mm assault rifle with a folded out stock, an Uzi. He pulled back the notch and let the clip engage then checked inside the firing mechanism. It was rigged to go fully automatic. He grinned as he playfully pointed at the wall, "Yeah...go in blazin'! Skyler will be my Bonnie and I'm her fuckin' Clyde! Hell to the fuckin' yeah!"

He inadvertently caught a glimpse of some old newspaper articles he had hung on the wall next to some old posters. Newspaper clippings of him and Dante, both high school, All-American, basketball standouts; they were supposed to take the city by storm. He eased the gun down, it had suddenly felt like it weighed a ton. It hit him, he couldn't possibly kill Mya. If anything, he had to look out for her. Get out clean and haul ass, that's what Dante would have wanted, but the head that tugged at him between his legs, wanted something else, Skyler. And the desire tugged at him harder every day as he watched her from afar. "Damn!" he threw the gun against the wall and dropped his hands in his head and wailed, "What am I doing! Dante! What..." He gazed back up at the clipping of Dante, and with wells of tears in his eyes said, 'I can't live my life...and yours, too."

"Okay...so, you're saying that we're leaving here Wednesday, right?" Hope asked, her adolescent mind, inquisitively, perplexed.

"Yes, baby."

"Here...in the Bronx right?" she shot back, still very much puzzled.

Mya let out a long, deep breath. "No...no. We're leaving New York."

"Until we get some money and then we come back...right?" Destiny asked.

"No. For good."

"Yes!" Hope jumped up and cried out, "Finally, we can leave the projects!" She dove into her mother's arms and squeezed her, "Oh, momma, thank you so much!" Mya hugged her back then looked over at Destiny. Her head hung low and face frowned up, "What's the matter, Destiny?" she asked, reaching for her she shrugged her hand away. "She just wants to be with those boys-" Hope blurted,

"So what!" Destiny shouted back, "Just because guys think I'm pretty! So what!" Tears had begun to formulate in her eyes, "For the first time in my life I'm noticed! You never noticed me before!" It stung Mya as she glared and pointed her way, "Destiny...I'm sorry, baby."

"Sorry! It's too late for that now, isn't it." she mocked, then stomped off towards a mirror that hung on the doors "You see, momma. I look just like you. Hope, looks like daddy and you treat her better than me, all the time." Mya was blown away, this was the first time Destiny had went off on this level like this. "She just wants some attention, that's all. She ain't nothing but a little drama, queen." Hope said sucking her teeth.

Destiny put her hands over her ears, tired of the attitude she was getting from her sister and screamed, "Shut up, Hope, shut the hell up!"

Mya watched in horror as the tumultuous, infantile scene between her children was played out in front of her eyes. She'd always watch them fight, nothing serious, juvenile at best. But this was different, the language. She recognized immediately what it was, Destiny was absolutely right. She did treat Hope better and unconsciously, ignorantly, whatever, it did have something to do with Dante. She, after all, was a dead ringer for him. Destiny, on the other hand, was just the opposite. Although she had her father's eyes, she was every bit of her mother; a reflection of her from earlier years gone by. Like looking into a mirror; she was just about her age when she'd first met Dante, and as she looked over at her crying uncontrollably, quivering, her mind immediately flashed back to when she found out she was pregnant. But things were much different then, distinctly different. Dante was a stand up guy, man of his word, and he quickly stepped up to the plate.

Soon after he was killed, after Destiny was born, she took up with Aziz; dreadfully at odds all the time and that's what these kids were raised on, Aziz's insanity. So it was only typical that it would show itself on her own kids, Dante's daughter's. God, her mind screamed out, what have I done? Dante would roll over in his grave if he had an inkling.

Coming back to herself, she rushed over to Destiny and instinctively hugged her, soothing her, "I'm so sorry for all that-"

"Momma," she said as she looked up in her eyes. The fear evident in her face, like a child scared, frightened, "Please, don't beat me..." That's all it took and Mya broke down. Hope kneeled down beside them, "Nobody's gonna beat you...not as long as I live! I promise you...I promise..." Cowering down next to both of them, Mya knew she had to have a heart to heart with them. A long talk and mutual understanding of each other's feelings. She had to be a mom.

After a bunch of napkins and some intense heart wrenching, rap, Mya had to let them in on the plan in order for it to go right, "You both need to be at the Port Authority at 8:00, Wednesday nite. Gate," she glanced at the tickets she had in her hand, "five."

"You'll be there, too, right." Hope asked.

"Of course. I'll be there. Now, pack what you really need. Everything else, throw away."

Destiny stood up and looked in a bag full of outfits, "Hold up...everything?"

Mya walked over and looked in, "Everything. Especially these old, hoochie mama, outfits-"

"Brought by dope boys, huh, huh." Hope taunted her.

Destiny threw a shirt at her, "You need to mind your business!"

"Ma! You saw that!"

Mya just nodded her head, they were okay now. It was going to be a time on her hands with them, but it would be well worth it. She grinned and chuckled as they threw clothes at each other. She hadn't seen them this cheerful in a long while. Skyler stood in the doorway and said "Y'all alright. Don't be tearing up my house and shit."

Destiny threw a shirt her way and Skyler playfully dodged it, "Alright now. I can't beat your ass but I'll tear a foot off in your momma's." Destiny laughed, doubling over then Hope asked the question that needed to be asked, "Ma...where are we gonna get the money?"

Skyler stared at Mya who just dropped her head, "What, ma...what's wrong?" she asked, worried. The curiosity from earlier vanished, and then panic seeped in. Skyler sat down near Mya and said to her, "We might as well tell them...everything."

Mya looked at both of them as they gawked, their mouths open, waiting, not knowing what to expect, except worse.

She knew to tell them would mean that it was all too real now. Their innocence would be forever lost and she was to blame. If anything went wrong, they could potentially be targets for retribution by Joker and his henchmen. "Damn…" she slowly picked her head up, "Okay, listen up and listen damn good…it's like this…"

Hope kind of sauntered over to the window and stared out silently while Destiny folded clothes. "Are y'all alright?" Mya asked hesitantly. Destiny shrugged her shoulders. Mya could see her tears as they danced off her cheeks. An uncomfortable silence congested the air in the room and Hope was choking on it and she couldn't take no more of it, she turned and responded, "No, ma. We're not okay. Why would you want to do something like that? You can get killed and then what."

"Yeah, ma…" Destiny chimed in, "Why can't we just leave without that happening?" Skyler sighed, it was too much for her. The emotions were too unbearable for her, "Mya…maybe we should call this thing off-"

"No! Hell no!" Mya angrily stood up and stalked over to Hope, hands flaring, "Everything that man has belonged to your father, and I'll be damned if he gets away with it!"

"But, ma…daddy's dead."

That sent jolts throughout her soul and took the air out of her, literally, but she countered, "Yeah…he 's dead, but baby, your momma caught pure-d hell from a man that didn't even love me…or you." She took Hope by the hand and walked her over to Destiny, "I'm doing this so y'all won't ever have to be in my shoes, ya hear." Skyler got up and quietly exited the room pulling the door closed behind her, then picked up the phone and dialed Steve's number, "Hey, wassup, baby . You got everything?"

"Steve paused and thought for a second before he answered, "Hey, Skyler. We might want to wait to pull this off."

"Steve…we've been through this. It's a go."

"Hear me out. I haven't heard from Gutter...seen him or nothing."

Skyler looked up, and Mya and the kids had come out of the bedroom and sat down next to her, "You got the guns?"

"Yeah, I do, but-"

"Look. It's simple. Whether he calls or not. Wednesday night," she glanced over at Mya, "it's a go, ya hear. If his big ass is in there, then he has to get it because he's the only one who can identify us. You understand me."

Steve pondered for a minute on that, she wanted Gutter to die, then said, "I understand." Nothing was said between them then he asked, "What about me and you?"

Skyler knew it would come down to this. She didn't have the time to sort through it all. What she felt for Mya, Steve felt for her, "We'll talk."

Steve had heard that song too many times before and he wanted to change the tune, "Naw...it's me and you...do you understand. I'm risking my life for your ass. It better be...me...and you. Got it?"

Skyler sucked it up, the choice was made for her, "I got it." then hung up the phone. "Well., ladies...we got some packing to do." She asked Mya, "By the way, were you going anyway?"

Mya continued staring out the window towards the George Washington Bridge overlooking New Jersey in a daze and said, "To Dante's family."

"Where's that, momma?" Destiny asked.

Mya turned towards them, "Charleston...Charleston, South Carolina."

chapter 17

DAY FIVE
8:34 A.M.

Groggy and coming out of a day old funk, Miles got a call from Joker early this morning. He wasn't crystal on Joker's ramblings, but it had something to do with some bad dope that had hit the streets. Word was that a woman had been found poisoned in a hotel with her dope laced with rat poison. It was one thing to have the good dope and people die from the fix; but it was altogether another to have tainted dope.

Once again, Joker's paranoid ass was distressed; thinking someone in the organization was trying to sabotage him. Miles thought too, that maybe it might have some credence since he had blabbed his mouth all over the city about selling off his spots and splitting; leaving everyone to fend for themselves after all the years of devoted service they'd given. For one, they should never had been that loyal and gullible in the game anyway, and to trust Joker was just stupid.

So now he was up, wide awake getting dressed, ready to make a run over to Flaco's, the mill house to find out what the hell was going on. He made arrangements yesterday for Mariah's body to be given to her next of kin, and then gave them the money to have her buried properly. He had finally made amends with it, now it was time to get on with the business of being Joker's lieutenant.

Aziz stared up at the facing of the building in quiet apprehension. He dreaded walking up the steps, his feet felt as heavy as concrete blocks. The front door was shut but the lock looked as if it had been jimmied open, perhaps by someone, a fiend maybe, breaking in and robbing the mailboxes by the looks of it.

A few tenants had timidly looked out their doors and nodded after recognizing who he was. He nodded back at them and not wanting any trouble, they closed their doors quickly and locked them, sending echoes of successive, clashing noises throughout the building. It was known that whenever Joker sent in his people to check out a building, more than likely it was going to be used as a spot. The only ones who stayed were either dope fiends or prostitutes. Either way they would have to contract their services out to Joker to make a profit; but with the traffic that came through copping dope, it was well worth it. But this time, this wasn't the case. The place was all too familiar to Aziz; after all, he was raised up in this hell hole.

Double stepping up the stairs to the third floor he glared down the hall at the apartment in front him, memories flooding his mind too quickly to shake, the door slowly swung open, beckoning for him to come as if it were waiting just for him. He sluggishly, dragged forward, pausing then taking a deep breath he stepped through, shutting the door behind him and hopefully this chapter in his life.

9:16 A.M.

Miles pulled up in front of the bodega and no one was out. He glanced around the perimeter and didn't see the regulars. It was strange, strange enough for him to reach for his gun. He got out of the truck slowly and stepped cautiously to the front door. Pushing the door ajar and hearing the doorbell atop the sign jingle, not a soul stirred. He pulled back the slide on his gun and pointed in front of him. He looked over the counter and the fat man was gone, but blood was splattered on the newspapers behind him. He swirled back around and crept towards the archway leading to the door of the basement. Sticking his head through, he saw no signs of the bodyguards that were normally posted. Inching gradually down the steps he glanced towards his left, the alleyway. The back door was wide open. Taking a look at the setting around him he saw no one, then heard someone call out his name; it was Flaco.

He pushed through the curtains and Flaco was on the floor, his face badly bruised and blood was seeping through a gash on his head, "Aw, man...Miles. We was robbed, man."

"Robbed. Who the hell-"

"Muthafuckas came in and started shooting A-K's. Fuckin' youngens!"

"Damn...which one!"

"Don't know the name." He tried to pick himself up but was still too groggy, "It was a inside job."

Miles pulled a chair closer to him, "Here ya, go. So...a inside job, huh. What, your people?"

"Think so, but they had help." He rubbed the graying patch of hair on his head and explained, "All I know is late, last night Aziz was supposed to pick up some mattes, like always. So, I waited a little while. I remember you were training some people...I thought maybe you were busy, so I called a few numbers here and there and got voicemail. I eventually dialed you up but your phone wasn't in service." Miles frowned up when he heard that. He was on the other side of Brooklyn in Red Hook and the metal canisters off the ship yards fucked up his reception. "The only reason I called Joker was a couple of people came and told me about some bad dope-"

"Yeah, he called me this morning. That's why I'm here."

"Hell. I told him last night."

"Fuckin' Joker." Flaco coughed and rubbed the knots on his forehead, "You alright. Maybe we should get you to a doctor."

"Naw...I'll be alright. Just cold. Where's Aziz any fuckin' way?"

"Man, Aziz's on some old bullshit. Bodies have been showing up all over Alphabet City. Hell, I believe he killed this girl I was fuckin'...maybe even Big E...Pancho."

"Damn! Not them...dead!"

"Yeah..." Miles looked off, "Joker's got a contract on him though-we'll get him."

Flaco reached over and grabbed Miles's arm, "Sorry about your boys. But...there's something you need to know."

"Know...about what?" Miles looked at him sternly, "You know who might have done this-"

"No...no. We'll get the muthafuckas who did this. All they took was dope anyway. They won't be hard to track. I'm talking about Aziz."

"Aziz was down with this!"

"No...listen. Aziz has a past. A dark past." He pulled himself up in his chair, "Hear me out..."

THE LONE FIGURE LEANED near the sink as Aziz sat down at the kitchen table, slowly sipping on a drink of water that was placed in front of him. He reached in his pocket and pulled out a prescription bottle and opened it. Took out two pills and swallowed them then drank some more of the water down. The glass was picked up and placed in the sink. Then, unexpectedly, out of nowhere, Aziz was slapped. He reeled back in his chair and put up his hands to shield himself, "No...no."

"Didn't I tell you to leave her alone? I told you to take your medicine..." He was slapped again, his barricade was ineffective, "And now...you beat her. You disgust me!"

Aziz straightened up after almost falling out his seat, "I tried to be good, but...I just can't-" he pleaded, but for his trouble he was slapped again.

"Couldn't what!" The lone figure stepped in front of him and Aziz averted his eyes to the floor and he was grabbed by the throat and forced to look up. "Look at me!"

Aziz slowly rolled up his eyes at the figure in front of him, face to face. A figure that he feared. The face he ran away from his own dreams.

9:42 A.M.

"There was this guy," Flaco continued, "I think he was Indian or something...came from across the water somewhere...India. Settled in the Midwest, Wisconsin somewhere on the outskirts of Illinois, least that's what he told me. Never knew why he came here. Said he was running, never told me from what and I never asked." Flaco reached in his pocket and pulled out a smashed up pack of cigarettes and pulled one out, straightened it up and put it to his lips.

"What does this have to do with Aziz?" Miles asked.

He searched around his pants pockets, "Wait a minute. Got a light?"

Miles reached in his jacket and pulled out a pack of matches, struck one and passed it to Flaco. He puffed on the cigarette to get it going then coughed, hacking up a little blood. "Anyway. I let him work with me for a minute. Nothing big time, stuffing packages. That's when I ran the spots over on 4th Street. Remember that, I was big time then." He grinned and his gold teeth flashed and sparkled through the darkened stains permeated with years of decay.

Miles checked his watch, "C'mon man. We need to find out who robbed this place," he looked around at the knocked over tables and scattered packages all over the floor, "clean it up, then call Joker. Let him know what happened."

"Then...you hear me out first."

"Man, this better be good." Miles said folding his arms.

"He had a family. Wife, little boy...girl. He seemed to be a square. He worked hard, didn't steal or even use, but he was strange acting. Kept using the bathroom and washing his hands and shit. He was obsessed with the prostitutes that came in here and copped, too...figured him to be a pervert. He always left late in the evening right after the time the girls hit the streets. I never paid it no mind. Next thing you know...the bodies were popping up everywhere." Flaco crossed his legs and looked out into space, blowing a cloud of smoke into the air, reminiscing, "Everyone that was killed...came into that one spot."

Miles's eyeballs exploded, "The killer!"

"Yeah...the killer."

"But...my sister."

"She'd come in and...uh, did her thing."

"I know what she did. "What about this guy?"

"I never knew where his kids were until," he looked over at Miles, "after you killed him, but..."

"But what!" Miles barked.

"When they took you to prison, I tracked them down. The girl and the boy still stayed in Alphabet City. Never knew what happened to the mother..."

Miles's patience had worn thin. "Who were they!" he hollered.

TEARS HAD FORMED, BLURRING Aziz's vision as he stared off into the eyes of the lone figure, his sister. The episodes were more severe, less sporadic, no longer controllable. She was becoming more and more like their father... insane. "Leave me alone!"

"Oh...is that what you really want?" She mushed his face and turned away from him, "That bastard, Miles, had you in his sights...ready to squeeze the trigger and it was me!" She turned around pointing her finger in his face loathing him. "Who saved your whiny ass!" she rasped.

He could only mull over how many times she had drummed up the demented, notion in her mind that she had to be his protector, at the expense of so many lives lost. Now, she was more like his father, obsessed with killing.

In their mothers' eyes, after their father was killed, she couldn't raise them any more with the stigma of what he had done. No one would hire her to work anywhere. No one wanted to have anything to do with the family. She couldn't even sell her own body, the scars revealed too much, too frightening to see. Their father left her broken down and useless, mentally. She did the only thing she could do to escape the pain and she was too selfish to take the children with her. She hung herself.

Aziz remembered the body as it swung in front of him. Her eyes bulged out her head rigidly fixed as she drifted back and forth in the air, motionless. He was a child lost now, scarred forever. His sister comforted him the best she could. Though she was younger, she was the more stable, mature acting. Cutting the body down together they buried it in Washington Square Park on a late cold winter's night, and forever walked away.

They would go to school by day, and his sister would work odd jobs at night until Aziz got to the age that he could hustle dope, make some quick money. They did well for a while, covertly, keeping their existence a secret. Aziz eventually hooked up with Joker and a guy he played basketball with, Dante. His sister liked Dante, but Dante paid her no mind. She didn't have the figure, the pretty smile for him, but her hair was long and pretty. The Indian in her showed, but not enough. He played her taking her virginity, then went for Mya. She was hurt and Aziz felt her pain and tried to get at Mya for himself, to get even, but Dante prevailed. It was then that it happened. Their young minds could take no more, the reaction from their parents' deaths were delayed and the response ultimately started to manifest itself. They both felt disheartened.

She would go missing for days at a time not telling Aziz where she had been, running from herself, her past, the demons. Aziz was left all alone haunted by the thoughts of his father pushing him in the bathroom and telling him to strip down. His father took joy in molesting him. His sister would watch as his mother let it happen. When she spoke up against it, he would beat her with a leather strap in front of the kids, further humiliating her by viciously raping her right afterward.

He was diagnosed in Elementary School soon after as having a schizoid disorder, and was eventually given the prescription medication, Risperidone. He took the drug frequently at first, but they noticed the side effects were too severe. He started acting erratically to the point where he didn't know what was real or what was not.

His sister on the other hand never took anything medicinal. The disorder worked on her in the form of multiple personalities. Her desire to be a daddy's little girl, blaming herself for her father's sick behavior: her mother's beatings and subsequent rapes: her brother's brutal molestation: her father's death. It all made her emotionally weak, disturbed. She killed to feel good, normal, escape the pain; finish what her father started and to protect her brother. She was sick, and now, she was getting worse, "I took care of you! I was the one that told you not to trust Joker, didn't I!" Her mind couldn't distinguish the past from the present. She was fucked up.

Aziz nodded his head yes. "But...you didn't have to start killing-"

"Killing! What! You dumb muthafucka! You started the killing! You killed that fuckin' Dante! You did, remember!" She sat down at the table next to him and spat in his ear, "You was supposed to get the book...the ledger, frame Joker, get the money; and we were supposed to go back home to India. Aziz, it was that easy, but...you killed him and we got stuck in this shit hole!"

"It was an accident!" Aziz said, banging on the table, rattling it, "He dissed me! Teased me!" Aziz stood up and wandered over to the window, "He didn't want to be my...friend." he said.

She was right behind him, rubbing his back amid his tears, "That's alright...you tried." She soothed him, but there was no therapy for her, nothing to control the other personalities that reared their unpredictably, erratic faces, "Now...you were fuckin' bad!" She reeled around and hypnotically, stalked into the living room. A blue, black .357 sat on a stand as she approached. She walked right by it into a room and reappeared with a long, thick leather belt wrapped around her fists, "Now...you have to be beaten!"

Aziz tried to make a break for the door, "Stop! Stop right there!" she commanded, the voice was almost unmistakably his fathers and instinctively he stopped in his tracks.

"Get over here!" He obeyed and like a child he doddered over to her, "Go in the room and strip." Tears ran down his eyes as he looked at the face that was no longer his sister's, but his old man's, "Now! I'll be in there in a minute!"

He walked into the bathroom and closed the door behind him. His sister sat down nervously pulling a cigarette out and lit it, "He deserves it..." puffing fitfully, she argued with herself, "Leave him alone," she shook her head as the voices got louder, "He fucked up. Beat him, beat him!" She jumped up and threw the cigarette to the ground and put it out, then turned towards the door and walked towards it. Turning the knob, tears streamed down her face, "I don't want to do this..." She opened the door and Aziz stood off in a corner, naked from the waist down, old whelps littered his back, "I have to do this, Aziz...I love you too much..." she said as she shut the door.

"Yes...mother." he answered back softly.

10:04 A.M.

Miles sat down shaking his head lethargically, as if in a daze, then leaned back in the chair on its hind legs tripping at the magnitude of the story Flaco just unfolded. "So, damn...you mean to tell me, Aziz's father is the one who killed my sister." It blew his mind.

"Yeah." Flaco said, keeping his voice down not knowing where Miles was going to go with this and played it safe. He continued puffing on his cigarette as the ashes on the tip grew longer like sand in an hourglass.

"This is some shit." Miles sighed, "All this time I ran with this dude and he never said shit." He leaned forward towards him and in a hushed voice asked, "Does Joker know?"

"Not that I know of."

"So, how'd you manage to keep this shit a secret so damn long? I mean, Aziz had to know that you knew something."

"Naw...he doesn't know a thing." Flaco got up slowly and walked over to the sink, ran some water, dipped a rag, getting it good and wet and said, "What was there to tell? Remember, he was thorough for a good long time...years. I mean, he just started bugging out a day or so ago from what you tell me. So again, what was there to tell?"

Miles turned towards him, "So why are you telling me this now then?"

Flaco wiped the dried up blood from off his hands then dipped it again, cleaned it off and washed off his face, "I'm tired of this shit. I want out."

"You need to be talking to Joker and not me."

"I need to talk to you...first." He turned facing him, "I need to clear my conscience."

"Your conscience...now what?"

Flaco walked back over to where he sat and pulled up a chair closer to Miles, "You might not like what I'm about to say-"

"Spit it out!"

Flaco took a deep breath, "Okay. Everything I told you is true, but I left out some things!"

Miles waved his hands at him, his patience waned and his curiosity kicked in, "C'mon now...spit it out."

"It's about your sister."

Miles reached into his jacket and pulled out his gun, cocked it and placed it on the table in front of him, "You sure you want to...uh, clear your conscience, or let bygones be bygones."

Flaco looked over at the semi-automatic handgun then at Miles, "Little bro. That don't faze me. I've been in this game before you were born; Cuba, Miami...Spanish Harlem. Believe me, do what you do, hell, I've lived a good freakin' life anyway."

"Then good. I won't feel the least bit fuckin' remorseful then."

Flaco grinned at first, then laughed. You're good. You should take this hell hole from Joker and make something of it."

"Look, Flaco, you're talking about my sister. I already had to kill one man, please...just tell me.

"I owe you this." He reached into the pack of cigarettes he had and lit up another one, then stood and walked towards a small side window and stared out, "You see. Your sister never got high. She was about her business. Hell, she even made her tricks wear rubbers" he chuckled, "regardless of how much money they promised to give her. She played the game well. Anyway, that night, she came in and rounded up her customers. Knocking them off, getting money, then she wanted to leave...go home. Said something about her little brother playing a ball game early in the morning. She wanted to be there." He turned and glanced over at him, "She loved you." then tuned into his thoughts, "But I was fascinated with her. I begged her to let me take care of her. Get her out the game, but she didn't want nothing to do with me...didn't want to get tied in with a drug dealer. I tried talking to her but It was getting late, so I gave up. Figured I'd surprise her in the morning by meeting her over at the Pitt. Your basketball game. Try to do the right thing."

"You really loved my sister, huh."

"Yeah."

"I'm sorry she didn't feel the same way, Flaco."

"It's nothing. Like I said it got late and I didn't want her to walk home by herself so I told her I would drive. I'd just bought a brand new Caddy, wanted to impress her." He tossed the cigarette out the window and walked back to the table and leaned over towards him, "I tried to do the right thing, Miles...I swear!" Miles grabbed his arm, "What did you do! Did you kill her?"

He jerked back, "No! But I might as well have." He sat in his chair, staring at the ground, "I told Nari, Aziz's father to walk her home-"

"You what!"

"I'm so sorry."

Miles got up and stood over him, with his gun in his hands, trembling, "You let a murderer walk off with my sister-"

"I didn't know he was a killer! I swear!" Flaco held out his hand and pleaded with him, "Please...believe me!"

Miles turned away from him then balled up his fist and smashed the wall still agitated and disturbed. He peeped over at Flaco with his head in his hands. He thought of his sister. Her pretty, bubbly smile. Long, jet black hair and slanted, chinky eyes; one deep blue and the other a bright, brown. She had a models figure and her stride matched her persona; soft spoken and friendly, Shayla.

He remembered before she left out that evening how she said she would be home early, go to the game with him. He remembered how happy he was and how even in the midst of everything they tried to live as a family. He remembered how he got up that morning and she wasn't there, how he'd missed the game waiting for her to come in, but it never happened.

They found her body in the gutter with her purse and money intact, raped and sodomized. Throat cut from ear to ear with a jagged bottle. He remembered the cops giving him her property, her purse untouched, and a Macy's bag with a brand new pair of sneakers just for him. He remembered it all so well.

He also remembered from his nightmares how he shot a man in his head as he looked up at him and begged for his life. How he emptied the clip in his brains from a piece that Joker had given him. How the man begged him, pleaded for mercy, told him he had a wife and...two kids. He shot him anyway.

He walked over to Flaco, "It's over with. You did...what she would have wanted."

"Do you forgive me!" he grabbed for Miles's arm and he jerked it back, "Don't push your luck old man." he put the gun back in his jacket, "Clean this shit up and call Joker. Tell him you got robbed and shit and I'm going after the muthafuckas who did it, okay."

"You want me to tell him about Aziz?"

"No," Miles walked over to the curtains and pulled them back, "Don't tell him shit." he walked through and paused, "Don't ever...tell no one, ya hear."

Flaco wiped his eyes and stood up, relieved, "I hear you."

"And oh, by the way..."

"Yeah."

"Miami looks good this time of the year...you might want to check it out."

Flaco shook his head, he understood the warning and he would take heed to it, after all, it was time to go anyway, "Maybe, I'll do that."

AZIZ SLOWLY PULLED up his pants, painfully, whimpering as he moved; more scars added to his already disfigured backside.

Long, thick and puffed up, the black blemishes were the momentums of his father's cruel brutality inflicted upon him as a child. The ripped skin and open wounds was a reminder that his father still lurked in his sister's mind, "Yoshi..." he called out to her.

"Yes," she turned around after laying the belt down on the bed and packed the back of a cigarette she had in her hand, "What is it, Aziz?" She reached into her worn, tattered, leather jacket and found a lighter and lit it. "Do you love me?" Aziz asked as she turned towards him.

Yoshi cocked her head ever so slightly at the remark and looked deep into the eyes of her brother before responding, "Of course-" she snickered, "Why do you ask?" His eyes glanced at the belt and she picked it up after noticing him staring at it, then turned to walk out the room and he said, "I would tell Mya the same thing, but," he buttoned up the front of his shirt and reached for his sweater, then looked over at her as he sat down putting on his shoes, "I don't think she ever believed me, though."

Yoshi swirled back around, that angered her, "To hell with Mya!" Aziz didn't even flinch, that was the response he was looking for, he stared off as he casually fixed up his clothing and she rambled on, "That bitch doesn't give a damn about you! All she ever wanted was the money you made hustling!" she searched around for an ashtray then stomped over towards him "She wants to take you away from me, then leave..." She sat on the corner of the bed and crossed her legs and rocked, "but this time she won't win. I'll make sure of that."

Aziz finished dressing then put on his jacket and walked towards the door, "Well, I think I've found someone else I love now anyway, so, Mya will be out the picture, soon."

Yoshi jumped to her feet and followed behind him, "Who? Who is this bitch now! Someone else trying to take you away from the family-"

"What family, Yoshi!" He turned and looked in her face, "What we do is not about family..." he walked over to the table and sat shaking his head subdued, "What we do is...insane, at best."

"Insane! Oh," she started to turn back towards the room, "You want me to get the strap again!"

Aziz sat, "Yoshi...just come here." She sighed but obeyed and came sluggishly like a child towards him, "Yeah!"

Aziz reached out and grasped her hands gently, "You need to get help."

"Me? No-no...I don't need that, you do!"

"I only take this punishment you give...for you. But it's over, now. It's not the same anymore." He stood up and kissed her cheek, "I found someone and I'm moving on." Yoshi stood despondent and in shock as her eyes welled up with tears, "No...Aziz, don't leave me..." uttered out her mouth. Aziz pushed his hands away and said, "Look...I'll come by later...I promise." He walked out the door leaving her dejected and mumbling silently to herself. She trudged into her room and opened up a dresser drawer, reached for the belt on the bed and neatly placed it inside. Wiping her eyes, she shook her head and bolted to the door putting her ear up against it, "No one will take you away from me, again. No one!" She ran back into the room grabbing for her coat then opened up another drawer and pulled out the silencer she had hidden underneath a folded stack of shirts and dug deeper pulling out a case of shells right next to it; picked up her keys and jetted right out the door behind Aziz. "We'll see if she takes you away from me. We'll see."

She reached the bottom of the stairs as Aziz jumped into his ride then dipped into the alleyway and hid, watching as he pulled off. Reaching into her pocket she pulled out her phone and dialed up some numbers and a loud squeal came across the speaker and the screen displayed a chart. A street map of New York City and a red beeping dot flashed intermittently as she pushed in a code. Instantly it traced the route Aziz drove. She dialed in a G-P-S sequence code earlier to track his cell phone, "Don't worry, I'll make everything alright." She turned and raced towards the back of the building and unlocked a chain that held the Honda moped she drove secured, then pulled out her keys and cranked it up, following the graph on her phone.

Aziz didn't suspect or have a clue that he was being followed. He picked up his phone and dialed Peaches, "Hey, baby..."

"Hey, wassup. What happened to you last night? You was supposed to come by."

"I got caught up."

Peaches sighed loudly through the phone sucking her teeth, "You wasn't with that other bitch, were you?"

"Naw. Just had to tie up a few ends. Look, uh...I'm on my way over. You got a little time to spend?"

"Oh yeah. I've been wanting to see you for a while. I'll be right here waiting, baby." Peaches said.

"Cool." Aziz closed his phone and tossed it over in the console pulling up to a traffic light, grinning ear to ear, not paying any attention to the black, motorcycle helmet that whizzed in and out of traffic three cars behind.

10:47 A.M.

chapter 18

YOSHI HADN'T BEEN IN this part of town for a long while and thought it strange that her brother would come here. She buzzed past a one time, outdated, butcher's market and peeped down the street adjacent to it and spotted a hoe stroll. Thriving, the hookers moved to and fro getting in and out of stopped cars. Tricks slowed down getting glances at their half nude bodies dodging vehicles and bartering their trade; sex. Fogged up windows and cars rocking back and forth, double parked, only adding to the shoddiness of the area and it got even seedier as she drove further along.

She remembered hearing about this section as a small child, but never actually seen it until the night she rode her bicycle over. She'd come up with a naive idea on how her family could be whole again and couldn't wait to tell her father. This same area where she peddled her bike to meet him was where she saw him walking up the street in front of her with a woman. A woman that wasn't her mother. A woman dressed like the women she'd just peeked at up the street. Her father didn't notice her; it was dark and she hid out of view. She watched as he tried putting his arm around the woman and she pushed it away. He laughed it off, then grabbed her playfully, but she continued to resist. He got angry and cursed her, then put her in a choke hold and drug her struggling body into the dimly lit, shadowy, alleyway behind them. It was late and no one else was around. He pushed her down to the ground and started slapping her. The woman put up a futile attempt to stop him but it was too much, she gave in, it wasn't worth the bruises she would have and the customers she'd lose. If she just let him get a shot of pussy, she figured he'd leave her alone; she'd settle up with him later after she told Flaco. Yoshi recoiled in horror as she watched her father savagely, rape the woman.

After the dirty deed was over, the woman pushed him off of her and tried to get dressed but he wouldn't let her up, he wanted more. He was entranced by her beauty, mesmerized with her looks. Yoshi didn't recognize him anymore, he'd changed. He shouted at her and she backed up against the wall, then tried to make a break for it. He grabbed her by her long, thick hair and tackled her to the ground, pinning her arms behind her back. She couldn't fight, it was useless as he pulled out again and fucked her brutally and hard in her ass. She cried out in pain, but no one heard her screams, except for Yoshi.

She put her small hands to her ears and cupped them tight trying to drown her out but it was useless. The woman caught a glimpse of her face and hollered at her to get help; but Yoshi stood still in her tracks, motionless, terrified. She slid deeper into the safety of the dark night. She watched in terror as her father reached into his black, leather jacket, the same jacket she wore now, and pulled out a six inch stiletto, gripping her in a headlock. He methodically, deliberately started slicing her throat. Staring, terrorized at the gruesome sight unfolding before her eyes she couldn't turn away as she watched the woman gag on the ground in agony as her father just stood and smirked. She tried grabbing at him but he kicked her in the chest and she fell backwards into the street, bleeding profusely into the gutter's drain. He heard a sound and looked over his shoulder but Yoshi hid from him, scared of what he would do to her. He searched somewhat, but left hurriedly not wanting to be seen as the woman continued to bleed in the street.

She remembered it all too well and wanted to get revenge on Miles for killing her father, after all his sister Shayla was just another whore that died that night, like all the others her father had murdered. All whores, dope fiends, trash, she said to herself as she snarled up her mouth, then watched as her brother's car pulled up in front of an old warehouse, converted to accommodate loft apartments and studios. She glared as a window opened upstairs and the woman who looked out and smiled at her brother looked no different than the whores she'd just seen; the whores her and her daddy killed. She made up her mind, she'd have to be the one to save the family, take care of the problem. Just like she wanted to tell her daddy to do that night, fix it.

Aziz parked his car around the side of the building and got out. He quickly hoofed it to the front of the building looking both ways before going in, cautious about his whereabouts. He stepped into the lobby and was buzzed in the door. He dashed inside noticing the elevator and pushed three.

The third floor was occupied by two other apartments, one overlooking the west side of the building facing the river and the other, the east side looking out into the city. There was a spacious studio in between them both; it was Peaches' condo and photography workshop. Aziz rang the bell.

Peaches swung open the door and flew into his arms, "Baby!" He was hugged and greeted with a wet, scrumptious kiss, "It's so good to see you..." Peaches cooed in his ear. By now his dick had started to get hard and Peaches reached down and played with it. Aziz weakened as her fingers tugged and played around the tip and he fell backward into a chair then gaped open his legs, "Peaches...I need you so bad." he said as he started rubbing between his legs.

Peaches knew it was time to call Gustavo before anything else happened to him like yesterday, "I will, baby...just need to step into the bathroom a sec."

"C'mon...now..." Aziz begged as he reached out.

"I'll be right back..." Peaches strutted into a room and picked up the cell phone that laid on a desk and dialed Gustavo's number, "Okay...he's here, and, you better get here quick. I'll hold him up as long as I can, you hear me!"

"I'm on my way, give me an hour or so-"

"An hour! C'mon now, work with me, Gustavo!" Peaches hollered.

"Now look, muthafucka! Don't rush me! You've been fuckin' him and taking all damn day any other time, so don't make this shit an issue! I got some things to do and I'll be on my way!" The call was sudden and Gustavo didn't expect it so soon. He had to ditch Joker, then pick up some bags to stuff the bodies in: Aziz's and Peaches. He figured he'd knock them both off at one time and pick the bodies up later on that night and dump them in the river. He also needed to find some help.

"Gustavo...please...just come. I can't do this by myself-"

"Okay-okay. I got you. Just hold him there. Do what you do...whatever, just hold him there."

"Okay." Peaches peeped over his shoulder and heard Aziz get up from the chair calling out his name. He adjusted his hair, makeup and strap between his legs and rushed out, "C'mon baby, you know a woman has to get right."

Aziz grabbed hold of him and felt the hormone enhanced, breast implants and squeezed them then started to reach between his legs but Peaches stopped him, "C'mon, baby. I thought you wanted me to suck your dick." and pushed him back down in the chair.

Aziz grinned, he was good and horny, "Oh yeah, but when you finish I want some pussy. Peaches sighed, hoping Gustavo got there quickly, if not, it might be ugly. This might be the day he'd have to reveal himself to Aziz if he persisted. He kneeled down and unzipped Aziz's pants and pulled them down and his dick shot out in his face almost slapping him. The veins were puffed up and pre-cum had already started to rise. Peaches could take no more. He hungrily grasped his mouth on it and swallowed it down then cuffed his hands around Aziz's backside and he twinged. He pulled up off of him and felt the whelps, "What is this, baby? You've been fighting?" Aziz blew, then said, "I'll tell you about it later. Please...I need to relax.

"Okay..." Peaches said and continued sucking. Aziz moaned and slithered in his seat as Peaches' head bobbed up and down rhythmically, steady stroking.

Yoshi had jimmied the lock on the door of the building open and snuck in. She noticed the elevator was still on the third floor and since she saw no one come out she assumed that was where Aziz was at.

Off to the side were some stairs and she opened the door and whisked up the steps. Reaching the third floor she opened up the door silently and stuck her head out. There were three other doors including the elevator and by remembering where the window was from outside, she chose one. She took out her picks and played at the lock until it popped open, then she crept into the apartment unnoticed. She heard noises of a sexual nature and walked softly towards them. Spying into the room she saw Aziz laid back in a chair with his legs cocked up and Peaches between them, sucking his cock. She walked in swiftly and said, "That's all you fuckin' want to do, huh."

Aziz's face turned two shades of white as he opened his eyes staring into the face of his sister standing, wide legged in front of him with her arms crossed, very angry. His dick immediately went limp. He knocked Peaches' head away and he fell backwards then turned around, "Who the hell are you!" he said as he jumped up from off his knees, "Who the fuck is this bitch, Aziz!"

Aziz hurriedly pulled up his pants, "I got it...I got it." and rushed over to Yoshi and started pushing her towards the door, "What the fuck did you do! Follow me!"

"Yeah...I followed your sorry ass..." she said as she looked over at Peaches, "and you're gonna wish you'd never...seen this...this...whore!"

Peaches balled up his fist, "Who the fuck you calling a whore...bitch! Aziz...is this Mya!"

Yoshi's eyes widened as she grabbed Aziz by the collar, "You mean...this bitch doesn't even know who Mya is!" She shoved him aside and scowled at Peaches, "This is gonna be a bad day for you, hoe."

Peaches charged first and swung, missing her target, catching Aziz on the back of his shoulder, he grimaced in pain, "Oww! Back up, Peaches! I got this!" Yoshi took advantage and elbowed him to the side then round-house kicked Peaches in his stomach and he doubled over grabbing at his gut. She then recovered and punched him square in the face causing him to fall back against the chair. Aziz tried in vain to hold Yoshi down but she shook him off, "You're just like your father." she said as she reached into her jacket. Aziz went for her hand and held on to it, "You have to be punished, but first..." she glanced back at Peaches who got up, running wildly towards them, "I have to deal with this problem, first." She tackled them to the ground sending them both sprawling all over the floor. Aziz struck his head on the side of a table and a gash spit blood spurting all over the furniture. He held his hands to the cut and ran for a towel on the sink. Yoshi whirled around and bounced to her feet much to the amazement of Peaches.

Yoshi knew her shit from hours of sitting in the theatres off of 42nd Street watching old, cheaply made, Kung-fu flicks until she fell asleep. She would run away from home long enough to muster up the nerve to go back only to be berated by her mother telling her she was a piece of shit. Yoshi would just run away again hiding out in the same dark, dingy movie theatres, cautious and mindful of the perverts who tried to get off, and kept her eyes open and trained to the movie. It helped her acquire the skills of a variety of choreographed stunts from movies from across the water, and not Jersey, but China.

Peaches swung again, and Yoshi side stepped and kneed him in the chest and he doubled over again. She kicked him in his mouth, he squealed out in pain as he sputtered out his front teeth. Yoshi stopped in her tracks, she knew something wasn't right but couldn't quite put her hands on it. Peaches charged again, and grabbed a hold of her trying to put her in a headlock. Yoshi grabbed for some hair trying to get a leverage and pulled. The wig came off in her hands as she pushed out of his arms and slowly backed away; looking at the clump of hair in her hands then back at Peaches. She knew it was something. Peaches was exposed.

"Oh, hell, no! I don't believe this shit! Aziz!" she shouted and he dashed back into the room from the kitchen covering the side of his head with a towel totally unaware of what just happened. He gawked over at the patch of hair Yoshi had in her hand.

"You mean to tell me you're fucking a man, Aziz...a fucking man!" She turned and walked over and slapped him, "Are you a fuckin' faggot, Aziz!" Aziz pushed her away, "No!" he quivered, confused as he still gaped over at Peaches, "I thought...I thought..."

"Thought what, Aziz." She grabbed him again and spun him towards Peaches, "Look... look!"

"Leave him alone!" he yelled at her, "It's my fault! I only showed him what he wanted to see! He didn't know!" Falling to his knees he banged the floor, "I wanted to tell him, but..."

"But what, faggot!" Yoshi hollered. "But what! You wanted my brother to think you were a woman, right...and then what!" Yoshi reached back into her jacket, "I ought a-" Aziz grabbed her arm again. "No...no...let it go."

Peaches tried covering his head but it did no good. Aziz yelled back at him, "What the fuck happened!"

Yoshi shook her head, she knew what it was and she went for the exclamation point. She charged him and tackled him down then reached between his legs and pulled at the strap. She tugged then ripped the panties off and the garment had exposed Peaches' genitals. Aziz looked and saw what appeared to him to be some mangled up pieces of meat; Gustavo's father had been cruel. Peaches, embarrassed, covered up with his hands and glanced up at Aziz, "Please...don't judge me. I can explain. I love you. I would have told you." He reached towards him, crawling, "Don't leave me. I love you I can get changed..." he pleaded and tears ran down his face as he doubled over crying uncontrollably. Aziz looked over at Yoshi then walked towards the door, looking back one more time and said, "I can't believe this..."

Yoshi hovered over Peaches as he cried, looking down at him with disdain in her eyes, "You hurt my brother..." she muttered.

Peaches climbed to his feet and started to cower back as Yoshi reached down and picked up the dagger her father used when he murdered: the dagger that was never found by the police, because she kept it for herself. "I'm going to kill you."

Peaches staggered backwards towards the kitchen looking for a weapon and spotted a pan and dove for it. He grasped the handle, rolled over on his feet and threw it. Yoshi ducked, but it was enough time for Peaches to rush up and grab her around the neck, choking with all his strength, "Bitch...you fucked my shit up!"

Yoshi struggled under the weight and force of Peaches' size. He grabbed her collarbone and squeezed. Yoshi twinged; he'd found a pressure point. She lifted her arm up in pain exposing the gun in the holster on her side. In one swift move Peaches pulled the gun and put it to her head. Pushing her away, he told her to drop the knife, "I got you now, bitch. I'm gonna kill you. I'll just explain to Aziz how you tried to shoot me-no...uh, it's Aziz, right." He started circling her, "I got him wrapped around my finger. He'll believe whatever I tell him...once I start kissing between his legs..." Yoshi was enraged now, not so much of the fact that Peaches had the drop on her, but because of what he was saying, it pissed her off. Peaches continued rambling and put the gun to her head and started to pull the trigger then heard a horn from downstairs. It was Aziz. "Yoshi...come on! Let's go!"

He hesitated and glanced towards the window. That was all the stretch Yoshi needed as she reached back and grabbed his hand twisting it hard then ripped the gun from him, angling it back towards him and pulling the trigger, *'Baaap!'*

The bullet ricocheted off the walls just barely missing Peaches' head as he ducked. Yoshi had the gun back and the dagger laid on the floor in between them, Peaches looked down at it then hesitated. Yoshi pointed the gun at him and stepped on it and kicked it away, then wiped the blood from her nose, "You really fucked up now." Peaches made a mad dash for the dark room in the back and slammed the door. Yoshi stepped to the window and pulled down the shades, "I'll be down in a little while. Me and Peaches are going to have...a little talk."

Aziz shook his head and sped off after seeing the window go black. Yoshi wasn't going to leave now and she no longer gave a damn about him. She was hurt, mentally confused, and mad and that made for a bad combination and Aziz knew it. Someone was going to die.

Yoshi stalked towards the door wiping the dagger's steel blade shiny with the rag Aziz had dropped and rasped, "Come here...bitch.

Miles drove around the projects over on 14th Street checking out his connects and some of his closest people trying to find out any hard information about the mill house being robbed. He wasn't too surprised at what he had heard. It wasn't confirmed but he was hearing that the dope was being repacked and put back on the Street. He knew that would happen, but he never would have suspected the parties involved. Then again, it wasn't that far-fetched. He figured he just needed to make a couple of more stops and if he heard the same rap then he knew he'd have to confront the dude.

He didn't want to say anything to Joker too early about what he knew until he had old boy lined up in his sights and his ducks in order. Then he had to have the gray haired, old timer at the Pitt to confirm the dope was theirs. He needed to get his hands on a package; one of his runners in Hampton Square Houses would have to find him a bag. He turned the corner onto Avenue A and sped up the street, then heard his cell phone buzzing in the console. He picked it up and checked the screen, it was Gustavo.

"Yo, wassup."

"Miles...it's me, Gustavo."

"Yeah, I know. What's going on? Why are you calling me?"

"I got a situation that I need you to help me out with."

Miles paused for a second, Gustavo sounded real urgent, desperate. He knew something had to be wrong, he lost his cool. He pulled the truck over and parked, "Talk to me."

"I got a lead on Aziz."

"I've been looking for that guy!"

"Well, I think I know where he's held up at."

"Where!"

"I'm outside the Pitt. Why don't you pick me up and we can go get him together."

"I'm on the way." Miles cranked the truck up and sped off towards the Pitt. Gustavo was standing up the block when Miles turned the corner; he pulled over and opened the door, "Come on in."

Gustavo jumped in, closed the door and reached over giving him some dap, "I believe I know where he's at right now."

"How?"

"I got connections." he shot back.

Miles put up his hands, "I didn't mean to get in your business..."

"Naw...that's cool, but the source I have is pretty credible. I got a call," he pulled up his coat sleeve and checked his watch, "about an hour or so ago."

"You think he's still there?"

"Well...I didn't get a call back saying he'd left, so..."

"Yeah, I hear you." Miles rolled past the Pitt and looked over at the office and saw the curtains draw back and Joker peep out, "What's up. Why didn't you let him take you?"

Gustavo smirked and said, "Your boss is on some old bullshit."

"Hell, I could have told you that." Miles chuckled. He pulled up to the stop sign on the corner and asked, "Where to?" Gustavo pointed towards the right and told him to keep going until he got to the West side over by the piers. "Over near the hoe stroll?"

Gustavo nodded. "There's some old butcher shops that were converted to apartments."

"Lofts and shit. Close to SoHo."

"That's the spot."

Miles drove up Houston Street and Gustavo pointed out an old, red, brick building. He looked up at Peaches' window and the blinds were pulled shut, curtains closed. He was keeping him occupied until he got there, he thought.

"Which building?" Miles asked.

They pulled in a spot across the Street and quickly walked over shrouding their face as someone walked out. They caught the door and dashed for the elevator. Gustavo pressed three, waited for the doors to close then pulled the stop button. He reached into his jacket and pulled his gun then cocked it, "You carryin'?" Miles reached and did the same, "Will we need it?" he asked.

"I think so." Gustavo sneered.

Miles thought about the bodies of Big E and Pancho when he'd found them, "I know that's right." he said. Gustavo pushed the stop button back in and the elevator resumed upstairs stopping only on three. They got off slowly looking around, they saw no one. Gustavo pointed to the door and he started to knock but pushed the door slightly. It was open. They pulled out their guns and silently crept inside. It was dim but some light escaped through the blinds as they tiptoed in quieting their steps as they moved. The living room was neat and tidy and showed no signs of anyone ever being there. Gustavo stepped off into the kitchen area and saw nothing. It was as clean as a whistle. Miles pointed to a room off to the back and they slowly headed towards it. Gustavo pushed open the bedroom door and no one stirred. The only room left was Peaches' studio in the back. They both moved cautiously towards the door and Gustavo turned the knob. He stepped through, Miles was right behind him and they saw a body sitting in a chair facing a light table. Gustavo put his finger to his mouth in a hushing movement and silently maneuvered to the side ducking out of sight. Miles was right up on him with his gun drawn, ready. The darkroom was pitch black and the studio lights showed the silhouette of a figure they couldn't quite make out, unmoving, deathly still. Gustavo pointed to a light switch and on cue flipped it and light flooded the room. They cringed back gasping at what they saw next.

Yoshi had hid in the closet unnoticed as they walked by. She was as quiet as a rat pissing on cotton as she listened closely to them through the wall.

"Oh shit, Miles!"

Miles moved up to get a better view, "Damn!"

Peaches' body had been propped up in a chair overlooking pictures he'd taken of Aziz. He still wore the same outfit he'd had on earlier; the skirt, blouse, but his legs were gaped open with a bloody trail that led to the floor. They looked down and saw that the carpet was saturated with blood, explaining the sopping sound they heard when they came in.

He was dead. His mouth was stuffed with something they couldn't quite make out. Gustavo moved closer and used a prop stick to pry open his jaws. The spasm from his muscle twitching made them draw back out the way as Peaches' body spit out what was in it. A blood soaked penis, and they got closer and noticed testicles. Miles shielded his eyes almost gagging, "That muthafucka' is sick!"

"You think Aziz did this!" Gustavo questioned.

"Let me tell you something. Every time I go somewhere where he's been at, a body shows up and believe me, this crazy shit is the norm. But why," Miles examined the body a little closer, "would he kill this woman and who's dick and shit is this?"

Gustavo pointed towards his legs and angled him around. The trail from the floor led up to a gash exposed where Peaches' dick and nuts were, "They belonged to him."

"Him!" Miles jumped back, "You mean this is a he-she!"

"Yeah...Aziz's lover!"

"Oh shit! Aziz was fucking a punk! You kiddin' me!"

"Naw...I'm afraid not."

"So...how did you know?" Miles backed up and looked at him cockeyed, "You knew this person or what? Was this your source and how-?"

"Whoa! Hold up." Gustavo walked away from the body and started wiping off his shoes on the rug behind them, "I grew up with this dude. I didn't know about him and Aziz until the other day. He was the one that called me and told me he was coming here. I assumed Aziz found out and killed him."

"Hmmm..." Miles said, "So, Aziz's hip to the fact that there's a contract on his head, huh. I can see why Joker wants him dead."

"I want him alive."

"But, why? Muthafucka's crazy."

Gustavo backed up out the room and guided Miles's steps, making sure not to touch anything, "Do you know where Joker's main stash is?"

Miles looked over at him strangely, "Naw...why?"

"Well, let's just say that it worth thousands...hundreds of thousands, right."

"Probably."

"I bet Aziz knows where it's at and if so, I can or...we...can get it. Get Alphabet City. Get control and get rid...of Joker."

Miles stopped and thought about the situation then looked over at Gustavo, "So...who would run Alphabet City then...you?"

Gustavo snickered as they walked towards the front door, "I have no interest. Alphabet needs a man that's on point. On top of his game." He looked over at Miles then pressed the elevator button and wiped it down afterward with a handkerchief, "You...if you're down for that."

Miles smiled at the thought of it. "We'll talk. Where are we going now?"

"Might as well go...talk, think so?"

"Yeah...let's do that."

Yoshi had heard enough of what she needed to hear and she dipped down the steps out the back behind them. She needed to hurry up and catch up to her brother before Miles or Gustavo saw him and let him know what was going down.

After hearing all that, she was glad she stayed over and cleaned up the mess they've made. On top of that, she was thrilled to death that she'd watched that punk ass Peaches beg for his life before she sliced off his dick and balls then shoved them down his throat.

Gustavo and Miles headed to a small eatery near Little Italy on Grand Street. An out of the way bistro visited by some of New York's most notorious types; they fitted in perfectly.

A table towards the back frequented by those who wanted to talk about things no one else needed to know was where they sat. Miles ordered a salad plate and Gustavo, pasta. After their meal, coffee was served up and Gustavo lit a cigar and offered Miles one, he declined. Gustavo crossed his legs, it was time for business.

"So...do you come here often?" Miles asked.

"Not much since I've been back in the city." Gustavo said as he admired the decor, "It is nice, though."

"It is." Miles pushed his cup to the side out of the way and leaned forward, "Okay, so, what's up?"

"I like you. Straight to the point." He put his cigar in an ashtray and took another swig of coffee and said, "I want to take over Alphabet City."

"Well, that's known. Joker said that, about five days ago. You wanted to buy him out right?"

"That was the plan, but...things have changed since."

"Seems like shit just went crazy all of a sudden. So, now...you don't want to buy..." Miles said snidely.

"I offered him a deal."

"Then, what's the problem?"

Gustavo moved in closer, "To be honest. I don't want to pay him."

"That's not business."

"It never was about business, anyway. It was all about taking it back."

"I don't get it."

Gustavo took another swig of coffee and beckoned to the waitress for some more before he continued. "Joker acquired Alphabet City by same real shady dealings. Well, my client...wants it back."

Miles's face was perplexed as he tried putting the pieces together. "Who? You mean...Akbar? I thought he was doing Fed. time or something." He started counting on his fingers, "Fifteen...eighteen...he should be on his way home in another what sixteen years or something. Hell I was a kid when he left."

Impressed at Miles's awareness, maturity, focus, he kept on, "Things have changed. He'll be here tomorrow-"

"Hold up." Miles leaned back in his chair, "In Alphabet!"

"Yeah."

"So...damn. He wanted you to buy back Alphabet from Joker, huh. Hell, why doesn't he just take it back. If Joker did that pussy ass shit to me, I'd be trying to kill him."

"You got it right." Gustavo said.

"So, you're really just trying to take the muthafucka out." Miles tripped on the whole scenario, "This whole thing about buying him out is bullshit."

"Something like that."

"So...now." Miles asked after some scrutiny. The pieces were coming together. "Where do I fit in?"

"Once Joker gets taken out, my associate needs a good man to run it." he answered.

"Whoa. Hold up. I'm no one's flunky. That shit is old." Miles picked up a napkin and started wiping his mouth, getting ready to leave, "I'm trying to get my own shit."

Gustavo reached over, "Hold up. Hear me out."

"I'm listening."

"Look. I got to know you since I've been here. I've also checked out things around here. My associate is just like Joker, and does this city really need another Joker? His style of dealing has played out, Miles. Look at the big picture. It doesn't have to just be about the dope. Man, fuck the dope. This shit here is prime fuckin' property worth millions on top of millions; and the good thing about it, you don't have to get your hands dirty."

It made sense. The Lower East Side was quickly becoming one of the hottest prime markets in the city, and the world. "I'm feeling that..."

"Okay, then. Let's do it."

"Do what? Man, I don't know nothing about running-"

"I got you."

"Then...why don't you do it?"

"Why? Once I acquire this, then I move on, and using this capitol, acquire more of this type of property. Trap houses...whole neighborhoods, cities...other places like Harlem, Brooklyn, Staten Island...hell. Jersey, Detroit, Chicago...man, even fuckin' California! This is just the beginning." he said as he banged his hand on the table rattling the coffee cups.

Miles contemplated for a minute on what he'd just said and responded. "Like I said. What has this got to do with me?"

Gustavo leaned forward into him, glaring in his eyes sneering as he spoke. "I know you know where Joker's stash is. With that money we can put what we just talked about in place. Now...we can drink coffee and shit all day, and I can tell you more about this plan. I can go on and on all evening long. But the bottom line is, I need the fuckin' money."

"You're good. But...how do I know you won't double cross me?" Miles snapped back.

Gustavo's sneer turned into a half-assed grin, "I like that. Well, you don't know, that's why we go half. The money...and the bodies...Joker's...Akbar's...even Aziz."

Miles nodded then uncrossed his legs and stood up, "Well then..." he held out his hand, "Let's get busy."

"So...you know where it's at?"

"How does a man know when his cowardice ends and his loyalty begins?"

Gustavo shook his head, "What..."

Miles straightened out his clothes and stepped by him and stopped, then whispered in his ear, "If you fuck me over, I'll kill you...myself. You understand."

Gustavo responded by nodding his head, "I understand." He had the partner of his dreams, Miles. He would take him to the money and then they would kill Akbar, Aziz and Joker together. He'd buy into the dope trade and lucrative, real estate, then when he was finished using him, he'd kill him, too. He chuckled, "Right behind you...partner."

He jumped back in Miles's truck and sped off towards Alphabet City. The sun had already started setting, and the nightlife began to blanket the city. Gustavo asked "So...where are we headed? To the stash?"

Miles snickered as he looked over at him, "Naw. It ain't that fuckin' easy. I don't get pimped." He made a left going to the poolroom, "We go to check out Joker...see if your story checks out." he stared off into the sunset, "If not...then we have a problem."

chapter 19

"AREN'T YOU LISTENING? They're trying to kill you!" Yoshi had been screaming at him for the better part of an hour and he still didn't respond. He drifted back and forth to the window staring out, looking off, "Aziz, what is wrong with you!"

He got up from the sofa and lethargically walked towards the room still not saying a word. Yoshi looked up at him and followed, bewildered as she stepped towards the doorway. He'd opened the dresser drawer and reached in retrieving the belt from earlier. He threw it on the bed and turned around slowly undressing himself. Sadly, Yoshi shook her head as she watched, then reached for the belt and he flinched. "No!" she said and ran into the kitchen throwing the worn, leather strap into the trash bin. Aziz was right behind her gaping at her in dismay. "Like you said, Aziz, it's over with. Now, it's just you and me and they want to kill you. You understand...take you away from me...and...I can't let that happen." She walked closer to him and embraced him, "We have to get them...first."

Aziz rubbed his hands through his balding head trying to get a grip, "B-b-but...what if they don't like me..." he uttered. He was starting to lose control of his faculties, resorting back to different stages of his troubled past. Yoshi knew what it was, he needed his medicine, but she'd thrown it away. She scrambled for the trash digging through in a last ditch effort to retrieve anything, but it was gone. She remembered she'd tossed the trash in the dumpster earlier right after she came in. She rushed to the window and looked out. It was too late, it was gone. Downtrodden, she sulked, then plopped down in the middle of the floor crying. It was starting to get away from her. The family she tried to hold on to, make perfect for her parents, was not happening, now and as she wept bitterly.

Aziz walked over to her and kneeled down beside her, caressing her long, silky hair, like their mother had, and said, "We can get through this, sis." She looked up in his eyes, smiled, then reached out and hugged him, "I know...I know..."

They sat for what seemed forever; crying cleansing tears in each other's arms, then Yoshi shook her head and threw up her arms, "No! We got a way!" She scrambled to her feet and ran off into the bedroom, Aziz hot on her tail, "What?" he asked.

She dragged the bulky black duffel bag from out of the closet, and with Aziz's help, dumped its contents onto the bed. Money flowed out, pounds of green paper weighing down her bed. She rummaged through it and found what she's been searching for, the ledger. "We still have this, Aziz!" she said as she held it out in front of him.

Aziz stared at it as his thoughts took hold, it sparked memories of the day Dante was killed. Known as a playa, he knocked off the young, teenage girls that ogled him whenever he got the chance, one by one. He did love Mya very much but he was still a young man, he couldn't stay grounded.

Yoshi was one of those such girls, she was a trick. He'd use her and eventually took her virginity and she loved him for it. He was her first true love aside from her father. He would go by the school and pick her up, ducking Mya. He would take her to one of the shooting galleries, an old abandoned warehouse and fuck, then drop her off on 42nd Street at a movie theatre leaving her by herself to walk home alone. She'd cry herself to sleep, he'd made her feel worthless and forsaken. He would call her the names her mother would: whore; slut; bitch, it didn't make for any emotional stability in a young, adolescent girl and seeing him with Mya only made her sicker.

Aziz himself was just getting a foothold in the game. Joker had confided in him, trusting him to do runs, some petty pickups here and there. Many times when he'd gotten drunk and Aziz drove him home, he'd tell him things about Dante, how he didn't trust him. How his sources told him that Dante was out to cut his throat, plotting his downfall, even going to the police and snitching. As far as Joker was concerned, he was getting too large too quickly, and he didn't like that.

It all seems to happen real fast. That day Joker had told him in secret he'd give him ten grand to take him out, dispose of the body, both him and his girl, Mya. He'd wanted her out the picture because by now she knew about as much of his operation as Dante did. He'd taken her everywhere and told her everything, maybe, Joker thought, even about his stash spots. He'd kill two birds with one stone. He told Aziz he'd make him his main man, his right hand and Aziz eagerly jumped on it. Besides, he didn't like the way Dante handled his sister.

He went home to tell Yoshi he was going to get large and eventually with the money to take them out of Alphabet City, perhaps Queens. He was feeling good, elated, but Yoshi wasn't home, she'd run away again. She'd argued earlier with their mother. His mother had made him go look for her, told him she wasn't finished with her. She wanted to beat her again, just like his old man did her. She took it out on Yoshi. He'd scoured all through Alphabet for her then he'd finally got a lead. Across from the Pitt was an abandoned building. He raced over there.

He remembered the voices as he crept up the steps, the shouting. He dashed into the apartment and Dante was standing over her, she was crying. He turned away when he saw him and started straightening up his clothes and said, "You need to talk to her..." She told him that she was going to have Dante's baby, and he wanted no parts of that. He spun around and started calling her names, names her mother had yelled at her earlier, "You stink ass, fuckin' cunt! I can't believe this bitch would think I would want a baby from her!" he stepped towards the door, "I got the finest girl in the hood...Mya. I don't want no...whore."

Aziz recalled how fast she moved, pulling out a dagger and slashing him with it. He screamed like a bitch as the blood spurted out onto the walls everywhere. Dante reached for his gun and Aziz jumped on him. They struggled furiously and the gun fell to the floor. Yoshi dived for it. Dante lunged at her and she shot him point blank in the chest and he fell hard to the ground dead.

The next thing you know they heard the sounds of someone coming up the steps calling out his name. It was Mya. Aziz snatched the gun away from her and pointed his sister towards the fire escape. She scurried down the steps and as he turned he knew he had to come up with something fast.

He told her Dante was being robbed when he came up on him. He said the jack boy jumped at him and they fought and a gun went off, Dante's. He claimed it was an accident, he was aiming at the other man as he got away down the fire escape. By that time he heard sirens so he snuck her out and they hauled ass.

Joker was glad Dante was dead, but he still wanted to kill Mya but Aziz gave her an option. Die or stay with him, be his girl. He could leave his mother finally and establish his own. Mya was scared and frightened, she easily went for it. Joker explained to him that as long as he kept his eye or her, she would be safe from him and that's how it's been, until now.

Yoshi blamed her for not letting her brother come home that night. Her mother beat her and he wasn't there to stop her. She blamed Mya for the miscarriage and losing the baby. She hated her ever since. It was Yoshi who was responsible for switching medications on Aziz, gave him hers. He didn't react well to the homicidal drug; hallucinations, paranoid delusions, she unleashed her abomination on Mya through Aziz. It worked.

Aziz grabbed her hand and pulled her close to him, "Okay, sis, it ends tonight. We kill them, get the rest of the money from Joker's stash and with the ledger...take over Alphabet City."

CHINO LOCKED THE SLIDING bolt across the door after he'd come in. It was late, and already they'd handled all the pickups for the evening, taking in at least 15 grand from all the spots combined. Petty cash. The stolen dope made everyone run off searching for it. It was being sold cheap, for little or nothing; get rid of it and make quick money. Joker was pissed. "If I catch this muthafucka..."

He looked over at the half empty satchel bag and growled like a bear. Chino calmly unlocked the door to the back and asked, "We still count, or what?"

"Count what!" he hollered, "This ain't shit!"

"True...but, the night's still young. Maybe, things might get better."

Joker nodded, he was right. It was still early and maybe he might see a surge later on once the other dope ran out. It was a good time to go over the books anyway. He'd been neglecting it lately. He wanted to see what Alphabet City was worth these days, see if the deal he made with Gustavo was worth it. Least take the last drop of money he could get from it before he turned things over, "You're right." He turned towards the bar, "Tempest! Let me get a bottle of Cognac!"

Tempest was in the back room fucking around with Blu. She stuck her head out, "I'm coming..." She was snatched back in and Joker heard her giggling. "God-damnit...now!" She rushed out with a bottle in her hand and grabbed two glasses, "Chino, you drinking with him?" He nodded his head, yes, and then she turned towards Blu who was coming out from the back straightening his pants, trying to conceal the hard on he'd worked up, "How bout you?" He reached over and squeezed her ass before he answered, "I'll take a drink."

Joker got up from the table and walked behind the bar into the storeroom. He looked around suspiciously as he pushed a shelf quietly over to the side revealing a safe. He dialed the combination numbers on it and it popped open, then reached in grabbing two ledgers and closed it back shut. He came back out and Tempest had already set up the table.

Both books were supposed to have contained the same count. Money that was collected daily from all his spots, and also all the dope that was taken there. At least, that was the plan. Gutter and Smack normally kept up with it, had it down to a science, but since they were missing and no one seemed to know where they were at, he let Blu take up the slack, he trusted him. Chino didn't want no parts of it. He was quite content with what he did for him, big boy, hard core, security.

Joker opened the books and started reciting the numbers randomly, coding, a system he'd devised, making sure everything was in order. He did well for about the first few days, but he noticed inconsistencies. Numbers were being forged. The product and the digits didn't add up. He looked at the spots written down and he knew good and damn well something was up. He asked Blu, "Why are the numbers off? Hell, I'm missing...so far, according to this...30-40 grand, easy. What the fuck is up?"

Blu leaned over and looked, "Maybe something ain't adding up somewhere." He looked down at his book and said, "My numbers are straight over here." Joker snatched the book from him and looked in it, then pointed to some erasures, blanks. "No...no...something's wrong, I tell you. This shit ain't right. Gutter and Smack never did no shit like this."

"No, Joker. You must have made a mistake-"

Joker reached over and snatched Blu up almost pulling him over the table, "Who the fuck has been skimming money!"

"Skimming money?"

"Muthafucka, don't play stupid. I've been in this game for damn near 20 years and believe me when I tell you! I know when a muthafucka' is stealing my money!"

Blu was deep in the shit now, up to his knees. He just figured he'd grab a few gee and let it be done with. Cop enough money to buy a nice ride, a beamer and find a nice condo in Brooklyn for Tempest. Set her up nice. He rationalized that they'd made enough money anyway and a few grand would be nothing. But, like Joker was saying, 30-40 grand was too much and he didn't have anything to do with that. He was being setup. "Joker...look...I can explain."

Chino shook his head. He didn't have a clue why Blu said something that stupid. He should have kept acting clueless, blamed the whole thing on Gutter, Smack, clean it up later, but hell, it was none of his business. He didn't have shit to do with it. When Blu mentioned it to him, asked him if he wanted to be down, he told him to get out of his face. He didn't want no parts of it or hear anything. Joker turned towards him, now, "You know about this!"

"I handle...business. Not bullshit." he replied candidly. Joker let go of Blu and smirked, "Well, then, if you handle business," he got up and walked behind Chino, "Take care of this..." Blu copped deuces, "Hold up, Joker! You're not even sure it was all me! All I got was a few gee to put on a car. I don't know anything else 'bout the rest of the money! Believe me!"

"You's a fuckin' thief. I liked you Blu, but damn, I can't have you stealing my money. I don't play that shit and you of all people should know that. So...how you wanna handle it?"

"Don't kill me. I can make the money back for you." Blu pleaded.

"Oh...you will and I'm not going to kill you, oh hell no. You don't get over that easy." He glanced over at Chino, took out his gun and placed it on the table in front of him, "Let him shoot you in the ass-"

"No fuckin' way! I told you I can work it off!" Blu backed up over near the bar where Tempest cowered behind it. He turned towards her, "Tell him, baby."

Tempest quivered as she stuck up her head up, looked at Joker then Blu and said, "I don't know anything about it, Joker. I mean, he gave me some money, but I don't like him like that-"

"You bitch! I gave you money to get a place! What happened to the down payment for the car, Tempest? What are you saying!"

She moved back away from Blu towards the back room, "Joker. I don't know what he's talking about..."

Joker grinned as he watched them both wiggle, like rats caught in a trap, his. "Tempest, Tempest, Tempest. You don't think I know about the fucking peep hole in the room next to the safe. You stupid, little bitch. Blu, you're fucking a whore. She doesn't like you. Hell, she just sucked my dick earlier and you steady tongue-kissing this bitch! She likes to use people like you, that's all." He laughed loudly, incensing Blu. Chino pulled open his jacket and the gleam coming from off his razor sharpened, stainless steel carving knives shined as Joker picked up his gun and cocked it. "No...what is it? Shoot you in the ass, or, hmmm, do I have to call Bezo.

Blu had remembered the horror story Miles had told him about what he did to Peanut and he instinctively reached for his gun. He swore he rather die than have that happen to him, and he meant that. "Oh, hell no!" Tempest dived behind the bar and cried out. "Just let him shoot you in the ass, Blu!"

Blu looked over at her and yelled, "Bitch I'm gonna kill you first!"

Joker fired his gun at her and the bullet whizzed over her head and ricocheted into a glass bottle shattering it, glass fragments flew all over the place. Blu shielded his eyes and shouted out, "What the fuck!"

"I'll be the one who kills her!"

Tempest shivered behind the counter screaming, "W-wha-what did I do!"

"Bitch...you've been stealing my money for years!" Hell, I didn't mind the grand or two here and there. You earned that!" He aimed the gun at her again, "But, 30-40 fuckin' grand...in a week! Are you kidding me!" He fired another round over her head. This time she stood with her hands held high, shaking, "Please, Joker, I just wanted a little something for myself. I can't work a fuckin' bar all my life!"

Blu looked at her and gawked, "You mean, you've been using me all this time..."

She inched closer towards the door looking for a way out, "Please! You're just another wannabe gangster! I had my fair share of them!" she said as she eyeballed the bolt that secured the doorway.

Joker lowered his gun and shook his head, "Tempest. All you had to do was ask. She stared at him then smiled, "Huh Well then, I can make it up to you, baby. The way you like it, right."

"Yeah, come over and bring those nice juicy ass lips and let me show Blu how you take care of me, huh. Maybe, Chino, too okay." Joker laughed as she nodded her head yes, and then Chino rubbed his groin watching her fat ass from around the counter. He'd always wanted a piece of that anyway. He was definitely going to punish it, "Yeah...know that's right!"

Tempest started easing her way from around the bar when Blu hauled back his arm and smacked her, sending her reeling into the back of the bar. She tried shaking herself off, recovering from the hit, but jerked as a bottle dropped besides her busting, then another. She'd broken the foundation on the mantle and it started to collapse. The mirrored, glass wall trembled for a moment, then it fell forward, sending bottles and the mirror crashing down on top of her. It shattered and ripped her face and arms to pieces as she cringed. Glass was stuck in layers over her body, Blu screamed out, "Tempest!"

She laid out on the floor among the broken glass; her body had spasms as blood pooled up around her heavily. Joker and Chino rushed over to the bar and looked down at her. "Aw, shit! Is she still alive?"

Chino looked at her stomach rise up and down laboriously as she gasped, "Barely. We need to get her to a hospital, fast!"

Joker put out his hand and stopped him as he tried to rush to the back room for a phone "No...she'll be dead soon. We'll get rid of the body. Clean this shit up, Blu. After all...it was your fault anyway."

Blu couldn't believe what he was hearing. There was no way he could let the woman he loved, just die, "No, Joker. We gonna call an ambulance!"

"Ambulance! Hell no! You stupid muthafucka!" Joker looked at him like he was crazy, "And have the fuckin' police come pouring through here looking for shit! Let her ass die!"

Blu pointed his gun towards him, "Chino...call the police, now!"

"Oh...that's how you want to play it, huh." Joker started stalking towards the side of the bar closer to the jukebox, "You want to kill me?" Chino went in the opposite direction leaning on the video machines by the doorway, his jacket still propped open. He reached slowly inside the holster and uncovered the sheaves that held his knives in place. "Do you honestly think you can do it, kill me? Hey, look...I'll find you some more pussy, okay. We can forget about this."

"Don't move!" Blu held the gun tightly towards Joker figuring Chino was no threat, thinking maybe he had to be up on him close to be able to use his weapons, but as the knife whistled through the air towards him and sliced his arm, severing it from the elbow, he knew he was dead wrong. "Awh!" he screamed out in pain.

Joker squeezed off three rounds quick, *'Baap!' 'Baap!' 'Baap!'* The bullets shattered the rest of the mirror that hung loosely in the frame and a sizable chunk dropped, landing on Tempest's head. Her face was ripped to shreds as the fragments sunk deep into her skull. It was over with, she was dead. Blu winced in pain as his arm landed on the floor in front of him. With his other, he aimed at Chino and started shooting wildly. All the shots missed tearing up the video machines in the background. Swiftly, Chino was up on him. Blu looked up at him in pity as Chino's arm was raised high above his head leveling off the six inch, pointed knife he brandished and Blu could do nothing but close his eyes.

It was quick, Chino kicked Blu's body over and his head dropped off, cut clean from ear to ear. He motioned towards Joker, "You alright?"

Suddenly, the front door was kicked open. Throughout all the commotion they paid no mind to the kicking and banging earlier. It was Bezo, finally getting the thick, steel door open. He glanced around at the bodies on the floor, the broken glass and then Chino, knife still in his hand and Joker standing behind him, waving. Chino turned and raised his arm to put his knife back and Bezo raised his gun, "I got him, boss!" he roared.

Joker put up his hand in an effort to tell him to stop, don't shoot, but it was too late. Chino's body spun from the .44 that twisted his body. Blood spurted out his mouth as he fell to his knees, the bullet pierced his heart. He tried turning back towards Bezo and reached for his knife, Bezo aimed again and fired. The shot hit him between the eyes as Chino fell face down to the floor.

Joker was shocked, he tripped out, "What the fuck did you do!" He ran over to Chino's body, "Damn...you killed him!"

"Boss...I thought he was trying to kill you! I did! I'm sorry..."

Joker shook his head. He knew Bezo didn't know what was happening and he was only trying to protect him. He couldn't even get mad, at least not at that. Now, he had to clean up this mess, then somehow cover it up, "Damn..."

Joker wiped his mouth worrying as he walked over to the bar and leaned. He needed a quick way to handle the disarray that was made, he had to make a call to Miles for help. Then he remembered that Gustavo had said he was coming by and he had to stop him; he didn't want him to see no parts of this. He might renege on his deal. He turned towards Bezo and snapped, "Go find me some carpet...quick!"

"Okay, boss." Bezo answered, then tucked the .44 he still displayed in his waistband.

"Okay...you know what this is!" Bezo turned facing three masked, heavily armed robbers coming through the door, guns raised, aimed at him moving very quickly. One approached Bezo at the bar, and the other two posted up behind a pool table close to where the video games were at. Joker looked up, "Now, what the fuck is this!"

Steve, Skyler and Mya made their move like they'd planned. Steve raised his gun up to Bezo's head and told him to kiss the floor.

Mya and Skyler held their guns at Joker, scanning the room for any traces of money laying around. Mya stared over at the bar and the clutter, then glanced near the opening and saw blood seeping out, she gasped, "Oh shit!" That was just enough time for Joker to take his gun back out, "Fuck this!"

He fired shots over at Skyler and Mya. They returned the gunfire and ducked behind a pool table. "Get down!" Skyler said as one of Joker's bullets barely missed her ear, she dived on the floor. Steve turned towards them and Bezo ducked the gun and sweep-kicked him to the floor. Joker hauled ass to the bathroom, the secret getaway. Mya and Skyler kept shooting as the bullets bounced off the walls, ringing steel claps throughout the air. Skyler got up and ran behind Joker. He turned and shot his last bullet. It struck Skyler in the arm as she cried out in pain, "Ahhhh, shit!" Mya ran behind her shooting at Joker as he ducked behind a pool table for cover. He looked over at the satchel bag filled with the 15 grand laying there. He waited for the shots to clear then dived for it. Mya saw the bag also and reached in her waist band and pulled out the knife she had and jumped at him, swinging. The dagger just missed, sticking right above his head into the green cloth of the oblong, billiard table. He released the bag and jumped back.

Skyler was winged but she managed to reload and fired some rounds at Joker, missing, littering holes on the bathroom door. Joker dived inside. Mya grabbed the bag and tossed it back over towards Skyler, "Here you go!" then jetted after Joker.

Bezo had Steve on the ground choking him. Steve gagged and wiggled trying to wrestle his way up underneath the weight of the big, burly, bruiser. It was no use. He reached down and grabbed his balls and squeezed, he yelled out, but still he didn't release his grip. He then remembered that his gun still laid to the side and tried to reach for it. Skyler looked up and saw Bezo on top on Steve and ran over, "Noooo!"

She jumped on his back and Bezo reached around and threw her head first into a pool table like a rag doll. She hit hard, knocking her out momentarily. That was enough for Steve to grab the gun. Bezo tried to snatch it from him but Steve angled it to his chest and pulled the trigger. One shot. Bezo slumped over and laid on top of him, blood spurted from a large hole straight to his heart. He died instantly. Steve pushed him off of him and rushed over to Skyler and picked her up grabbing the duffel bag with the other hand.

Mya hesitated before she entered the four stall, bathroom. Joker struggled furiously pushing the toilet bowl to the side revealing a sliding, metal, stairwell that led downstairs to a door to the alleyway out back. Mya crept around and looked underneath the stall, gun still in her hands, smoking. Joker got it open, Mya spotted him. Joker jumped on the stool as Mya fired three rounds at his feet. He looked at the hole and the stairs and jumped through. Mya got up kicking the stall door open. Looking at the hole she looked in and saw Joker as he scrambled down the steps. She took aim and fired. She missed as he busted through the door falling into the street. She started to climb in, but heard Steve call out her name. She mean-mugged Joker and hauled ass back out to the front.

Skyler had the bag clutched tightly in her hand as Steve motioned her over, "C'mon, we gotta get out of here!"

"We got the money?!" Mya asked.

Steve looked at Skyler, still groggy from the toss and bleeding heavily from her arm and said, "We got something...let's go!"

They all turned towards the door and suddenly stopped in their tracks as Miles and Gustavo came through. "What the hell is going on?" He surveyed the room and saw the damaged wrecked room, torn up bullet holes strewn throughout the wall, then looked over at them and saw the satchel bag in their hands. He knew what it was. He drew his gun, "Jack boys! Take cover!"

Gustavo dived for the floor and pulled his gun as Miles rolled around to the back of the bar. He stared over at Tempest's mangled body, then wailed, "Aw shit! You muthafucka's gonna pay for this!"

Steve pushed Skyler to the ground and Mya grabbed her and started back-peddling towards the bathroom recollecting the hole Joker had escaped from. She knew it was an out, but what she didn't know was if Joker was out there waiting. She had to chance it. She smacked Skyler who was starting to lose consciousness, "C'mon girl, wake up!" Skyler came to, but Miles had heard their voices, "I know who you are!" Mya paid it no mind and started towards the bathroom. Miles got up and aimed his gun their way. Steve saw him and aimed his gun at him. He paused and Skyler and Mya continued to run. Gustavo jumped up, aimed and shot Steve in the arm and as he whirled from the shot, Miles caught him in the shoulder. He dropped. Gustavo got up and started running full speed towards Mya and Skyler. Mya dropped Skyler and let off a couple of rounds his way slowing him down. Skyler had regained her senses long enough to remember she had the Uzi in her backpack. She reached inside and put in a clip, got up and started spraying. Gustavo hit the ground and started rolling from the rain of gun fire that chased him. Mya glanced over at Steve as he tried crawling their way, Skyler gave him some cover fire. He got up and ran towards them. Gustavo took aim and shot him in the back. Steve fell to the ground grimacing in pain as he yelled at Mya to go, to get Skyler and haul ass. Skyler backed up and tried to help him, but he couldn't move, the bullet paralyzed his legs. "Goooo! Get out! Pass me the Uzi, I'll cover you!" he continued to shout.

Miles had gotten closer to him and called out, "Steve! That's you!" Steve ignored him as he looked up into Skyler's eyes then took off his mask and smiled, "You know I always loved you, right..."

"Shhh, Steve, be quiet. Don't talk. We'll get you out of here." Skyler said as she cuddled his head in her arms.

Steve reached and grabbed at the Uzi and she wouldn't let it go, "Come on, baby...get out of here!" She let it go unwillingly, he propped himself up against the door casing. "There's some money at the crib. I made a quick lick...it's yours. Leave this place-"

"Steve!" Miles shouted out, "I know it's you. Come on, man! Don't go out like this! We homeboys! We can work this out!"

Steve shook his head, more from pain then what Miles had said, but it hurt, too. Miles had recognized him. "Naw, man...it's my turn to get paid now. You and Aziz been getting yours all these years!" he hollered back.

"You played that card. You knew good and damn well, me and Aziz would have brought you in-"

"What! As a fuckin' flunky! I'm better than that. You know that!"

"I feel you. But, you got to do better than what you're doing! I know you robbed the millhouse!" Miles stuck his head up after reloading his gun getting a head on him, waiting for a response, "Just give me back the money and the money from the dope you stole and we can work something out, okay!"

Steve pulled Skyler close to him and kissed her as Mya pushed open the bathroom door, "I love you."

"I love you too, Steve..."

He shoved them away and shouted back, "Like you did Peanut, right. Fuck that!" He pushed himself up and started to spray heavy gunfire at Miles and ducked, then thrust the girls through the door, "I'll die first!" and he started shooting again, totally oblivious to the shadow that approached him off to the side, it was Gustavo. He pointed his gun to his head, "If that's what you want..." then pulled the trigger. Steve's head exploded like a melon. Gustavo kicked his body away from the door.

Miles got up and ran over to him, "What the fuck did you do that for! He would have given up!"

Gustavo looked at him and said, nonchalantly, "He waited too late. Now let's get the others."

Miles watched as Gustavo slipped through the door, he was behind him as he gave one last look at Steve.

Mya opened the stall and pushed Skyler through, then pointed down into the hole. Skyler tossed her the duffel bags "No! You go! It's gonna take me some time to get down. My arm is too sore."

Mya nodded and jumped into the staircase and made her way to the door then motioned for Skyler to come down, "C'mon on." Skyler shooed her off and leveled the gun Gustavo's way as she heard them come through. "You need some time. Go get the car!"

Mya threw the bag out the door and dived through. Joker was hiding, ducking behind a trash bin. She picked up the bag and hauled ass to the car parked out front.

Gustavo ducked the shots as she fired at him then dove to the floor and spotted her feet. He shot and she stumbled then fell into the hole on her back. She winced in pain and looked at her ankle, it was broke. She tried to crawl to the door but it only hurt more. Gustavo looked in the hole and put in another clip and pointed. Then, his eyes bulged open and he turned around feeling his chest. He had been shot. Miles had the gun raised to his head. It was still smoking as the sulfur seeped out the muzzle. Gustavo looked at him in shock, disbelief, wondering why, "What the fuck!" he said as Miles pulled the trigger again and he fell against the side of the stall falling face first into the toilet. Miles looked down at him as bubbles rose up from the murky water and said, "That was for Akbar..." he spit on him, "and Steve."

chapter 20

AZIZ AND YOSHI WATCHED silently as it all unfolded before their eyes. In disbelief they shook their heads as they watched across the street from the alley next to the Chinese restaurant. A still masked Mya ran out in front cranking up the car making a U-turn, then skidded off into the alleyway.

Blood was showering down on Skyler from Gustavo's body, but it was so dark and dim she didn't know what it was and wiped at it. "Ewww it's nasty down here..." She struggled to get her bearings as she turned her body around gritting her teeth in pain from her ankle swelling up, cursing as she moved. "That fuckin' Mya. "When my foot gets right, I'm gonna kick her ass-" The door swung open. It was Joker. "I knew it was a bitch" he said. He held the gun and reached up ripping the mask from off her head. "Hmmm...you look familiar. I can't quite place you though."

Not knowing what he would do, she figured like all men he was just horny and he'd rape her, but Joker was a different type of man. He pulled the trigger back and pointed it making her face change quickly. She put up her hands and begged.

"Please...don't." He backed up, "Bitch...you're gonna wish you never robbed my place." He aimed a little lower at her leg and said, "I won't kill you, though." He looked at her breast as it heaved up and down, panting. I might have plans for you. You've got lots of nerves, to fuck with a beast like me."

She heard the car skid from out front and listened attentively as it turned the corner. She had to let Mya know not to shoot. They might just have an out.

Mya whipped the car around the corner and gasped as she saw Joker at the door with a gun in his hands. She knew he was pointing at Skyler. She trained the car his way and stomped the pedal. Joker looked over at the lights, blinding him as they got larger and larger as the car approached, "Oh shit!" he yelled. At the same time the gun poked Skyler in the chest and it went off. Joker jumped back inside the doorway as Mya wrecked, careening off the building into a trash bin. Skyler's body was slumped over in his arms, "Damn...nice piece of ass, too..." He dropped her body to the ground and fled out the door running into the Street.

Mya jumped out the car and dashed to the doorway. Skyler was breathing heavy and she struggled to her feet, "H-h-help me u-up..." she said as Mya lifted her up and drug her to the car. She gunned it to the backside of the dead end alleyway, pulled the brakes and spun all the way around and headed for the street.

Miles had finally made it down the stairs. He ran out and stepped right in front of the car speeding towards him full throttle and aimed his gun, shooting into the windshield. The bullets missed Mya as she drove wildly, crashing against the walls, sparks flying all over. Miles jumped to the side, the car barely missing and she turned up the street towards 14th Street. Miles got up dusting himself off, "Damn...they got away." he looked on the ground at the blood near the door, "Someone was shot...they'll show up." He heard the sounds of sirens coming up the avenue; "Fuck! The goddamn police!" and he took off running towards his truck looking back at the pool room. "There's gonna be a lot of questions asked."

Aziz watched closely as the car turned the corner in front of them. Mya reached and took off her mask. Aziz tried to get a glimpse, but it was no use, he couldn't quite make out the face. Yoshi watched Joker as he ran off. He was headed to the school, his stash spot, figuring to clean it out, collect Gustavo's money and get out of town before the police came asking questions. He had no clue that Gustavo was already dead. Yoshi followed behind him, smirking "Now, I can take him out."

Aziz turned and watched her run after him then yelled at her, "You better kill him!"

"He deserves to die! All this shit happened because of him, anyway." she muttered, then stopped, turned, and shouted, "Go to the house and wait for me. It won't be long, okay!"

He looked down at the full, duffel bag at his feet and swung it over his shoulder, "Alright...but be there!" and ran towards his car.

Nearing the corner by the park she could see Joker unlock the lock to the window and shimmy inside. She checked her waist for her gun and remembered she'd left it with Aziz, but she still had the dagger. That would have to do.

Aziz threw the duffel bag in the trunk of his car and took off to the apartment still trying to get a picture of the image of the person he saw in the car out his head, "Damn...I know that face.

Mya drove up 14th Street, then pulled over by Avenue D and dipped into a secluded side parking lot. She put the car in gear and looked over at Skyler. "Skyler! Yes, bitch! We did that, we got away! We got to go somewhere, change and hide the money. Then I need to get the kids ready-" she rambled on then looked over and Skyler didn't respond or move. She shook her, "Skyler, come on, wake up! Stop playing!" Skyler fell over in her lap and only then did she see the blood on her forehead. The hole in the windshield told the story.

Mya tried to bite her lips, but it was no use. She cried bitterly and long but she knew she had to get rid of everything. The sun was going to be up in a couple of hours. She cranked the car up and drove towards the boardwalk to the East River and dragged Skyler's body out. She kissed her cheek then reached into her pocket and put some lip gloss on her lips and straightened out her hair, "When you meet your makers sweetie, I want you to look as you say...like a fucking bad ass diva!" She dumped her body into the river and watched it disappear then unresponsively walked back to the car not looking back.

Yoshi waited until the window shut then she snuck over and looked in. It was dark but she could make Joker's figure out as he made his way over to the back of the room. She saw a spark; he pulled out a lighter trying to get some light. Feeling around the walls for a light switch he found one. The overhead, fluorescent light flickered for a brief minute then illuminated, brightly helping him make his way to the boiler and exposing the hatch.

Yoshi had taken full advantage of the darkness and climbed through the window taking her time not to make any noise. Once in, she stayed close to the walls and tiptoed around to the back of the boiler room. She'd been down there so many times lately, even just recently this evening. She picked a spot catty corner to the rusted out steam tank and watched, waiting and pulled out her knife.

Joker got to the boiler's door and wiped the front of it off looking for the handle, then he pulled back hard on the door and it popped open effortlessly. He was surprised, it pulled too easy almost causing him to lose his grip and fall backwards. Yoshi could read his lips as he did; he cussed at every step he took. She moved closer to him. He looked around inside, the bottom, top and saw nothing. The money was gone. He slammed the door shut and yelled out, "I got robbed...twice! Somebody's gonna fuckin' pay!" He kicked the door and turned towards the window then he saw a shadow, and he stopped in his tracks tracing it back to its source. Yoshi had stepped from behind the boiler, "That's a wrap. The money's gone."

"Who the fuck are you?" he asked as he gaped at her up and down.

She flashed her knife and started to encircle him, "Your worst nightmare!"

Joker squared her off and started to move along with her, "Oh...you had something to do with tonight, huh. You must have been with that other bitch."

"No. Matter of fact, I wasn't, but I saw how you shot her..."

"Hmmm, then that makes you a witness." He rolled up his sleeves and took up a fighting stance, balling up his fist he swung, "We can't have that."

Yoshi bobbed and weaved then shot a jab straight to his face. "I see you got skills." he said. Joker took to his toes and started skipping, "I'm gonna beat your ass and you know what, then," he threw a left catching Yoshi on the side of her stomach and she doubled over, "fuck the shit out of your ass. How about that, huh." he mocked.

Yoshi had the knife tucked close to her arm and swung it outward. It sliced through the air missing Joker by a mile. He continued to talk shit, "That's all you're working with. C'mon, give it another try..." She swung again and he threw a right left combo, swelling up her eye. "C'mon, bitch you gotta come better than that. Remember, get right or I'm gonna fuck the shit out of you." he jested as he continued to pick off her advances.

Yoshi kept her composure even though her eyes were stinging from the hits she took to the face. "You little dick muthafucka-" she said and swung blindly, this time she connected and sliced a line through his shirt. Blood dripped off the knife and he stopped dancing. "Oh shit! You muthafuckin' cunt. I was just playing with you but now I'm really gonna punish your ass, you stank ass hoe!" He charged at her and she sidestepped and swung the knife again opening up some more skin across his back.

Joker fell against the boiler in pain feeling his back then looked down at the blood dripping to the floor and shook his head. He snatched off what was left of his shirt and wrapped it around his fist and started bouncing again, "I'm gonna beat the shit outta you..." He swung and connected to her chin, "But I'm still gonna fuck you cunt. Hell, I'm damn near turned on."

Yoshi fell to the floor, rolled and got up, "I'm tired of playing with you." She rushed at him and he side stepped like she expected, then ran to the wall and jumped against it and flipped backwards, landing to his surprise directly in front of him. He swung and she ducked then shoved the knife into his stomach and pulled it back out, just as quickly, just like in the movies.

Joker grabbed at his stomach and the blood started pouring between his fingers and he sat, "Aw, shit...it hurts... fuck you!"

She got to her feet and walked over to him wiping the dagger off, "Any last words..."

Joker looked up at her face, "Who the fuck are you?"

She hesitated then answered, he was going to die anyway, so it didn't matter, "Aziz's sister..."

"Aziz? I didn't know he had a sister, but why do you want to kill me?" he asked as the blood began to flow more freely from his wounds.

"It's a long story and you don't have that much time, but I will say this..."

Joker slumped over towards the boiler, the pain stinging in his stomach gave him hell as he tried to breathe. He put pressure on it, Yoshi continued, "You should have let Miles rot in jail."

"Miles, that nigga? He did me a cold favor. He killed the muthafucka that was killing everyone in Alphabet City and no telling where else."

"Yeah, well bitch nigga... that *muthafucka* was our *father.*"

"Oh, shit...you're fucking with me! Aziz's old man? And *you're* the sister. It fuckin' figures, damn!" He coughed and spit up blood then looked over at the boiler, "What happened to all my money?"

Yoshi looked over at the boiler too, then glanced back his way, "We got that...all of it."

"You muthafucka's got my money!" He started to struggle to his feet and Yoshi kicked him in the chest sending him tumbling to the ground then swiftly jumped behind him and reached into her back pocket and took out some zip ties. She caught his wrist and tied it to a pipe. There was no way out. He swung at her frenzied and she jumped out of his way, "This...cunt...bitch...whore, has got plans for you." She tossed him some of his shirt, "Here use this to apply pressure. I don't want you to die just yet." She backed up near the window and pulled out a cell phone and dialed some numbers then waited for the person on the other end to pick up. "So? I guess *you're* calling the Police, huh. That's okay. Those are my people. I'll be out of jail in a few days. Then I'll be looking for you. You bitch!" He pulled at the plastic wire cutting through his skin and hollered, "When I see you I'm gonna tear your ass up!"

She got an answer, "Yeah? Shut the fuck up...listen up and listen good, you hear me! That muthafucka that raped your brother tell your peeps he's locked down in the boiler room at the school over on 12th street, PS-7, right fuckin' now! If you want a piece of him...do what it do!"

Joker screamed out, "Fuck you! Fuck them! If they come, I'll kill them, too!" he struggled at the pipe, pulling. The blood came out more now squirting on the steel making it wet and slippery, "You just wait...you'll see. Nobody fucks with Joker!"

Yoshi had the phone held up and put it back to her ear, "Is that enough proof?" She looked over at him and nodded, "There's a small window over by the playground next to-okay, you know where it is." she smirked at Joker. "Who me? Don't worry about that. I just hate the muthafucka too, but I know you wanted some get back, but you better hurry. I already stuck the pig in his gut-hello, hello..." she closed her phone and laughed. "They're on the way." She walked up to him and he swung at her and she dodged it, "I'll kill you bitch and your fuckin' pussy ass brother, you hear!"

She spit on him as she walked off and climbed out the window back into the street hearing the shouts and obscenities he hurled her way. She smiled, then looked up the block and she could already see the bright lights of the car speeding up the street. She dipped into the playground and hid behind some monkey bars. The car had pulled over, and a couple of people jumped out quickly. Two males and one female. One of then pointed at the window and nodded then looked around to make sure no one was trying to set them up. The other person held the window open and yelled out to the man that stood off to the side looking around, "C'mon Peanut...he's down here." Yoshi grinned with pleasure as she watched. She recognized the woman. She went to school with her. India, Peanut's sister. She had befriended her when no one else would and even let her stay the night at her place more than once. Yoshi stood up and she spotted her. Yoshi smiled and turned away, making it back to the apartment.

Joker still struggled with the cuffs and the pain from the knife stab only made him more frustrated and angrier. He looked up and saw the shadows coming through the window. He stood up and looked around for something to fight with. He grabbed a handful of dirt thinking, maybe he could blind one and tackle, then take the weapon. "I prayed for this day..." one of the figures said as they came closer into the light and Joker saw who it was, his plan was out the window. The only weapon he could see was the long, slender wooden pool stick Peanut had in his hands, patting his open palms, "Now you can either take it easy or hard, but one thing's for sure..." Joker's eyes widened, "You gonna take it. And oh yeah...there's no grease. Payback's a bitch."

Yoshi stopped and wriggled her head around and held up her hand to her ear and giggled. "I know that's right!"

A couple of car alarms had gone off and a few lights came on, as the only sound that filled the air in the early morning hours as the sun started to rise over Brooklyn, was the shrill, shrieking echoes of Joker's screams as he cried out. Then as swiftly as they came, they were silenced. Forever.

Mya woke up behind the wheel of the car, her body ached in pain. The sun was high above her head and sunrays flooded out the car causing her to rub her eyes, it was well into the afternoon. She looked around and found herself at a dead end overlooking the water across from the Harlem River Drive. She didn't remember how she got there. She looked around then over at the passenger seat and thought about Skyler, remorse seeped into her already confused mind as she pouted. She looked in the back and saw that the duffel bag was still there. This wasn't the dream she hoped it might have been.

There were no signs of life creeping outside but she peeped around cautiously anyway. She crawled into the back seat and hunched down then looked into the bag. It was all there, the money. She pulled out a bundle of 20's, then 50's and rummaged through it. She couldn't get a good count but estimated it to be roughly ten grand or so, give or take.

She shook her head in despondency not believing that Skyler was killed because of this little bit of money. She banged the back of the seat then thought about Steve. Did he make it, too? If Joker got away she knew he would be looking for him, and her. She checked her watch and it was already past four o'clock in the afternoon.

Damn, she thought, the kids. She was supposed to meet them at the Port Authority. She climbed back into the driver's seat and cranked up the car and it wouldn't start then checked the dashboard, it was out of gas. She bit her lip in disgust then reached through her pockets grabbing her cell phone and the battery was dead. She hit the steering wheel and it honked loudly as tears welled up in her eyes.

She pulled herself together and wiped her face with a rag she'd found on the floorboard underneath the seat then got out the car and put it in neutral and pushed it towards the pier overlooking the water. She let it go jumping out the way, and the car splashed into the river. Bubbling and rocking before the air pockets flushed out, it nosedived and went plunging straight down into the murky black waters. She tossed the duffel bag over her shoulder and took off walking towards the highway.

Mya gave the truck driver that picked her up a stack of twenties and he pulled over and dropped her off at 18th Street on the FDR Highway. She thanked him and made her way to a pay phone and dialed Hope's numbers hoping she would answer. She did.

"Momma! Where are you! We waited and waited! We thought something had happened!"

"I'm alright. Listen to me, and listen good. You still have the bus tickets right?!"

"Yeah!"

"Okay. Then...go back to the bus station and wait for me."

"But, ma...we did that and you didn't show up."

Mya reached into her jacket and found a pack of cigarettes. She pulled one out and lit it, "Hope...hear me out. I'm okay. Just do what I ask."

"Yes, ma'am."

"I have to stop by the apartment and pick up some things so I can change clothes. I gotta get all of my I-D, and make sure that

Dante's stuff is trashed, incinerated and flushed...okay." She knew Joker would search there first.

"Okay, momma. I understand. You need me to help-"

"No! Just stay in the house until it gets dark and then go. Take a cab! Now, where's Destiny."

"She's..." Hope yelled out her name and she answered and stuck her head out the bathroom, "Is that momma?" and ran to the phone snatching it out of her hand. "Momma...you alright!" Hope grabbed the phone back from her, "I got it!" Destiny shouted at her and Mya sighed a breath of relief, they were okay. "Hope!"

"Ma 'am!"

"Now, don't forget. Be there. I'll be there, too...I promise."

"Okay momma. Where's Steve and Ms. Skyler?"

Mya took a long draw off the cigarette and thought about the question then answered, "We'll talk later, just don't forget. I gotta go, now!"

"Okay, momma. I love you!"

"I love you, too." Mya hung up the phone and swung the bag on her back and headed towards the projects, the way back, so she wouldn't be seen.

Aziz had waited a while for Yoshi and she didn't show. He started getting a headache and looked into the bathroom cabinet for some Tylenol and he didn't find any. He remembered he had some pills at his own apartment, but he didn't want to go anywhere until Yoshi had come in. He tried calling her cell phone and she didn't pick up.

He left the bag of money in the car along with the other one and figured he'd go downstairs and bring them both up, maybe count the money, kill time. He started walking out the door and spotted the ledger on the table. He grabbed it and opened it up flipping through the pages. There were names, dates, and places of Joker's pick ups and people from city council and the police department he'd paid off. Dante had it all written down right there in front of his eyes. Yoshi was right, they could write their own check with this. He tripped then accidentally dropped it on the floor, and it popped open to a page. He picked it up and looked closely; it was a note scribbled to Mya. He read it and it explained to her where to go once he blackmailed Joker. There was an address on the bottom, but the pages were dry rotted, and he couldn't quite make it out. He knew if he could find the address, then that's where Mya would be hiding out. The only place he could find it would be at the apartment. He snatched out a page and jotted down a message to Yoshi where he was going, and tucked the book underneath his arm and left out.

Yoshi yawned as she awoke in a theatre over on 42nd Street and 9th Avenue. She wandered over there unconsciously to relax her mind, think things through like she would always do. Figure out what she was going to do next; her and Aziz, but instead she dozed off. She reached in her jacket to check her phone and realized she had no reception, it was a dead zone. She got up and walked into the bathroom and washed her face then went outside waving goodbye to the crew that worked there. She'd known them for many years, and they all knew to leave her alone when she came in making her way up to the secluded aisles of the balcony, to meditate. Aziz's number had come up frequently as she checked and she knew he was probably worried to death. She hailed a cab to her place.

The gold and black, gypsy pulled up in front of the building and she got out and rushed up the steps barging through the door. She called out his name, but she didn't get an answer, then looked into the rooms. She didn't see the duffel bags, and then she remembered she didn't even see his car. She was confused and sat down at the kitchen table wondering where he'd gone, then looked down and saw the note and read it. The medication from earlier, that's probably what he went to get. He would be sick if he didn't get it and she needed to go help him, so she thought. She showered quickly and put on some fresh clothes then grabbed her keys and ran out the door.

ᚖhe Finale

DAY SIX.

The haze cleared and Mya opened her eyes up. Aziz was standing with his gun still pointed towards her. He had a sizable hole in his chest and blood leaked out from it. She looked at her gun and it was smoking; she must have shot him.

He wobbled as he looked down at the hole in his chest then at her. His eyes grew faint and tired as he tried to take a step then fell to his knees. That's when he saw Yoshi. She also had a gun in her hand with smoke coming from out the barrel. Mya backed up a little not recognizing who she was, thinking maybe she was going to shoot at her, also. She didn't know, and at this point she wasn't sure of too much.

Aziz felt at his chest and said to Yoshi, "You...you...shot...me...in the back..." Yoshi put her hand to her mouth and dropped the gun, then ran over to him. He tried talking, she hushed him but he kept on, "That night...the night...I saw Dante. He wa-was going to hide the ledger. Joker knew he had it...he wanted me to kill him."

"Please...shhh, don't talk..." She looked up at Mya and yelled out, "Call an ambulance..." then lowered her voice, "please..." She held him closely as he coughed up blood, slowly dying, "Hold on...hold on..."

Mya took out her phone hesitantly and dialed 911. She told them there had been a shooting and gave the address. She knew she would have to leave soon, as quick as possible because they would definitely be on the way, fast. She threw the gun to the floor and waved her hand, "Please...let me...go..."

Yoshi looked up at her, "Let you go...let you go..." She snatched the small .25 from Aziz's grasp, and rushed at Mya. She tried to run, but she grabbed a hold of her hair and pulled her down and put the gun to her temple, "You made me shoot my brother...he jumped...in front of...me...it was your fault."

"Brother?" Mya gasped. She turned her head slowly and looked at her, "I never knew he had a sister."

Yoshi stood up and leveled the gun at her and said, "There's a lot you don't know about..." She looked at her with malice in her eyes and searched her face, then caught the marks littered around her neck. She cocked her head to the side and stared as Mya lowered her head and sobbed.

Yoshi ripped her shirt down from the collar and saw what she never would have expected. Bruises. Whelps. Scars. Just like her mother would give her from the beatings. Just like the ones her father would give Aziz, Aziz. "Where did you get these!" she said as she traced her hand along her back.

The touch made Mya twinge, they were still fresh and sore, "Your brother, that's who. He beat the shit out of me! Every day! Even when I tried to do everything I could to please him...he beat me...even in front of my kids! Now, go ahead...shoot me if you want! I'm tired of this shit anyway!"

Yoshi pointed the gun to her head and looked at her clothes. She was the one who ran away from the pool room last night. One of the ones that stuck the place up. "Why did you rob the pool room?!"

Mya raised her head slowly, "Because...I don't have anything else..." she looked over at Aziz, "to lose." then picked up her hands and grasped the barrel of the gun and pulled it closer, "Just shoot me...get it over with..." she said as she waited for her impending execution.

Yoshi yanked the gun away and screamed out and listlessly walked over to the sofa and sat, quivering as she thought about how bad her mother would beat her. How their father would march them all in the back room to watch him beat Aziz. She sighed as she looked over at Mya, she felt empathy for her. "We don't get to pick who wins..." she said as Mya looked over at her oddly, "even...if no one does." She got up and walked over to Aziz bent over, digging in his pocket pulling out a set of keys, and tossed them over to her, "Take these. You'd better leave before the cops get here."

Mya eased her head up and started to rise slowly from her knees. She didn't understand what she had said or what she was doing or even what was going on, "You don't want to kill me-"

"No!" she shouted as she gingerly picked up her brother's head and cradled it rocking him back and forth, "Just...go..." Mya stood up quickly now and grabbed the bag of clothes she had gathered and tiptoed past her. Aziz reached out grabbing her leg, "Don't leave...me..." he said. Mya looked down at him and then Yoshi and said, "You're gonna be alright..." then pulled free and headed for the door. Yoshi continued to sway her brother confronting him and he gazed up at her, "It hurts so...bad...mother..." The tears streamed down Yoshi's face from her eyes as she picked up the .44 Mya had thrown down and cocked it and put it to his head as his eyes rolled up in his head, he was delusional, "You're not gonna let daddy beat me, are you? I promise I'll be good..." he said.

"No...he won't ever beat you again..."

"You promise..."

"I promise..."

Mya ran down the steps as fast as she could, almost stumbling and falling out the door when she heard a shot. It was the strong sound of a powerful gun, like the one she dropped to the floor; the gun she left upstairs with Aziz's sister. She glanced down at the keys that jingled in her hands and recognized them as Aziz's car keys. She didn't have to go far to look for it, it was parked right in front of the building, the flashiest car on the street. Junkies had already started flocking to it, looking for Aziz, the drugs. All the cheap dope had run out and now they looked for their regular fix. She waved them away and got in. The cops were coming up the avenue in droves and she rolled up the dark, tinted windows and drove off, riding right past them unscathed. She looked in the rear view mirror and saw them rush into the building with their guns out. She wondered if Aziz's sister was going to try to leave or stay. Maybe, she was being set up by her. She might tell them she robbed them, then shot Aziz and give them a description of the car. She punched the gas and nervously searched the console for a cigarette, but Aziz didn't smoke.

She turned on Avenue A going across town and ran straight past Miles's truck coming up the opposite way. He recognized the car and flashed his lights. She didn't pull over so he followed her and blazed in front, cutting her off and she skidded to a stop. He jumped out and rushed to the window and banged on it, "I know it's you! Roll down the fuckin' windows!"

She did and Miles gawked at her. Her clothes were tattered, her hair looked like hell, and she still had on the same outfit from last night; as he recollected the robbery and Steve, "Damn, Mya...what the hell was y'all thinking about!"

Mya shook her head in a daze and answered, "We didn't..."

Miles reached in and held her white, knuckled hands as they gripped tightly on the steering wheel, trembling, "Look...I'll clean up everything. I think Joker's dead. I don't know what happened to Aziz...hell I thought you were him-"

"He's dead...too."

"What!"

"He tried to kill me. I had a gun, too. I shot him. He was shot, but I don't think I shot him. I missed, but he was shot..." she babbled on and he stopped her.

"You're not making any sense."

"His sister...she shot him!"

"His sister! Yoshi! She's still around..." Miles was thoroughly confused now. He thought Yoshi had left the neighborhood for good years ago after he got out of prison, "Damn! Where are you going now? And, for gods' sake...where's the money you guys took?!"

It dawned on her that she'd left the money upstairs and punched the dashboard. "I left it. I fucked up!" she cried out. Miles rubbed her back and said, "I'll go see what's going on and I'll call you, okay. We'll work it out...trust me." He jumped in his truck and she gestured him back. She reached under the seat and grabbed the ledger and gave it to him, "Here...take this. I think Dante would have wanted you to have it." He grabbed at it and jumped in his car and took off heading towards the projects. Mya watched as he left and recalled his words. The same words Aziz had said the night Dante was killed. She gritted her teeth and said, "Fuck that! I'm not going through this shit again!"

Once she got to the Port Authority bus station, she parked the car down a side street a block over and reached into her bag for a change of clothes. She stepped outside and opened the trunk so no one could see her and spotted the two duffel bags. She looked in and almost fell out. She reached in and pulled out bundles of money, both bags were full of it. She yelled out in joy, then muffled her voice as she concealed herself. She checked her watch, "Oh shit, I gotta make it!" She changed clothes quickly and grabbed both bags and drug them up the steps and through the terminal to Gate 5, the regular bus to South Carolina, and sure enough, Hope and Destiny stood there waiting. They spotted her and ran to her, hugging and kissing her, "Momma...you're here! The bus just pulled up!"

"You got the tickets, right?!" she asked.

"Yeah, but they say we still owe a little more money. You got any money?"

Mya opened up one of the bags and reached in and pulled out some twenties, "Give them that...hurry." She gave the money to Hope, and Destiny dragged the bags to the bus and watched as they got tagged and carried to the luggage compartment. "Make sure you keep an eye on them..." Destiny nodded her head yes, and they got on.

They made their way to some seats in the back and Mya sat down and sighed, "We're gonna be alright...right..." then started crying. Hope and Destiny hugged her and looked outside at the skyline over New York as it got smaller and smaller as the bus left the Lincoln Tunnel in New Jersey making its way down south.

MILES STOOD ON THE rooftop opposite the Pitt overlooking Alphabet City gazing over the neighborhood. *'Buy some of those abandoned buildings an*d *remodel'* he thought as he imagined becoming a real estate Mogul in Alphabet City. He pointed towards 14th street and said, "We need to control more of that territory..." The man who stood next to him glanced over his shoulder, "I'll work on it...boss."

Miles was now in control of Alphabet City. He used the ledger as leverage with some influential people and cleaned up the mess Joker had made. No more penny-ante change for him. He used some of his revenue and secured a nice penthouse apartment over on the east side of New York University. He was a higher, upscale sort of dealer now, but his hustle wasn't dope this time. He changed the game. It had been in the making for years, since he'd been in prison and met Ace, his cellmate. The one man that had his back while he did time. Ace had approached him with the plan, and told him he was one of the people Joker had snitched on. He was angry, upset, but Miles agreed to his plan and told him to hold on, once he got out he'd handle the business. He kept his word.

There was one problem. Alphabet City wasn't totally drug free like he would have liked. They still had a partner. A sort of, silent type of partner. He wanted desperately to buy him out, get rid of him for good, but he couldn't. A deal was made. His cell phone rang, "Hello..."

"Yeah, this is Akbar."

"What's happening? I told you we had a meeting to go to-"

"Naw...you go to those ciddity, gay, fuckin' meetings with your well to do punk friends. I'll see you later on tonight."

"Look, Akbar. We're trying to be respectable business-"

"No. You're trying to be respectable. I'm a fuckin' dope dealer, ya hear."

"I guess so-" he sighed.

"I'll talk to you later. I got pickups. Hell, somebody gotta wash the money you front with!"

Miles hung the phone up and shoved it in his coat. His assistant asked him who it was seeing how incensed he'd gotten, "Akbar, huh..."

"I wish I knew a way to get rid of him...besides killing him my damn self!" he said as he balled up his fist.

"Don't go there...he ain't worth the trouble or time in prison. Don't worry...somebody will get him...it always happens that way."

"You're probably right." he said as he walked towards the rooftop doorway then looked back over the city and slammed it shut.

Akbar was in the basement of a shooting gallery over on Avenue C standing over the body of a half-naked junkie. She was well dressed, well kept, more than likely one of the professors that wandered over from New York University looking to cop some dope. This one had fucked up, she came short. Akbar wanted to make up the difference. He unzipped his zipper in front of her face and she reached in fumbling with his dick getting it hard and pulled it out. She opened her mouth wide and moved forward then felt his body jerk. She looked up at him and his eyes were bulged and his mouth open, gasping for air. Scared, she jumped back then saw the dagger come pushing through his stomach and blood gushing from it. She hurriedly got up and took off not paying the figure in the leather apparel behind him, that pushed the knife through, any mind. The blade stopped then made its way up splitting open his spleen. Akbar struggled to breathe as blood spit out his mouth and started to clot in his throat. He fell face forward to the floor, with the dagger sticking out his body.

The lone figure looked over him and spit, "Bastard..."

Akbar's breathing slowed down as his heart stopped breathing and blood poured out of his body pooling up on the floor, he couldn't understand why he'd been stabbed. Why would someone want him dead? He asked the million dollar question as his mind went black. The last words he would know in life. The answer. I don't know, perhaps, it was real simple, only because, after all, Yoshi kept it that way.

Maybe, it's because that's what killers do... *kill.*

The End

Also by Dean Hamid

Part One
Lovin Safari

Part Two
Lovin Safari: Gunzz and roses

The Bushwick Chronicles
Dunya 2: Rasheed's Redemption
Dunya: The Do or Die

Standalone
Hell has no fury